"I WILL BE FAITHFUL TO YOU ALL MY LIFE."

Ian drew her closer and their lips met, their bodies moved together, hard muscle against soft skin. He reached out to touch her cheek with a gentle hand as he took his mouth from hers.

"If you want to stop, you must tell me, my love."

"No, my lord," she said, her voice soft and shaky. "I very much want to give myself to you."

His hands traveled her small body, sliding over her damp, silky skin, finding her thrusting breasts. He caressed her, his big hands trembling. Passion drummed in his wild heartbeat. He felt a towering desire for his woman, but still the desire came with an awful fear of frightening her, of hurting her. . . .

"Ian?" Her voice was hushed and passionate, like words said in a dream. "Take me now. I ache inside, and 'tis as if I want you there. . . ."

A LOVE SO FIERCE
"A rousing good tale!"*

"Joanna McGauran brings the Middle Ages vividly alive with this sensual love story."—Katherine Deauxville*

"*A Love So Fierce* is a well-written book full of the gaiety and the intrigues of Edward's court, the flavor of medieval times, and, most important of all, a young woman who wants to be loved for herself. Ms. McGauran joins the ranks of Roberta Gellis, Anita Mills, and Katherine Deauxville as a writer of medieval novels."
—*Romantic Times*

"Ms. McGauran has created a memorable love story, one that crackles with tension and sizzles with passion . . . sharp, often witty dialogue makes their verbal sparring an exciting match of wits. This one is too good to miss!"
—*Affaire de Coeur*

"It's a fascinating glimpse into another time, when men and women's passions were exactly as they are today."
—*Rendezvous*

Also by Joanna McGauran

TO TEMPT A MAN
BY MY LADY'S HONOR

Joanna McGauran
For My Lady's Hand

A DELL BOOK

Published by
Dell Publishing
a division of
Bantam Doubleday Dell Publishing Group, Inc.
1540 Broadway
New York, New York 10036

ISBN: 0-440-22163-3

Printed in the United States of America

Published simultaneously in Canada

April 1996

10 9 8 7 6 5 4 3 2 1

OPM

It's about time for me to dedicate a book to the agent/editor I've had for ten years—or is it longer, Maureen? Maureen Moran, of Donald MacCampbell, Inc., has encouraged me, harassed me, and made me laugh more than once. Sometimes at myself. Who could ask for more?

1

 Ciel Valoir had risen at first light to ride the two-year-old Percherons, young warhorses she and her father were training for the yearly sales. There were three of them ready for market now; two of them eager to learn, one of them too wild and fierce for a stranger to handle. Ciel rode him last; it was easier to calm him if his belly was stuffed with the mash and grain she brought them. But still he was stubborn. Two thousand pounds of disobedience, yet so beautiful. Skin like gray satin, eyes like deep pools of loving innocence. He followed her like a puppy, stood still for his grooming, and was gentle as a kitten until he felt her slight weight on his broad back. Then he acted as if a devil had entered his heart. But Ciel never gave up. Gentle but firm, she continued to teach him. At seventeen, she had learned patience.

Now, turning him toward the home barn, she knew he was full of mischief this day, and so she avoided the patches of woodland, though it was cold, and she wished for shelter from the north wind. But, if Devil had the slightest chance, he would rear and rub her off against one of the gnarled oaks. Her caution disappointed the two men hidden in a thicket of trees near the winding road but didn't surprise them. Their horses, two mangy-looking, half-starved animals, were tied on the other side of the thicket they were in, well out of the way of the warhorse. The men had watched the girl now for over a week, and she had never changed her habits. Always the disobedient horse last; always through by midmorning. And, to their great satisfaction, always alone in this far pasture.

The men were extremely careful. They knew the girl's father, Vincennes Valoir. He was a hard man, a hard worker, and proud. His family carried noble blood, and his sons were making their way in King Louis's army. It had been said in the village that Ciel Valoir would never be allowed to marry unless her father found a man with noble blood who wanted her.

In the opinion of most of the villagers, the Valoir family was too proud, too certain that they were better than the others, and these two men were set to cut them down. And, in the act, have the incomparable thrill of taking a reluctant woman. When they got through with Ciel Valoir, not even a respectable farmer would have her. She would be ruined. She would be laughed at and mocked in the village. And they could brag of their conquest. Even the other girls would laugh, and no doubt admire the men for their enterprise.

"She is coming closer," one of the men whispered, dry-mouthed and eager. "Be ready. It will take both of us to drag her from the horse. If she screams, gag her at once. *Mon Dieu*, I begin to stiffen . . ."

"You may be first," the other man said, grinning, "after me. I am not so slow. I have been stiff as a sword since she came in sight."

"Now," the first man said, excited. "She is as close as her path allows. Run!"

They broke from the shelter of the thicket and came flying in great long strides toward the big horse and the young woman on his back. They were silent, and for a moment Ciel paused, staring at them in surprise, then instinct took over and she reined the big horse away from the hot evil she saw in their eyes. She kicked Devil's sides and yelled at him: "Run, *mon enfant!* Make haste!"

Devil chose that moment to sulk. Ciel's small heels beating a tattoo on his heavy ribs meant nothing to him. He stopped, turned his head, and gave her a disgusted look from his magnificent eyes. At that instant the men were on them, leaping upward, grabbing the girl and pulling her off the horse's broad back. They ended in a heap of kicking legs and grasping arms, the girl's shrill cries echoing in the still morning air for only a moment. A grimy hand stuffed an equally grimy kerchief into her mouth and silenced her. Then they sat her up and tied her hands behind her back.

"There." The man grinned at her furious mumbles, her hard stare. "Come now, Ciel. You'll have some of the fun, wait and see. Once we break your maidenhead, we'll give you plenty of pleasure." He got to his feet and reached down to help her stand. She kicked him hard, aiming true. He screamed, his voice high as a woman's, and grasped his bulging loins. Then he kicked her, aiming for her slim belly but missing his mark as she rolled away. The other man grabbed his arm.

"*Mon Dieu!* Don't kick her, you idiot! Her father will never believe she consented if she can show him bruises. Come, we'll drag her to the thicket."

"What of the horse?"

"He'll stay. The dry grass is good here, and he's already eating it. He thinks with his belly."

They each grabbed an arm and dragged the girl through the bending grass, heading for the thicket. Halfway there, the man Ciel had kicked slowed and reached down to pull up her loose tunic and expose her breasts. He let out his breath and gave an excited giggle.

"Look at these, friend. No old whore's hanging dugs for us today." His eyes swept from the high young breasts to the blue-green eyes above the grimy gag, staring at him with pure hatred. He looked away and began moving faster, his jaw grim. He still ached, and he wanted revenge.

Inside the thicket the men relaxed. No one could see them from the road; no one would hear Ciel's muffled cries. They could take their time. They took off her boots and her skirt and folded the skirt for a pad on the damp ground. She was left with only her tunic, her short petticoat, and a growing rage that was burning away her fear. The men could not stop touching her, pinching her breasts, rubbing her lower belly, her crotch. Then, crazed by their passions and sure she was starting to want them, they decided to take off her tunic, and of course they had to untie her arms and pull it off over her head. Her hands in the air, she allowed them to remove it.

Laughing, they stumbled backward away from her, and her hands came down and pushed them hard, so that they stumbled again and fell. Grabbing up her skirt, she ran like a deer, bursting from the dark thicket into a bright, noonday sun, flinging her gag away, her hair flying, her breasts bare, her slender legs flashing beneath the thin short petticoat. And the men right behind her, red-faced, angry, running as fast as she but not gaining yet. But she knew they would; they were stronger, their legs used to running . . .

A thunder of hooves came from the nearby road, and she looked around. One of Lord Rodancott's black war-horses, but the rider a stranger. Still running, stumbling . . . she turned again and saw the two men slowing, looking toward the rider, looking frightened . . . and the black horse was stopping, the man who rode him looking from her to the two men, and, oh, *mon Dieu,* thank all the saints and angels! He had turned his black horse into the meadow and was coming toward her at a slow trot.

Facing him, clasping her skirt in front of her to hide her nakedness, she stood and waited in the knee-high grass. She was full of awe. She had never seen a man like this one. No man as tall, no man with hair the color of shining bronze, no man with shoulders that wide. No man with the face of a young god. He stopped and smiled, and tears welled into her eyes.

"Thank you," she said, and her voice trembled. "They were—were going to rape me. I had gotten away, but they would have caught me. *Le bon Dieu* sent you, I know."

"I am glad to be of service," the man answered, and sent a look toward the thicket where the men had disappeared. They both watched as the men burst forth on their ragtag horses and, gaining the road, took off in the opposite direction. The man's dark blue eyes came back to her face. "Do you know them, my lady?"

She nodded. "They are from the village. My father will bring charges against them, though it will do little good. The villagers are not fond of Vincennes Valoir

and his family." She looked around and saw Devil crop-
ping grass, paying no attention to anything else. "I was
riding that horse over there, helping my father with the
training, and I suspect those men have been watching
me long enough to know I come here alone. It was foolish of me."

"I see." He studied the way she held the voluminous
ripped skirt. One slender hand pressing the waistline
against her throat, one arm holding the full skirt to a
narrow waist. "Where are the rest of your clothes?"

She blushed heavily. "In the thicket. But, you see, I
cannot go and get them until you leave."

For a moment he looked puzzled, then his face relaxed
into humor. "I do see. But I have a remedy." He swung
from the saddle and took off his cloak. Ciel gasped. The
cloak was beautiful, a soft gold wool lined with vair,
with a jeweled clasp and a hood that hung down the
back. Grasping it by the collar, he swung it around her,
hiding all of her except for her pink, astounded face and
her shining, wildly tangled black hair. Fastening it se-
curely, he grinned.

"You look like a golden haystack, my lady. But it
will keep you covered while you gather your clothes and
put them on. Then, if you like, I shall see you safely
home."

Ciel's gaze was almost reverent. Once he stood on the
ground she had realized he was even taller than she
thought, taller than any man she had ever seen. To her
mind, there was an aura of magic around him, a faint
but glowing circle of light. She remembered the ancient
fables her mother had read to her when she was a child.
All true heroes in the past were identified by what was

known as the hero light that glowed when they did their good deeds.

"I'll hurry," she got out. "I'll try not to keep you waiting long . . ." She was gone, running like a child, the cloak fluttering over the bending grass, her small white feet appearing and disappearing, kicking up behind her, smeared with the damp black earth . . .

Ian Stewart allowed himself a grin. She was a charming girl, with charming manners. Hardly a peasant, but what else could she be? Something, he thought, betwixt and between. Neither peasant nor noble. The daughter, then, of a horse breeder. And a rare beauty, at that. He looked over at her horse and amended part of the thought: a successful horse breeder. The gray was a superior animal.

He waited, looking over the rolling meadows, the thickets of growing trees. The land was still tinged with green even in December, due, he had heard, to the warmer air near the coast. In spring these lands would be rampant with new and tender grass, and the pregnant mares would be let out to eat their fill and make the rich milk that the new foals needed.

He sighed. His own home, which he loved, was suitable only for sheep. Sheep thrived on anything that grew. The Stewart holdings in England's Northumberland were mostly barren and rocky, but the wool from the sheep made a good living in most years, and the problems were small. The horses he kept had to be fed on grain, mostly oats, bought from men who lived in greener fields to the south.

He came back to the present and looked up as the girl, half running, came from the thicket. She was carrying his cloak, neatly folded, over one arm and was dressed

in her wide skirt and a tunic, with a warm shawl about
her shoulders. Her clothes were all smeared with mud
from the damp earth inside the thicket, and as she approached he kept his eyes on her face, pink with embarrassment.

"Are you warm enough, my lady?"

"Oh, yes. I am very warm." She hesitated and then
added: "You flatter me, my lord. It would be best if you
addressed me as Mistress Valoir. We are not nobles,
though it is true that we sprang from noble blood."

So that was the answer. The blood, but not the name.
It wasn't an uncommon thing, especially in Normandy
and France. Some nobleman in the past had seen a beautiful woman amongst the families of tradesmen and mer-
chants, or even a maid in his own castle, and had taken
her. This little one was direct and honest, not wanting
to lie nor play the lady. He smiled. Oddly, he felt a
certain admiration for her open, matter-of-fact explana-
tion of her background. He lost no time in saying so.

"You are beautiful enough to have sprung from a
union between Venus and Apollo, Mistress Valoir, and
as honest and true as any knight I have ever known. I
am Ian Stewart, laird of Stewart Castle in Northumberland, England, and here in Normandy to visit my sister,
Lady Aylena Rodancott, and her husband, Lord Rodancott of Castle Cheval Noir."

She curtsied, a small curtsy. A quick dip of knee, a
bowing of her shining head, and then a direct look from
her brilliant turquoise eyes. "I should have known, for
I know your sister well, and there's a look of kinship to
her in your eyes. I will never forget you, Lord Ian. You
have saved me from lifelong shame. You will be in my
prayers from this night onward."

Startled, Ian bowed in return. He had done so little. But he understood now just how she would have felt—soiled forever by those stupid peasants. "I will escort you to your home, mistress, and make sure no one attacks you on the way. And I'd have a word with your father, if you don't mind."

She looked down, wincing at the muddy shoes that peeked from her skirt. "I don't mind. He will punish me whether you do or do not speak of what happened. I am not supposed to wander this far from home without taking along a servant as a guard."

"Then come along and I'll help you mount your gray. He's a beautiful horse."

She shook her head. "I must go to him alone. He's young and not yet trained, and will run from anyone but me. Stay here, please, until I've mounted him."

Ian nodded and mounted his own horse, a huge black stallion. He watched as Ciel took the gray's dragging reins in her left hand, disappeared behind the solid wall of his body, then grabbed his mane and swung herself into view on his back. She straightened her muddy skirts, then turned the heavy horse with ease and kicked him into a trot toward Ian.

"We go to the north, perhaps a mile or more, and we'll be at the farm. If my father is in the fields, we will see him from the road."

Ian nodded and followed her to the road that wound to the north. They rode in silence for some time, and then Ian put his stallion to a rocking trot and was pleased when the gray copied it smoothly. He glanced over at Ciel and saw that she looked delighted.

"As always," Ian said, "a young horse will take lessons from an older horse much faster than from a human. Lord Rodancott likes to have his horses ridden, and I would be happy to ride with you while you train your gray. I will ask your father if I may.''

Ciel was shocked. "My father would never agree to that. You, Lord Ian, are a noble. He . . .'' She stopped, her cheeks red. "Let me put it plainly. He will not act above his station, nor would he wish me to do so.''

"Perhaps he has good reason,'' Ian said, staring at a large and well-made house appearing in the distance, "but still I will ask. Is that your home?''

"It is.'' She was struck by a sudden shyness. "I see my father now, there on the knoll behind the house. I hope he will not be—be rude to you.''

Ian grinned at her. "I hope the same, but if he is, I will not take offense. A man with a daughter as beautiful as you must always be on guard.''

She gave him an astounded look, and then, leaning to open the gate, she was pink and silent. She waited as he rode through, went in herself, and shut the gate again, maneuvering the big gray like a puppy. Ian, waiting for her, wondered if she knew that few men could ride bareback as well as she. Her father, he thought, was a fortunate man.

"Do you have brothers?'' he asked as they rode toward the solitary figure on the knoll. "Or sisters?''

"Two brothers,'' she said, "both in King Louis's army. Fine soldiers. They are much older than I, and my father is very proud of them.''

"Of course. As he should be.'' It suddenly seemed strange to Ian that here in Normandy there were men who followed Louis and men who followed Henry, and yet they lived together without argument or hate. He glanced up and saw that the man they approached had seen them, and was staring at him. As they came closer, Ian was startled by the imperious look, the lack of servility in the reddened but proud face. The man looked very familiar to him, yet he had never seen him before.

"Father," Ciel said, and slid from the gray's back to kiss her father's cheek. "I have brought Lord Ian Stewart, brother of Lady Aylena Rodancott, to you. When you learn why, you will wish to thank him."

The man's face softened as he looked at her and then at Ian. "Dismount, Sir Ian. I will hear more of this."

He turned back to Ciel as Ian dismounted. "What foolish thing have you done this time, my child? You are covered with mud. Did Devil throw you?"

"Indeed not." Her clear skin reddened as she looked at Ian and then at the ground. "I was much more foolish than that. I took Devil out to the far woodlot, hoping he would pay more attention to me when away from the other horses."

Her father took her chin in his fingers and brought her face up so he could look into her eyes. "And did he?"

That she could answer. "Yes, sire. He was more attentive. But once I was ready to leave . . . he wasn't. He would not run. Or even walk. And . . . they caught me."

" 'They'?"

"Laron and Olaf Todden, from the village." Tears came to her eyes, but she went on. "They pulled me off Devil and—and . . ."

"I will kill them!" her father shouted, and turned purple with rage, stamping a few feet away and stamping back, his hands doubled into fists and shaking with his anger. "I will hang them on the village gibbet and leave them there to swing and rot! No villager will despoil my daughter and live!''

''Father.'' Tears wet on her face, Ciel laid a pleading hand on his arm to halt his pacing. ''They did not despoil me. 'Twas their intention, surely, but Lord Ian came riding along the road and—and scared them into leaving. He has given me a lecture about being alone in an unprotected spot and has brought me to you. And— and you should thank him, as I have done, for s-saving my v-virtue.''

Silent, fascinated, Ian wrestled with an impossible impression that grew by the minute. He now knew why Vincennes Valoir looked familiar to him. Except for brown hair instead of red, and except for long, straight legs instead of bowed, the man looked and acted precisely like Henry II. How many times had he watched the king stamp back and forth in a rage just like that? Ian turned away, afraid that the man might see his thoughts in his face. Surely he knew who he looked like . . . and what people might think. Geoffrey Plantagenet, Henry's father, had been known in both France and England as a man with a terrible temper and an enormous appetite for sexual adventures. This man had to be his get.

A hand fell on his arm, heavy but unthreatening. He swung around and smiled. God help him if he forgot and bowed to this farmer.

''I am in your debt,'' Vincennes said gruffly, ''and will always be. My daughter is foolish, but this will help her learn. There are those in the village who would like to see her humbled, though 'tis I they want to hurt. They envy us.''

Ian nodded. ''Of course. You are far above them, and

are educated. That was clear to me when you first spoke. There will always be jealous men around you. Your daughter has told me of your sons; she is as proud of them as you must be.''

Vincennes smiled, and Ian looked away, hiding shock. Smiling, the man looked even more like the king.

''Indeed,'' Vincennes said, ''I am very proud of them. And of her. She has learned today, and, thank the good Christ, she had help from you. I am deep in your debt, and I acknowledge it. You will be welcome in my home, Lord Ian, for as long and as often as you wish.''

Riding back to Cheval Noir, Ian was amused. He felt as if some great official had handed him an accolade for excellence. But Vincennes Valoir had clearly meant what he said. Like his daughter, who from now on intended to mention his name to God each time she prayed, he had a great sense of gratitude. Which, Ian thought as he came in view of Cheval Noir, is one of the rarest of virtues. He thought of his sister, Aylena Rodancott, waiting for him in the castle, and began thinking what an amusing story he could tell her this night. About the young brave girl treated so badly and so grateful to be saved. And her father, who looked enough like Henry II to be his natural brother—and likely was, on the father's side—who invited him to make himself at home in his farmhouse while he was in Normandy. Aylena would love the tale . . .

But somehow he didn't tell it. And later, while he drifted off to sleep in the room his sister had given him, he knew he was right. It wasn't a joke, or a story song for a troubadour. It was an understanding, between him and a man and the man's daughter, that would be kept secret.

2

 At dawn, the ancient sprawl of Thor Rodan-cott's gray stone castle was lit in sharp outline by the cold yellow light of a rising winter sun. The castle faced west, as if on constant guard for raiders landing on the unseen beaches of the English Channel a few miles away. Tall, crenelated towers and menacing walls frowned in deep shadow, staring out across high rolling meadows and dense forests. Inside the walls men and women hurried, sleepy-eyed and yawning, beginning their working day. And, from a high turret, a black and silver pennant fluttered in the air, announcing the presence of the noble owner within the walls.

Stepping out into the cold from the warmth and tempting odors of the kitchen, Thor Rodancott carried a steaming cup of mead and a small loaf of coarse bread, speckled with dried bits of sweet currants. Rodancott was forty-five, but he showed little sign of aging. At most, the few silver threads at his temples only accented the rich shine of his black hair and beard. His body was as muscular and strong as in his youth, his handsome face alert and contented.

An elderly man, warmly dressed in a heavy sweater and coat, was working in the kitchen garden, turning soil. He looked up and smiled, snatching off his cap to bow and putting it on again with alacrity. His ears were red with the cold.

"If you are looking for Lord Stewart, sire, he was out at the first sign of light," the old man said, and leaned on his shovel. "He is bound he'll master Rogue."

Thor laughed. "He'd find the task easier if he followed my advice and confined the training to afternoons, when the horses are drowsy and settled. But a young man is always impatient, Piers."

"Yes, sire. Still, he shows a rare patience with a horse. Rogue will stand to be saddled now, and ridden, though only by him. I believe the horse knows he has met his match."

"Good." Thor broke the loaf he carried and handed half of it to Piers. "That strong horse needs a strong man, and my young brother-in-law is certainly that. Eat, man. Your work will wait, and cook will pour a mug of mead for you. I'm heading for the stables to have a word with Ian."

"He'll not be there now, and it's likely that he'll not appear until past noon. He said he'd ride to the east road, ride north, and 'twould be late before he comes home."

Thor's black brows rose. "Again? He's ridden that way for almost two weeks. Is he hunting? There are very few boars in those open meadows."

Piers shook his head, half smiling. "Who knows? Your lady's brother is a man who keeps his thoughts to himself. But for a single man of his age, there are other things than boars to hunt, and the Valoir family has a very pretty daughter."

After a moment of astounded silence, Thor laughed. "And so they do! But it is to be hoped that he is not courting her seriously. Vincennes Valoir will never allow Ciel to leave Normandy, for his wife is long dead and there is only the one daughter. He prizes her as much as either of his sons.''

Piers chewed thoughtfully. ''Still, he might give in if Ian asked for her. It has always been said that her father would never give her to any man unless the man had noble blood. Of course, he may have meant a French noble, but there have been no offers from one of them. I would think Vincennes might jump at the chance of an English lord.''

Thor laughed out loud. ''Piers, you're as gossipy as an old woman! Where do you hear these things?''

Piers grinned. ''From my old woman, sire. An 'tis true, she is a terrible gossip.''

''Is that so? Then I will give you a tidbit to carry to your old woman. She will thank you for it, and tell everyone. King Henry himself is coming to Bures for Christmas Eve Mass and will be reunited with Queen Eleanor—though only for the Holy Night celebration.''

Piers's eyes were round and blinking, full of awe. ''And you, sire . . . will you attend the king again?''

''As always in France,'' Thor said, and patted the old man's shoulder, ''and often in England, I am the king's man. I, my wife, and her brother will attend, with Margit and James to look after the baggage and mounts. We will leave in one or two days, depending on the weather. Now you know what no one else in the castle knows. Go and start the gossip spreading. And you might tell the laundress first. We will need clean clothes to pack.''

''Yes, sire. Right now.'' Piers shoved his spade into the ground and left, making a beeline for the busy courtyard. Thor turned to go back into the kitchens again, then hesitated. It was a brisk but sunny morning, and his old mount, his Frère d'Armes, was nearing eighteen years of age and needed exercise. He'd take a quick ride and see what his young brother-in-law found so enticing at the Valoir farms.

Vincennes Valoir had trusted Ian Stewart from the moment he laid eyes on him. But the glowing reports Ciel brought back from the training field had roused his professional interest. And when Ciel told him how Devil had learned to gallop on a straight line without the help of reins, as warhorses must do in battle and tournament, Vincennes came to the field and watched. He was amazed at how much young Ian knew and how patiently he taught the horses. Then he asked about Ian's fighting experience and found it was all in tourneys.

"No battles?" Vincennes was amazed. "I have heard you alone hold the boundary between England and Scotland. How can you manage that without fighting?"

Ian reddened. "In recent years the Scots prefer fighting each other to fighting England. Five years ago, when Malcolm the Maiden died without issue, his eldest brother William took the throne, calling himself William the Lion. So far he has spent his energies and time ruthlessly suppressing the many quarreling Scots who wish to be king in his place. He is doing quite well."

"But . . . who watches the border while you are here?"

Ian grinned. "The rest of the Stewart clan. There are many strong warriors amongst the Stewarts, Vincennes. And all of them true to me. They would not allow the Stewart castle to be taken."

"Then you are not English, I take it."

"By blood, three-quarters English. By heart, a Scot. But true to King Henry. I have sworn fealty to him."

"Well, you are a mixture, then. Some day you will have to choose, Ian. Choose well and carefully."

"Father."

Vincennes turned and looked at Ciel, frowning. "We are men talking of things that do not concern you, daughter. Continue your practice."

She smiled. "I will, of course. But I thought you might wish to greet Lord Rodancott, who is crossing to us from the road."

Vincennes whirled to look, then kicked his mount into a canter toward the huge black horse and the man on his back. It was seldom these days for the legendary Frère d'Armes to be under saddle again, though from his easy rolling gait he was as strong as ever and enjoying a day out. Vincennes approached him with much pleasure, and no little jealousy. Smiling, he doffed the cap he wore and bowed toward Thor.

"As I said when we first met, Lord Rodancott, name the price of that black stud and I will pay it."

Thor grinned, his teeth white in the black beard. "And I will give you the same answer that I gave then, Vincennes. I do not sell the members of my family." That ceremony done, he motioned across the field at Ian. "My brother-in-law is young and enthusiastic. If he intrudes . . ."

"He does not intrude. He is more than welcome, and very knowledgeable. Our horses will sell this year with battle skills that will bring top prices. Even Devil has responded to his teaching." He laughed a little. "Devil takes it seriously. Before Lord Stewart began his teaching it took a strong man to keep him from fighting on a peaceful road, yet my daughter can now handle him with ease." He paused, frowning. "It is too bad that Devil didn't have that training when those villagers attacked my daughter. He could have killed them with his hooves . . ."

Thor's face froze into grim lines. "Villagers attacked Ciel? Who were they?"

Vincennes looked amazed. "Lord Ian didn't say? Why, I knew he wouldn't gossip, but I did think he would tell you and your lady, surely. By the grace of God he came along when two of the village vermin had captured Ciel and would have raped her. Most young men would have bragged on that good deed."

Thor nodded. "Most would. But Ian hides his light. He never brags, yet he is a young man with many talents and immense strength. At times, a man will underestimate him and offer a challenge." He smiled grimly. "They are always sorry. He seems peaceful and calm, but when he is truly angry—which, thank God, is seldom—he is like a berserker."

Vincennes stared, somewhat disbelieving. "I've not seen that, my lord, nor do I wish to. A man his size could kill with a blow of his fist. I am glad to say he's a friend to us and will always be."

Thor nodded. "Knowing you both, I believe that true. Now, since I see your daughter riding the gray, I'd like to move to that end of the field and watch her put him through his paces."

"Then come," Vincennes said, smiling again. "We will watch the young perform. I am not like Ian. I do brag, and often concerning my daughter."

Later, riding back to the castle at noon, Thor and Ian talked of how well Ciel handled the horses.

"She is small," Thor said, "but she has a way with them. It is as if she speaks in silence and they hear her meaning. I couldn't see what trick she used to make Devil back up for half the field, nor what she did that made him rear and paw at the air as if at an enemy. When he is sold, as he is bound to be, she will have to teach his owner."

Ian smiled. "He will not be sold, Thor. She wants him for her own, and believe me, what Ciel wants Vincennes rushes to fulfill. He pretends to be a harsh father, but he is soft as a feather bed."

Thor cocked an eye at him. "And how do you feel about the girl, Ian? Aylena thinks the world of her and sees her often when the lazy summer months allow visiting. Does she make your heart beat faster?"

"I think her charming, beautiful, and warm. She has become a true friend, and, I do admit I find her tempting, to say the least. But I am careful not to become too close."

"Why? I know you aren't put off by her lack of a title. What other thing does she lack?"

Ian smiled. "She lacks nothing, Thor. But, strangely, I feel that I have already seen the woman I want. When I landed at Calais on my way here, I left the ship in thick, swirling fog. Then, momentarily, the fog parted before me. For a few moments only it revealed a woman with long, golden hair and a face so beautiful it was like a dream. She rode away on a gentle warhorse, accompanied by a dignified old man whom she called father. When I found a horse to ride she was gone, and no one I asked knew anything of her. I now dream of finding her, courting her, marrying her, and settling down to live my whole life with her as my father did with his beloved, and as you have been and are, with my dear sister, even though she is a Scot.''

Thor smiled, but gently. ''You speak of a lovely dream, Ian. But a dream can turn into a nightmare instead. When you decide on a wife, be sure that what's inside is as lovely as her face.''

Ian laughed. ''Perhaps she is only a dream, and I am foolish. I need time. Say another eight years? As I recall, you were close on thirty years old when you married Aylena.''

''But I knew she was mine when first I saw her,'' Thor said, and smiled, caught up at once by the memory. ''And, at the time, she was trying her best to bite my wrist in two. And when that didn't work, she spat my own blood at me.'' He laughed out loud. ''And I still knew! Perhaps it will be the same for you when the time arrives.''

''Possibly,'' Ian agreed carelessly. ''It could happen at any moment. But it hasn't yet. Even though I hope to find the woman in the mist, I cannot say she won't be the one, nor can I say she will be. Now, tell me if the message has come from the king. Are we, or are we not going to Bures?''

''We go, leaving soon. We will take Margit and James and several men-at-arms, if only for show. We will be there for perhaps a week, and, if all goes well, we'll return home before the new year. But Henry smells trouble from Canterbury again. He is seeing more and more cases when men who murder and steal go unpunished. They run to join the priesthood and hide behind Becket's holy robes.''

''How can that be?''

''Becket has declared that his priests cannot be tried

in secular courts, only in the church's courts of justice. Scoundrels have learned to quickly join the church, and he absolves them in the name of God. Whether he realizes it or not, he is building a nest of thieves who will pull him down.''

"But he must know!"

Thor shook his head. ''He believes his holy hands will heal them of all sin, and they will become angels of light. So far, three of them have killed again, for profit. He has heard their confessions and has declared them innocent once more.''

Ian was silent. In spite of what he had been told, he would not curse a churchman. And other than that, there was nothing more to say. Perhaps in time Becket would learn that hardened criminals who are truly evil and profit by it are hard to change by a simple laying on of an archbishop's hands.

The castle was a beehive. The laundresses were washing and ironing; the armorer was cleaning the shirts of mail and putting an edge on axes and broadswords. Aylena, her thick mane of brilliant red-gold hair in two long braids, her smile wide and happy, was directing the filling of baskets and boxes of wine and loaves and preserves. It was not a long or tiring journey to Bures, and there were friends along the way who would take them in, feed them and amuse them, and so she wanted the finest of foodstuff to give to them as gifts.

Especially she wanted the finest of all for two noble families who lived along the Seine—the family of the Comte de Flanders, where her first son, Thorwald, was a page, and the family of Baron William Capet, where her younger son, Bruce, had been taken in for training.

She was joyful and excited, knowing she would soon see her sons. She came running down the stone steps from the gallery to greet Thor and Ian with hugs.

"This is wonderful, Thor! I had no idea until old Piers came to me and told me the news. When did the message come?"

"Several days ago," Thor said, and grinned at her open mouth. "I know, you are angry because I didn't tell you then. But"—he waved an arm at the scurrying servants and the din of excited voices—"a day or so of this is enough. I am an old man; too much excitement is not good for me."

Both Aylena and Ian burst into laughter. "Old," Ian repeated. "Your man is *old*, my dear sister. Am I a weakling because I cannot win over this old man in the lists? In the last tournament he made me look like a fool. How do you rate him in his own home?"

Aylena's eyes danced. "Why, perhaps he shows less ardor in the marriage bed, but . . ." She shrieked as Thor tossed her over his shoulder and struggled to be free. "Put me down, Thor! The buckle on your shoulder digs into my belly . . ."

"Not for long, my sweet." Thor's long legs were taking the steps to the gallery two at a time, and rapidly. Aylena's hair swung down his back like a golden banner, her fists played a tattoo on his broad back, her voice continued her lament.

"I warn you, Thor! Put me down!"

His deep voice came rolling and laughing down the stairs as he turned toward the solar. "I cannot! I am a slave to my love for you, and my lost ardor has returned in full force. I am not as elderly as I thought." Ian, laughing, turned away and went toward the kitchens. He felt a small pang of jealousy; he knew, as everyone knew, that the ties between his sister and Thor Rodancott were impossible to break, too strong to be cut until death came to one of them, and perhaps not even then. Their marriage was a miracle in the world they lived in, where nobles married for lands, fortunes, connections, and political strength, and found a pale, transient love in other, carefully hidden places. He sighed, going through the kitchens and, by habit, snatching a chunk of hot bread to carry outside. Their kind of marriage was truly rare, yet he felt he'd never be satisfied until he found a woman who could make him feel the way Aylena made Thor feel. So far, only the one in the swirling fog seemed to match the dream.

The old man Piers was in the kitchen garden again, slamming his spade down, turning the dead thatch under the rich dark earth. He looked cold; he looked feeble, and Ian was suddenly sorry for him.

"Why do you dig now, Piers? 'Tis months before the time of planting. Go warm yourself by the kitchen fires."

Piers leaned on the shovel and grinned at him. "You are young, Sir Ian, and no gardener. If I don't turn the thatch down now, it will not rot and make the soil deep and rich in the spring. I am indeed old, but I know my work."

Ian smiled with sudden warmth. "I see. I was thoughtless, not knowing the importance of what you are doing. But there is a limit to any man's strength. If you need help, there are several young lads around the castle, well muscled and with time on their hands. Tell me when you need one of them."

"Not soon, Sir Ian—but you may be looking around for a boy. I could teach a boy much. I'll think on't."

"Good." Ian went on toward the stables, realizing he could have no more than a day or so here at Castle Cheval Noir if he had read Thor aright. Thor knew much more about the king than he ever said, and Ian had seen his thoughts in his cool gray eyes. Thor thought there would be trouble in England soon—and that meant he'd be traveling back with King Henry. And, naturally, Aylena would go along. Since their marriage, they had never been parted. If both of them were going to England, Ian knew, there would be no reason—or excuse—for him to stay here.

Stepping into the shadowy stables, redolent with the odors of grain, sweating horses, and manure, he nodded to the chief ostler. "I believe Rogue is trained well enough to have him as a mount on the road to Bures. Also the three-year-old I rode when I came here. I cannot think of his name . . ."

The ostler laughed. " 'Tis understandable, Sir Ian. His name is Digne de Foi, which means one can trust him to be courteous, but few remember it. We call him Foi, and he answers to it, so it is good enough."

"Then, unless Lord Rodancott has a wish for either of them, those are the two I will take. Will you ride with us, Dirk?"

"Indeed, my lord. I and two others of my station. We will be ready."

"Good."

So, there was nothing more to say. Feeling empty and lost, Ian wandered out again and stood looking north. How long had it been that he'd been spending his days in Vincennes Valoir's pastures? Not quite two weeks, he thought, counting back. It seemed longer than that. But not long enough. There were more lessons that needed attention—more disciplinary work with Devil, more help and information that he could offer to Ciel. If, he thought, I had known we would be leaving soon, I could have said more, done more. She was so appreciative, and so easy to teach.

He sighed, thinking of the future. She would likely be married and a mother by the time he came to Normandy again. Northumberland was many days away, and he couldn't ask the clansmen to take over the work at the castle often, for their own work would suffer. He shrugged and turned, head down, starting for the kitchen. Small, thin Piers, immersed in his work, saw Ian's big body bearing down on him just in time. He leaped out of the way, considerably more agile than anyone thought he was, and said in a high, angry, frightened voice: "Watch your step, m'lord! The ground is mucky where I've dug it up."

One boot immersed in deep muck, the other high on the two inches of frozen ground, Ian cursed, softly but with feeling. "Indeed, I see that is true. Sorry I frightened you, Piers. I wasn't looking."

"That is also true, Sir Ian. Not even a glance did you give me. I'd leave that one boot at the back door, if 'twere mine. Someone will clean it."

"I'll take that advice." He said it humbly, wondering why he felt so gloomy and detached. He hadn't even seen old Piers.

At dinner, Thor and Aylena came to the decision. They would finish their preparations and leave at noon tomorrow, spending the first night with the family of the Comte de Flanders, where they would visit Thorwald, their elder son.

Thor raised his heavy brows at Ian. "I agreed to Aylena's wish. She will have one more, which she hasn't brought out yet. Bring it out, Aylena."

"Certainly, my love. On the following day, I wish to visit the Baron William Capet, and see how Bruce is faring. Since the two men live but a half day's ride from each other, it should be an easy trip."

Thor sighed. "I do not envy either the Comte de Flanders or the Baron William Capet. They will have two young boys acting like princes of the realm for a week after we've gone. You know how our sons get above themselves when you are around, Aylena."

"When *I* am around? It's *you*, Thor, and you know it! The first flattering welcome to the Lord Thor Rodancott, and both of them start walking like you, talking like you, and looking down those Rodancott noses at everyone in sight!"

Ian roared, and the maid serving wine turned giggles into a cough and left the room. Thor kept a straight face, but his gray eyes met Aylena's defiant gaze and softened into humor.

"You may be right, my love. I have noticed the strutting. But to my mind, they are trying to impress you, not the others around them."

After a startled moment, Aylena laughed. "I'll take the blame, my lord, if you'll allow the visits. I ache to see my sons."

"Then it is done."

After dinner Ian went outside in the dark air. The castle walls loomed black around him, keeping enemies out, penning him in. Far overhead, in a blur of misty dark clouds, the winter stars looked pale and frostbitten, too small to give much light. He felt unaccountably gloomy, like a man with no home or family. He knew he was going to miss Vincennes Valoir and his hearty friendship, but even more so the bright face of Vincennes's daughter. Ciel was so charming, so easy to teach, and so beautiful. He hated the thought that their warm friendship would be weakened—as all friendships pale when people must be parted for a long time. She would undoubtedly marry soon . . . some fine fellow Vincennes would find. The thought made him feel even worse.

"Pick well," he whispered, thinking of Vincennes. "Choose a man good enough for her, if one lives . . ."

"Ian?" The heavy door leading to the kitchen swung open, a golden light sprang out and gilded the dark, frozen ground. Wonderful scents floated in the air, and Aylena's slender form appeared, her hair a golden halo. "Ian! Come in! We have a steamed plum pudding yet to eat, little brother."

He turned and smiled. Little brother. He didn't mind the words, as long as they came from his adored Aylena. "You have tempted me, Circe. I'm very fond of plum pudding."

Ian awoke early and put on the clothes he meant to travel in. The servants had packed his other clothes and necessaries the evening before; his weapons, along with Thor's and Thor's knights, were in the great hall below. He went down and took his sword and ax, then told the seneschal, Robert of Lyons, that he would be back an hour before noon.

The seneschal nodded. "Indeed, Sir Ian, the Valoir family would wish to say a prayer for your safety on the road and your good health. They speak of you as of a close friend."

Ian left, heading out to the stables for Rogue and thinking that his friendship with the Valoirs had become common knowledge.

As it turned out, he was in the woodlot field before the Valoirs arrived. And, from an even denser thicket than they had used before, Laron Todden and his brother, Olaf, watched him with hungry, angry eyes. They saw him dismount, tie his black stallion to a tree, and wander away, looking north along the path that came from the Valoir homestead.

Laron grabbed his brother's arm and pointed. "He wears no dagger," he whispered, "and he has left his war ax and sword hanging on the saddle. We can get him, Olaf! Without weapons, he will be no match for two men and two long knives!"

Olaf's eyes gleamed. "And then we shall have his ax and sword, Laron. And the woman he plans to meet."

"Maybe, but if her father comes with her . . ."

"He will not come." Olaf stood up and pulled his long knife from its sheath. "You forget—this morning Vincennes goes to the horse market and will be gone for two days. Come, let's get this big fool!"

They burst from the thicket with wild cries and rushed toward the tall figure standing in the morning sun. Ian turned, recognizing the wiry men, noting the hatred on their thin, dirty faces, the glint of knives in the morning light. Knives. He hated knives. He thought of them as hidden sins, as treachery for cowards to use. And suddenly his handsome face changed, becoming a harsh and ugly mask. Then the fingers of his big hands curled like huge claws, and he faced them fully, waiting. In seconds they were upon him, their eyes wild, their arms raised, their knives flashing in the air, their lips stretched thin, a wolfish snarl of stained and broken teeth . . .

Ian's skill and strength blended with his fury. His hands flashed to their skinny arms, passing the long knives in a blur, taking an immovable, iron grip on their forearms. He flung the two men high in the air together, and, as the thin arcing bodies swung overhead in his iron grasp, he heard their bones snapping and their screeching agony. He loosed them, letting them fall behind him. Then he turned and looked down at them, sprawled in the tall grass behind him. Bloody ends of bone protruded from their crooked and broken arms. They shrieked and groveled, their bodies jerking back and forth in agony.

Ian watched them without compassion, then looked toward the path, hearing the rumbling trot of Devil bringing Ciel Valoir to the field again. He stepped away from the screaming men and stopped her with an up-raised hand.

"Is Vincennes with you?"

Ciel shook her head, her eyes huge. She could hear the howls and screams only too well, and she was frightened, more by the look of implacable anger on Ian's face than by the sounds of pain. There was no pity in him, no mercy.

"This time," Ian said, "the rats need a wagon and a man. Laron and Olaf have had a lesson. Will you see to it?"

Still silent, she nodded and turned, putting Devil to a full, pounding gallop.

Later, after the two villagers had been taken to their homes, Ian—calm and pleasant again—had a brief half hour with Ciel, standing in sunshine and knee-high, shriveled grass while their horses grazed.

"I had hoped for a longer visit," he said after he explained that Thor, Aylena, and he were leaving at noon. "There is so much more I had wanted to tell you." He was uncomfortable because her eyes were wet, and because they were standing close and he wanted badly to take her in his arms and comfort her. His whole body ached with the need to hold her, to kiss the tears away. But he thought he must be wrong in his desires, for there was nothing like that between them:

"But"—Ciel looked away, ashamed of her tears— "you will come back, will you not?"

"I think not," he said, and felt a sorrow that filled his throat with a strange thickness. "I think, in fact, that we may go from Bures to London, and then, of course, I must see to my own demesne in Northumberland."

"I see." Still turned away, she wiped her eyes and turned back to him, forcing a smile. "Our homes are far apart, Lord Ian, and I regret it. But I will always be grateful to you, both for your protection and your knowledge. I know my father will also feel as if he has lost a friend."

"Not you nor he has lost this friend," Ian said abruptly, "nor ever will. If I am ever truly needed, you must tell my sister, and I will come." He took her small hand in his large one, bowed, and kissed it. Straightening, he reached for Rogue's reins.

"Good-bye, my lady."

She smiled bravely, her heart throbbing with pain. "You are flattering me again, Lord Ian."

He bowed to her from the saddle. "No flattery, Ciel. You are much more the lady than most of the ladies I know. May God bless you and your family."

She watched through her tears until he was out of

sight, his tall, striking body shimmering away in bright sunlight and then passing into the deep shadows of the oaks overhanging the road. To Ciel, there was still the hero light about him, even in the shadows. And as she turned to make her way home, she knew there would be no other man who would ever own his place in her aching heart.

3

Bures, Normandy
Christmas Eve 1170

 An icy north wind blew along the gentle Bethune River, swept into the black streets of Bures, and chilled King Henry II and his still-beautiful queen, Eleanor of Aquitaine. They had attended a midnight mass after a day of fasting, and were arm in arm as they left the cathedral into the frigid night, followed by a crowd of fifty or more nobles who had been invited to attend.

There were men with flaring torches, great golden flames lighting the avenue, waiting to guide the royal couple to the huge inn where they were staying. The torchbearers, seeing them leaving the church, divided into two outside lines, so as to protect them as well as to light their way.

The crowd that stumbled along after them on the cobbled street wore clothes chosen for richness and style rather than for warmth, but they hardly felt the cold. They were too interested in the royal couple to give much thought to their own discomfort. For the first time in two years, the king and queen were together in public.

Amongst the crowd of nobles, some were disappointed in this turn of events; others hoped for a final reconciliation between the two. And some curious few were merely eager to learn what would come of it. Gossip about the royal couple was always exciting.

It was barely a ten-minute walk to the large public house where a joyous gathering was to take place. Following the pace that Henry set, the others were soon warm. Always, Henry II walked fast, rode hard, slept little. He was strong as a mule and, it was said, just as stubborn. Red-headed, bowed legs, tremendous shoulders and chest, the king had a talent for winning victories over other countries and, it was often said, over beautiful women. At thirty-seven he was at his physical peak. And Eleanor, in spite of her smooth and unlined face, was forty-eight. There would be no more additions to their flock of children, nor were any needed; his three sons were rapidly growing into rivals for Henry's power.

Right behind the king—close enough to touch him— was the king's man, Thor Rodancott. Thor's cold gray eyes never looked at the king, only at those who crowded around him. His right hand rested casually on the hilt of a long, slim dagger in a loose sheath, and there was no doubt in anyone's mind that he knew how to use it. With Thor at his back, the King of England and ruler of most of France was safe amongst his enemies, no matter the number.

In the middle of the procession, Thor's wife, the Lady Aylena, walked with her brother, Lord Ian Stewart. Aylena's attention had sharpened on Ian nearly as intensely as Thor's on the king's possible enemies. She had seen, as all women can see, the look of a smitten man on her beloved young brother.

Ian's attention had as his target a young, slender woman in the group directly following the king. Dressed in a green velvet gown, trimmed with gold braid, she wore no jewels except for a gold crucifix set with pearls. She had long, shining red-blond hair and her eyes were the color of pale sapphires—not one fleck of green or gray in that blue, Ian would swear to it. She had risen from her seat and faced him as they left the cathedral, and when he saw how beautiful she was he had stumbled and nearly fallen at her feet. 'Twas the woman he had seen in Calais, leaving the ship in the fog. And perhaps she had also seen him, for she had looked away quickly, her face flushing pink, whether in amusement or embarrassment, when she saw him staring at her.

Every feature, Ian thought wildly, is lovely. A small, straight nose, just the right length. A cushiony, soft mouth, beautifully shaped and just right for kissing. And, though slender as a swaying reed, her body was deliciously curved.

Ian was dazzled. He felt she was perfect for him. Fate, he was sure, had led him here to find her. And she had seemed at least a little interested in him.

"Ian."

He started and turned to look down at his sister. "My lady?"

"You might annoy Lady Serena Bertran if you continue to stare at her. Not that I blame you; she is well worth a good stare. But she may be embarrassed by your devoted attention."

"She canna see me watching her, Aylena."

"I have no doubt that she can feel the warmth of your gaze, little brother."

Those last words were delivered with a half smile that tugged up a corner of Aylena's beautiful mouth. The word "little," she thought, was not a word anyone else would use to describe Ian Stewart. At the age of twenty-two, he stood a soaring six foot five inches, a giant amongst his peers. And strong? She had often thanked a thoughtful God for giving Ian a hard-to-rouse temper and a conscience to go with his tremendous strength. Thor had been Ian's instructor in the arts of tournament fighting, and, since Thor believed in being skilled and ready for war even in times of peace, Ian had also learned the deadly arts, and learned them well. Not that he was eager to use them. He was a peaceful man. On the other hand, he was no longer a little boy, and he continued to watch the Lady Serena with a look of great pleasure.

"Perhaps," Ian answered her, "she enjoys the attention. Most beautiful women do. When Thor admires you with warm glances, you become more pleasant than you were just now."

Aylena felt the heat of embarrassment, caught again in a habit of instructing her young brother as she had done when he was a motherless babe. Looking up at him as they approached the huge Chetexe Inn, she gave him an apologetic smile. It was true; likely the young woman Serena did enjoy Ian's rapt attention and would miss it if he looked away. And she would do him no harm in any case. But he was not used to the guile and the secrets, the ambitions, the schemes and lies that flourished like poisonous weeds among these nobles. Those were the things Aylena hated, and she hoped he would never come in contact with those who invented and used them. She made up her mind to find out what connections and friends the Lady Serena had about her. They had once been introduced, but all she really knew about the girl was her name.

They had come to the steps leading up into the huge

inn, and Lord Thor Rodancott, having seen the royal couple safely within the doors, came back to Aylena and offered his arm. Ian was away at once, hurrying to catch the lovely Serena before she reached the doors and disappeared in the crowd.

Aylena took Thor's arm and leaned toward him gracefully to speak in an undertone. "Since I know you and Philippe Bertran are in the same business, you must know him at least. How well?"

"I know him well enough. Why?"

Aylena shook her head in amusement. Thor never noticed warm glances or flirtations. But, on the other hand, he was quick to note a nearly hidden scowl directed toward Henry II and quick to hear a muttered lie or scheme. Foremost in his mind was his duty.

"Then I will ask this: Is the Bertran family of good blood?"

Thor hesitated on the broad steps to allow others to pass around them. Once they had, he lowered his voice. "Why do you ask?"

Aylena watched Ian as he entered the inn, still on the trail of the young beauty. She lowered her voice in turn. "Ian is fascinated by Bertran's daughter. It would not surprise me at all if he fell in love with her."

Thor rewarded her with a gentle smile, an odd smile on his hard face, and one he kept for her alone. "You leap far ahead in the stories of love, and you are often right. But I believe the young lady is ambitious, and she may tell Ian to take his attentions elsewhere. Wait, and we'll see."

Aylena's clear brow wrinkled. "Can you not answer my question, Thor? Surely I am worthy of your trust."

"I hesitate. It may not be what you wish to hear."

"I would hear the truth."

"Then you will. There is plenty of noble blood in Bertran's veins, but there is a bar sinister across his war shield. She hides it as well as she can, but 'tis true. Her father, like Vincennes Valoir, is one of the Plantagenet's by-blows."

"Oh." Aylena looked down and began again to climb the steps, trailing now behind the other, more eager guests. "Thank you for telling me." The tone of her soft voice was sad. "But if that is true, why was she welcomed to the king's Christmas Mass and the gathering now?"

Thor smiled faintly. "In this case, he simply allows his 'cousins' to attend his fetes and parties."

"I see," Aylena said, "but I don't approve!"

Thor laughed out loud, taking her hands and holding her still outside the double doors. "How shocked you look! You can't blame our king for this. Only his father. As everyone knows, all the Plantagenets left behind many royal bastards, and one of them was Henry. Henry is but showing kindness to a lovely relative, one of many fruitful sins of his lustful father."

"I see." Aylena shook down her cloak and turned to the door. "A tangled web indeed. And she claims a title? I do hope Ian isn't seriously interested."

They were the last to enter the large but crowded hall of the inn. Ian, still with an eye on the beautiful young woman, was halfway through the crush of excited, talkative guests. Wine was being offered; servants passed around the edges of the crowd with brimming goblets that were welcomed with eagerness after the day's fast. Long tables had been placed in the huge hall; a smaller one on the raised dais at the end. Hot food was being placed on all of them. This had been a long day of fasting and prayer; now came an evening of feasting and revelry.

Slowly Thor and Aylena made their way through the crowd to the high table at the rear and found seats kept for them near to the king and queen. The faces around them now were flushed and happy, the voices rose to a deafening swirl of talk and loud laughter.

"There," Thor said, bending to Aylena's ear, "Ian has reached his admired lady and is talking to her. She seems cool toward him."

Aylena looked. It was easy to pick out Ian in the crowd; he stood half a head over the tallest of the other men. And, from the dais, Aylena could see that the look on Serena Bertran's lovely face was cool, as Thor had said. Cool and distant, though polite. Aylena sighed and looked at Thor. Ian had been persistent from his childhood on, they knew that well.

"At times," Aylena said softly, "I wish for a daughter. It is hard to be wife, sister, and mother to four determined men."

Thor laughed out loud. "What? You call our sons men? Perhaps Thorwald nears man's estate, he will soon be sixteen, but Bruce is only ten."

"True," Aylena admitted. "I should have said males, not men. I need an older daughter, and I expect Ian to provide me with one by marrying. But this young woman seems very cool toward everyone." She looked again and saw Ian leading the Bertran woman and her attendant toward one of the long tables. There was a happy flush of success on his bearded cheeks.

Ian had taken no chances. He had approached the lovely young woman carefully, looking around her for her parents, perhaps, or a brother. But except for a plump older woman who seemed glued to her side, he saw no one who spoke to her; even the younger women who passed gave her no more than quick, wondering glances. So, he made his plan and began it. He went to the older woman and bowed.

"Let me find you seats at one of these tables," he said. "I would enjoy the company of the young lady you attend, but I would also wish you to take a seat with us, for propriety." That last was an arrant lie, and the companion knew it as well as he. Still, it was the proper opening. The companion, a gray-haired, plump, and jaded woman, gave him a conspiratorial grin.

"Indeed. It would be helpful if you can find us seats. Don't you agree, Lady Serena?"

Serena looked at the woman and then at Ian. Suspicion gathered on her lovely face, creating a faint frown. "Will you say your name, my lord?"

Ian bowed deeply. "Ian Stewart, laird of Stewart Castle, in Northumberland, and I am at your service." He would have appreciated a smile, but the beautiful face stayed somber and questioning. He added more words, quickly. "I am a stranger in Normandy, as you must have guessed, but you may know of my sister, the Lady Aylena Rodancott."

The frown eased. "Rodancott is a name I know. My father, Philippe Bertran, counts Thor Rodancott as a friend and respects him highly as the king's man." She hesitated, and then, as if realizing there was nothing to fear in this situation, smiled stiffly and added: "I am the Lady Serena Bertran, and this is my aunt, Madame Therese Pernoud. My aunt and I will appreciate your help in finding seats."

Ian looked at her and saw nothing but perfection. He bowed and offered his bent arm. She took it, but made sure she maintained a proper distance between their bodies. At the table she sat beside him, with her aunt on the other side, listened to his conversation and compliments, ate daintily and drank little. And, afterward, she willingly went with him, her hand on his arm, to be introduced to the Lady Aylena.

Aylena was gracious; only Thor recognized her doubts. He bowed, and, since he had news from the king to give to Ian, drew him away and left Aylena with Serena Bertran and her aunt.

Thor and Ian found a spot near the entrance where the air was so cold no one cared to wander there or try to listen. Thor's face was grim as he told Ian there was trouble ahead with Ireland, where Norman Marcher lords had at last captured Dublin and were overrunning the eastern coast as far south as Waterford.

"And there is more trouble brewing," Thor ended, "Henry spoke foolishly when he came here, cursing Thomas à Becket and saying he wished someone would rid him of that turbulent priest. We have had word in the last half hour that some of his most loyal men are on their way to drag Becket from the cathedral and send him back to his friends in Rome. If they use force, Henry will be censured by the pope."

Ian listened with only half an ear. He was usually interested in any news of the king, but tonight he could see only one face, hear only one voice. He excused himself as quickly as he could and made his way back to Aylena's chair and the young woman he had left with her. Serena gave him a cool, short-lived smile.

"I must be going," she said, rising from her seat.

"My aunt is tired, and my parents will be wondering why I have not returned. But I wished to wait and thank you for your courtesies, Lord Ian. It was pleasant to talk to you."

Ian bowed. "May I request a later meeting, my lady? I would value the privilege."

She looked suddenly amused. "Indeed, why not? It must be like a holiday for you to be here in our beautiful country. Your sister has been telling me of the place where you live. She says it is in a barren land, and cold in every season. But she also says it is beautiful in its serenity." She put forth a hand and took his. "While you are here, Lord Ian, you will be welcome at my father's home."

"May I see you to your horses?"

She gave another trill of cool amusement, as if she laughed at his excessive concern. "Tonight we stay at another inn, only a short walk from here, and my father's men await us to see us there safely. Good night, Lord Ian."

The large hall was emptying; Ian stood to watch her slim figure make a way through the few knots of chattering people and disappear. Then, disappointed, he turned back to Aylena.

"When will you and Thor return to your castle?"

Aylena smiled wryly. Ian would want to stay in Bures and devote himself to courtship. She had seldom seen a man so struck by a pretty face, nor so oblivious to chilly manners.

"We shall surely stay through tomorrow; and, if the king has need of Thor, then longer."

Ian's strong features finally relaxed into a smile.

"Good. Now I must find directions to the home of Philippe Bertran. I wish to visit the Lady Serena."

"Thor will be able to help you with that," Aylena said, and hesitated. "He knows the Bertrans, and their history."

"Their history?" Ian laughed, his whole eager face lighting up. "I am more concerned with the Lady Serena's future."

"Still," Aylena added, frowning, "it is wise to know as much as possible about their background. For instance, Philippe Bertran is—uh, a horse breeder." She had meant to mention the illegitimacy and had lost her courage in the end.

But Ian was off, searching the crowd for Thor. Then, seeing him standing in frowning attention as King Henry spoke to a silent circle of men, Ian turned away. Best to stay out of that, he thought, and turned back to join Aylena as she left the dwindling groups and headed for the steps that led up to their suite on the second floor. When possible, Thor stayed in the same inns as the king when Henry traveled around his huge demesne.

Aylena greeted Ian with a smile. "A few hours of sleep will do you no harm, Ian. If this north wind moderates with morning, I'll want a ride along the shore of Bethune River. Perhaps you will accompany me."

"With a will, my sister. And later you can inquire for me as to the inn where my Lady Serena reposes. Tell the truth, Aylena—have you ever seen a more beautiful woman?"

Climbing the stairs, Aylena looked over at him and thought before she spoke. "None more beautiful, Ian, but many much warmer. 'Tis a cold eye your new friend has."

Ian frowned. " 'Twill warm as she knows us better."

"Perhaps." And it was possible, Aylena thought. This young woman, hoping to be taken into the highest society, would be careful and cautious—particularly because of the stain on her father's birth. There would be many jealous mothers of less attractive females who would point out the Bertran family's bar sinister at every opportunity. It might be countenanced by the king, and it did hold the boon of the king's own Plantagenet blood, but always gossip can hurt a young woman's chances . . .

They parted at the landing, each going to their designated rooms. In Aylena's room her maid Margit, who now had streaks of silver in her dark hair, waited patiently for her mistress. Plump and smiling, Margit took down Aylena's mane of red-gold hair and brushed it thoroughly.

"Tell me," Margit said as she brushed, "does the queen seem happy? Do you believe they will reconcile?"

"In heaven perhaps. But never in France. Or, for that matter, in England. She is even more bitter than before."

"She is jealous of his Rosamund, you think?"

"Heavens, no. She is jealous only of Henry's power. Eleanor of Aquitaine will never be happy until she rules a large portion of Henry's lands."

Margit laughed. "No doubt she will—through her sons. They have been promised much by their father the king, but they will listen to her."

Aylena nodded. "They will indeed. Especially Richard, whom she has always intended to honor. He is already the Count of Poitiers, and the king has promised him Aquitaine." She yawned and motioned Margit away, taking the brush in her own hands.

"Go, Margit. I'll not keep you gossiping here while James is wondering if you'll stay up all night. Go warm his bed."

Margit laughed easily. She and her mistress had long been confidants and friends. "Indeed, I believe you think of James's comfort before mine own. I'll lay out your night shift and be on my way."

At dawn Ian was at Aylena's door, ready to accompany her on a morning ride. Up and dressed, Aylena went with him to the common room of the inn below, where they drank warm ale and ate coarse bread smeared with butter and preserves. Then Ian set out for the stables behind the inn and brought around their horses, the quick and slender black Arabian Barb Aylena owned and the gentle Foi for Ian. They set out at once for the shore, a mile or so away. They were in sight of the sliding dark water of the Bethune when a shout behind them stopped them both. They both turned to look and smile.

"I thought it odd that you managed to leave Thor behind," Ian said as Thor came galloping up to them. "But, as always, he has refused to let you stay out of his sight."

Thor's black bearded face was calm and amused. "I am more in need of fresh air than either of you, I vow. The meetings last night stank of jealousies, greed, and plots. I decided I needed the company of thoughtless innocents, and here I am. Shall we proceed to the river?"

"At once," Aylena said, and put her heels to the sides of the Barb. She was off, in a mass of fluttering skirts and her wool scarf waving good-bye. She won the race as she had known she would, the quick little horse leaving the heavy warhorses far behind. She laughed at them as they came up, the thunder of the great, galloping monsters shaking the ground.

"Now I am happy." She gasped. "I believe I have banished all the suspicions and evil stories I heard last night. They poured out of my ears as my black butterfly flew and fell in the dirt where they belonged. Ah, but I do hate the whisperings and plots."

"And I feel the same," Thor said heavily. "I rue the day I promised Henry to be his man. Soon I will ask for my freedom. Come, let us ride along the shore and dream of summer."

Ian joined them as they moved away, taking a place on Aylena's right. "I will ride with you, Thor, for a few moments. But I will dream of another golden-haired woman as beautiful as my sister. I need to find the inn where the lady Serena Bertran stays. Do you know it?"

"Yes, of course. The Bertran family owns it and uses it when they come into Bures. 'Tis a small inn, no more than a five-minute walk from the Chetexe where we are staying, and I know it is comfortable. I have stayed in it myself when I came here alone."

"The name?"

"Sans Sottise. Head south from where we are staying and then east, no more than a stroll away. You will see the sign, which has the shape of a flying swan. The building itself is of wood over stone."

"Good!" Ian's face was joyous. " 'Tis early yet to call on her. I'll ask for her only after the hour of ten. But I will see to the directions first and be sure of the place." He turned back, lifting a hand to them in farewell, his white teeth shining in a broad smile, the bronze beard glowing in a ray of sunlight.

Aylena stared after him as he rode away. "He is not thinking with his head, Thor, only with his heart. She was cold to him, taking advantage of the only man who approached her last night. Why did the girl come to the festivities with only an old female companion?"

Thor sighed, riding on. "I know very little of women, my love. But I would guess she and her aunt came against the wishes of her father, who is no more ambitious of a place at court than our friend Vincennes Valoir."

"You confuse me. What does Vincennes Valoir have in common with Philippe Bertran?" Aylena, her hair blowing loose in the wind from the water, tied her reins to the pommel of her saddle and began tucking the long golden strands into her scarf. "Of course, they are both horse breeders, but so far as I know, the king doesn't knight men for breeding good warhorses . . ."

"Philippe and Vincennes are not likely to tell you this, but they are both half brothers of Henry, my love."

"What? Why . . . why that is shameful! Who was the mother?"

"There were two mothers, both beautiful women, who were married off to decent men and given a good sum of money to be their dowry. It is a common thing amongst royalty, Aylena. Don't be upset. Both men are sensible and hardworking, and neither has asked favors from the king. Haven't you ever noticed the resemblance between Vincennes and our king? Philippe, at least, looks like his mother's family."

Aylena was silent for a few moments and then burst forth again. "What you have told me only deepens my concern for Ian. This young woman may encourage him only to put herself into the crowd of fawning idiots who surround the king and queen. I am sure she would never consider being the wife of a young lord who can only offer her love and an ancient castle in Northumberland. She could break his heart."

"She could not. Ian is not a soft-headed fool. I am surprised at your thoughts."

Aylena looked at Thor, amazed. "And I, at yours. Why, he's head over heels in love with her now."

Thor laughed. "He is head over heels in love with his dream, darling, but he will wake up later. The woman has long, beautiful red-gold hair. She is slender and graceful; her eyes are a true blue. In her looks, and in her looks only, she is very like the sister he adores, the sister who raised him lovingly and well. Ian will see the difference in time."

"That," Aylena said angrily, "is outright foolishness! I have nothing to do with any young man's dream, for heaven's sake. I am a—a—dowager!" She turned her horse and rode back toward the Chetexe Inn, her back stiffly straight, her golden head high, pretending not to hear Thor's laughter.

4

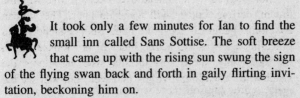 It took only a few minutes for Ian to find the small inn called Sans Sottise. The soft breeze that came up with the rising sun swung the sign of the flying swan back and forth in gaily flirting invitation, beckoning him on.

Ian's heart lifted even as he turned away from the clean, prosperous-looking establishment. The morning was glorious with sunlight and brightly colored silk pennants put out in honor of the English king, but he was wise enough to know that the ladies within would spend the morning hours in gossip with other ladies as their maids catered to them. It was not fashionable to appear until ten even among England's noble ladies, and 'twas rumored the French often slept until noon.

At the Chetexe, Ian first headed into the kitchen for a solid breakfast of warm ale, cold fowl, and a fruit pie. Then he sought out the innkeeper and ordered a bath brought to his room. A half hour later he luxuriated in a big wooden tub, lying back in the warm water and dreaming of some day sharing a bath with Serena. In his dreams he saw a pale, curved body gleaming in the water like smooth alabaster, the tight pink buds of nipples on her breasts, the smooth curves of her slim hips. He forced his heated thoughts away and began drying himself with linen towels, rubbing roughly until his skin was dry and warm. Then he dressed, choosing a long, loose velvet tunic in deep blue, set off with a broad gold belt, to be worn over his cream-colored chausses. He put on soft and supple leather boots, which he laced up along the inside of his ankles. His fur-lined cloak, the same gold wool cloak he had swirled about Ciel Valoir to cover her small half-nude body, was next. He smiled as he put it on, remembering how grateful she was and how fast she ran, her white, mud-smeared feet flying up behind her . . . and, suddenly, he was conscious of a strange feeling of emptiness and loss.

He wondered at it and then tried to shake the feeling away, telling himself there was no help for it. It was as she had said. Their homes were too far apart for a close friendship.

The last bit of holiday attire was a new gold wool Phrygian cap, trimmed with jeweled medallions on either side, matching his swinging cloak and peaking up at the crown of his head, fitting smoothly over thick bronze hair that brushed his shoulders. Leaving the room, he glanced into the buffed steel mirror. He had trimmed his short beard and moustache before he took his bath, and he thought he'd done rather well. Perhaps he wasn't as fashionable as some of the French nobles, but he was clean and wearing his best. In Northumberland, French fripperies had never been important.

Seeking out the Rodancott horses in the huge stables behind the Chetexe, he asked to have both Rogue and the gentle Foi saddled and made ready to ride. Few noblewomen ever brought a horse just to ride for pleasure, and he was sure Foi would please Serena. He set off for

Sans Sottise with a light heart. There had been many times in the past few years that he thought he'd never find the woman he dreamed of, and now that the miracle had happened, he felt wonderful and told himself it was meant to be.

Serena Bertran had not been idle. Other nobles and their knights had chosen to stay at Sans Sottise instead of paying the exorbitant prices of the Chetexe. Among them, Serena had several acquaintances, including some older women. They had all met for breakfast in a private room and the gossip flew. Sly laughter warmed the chilly room.

Serena, wise in the company of older noblewomen, had been careful. She had mentioned the Lady Aylena and had only to listen as the others talked of Lord Rodancott, Lady Rodancott, and the regard in which the king held them.

"And also the Lady Aylena's brother!" One dowager spoke as if sharing a secret. " 'Tis true that Lord Ian Stewart owns a wild and uncomfortable demesne bordering Scotland, and knows but little of court life, so that some are inclined to laugh at his youthful ignorance. But within a year or two we should expect to see Lord Rodancott step down from his position and put his young brother-in-law in his place as the king's man. If so, you can be sure he'll learn very quickly and cut a swath amongst the young women at court. He is a handsome and virile young man."

"Can that be true?" Another elderly lady was incredulous. "He is so young! And while I hear he is quick with weapons in the tourneys, he may lack the judgment a man earns in war. The king needs a seasoned warrior at his shoulder always."

The first woman shrugged. "All I know is what I hear. And I have heard on all sides that Lord Stewart was trained by Lord Rodancott from his childhood on. If that is the case, I think we can be sure he will make an excellent king's man."

Serena kept her eyes down but listened attentively. It seemed that Ian Stewart, in spite of his laughable innocence, had been taken into the king's inner circle. Though she had no intention of marrying a man who lived in cold, desolate Northumberland, it appeared that there was more to be obtained from his interest in her than she had thought. She looked up, signing to one of the servants to come to her. The maid came, curtsied, and waited.

"If someone asks for me," Lady Serena whispered, slipping the maid a coin, "ask him to wait and then let me know he is here. I expect a visitor."

The maid smiled, pocketing the coin and lowering her voice. "A tall and handsome lord who mentioned your name is already cooling his heels in the solar, my lady. What shall I tell him?"

Serena's smile glowed. "Tell him I will join him soon. I don't want him to leave."

"Yes, my lady."

The solar of Sans Sottise was, of course, on the second floor and on the south side of the popular inn. It was a narrow room, but stretched from the plain rear wall to the usual stone and wood facade, with glazed windows to add light and warmth. After a quick trip to her room to change her gown and have a maid dress her hair, Serena hastened there, coming in silently and looking around. A small smile curved her perfect lips. Standing at a sunny window, Ian dwarfed most of the men in the crowded room, and his face was as handsome as that of a Roman god. Serena was suddenly pleased with his appearance; 'twould reflect well on her if he showed a preference for her company when others were about. She went toward him with a much sweeter expression than she had shown him before, determined to charm him.

"My Lord Ian, you have surprised me. I was sure you would have forgotten me before the night was over. I am flattered by your visit."

She put out both her small hands, and he took them in his, amazed and delighted by their softness, by the white skin and rosy fingernails, so feminine and tender.

"I could never forget you, Lady Serena. You are both beautiful and gracious. I have come to ask you to ride with me so we can talk."

She frowned a little. She hadn't thought to leave the cozy inn in such weather. "I would be happy to comply, my lord, but I have brought no saddle horses with me."

"I took the liberty of bringing along another warhorse besides my own, in case you accepted the ride with me. He is extremely quiet and well mannered. Would that suit you?" She shrugged and smiled, not particularly pleased but wanting to seem agreeable. "I have ridden warhorses all my life," she told him. "My father, like Lord Rodancott, raises Percherons. However, I choose only the best trained and those of meek nature. In fact, I am truly a coward."

Ian smiled. "Then I've brought the mount that will suit you best of any I can name. His name is Digne de Foi, and he lives up to it. Come, put on a warm cloak and hood, and we'll ride together."

"No hood," she answered, amused by his ignorance of fashion. "I am neither a monk nor a peasant. I will have my maid wrap me well in a woolen wimple and find my warmest cloak. The day is raw.''

They left the inn a half hour later; the Lady Serena gowned in a green velvet tunic over a white undergown of pleated silk, with a full fur-lined cloak of supple yellow leather over her slim shoulders. Her slippers also were of yellow leather, and her wimple, made of thick silk, matched the green of her gown. Ian was sure he'd never seen such a beautifully robed female in all his life, even in the king's London court.

''Each time I see you,'' he said, helping her mount the huge Foi, ''you are more beautiful than before. Soon you will have all of France and England at your feet.''

Serena laughed. For once her laughter was clear and merry, without a sign of concealed bitterness. She settled herself in the big saddle and disposed her full skirts about her neatly, her face still shining and happy as she took up the reins. ''If you can bring that about, Lord Ian, I will surely bless you in my prayers.''

''Then I shall surely try,'' Ian said, and, for once, mounted Rogue carelessly. Always ready to take advantage, Rogue reared and whirled in the air, trying to dislodge him. Ian, aware of his mistake, stood in his stirrups and brought him down calmly, rubbing the thick, bowed neck and speaking softly. Rogue stood still, quivering, and Serena smiled.

''You have a gentle hand with a warhorse, my lord. I believe he knows what you say.''

''He also knows when my attention is elsewhere,'' Ian said, and laughed. ''We teach each other. Come along to the river shore and I'll shake out Rogue's disobedience on wet land.''

Serena nodded. She knew enough of horses to realize

that Rogue would cause trouble in town unless he used up some of his rested strength and waywardness. She turned to the city gates and set a smart pace toward the river.

Ian grinned and followed, holding Rogue back. Like all warhorses, Rogue hated to be held behind another, and this was another lesson that would do him no harm.

The river, low because of little rain, exposed a wide and solid shore. Serena stopped Foi and waited until Ian came up, grinning and holding Rogue to a fast trot.

"Now," he called out, "I will give him his head and hope I can turn him before we reach the English Channel!"

Serena laughed, excited. "Go, then! We'll see who wins, you or your horse!"

Grinning, Ian settled himself in the big saddle, loosened the reins and pressed Rogue's huge sides with his heels. "Charge, *mon ami!* Go!"

Rogue responded with a burst of speed, hurtling himself forward with all his strength. Among all of the Rodancott warhorses, Rogue was the fastest, and the hardest to turn. He grew drunk on the freedom of running wild, and Thor had often said the horse would burst his own heart unless someone stopped him. And here on this long, straight, sunlit shore, he seemed clearly determined to run until he dropped.

Serena, who knew enough of warhorses to understand how dangerous this could be for Ian, watched excitedly. Her heartbeat accelerated with every minute. If the horse dropped; if the man were killed, 'twould be a magnificent story to tell . . . and when she told it, everyone would realize that the young lord was racing the horse to gain her admiration. Not that she wanted Ian Stewart to die; but if he were foolish enough to take the chance, why, then she could easily embroider such a wonderful tale to her advantage!

But no. She relaxed and took in a long, leveling breath. The horse and his rider had come to a distant point to the west, far enough from her that they seemed a toy horse, a boy in the saddle. She shook her head, marveling. Few of the heavy warhorses could run at top speed that far, but Rogue was coming back almost as fast as he ran away.

And then she put on a wide smile and kicked Foi into a trot to meet them. "That was indescribable, Lord Ian! You managed him wonderfully well. Few men would dare to give that horse his head, I am sure."

Ian flushed with pleasure, patting Rogue's thick neck, now gleaming with sweat in the bright, chilly air. "Nor would I, had I not helped to train him. But after his run, he's ready to behave. Where can we go to ride together?"

"There is an open woods once you pass the center of town. Come, and I'll show you how to get there." Serena spoke rather indulgently, as if reassuring a child, but Ian didn't mind. He was too happy in her company to object. He followed her lead to one of the open town gates and passed in to the narrow streets and the long lines of crowded dwellings that led to the center of town.

Away from the cold wind and protected by the town walls, they rode side by side in winter sunlight. Ian scarcely saw the people around them, nor the houses and gardens giving way to brick-laid streets with markets and stores. He was only aware of the woman beside him, the woman of his dreams. She seemed wonderful to him with her glorious red-gold hair, her deep blue eyes and small, trim figure.

Serena's pale face took on the warmth of the bright day; she smiled gaily when she saw other noblemen and ladies nodding pleasantly as they passed. She was never truly snubbed by the nobles of King Henry's court, but usually the greetings that came her way were formal and cool. It seemed that the presence of Lord Ian Stewart made the smiles more genuine, the greetings warmer. She was surprised by that, since he was so young and untried, but she was learning that he was very well liked. She began to feel that he might be the key to her own good fortune . . . in England.

"A fool," Ian said suddenly, and laughed. "There, my lady, amongst those gathered in the market square. I can hear their laughter and his jingling bells from here. Shall we go and see the comedy?"

She looked at him, dumbfounded, and then shrugged. "Why, if kings can have their fools, so may we. I have never watched one in the town, so it will be a new entertainment to see."

"Then come. If the fool's jokes are too rough for your ears, we will leave at once."

The crowd parted to let the nobles on horseback enter the circle around not only one but two fools, one dressed in motley, with dangling strips of red and yellow cloth sewn with bells that jangled and clashed constantly as he whirled in a dance. The other man, foolishly grinning, drank from a jug and swung a long rod with a distended pig's bladder bobbing at the end, aiming at every man within his reach and bouncing the bladder on his head.

"There! And there! If the bladder splits, sirs, it will sharpen your wits and scent you with a new parfum,

sickly but strong, which will send those about you running away . . . come now, throw us a penny and I'll not
threaten you more with my dangerous weapon.''

From the laughing onlookers copper oboles flashed
into the cold, sunny air and scattered themselves at the
dancer's feet. The man stopped dancing to look around
him in pretended awe, scratching his head and mumbling
as if to himself:

''Ah-ha! The goodmen of Bures and their goodwives
wish to appear generous today, flashing their coin before
the lovely face of King Henry's favorite . . . ah, shall we
say it more politely . . . one of his favorite cousins?''

Faces turned toward the two warhorses, wondering
eyes flickered over Serena's face. A happy flush warmed
her cheeks and she smiled, preening a little. Ian's expression changed; he saw a dull anger and scorn growing
in many of the eyes turned toward Serena, and knew she
hadn't noticed it at all.

''Come,'' he said, and turned his horse carefully in
the crowd, motioning her to follow him. Serena frowned
a little but obeyed. Once they were free of the others,
she came to his side.

''They meant no harm,'' she said carelessly. ''Everyone in Bures knows the Bertran family, and they all
respect us. Perhaps a few are jealous, but that is natural.
They, too, would like the benefits we receive from King
Henry.''

''It is often wise to leave a crowd when a fool is
pointing you out,'' Ian said, ignoring what she said. He
was surprised that Serena wanted to stay and listen to
the fool calling her—and her tentative position in court
life—to the mob's attention. Then, glancing again at her
pleased expression, he thought to himself that she was

still a child in her pleasures and had no thought of raising jealousy or scorn in others. But he could watch over her and keep her from harm.

He smiled at her and pushed away his concern. "Shall we find those open woods and ride in them? It's a perfect day. The air is so cool, and the sun's warmth is just enough."

She laughed gaily and nodded. "There may be friends of mine in the woods. If so, I will present you to them."

"I shall be honored."

They rode on, coming finally to a small forest reached through one of the open but guarded gates to the town. These woods were splattered with sunlight, many of the trees were bare of leaves, but still numerous pines shadowed the trails. There were the sounds of laughter and conversation that proved other nobles, drawn from both Normandy and England, were there for amusement or flirtation. Serena sat forward in her saddle and peered around, her eyes sparkling with anticipation.

"Come," she said, "we must find them! Listen to them laugh. They are likely in the valley below us, and we can join them quickly. What a happy chance!"

But Ian had recognized the voices. "We'll not be welcome in that group, Serena. Queen Eleanor is among them, as well as her son, Richard."

Serena's eyes rounded. "Are you so familiar with the queen and her son that you can so easily recognize their voices among the others? Or"—she added, suddenly suspicious—"is that merely an excuse because you want to be alone with me?"

Ian reddened. "I do not lie, Serena. Neither do I take advantage of my friendship with my country's queen.

Had she wanted me with her, she would have sent a man to say so.''

Frowning, Serena looked away. "I see. Possibly you are telling the truth, but I doubt it. Besides, this cool air is becoming cooler and less inviting. Shall we go back?''

"We shall, if you wish.'' Ian was surprised at Serena's obvious distrust of him. He turned as she turned gentle Foi, jerking the reins angrily. Then he was silent as they headed toward the town again. In a few moments, Serena gave a small, embarrassed laugh.

"I am sorry to have said something so rude," she said sweetly. " 'Twas disappointing that you thought it wrong to join the queen's party, and I'm afraid I spoke too quickly. Will you forgive me?''

Ian let out his dismay with a long, relieved breath. "I forgive you most willingly, my lady. I will ask if Queen Eleanor will receive you if she stays for another day or two. She may refuse, but I will tell her you have the kindest feelings for her, and a deep loyalty.''

"Indeed," Serena said piously. "Indeed I do. My whole family is deeply loyal to both King Henry and Queen Eleanor, in spite of the trouble between them. 'Tis a pity two such remarkable and glorious rulers cannot agree.''

"They agree on much," Ian said, "but disagree on many serious matters. Both are strong-minded.'' He smiled at Serena as he added, "Few women are brave enough to defy a king, yet our queen disagrees with him both often and loudly.''

Serena nodded, laughing a little. But after a few moments Ian looked away, his smile fading.

" 'Tis a pity," he added slowly. "For, could they agree, they could rule all of Europe.''

"Then perhaps it is good that they disagree." Serena's voice held a tinge of sourness. "The rest of Europe would not like bowing to tiny England."

He looked at her, surprised, and then nodded. "You have the right of it, Lady Serena. Every man loves the land he springs from and hates the conqueror who takes it by force. But many Normans such as yourself have moved into England since William the Bastard conquered her, and now few of the English resent the Plantagenet line."

Serena's small mouth curved in a satisfied smile. "Ah, I am happy to hear that. I may carve a niche for myself then."

Puzzled, Ian glanced at her and then away. The expression on her small face was secretive but also triumphant. He was silent, waiting. If she wished to say more he would listen, but he would not ask.

At Sans Sottise Ian lifted Serena from Foi's back and set her on her feet in a swirl of cloak and fluttering gown. He had tied both of the warhorses to the posts along the front of the small inn and now intended to escort her in and to the sunny solar where she had found him. He took her arm and led her up the steps to the wide door.

"I will return you to the care of Madame Pernoud," he said, "and beg her pardon for stealing you away without her. It was too great a temptation to resist."

Serena laughed. "Had I wanted a dowager with me," she said, "I could have found too many to count. But here, in Bures and in the light of day, I need no chaperone."

"Still," Ian began, entering the inn, "I would see you to her charge . . ."

"Oh, no, m'lord Ian, you need not . . ." Serena had taken her hand from his arm and moved a step away, her eyes on a laughing group of men and ladies in the shadowed foyer. "I will be fine, and indeed safe. I have many friends here in my father's inn."

Ian had forgotten that little detail. He flushed a dark red below his tanned skin. "Of course, my lady. When shall we meet again?"

"Undoubtedly at one of the gatherings planned as a tribute to King Henry," she said, moving away from him and looking back with a smile. "There are many, I am told."

Ian was not satisfied, but there was little he could say. He bowed; she gave a quick little nod and went on, heading for the group in the shadows. One or two of the men were smiling in her direction; the other men and all of the women were chattering gaily and paying no attention to either Serena nor Ian.

Strangely, Ian recognized none of them, though he knew most of the nobles from France and Normandy who visited King Henry. He watched Serena blend gracefully into the group and then turned away and went out again into bright sunlight and cool air. After mounting Rogue, he leaned to untie Foi's reins so he could lead him. He felt extremely confused as he left Sans Sottise and began to move along at a fast clip. This courting, he thought, kept a man on edge. It would take considerable time to feel at ease with someone as beautiful and as strangely cool as Serena Bertran.

5

 The young king, Henry III, who had been crowned this very year at the insistence of his father, Henry II, met Ian at the entrance of the Chetexe, hastening outside as he saw him dismounting from Rogue. Young Henry's face was pale, his eyes red from lack of sleep and frightened. At once Ian was struck by a feeling of impending danger. He bowed, as he must in the presence of royalty, but then grasped young Henry's forearm, fearing trouble had come to the boy's father. Though nearing sixteen, Henry was clearly shaken.

"What has happened, my prince? Why are you here?" Ian knew the young king liked to stay in England when Henry II traveled. It would take a catastrophe to move him from the royal seat at Winchester, where he played at being king, even though his father always named a justiciar to reign in his absence.

At times, Henry III demanded nearly as much pomp and consideration as his father, the present king, asked of his subjects. But this was not such a time. The young king put his other hand over Ian's hand on his forearm and grasped it tightly.

"Thank God and all the angels for you and Lord Rodancott, Ian! There will be angry men from all of Christendom trying to kill my father and perhaps even me, for four of his most trusted magnates have killed the Archbishop of Canterbury, and have most viciously spilled his brains in front of his own altar!''

Taken aback, Ian first stared, wordless, and then shook his head. ''It cannot be. The king would never give such an order.''

''I well know that! But the death is from a beating witnessed by the monks, who swear they recognized the men. My father's enemies have accused him of sending his men to rid him of Thomas à Becket while he hides from the heinous crime here in Normandy.''

''That is not true!''

''I know it is not! But others will believe it. The priests and other dignitaries of the church have created a huge uproar, for this has frightened all of them. They are solidly against my father, and the feeling will spread to take in our whole family.''

Ian heard the fear in the young king's voice and glanced about. He saw men edging nearer, trying to hear. Their faces were full of avid curiosity.

''Let us seek privacy,'' he said, ''and your father. Is Lord Rodancott with him?''

''Indeed. As is William the Marshal. He is very well protected at this moment. Come, we will see what they have decided to do.''

They went inside, young Henry leading the way up the wide stairs to the suite of rooms where the royal couple were staying. He opened the door without knocking and declaring himself, and was met by two big men on their feet, their chairs kicked over behind them, their swords in their upraised hands. Thor and William lowered their swords and looked at each other before turning back to their seats. Young Henry's pale face grew red as he apologized to them and to his father for daring to enter before he had knocked and given his name.

"I have brought Lord Stewart to you," he added. "He knew nothing of what had happened. I thought you would want him here also."

After shutting the door, Ian turned and went to the king. Going down on one knee, he offered his hands, pressed together, to be enclosed by the king's hands in a sacred vow of fealty. The king's hands, usually warm and strong, were cold and trembling against his.

"At your command," Ian said formally, and rose, going to a chair behind Thor and William and sitting down quietly. The young Henry took a chair near his father, but behind him.

"The king does not want to return to England as soon as we had planned," William said abruptly. "He intends to let the anger die down, and allow time to the wiser of our men in London to find who did this crime, and, to find out why the king is being blamed for à Becket's death."

A rapid mumble of prayer was heard from King Henry's lowered head. His head came up; his eyes—always so fierce—stared at them wildly, looking from one to the other, as if to make sure he was heard.

"We must pray for the soul of Thomas à Becket. All of us. Our enemies will lie and say we caused Becket's death, but that is untrue. Remember that! Remember it when others speak of it, and tell them the attack was not of my doing! Remember!"

"We will remember," Thor said soothingly. "All of us will remember and pray for the soul of Thomas à

Becket. But we must also plan our return to England. We must not wait until the people begin to think their king is hiding guilt.''

King Henry jumped to his feet and began pacing back and forth before them.

''Another few days will not hurt our chances. There will be violence waiting to be done against me and my sons,'' he said, his voice strained. ''But none against Eleanor, for they know she's apart from me. The priests will know that they can injure me and my children with impunity—the pope will not punish them for it. He will be far more likely to praise them.''

Thor stood up, his cool gray eyes full of pity. It was rare to see Henry II disturbed—and, for the first time, frightened. Not so much for himself but for his sons.

''You must send a message to Pope Alexander, my king. He must be told that you did not plan the death of the archbishop nor did you send the men who attacked him.''

William the Marshal got to his feet. ''Indeed, Rodan-cott has the right of it, sire. Only the pope himself can call off the priests of his church.''

Henry flung himself into his chair again, his eyes wide and burning blue. It seemed his panic was changing into a wild desire for action. ''Then bring me a messenger, William; bring me paper and ink! Let us begin! You stay, Thor. And you, Ian, will go about amongst our followers and guests, and learn what you can of what they are saying. I can trust no one except the men in this room.''

Outside the door, Ian struck off toward the rooms taken by Thor and Aylena. Aylena, he knew, would have heard of the murder, and he was anxious to hear her opinion of it and what she had heard from others concerning the news. He was sure now that they would all go to England. King Henry would want the three of them: the king's man, Thor Rodancott, the famous William the Marshal, and Ian Stewart. The lovely face of Serena Bertran came into his mind and his heart dropped. Had he come all this distance to find the woman he dreamed of and then leave her?

Ian's face was long as he knocked at Aylena's door, quickly opened by Margit, who was dressed for traveling. Margit looked at him and nodded. "You've heard, then. James and I are heading for Castle Cheval Noir, and your sister is beginning to prepare for the trip to England. Do you wish to speak to her, Lord Ian?"

"Yes, I do." He sounded serious, and Margit asked no more. She went into the adjoining room and returned with Aylena, who looked solemn and tired. She came to Ian and put her arms around him, kissing his cheek as he bent to kiss hers.

"I see you've heard the news, little brother. I have heard nothing except for the message that came; and that was enough. A horrible death for a troublesome man, and one that will bring hate and more grief. Still, we must go."

"You are leaving Margit behind?"

"Indeed. I will not separate those two. James must handle the breeding of the horses and supervise the training, and he would not be happy without his wife."

"You will have no friend, no lady's maid?"

Aylena hesitated and then smiled. "There are many lady's maids to be had when one needs them, Ian."

"True. Have you heard anyone blame our king for the beating that killed à Becket?"

Aylena waved a dismissing hand. "Only in servants' gossip. They argue stormily; some for the king, others for the archbishop. The nobles—whether Norman, German, or English—are careful not to cast blame in any direction."

Ian nodded, turning away. "I will stroll through the inn and out into the gardens. I was away from my duties this morning; I wish to make up for it. I may find someone who is willing to talk."

As the door closed behind him, Aylena turned to Margit. "Don't fail me, Margit. Be as convincing as you can with Ciel Valoir, and let James talk to her father. I believe Vincennes Valoir, strict as he may be, will allow his daughter to travel as my companion and lady's maid in London."

"I will do as you say, my lady, and no more. If she refuses, I will not try to win her over. The child is happy to be a wealthy horse breeder's daughter and has no desire to put on airs and pretend to be of noble blood."

Aylena sighed at Margit's hectoring tone, then crossed to the wardrobe and opened the doors, beginning to take down the clothes within.

"I wonder that I put up with your advice and arguing," she said, "since I asked for neither. Simply tell her I would like her companionship on the trip and her help in the packing and unpacking. Also, I would be glad to have her along as a true friend I can trust. If she can come, send her here before the end of the week, with James as her guard."

"That I will do, m'lady."

By evening, King Henry had regained his usual confidence. A missive had been sent to Pope Alexander III, denying any involvement in the death of Thomas à Becket and expressing great sorrow at the loss to the church.

"He'd not believe that I sorrow for Thomas," the king told Thor Rodancott, "nor any other man will, for all know Thomas had become a thorn in my side. But we have done all that we can. I only trust the pope will not take revenge on England by withdrawing the sacraments of the church. The common man would be in an agony of fear, expecting eternal hellfire unless a priest prayed for him at his death."

Thor nodded. "True. But I doubt he will go that far, my king. The income from England adds greatly to the coffers of the church."

Henry almost smiled. "Indeed, that is a telling point. Now, what have you heard from Eleanor on this subject?"

"Nothing, my liege lord. She has quitted the inn and is undoubtedly on her way to Poiters. She is much too wise to stay at your side after that terrible news. She'll not want to share your guilt."

"Indeed." For a moment the bold blue eyes of the king darkened with a memory of pain, then cleared again. "She is also too wise to cast blame on me. I trust her in that. I suppose Richard is with her?"

Thor inclined his head. "As always. But young Henry came as soon as he heard and is remaining with you."

The king sighed and shook his head. "Eleanor has weaned all of my sons away from me, by promising them everything they could wish for. Ambition drives my son Henry, not affection. Still, I am glad for his company whatever the reason. Seek your food and rest, my lord Thor, and ask my steward to see to mine. We will stay in Bures long enough to let the gossip and tumult die down in England.''

"I think him wise," Thor told his wife in their rooms. "Cooler heads will come to those in England who are blaming him now, and he will be believed, at least by some, by the end of a week. But we, and Ian, must travel with him and stay near him, likely for some time. We want no criminal turned priest to hunt him down and kill him, then claim a pope's pardon."

Aylena nodded. "True. The next month or so will be dangerous for him. Then the public, seeing that no avenging angel has come to rid England of a murdering tyrant, will decide him innocent."

Thor heard the faint sarcasm in her words. His brows rose. "You tire of the lies and treachery around the royal family, I know. And so do I. After this last effort, I will turn over my duties to Ian—if he wants them."

Aylena smiled without humor. "He will want them. He is full of love toward country and king, and his sense of duty is strong. However, this trouble is strong too and enough to teach him much and change his mind. Now that I know more about the duties of a king's man, I pray it does."

"Where is he now?"

"Listening to other men. He tries to discover which men amongst Henry's closest friends are missing. Then he will know who the murderers were."

Thor shook his head. "That is the last thing Henry wants. He will wish to protect them."

"Ian sees only black and white, my lord."

"If he wants to be the king's man, he must see gray and learn the varying shades of that useful color. The king is blind to an enemy's blood on the hands of his friends.''

Aylena sighed. ''But Ian will see it clearly.''

After a moment Thor nodded. ''True. I must find him and tell him to keep the names a secret. I know he'll not lie, but perhaps I can persuade him to be silent.''

''Go, then. He will listen to you.''

Thor found Ian in the stables, looming over an ostler, who stared up at him fearfully. He turned from the man with a satisfied expression and came to Thor. ''There are four men, Thor. And not mere knights. They are magnates, and close friends of the king. Their names are—''

Thor grasped his arm, his dark face grim. ''Quiet, my brother. Neither I nor any other true friend of the king wishes to hear the names. Undoubtedly King Henry will take the blame whether the identity of the men is told or untold. 'Tis best to let the matter drop.'' He let go of Ian's arm and went to the ostler.

''You will say nothing more, Ludoc. Neither the men's names nor their time of departure from here. Do you understand?''

Ludoc sagged with relief. ''Indeed, my lord. They said the same. And I have said nothing to anyone except to yon giant, who said he came in the name of the king.''

Thor couldn't hold back a grin. ''The giant did not lie, nor will he betray you, Ludoc. He was—mistaken as to his duties.''

Walking together from the stables to the Chetexe, the two men were silent, Thor wondering how to explain to Ian why the culprits should remain unnamed, and Ian, shamed to his soul, wondering what he had done wrong.

''Why?'' Ian burst out as they began climbing the

steps to the inn's entrance. "Don't we need to know the men's names?"

"I know them," Thor said patiently. "I have since the beginning. But we will never name them. Without names, the crime itself will be suspect. After the first shock, the king's loyal subjects will decide 'twas all a lie." He smiled without amusement. "They may even decide that the archbishop was killed by thieves he surprised in the cathedral."

After a silence, Ian stopped at the wide entrance, his eyes on Thor's face, his own expression washed with a painful acceptance. In a strange way he looked older. "I think not. There has been too much hatred between them since Becket became archbishop and declared himself and his priests beyond the king's rule. But I believe I understand. 'Tis the king himself that you and I are sworn to protect, not England nor England's laws."

"Now you have it," Thor said, and the worry on his face eased into a rueful smile. "Though you must remember that England and England's laws become of great importance to us once the king is safe from all harm. Now that you've seen the future with that understanding, you will be able to decide whether you wish to be the next king's man."

"That," Ian said slowly, "will take a deal of thought. In the meantime, what do we do?"

Thor's worried expression eased. "As for now, we wait for the king's decision. Be ready to leave at the end of six or seven days." He swung open one of the great doors and went in, striding across the open hall and toward the stairs to the solar.

Ian followed, nearly half a head taller than Thor,

weighing at least a stone more, but feeling like the seven-year-old boy Thor had taken to raise over fifteen years ago. He had learned much from Thor, but now he knew there was far more to learn about being a king's man.

6

 The violent death of Archbishop Thomas à Becket settled like a stifling fog of suspicion and doubt on Normandy. The horror of it chilled the blood of every man. A great priest of their mother church, it was said, had been killed in cold blood by noblemen sent to do the deed by the English king. Some of the Normans avoided Henry; many more made special trips to see him, some to declare again their allegiance to him and some wishing only for favors, knowing he would be granting more than usual, or hoping to be seen in a favorable light. One of these last was the Lady Serena Bertran, led into his presence one morning by her father, Philippe Bertran, who then left and waited for her in the entry hall of the Chetexe.

Serena, dressed in a new and very lovely blue silk gown that showed off the smooth white skin of her neck and her fragile shoulders, was full of graceful compliments and respect for her king. She ended with a blushing admission that she had a great attraction to one of his king's men, Lord Ian Stewart, who had offered her marriage.

"As yet, your Highness," she ended, "I am not ready to answer yes to Lord Stewart's proposal, but I feel ever

more attracted to him each day. Now he has said to me
that if I will not accompany him to England, he will stay
here until he wins my hand. Since I know you want your
champions around you at this time, I came to say that
if you wish, I will travel with your court to London. My
father has agreed to let me go, but only in the royal
train.''

Bemused, King Henry stared at her. She was quite
beautiful, and extremely inventive as to her problem,
which he recognized at once contained a lie; he knew
Ian Stewart would never desert him to stay and court a
lovely liar. But he also knew the girl carried noble blood.
She was as close to him in blood as a cousin and would
have been honored as such had her father not been a
bastard. She carried the rich red-gold hair of the Plantagenets and the cool, at times icy, light-blue eyes so
like his own. Remembering the man who had fathered
him as well as Philippe Bertran, Henry wondered if this
young woman also carried Geoffrey Plantagenet's sexual
appetite. If so, the young Stewart might regret his
choice. Still, the man was more than faithful to the
throne, and, if he wanted her . . .

''Granted,'' Henry said, and smiled. ''We will provide you with transportation and a place in London
amongst the young ladies of the court. You will be no-
tified of the time of our departure.''

Serena's mouth fell open. She had fully expected to
be forced to ask for Ian Stewart's help before the king
gave in to her wish, and then his words came so easily!
She curtsied deeply, her cheeks red with triumph, and
gave the king words of utmost gratitude.

''I will never forget your kindness to me, nor will my

father," she ended, "and I intend from this day forward to be your most devoted subject."

The king smiled as she curtsied again and left. She hadn't expected his agreement, he knew, and her surprise and pleasure had made her seem younger and less practiced in her deceit. But she was, he thought, completely deceitful. He had seen and known well many young women like Serena Bertran, and they were all the same.

Rejoining her father in the hall of the inn, Serena was glowing. Ignoring curious glances from others, she leaned toward him and whispered into his ear.

"I have all I asked for," she said, "and more. I believe the king has taken a fancy to me! Is that not wonderful?"

Philippe's face was a study as she drew away and took her cloak from his arm to put it on, ready to leave. Hurriedly he moved aside and donned his own sweeping garment of heavy dark wool, which nearly hid his face with its hood.

Philippe Bertran was a slave to his daughter; all knew it, pitied him, and, in turn, scorned him for his weakness. Men of Bures, waiting themselves to be called to the king's room, watched him now and knew he was again giving his daughter her own way. Had she asked for an audience with Almighty God, one man whispered, Philippe would have tried to arrange it with Pope Alexander.

But, they all agreed, Bertran was an honest man; they would all deal with him with confidence, but not one of them with a son wanted Philippe's daughter in the family. They watched, amazed, as Lord Ian Stewart entered the hall and stopped, staring at Serena Bertran as if at a vision. They watched her smile at him and shook their heads as Ian went eagerly to take her hand.

"My Lady Serena! May I see you home?"

Full of new confidence, Serena laughed. "Indeed, if you wish, Lord Stewart! But first let me present you to my father, Philippe Bertran."

In the folds of his hood, Bertran colored painfully. "But you must present me to Lord Stewart, Serena. You forget your manners. I am not a noble."

"I am honored to meet you, Philippe Bertran," Ian said, ignoring his words, and bowed. "I have heard of your fine horses from my sister's husband, Thor Rodancott." He looked back at smiling Serena and his voice softened. "I will see your daughter to Sans Sottise, if you will permit it."

Philippe's shadowed face relaxed. "I know who you are, Lord Ian, and you have my permission. I have business to transact in the town, and very little time. Thank you."

Serena could hardly wait until she and Ian were away from the Chetexe Inn and walking alone in brilliant sunshine, though the breeze from the Bethune River was crisp and cold. Glancing around the pleasant streets and seeing no one close to them, she burst forth. "King Henry has invited me to join his court, Ian! I will be in London as soon as you are."

Ian's eyes widened, his close-cropped bronze beard split in an amazed, white-toothed grin. "Wonderful! We will be together, after all. I was afraid it would be months before I saw you again. As it is, we shall be closer than ever. Lord Rodancott and I will be constantly on guard at the palace until the threats against the king die away."

A small frown creased Serena's smooth forehead. "Ah, yes. But you must not expect to command my attention overmuch, for there will be duties for the ladies of the court, and I wish to . . . to show my gratitude by fully entering into them."

"Naturally. I too will have duties. But we will be together often. The so-called duties of the court are not in the least tiresome, Lady Serena. They are often pleasant."

"Indeed, I am sure of that," Serena answered with a meaningful smile. Her eyes glistened with anticipation as she raised her gaze to his handsome, admiring face. "It will be wonderful too to meet the magnates and great lords of England. Oh, I am so glad the king invited me!"

They had come to the entry of Sans Sottise, and Ian hesitated. "I will see you to the door," he said, taking her arm and turning to the flight of steps that led to the entry. "Then I must hurry back to the Chetexe. Thor will be looking for my return."

The corners of Serena's pretty mouth drooped. "Can you not take me to my own door? I have a little suite, and we could toast my wonderful luck in a glass of wine. No one would know."

Ian smiled down at her. "How I wish I could, my lady. But I must go. These days are hard for us, with so many against our king. We can take no chances." He took her hand in both of his, holding it warmly. "We will have our time together, Serena. I hope 'twill be for many years."

Serena turned away, her golden brows drawing together. "Perhaps," she said, "and perhaps not. We shall see."

Striding rapidly toward the Chetexe again, Ian told

himself she was still very young, and he had disappointed her wish to celebrate with him. That, undoubtedly, was the reason for her last remark—a tiny bit of punishment for his haste in leaving her. It would take time for Serena to grow, to understand, to realize he had duties. But he could wait. She was the woman he had dreamed of, and he would be patient with her. He ran up the steps of the Chetexe Inn and into the entry hall, seeing Thor and William the Marshal talking to three men-at-arms who seemed travelworn and weary. He joined them, in time to hear that the men had come from England to tell the king that Norman Marcher lords from Wales, who had been fighting in Ireland, had finally captured its richest town, Dublin.

"Come," Thor said, and grasped the right arm of the leader. "All of you come. The king will want to hear of this."

That evening Thor and Ian went secretly to Ian's room with William the Marshal and drank to the health of the enemy—the Norman Marcher lords.

"Our king has recovered from his unnecessary shame," William said. "We should be thankful for the grasping hands of the Norman lords in Wales. We will be leaving Bures and its memories. Before long, Henry will throw himself into the battle for Dublin and forget his problems in London. Thank a good and merciful God!"

"Indeed," Thor said, satisfied, "Henry was ever a man of action, not a worrier. I would say the worst is over. Now, to get ready to sail . . ."

In two days, they were ready and waiting. On the third day, James arrived late in the afternoon with luggage packed with extra clothing and money. He gave Thor the news that Castle Cheval Noir was in fine shape, as were the horses, and, to Aylena's great relief and secret delight, James also brought Ciel Valoir riding her warhorse, Devil, ready to sail to England and assist Lady Rodancott in every way possible.

Ciel was welcomed with a happy laugh and a hug from Aylena. The young woman was glowing, her turquoise eyes sparkling with joy, her lilting voice soft but clearly excited. "Never did I think I would see England, Lady Aylena. It was wonderful to hear you wanted me to take Margit's place! When I told my father I had been invited to go with you, he gave me permission immediately."

"And I am thankful," Aylena answered, smiling. "I promise you I'll not be a hard taskmaster. You will have time for your own pleasures." She turned to James, who was standing by and grinning. "Go, James, and find Thor. He's outside near the stables, watching men load a wagon for us. He'll want to know the space he'll need for what you've brought."

"Could I help?" Ciel swung around and looked at James. "I am strong enough, and more than willing."

James laughed. "Then, if the Lady Aylena doesn't need you, come along."

An hour later, after adding Rogue to the several warhorses being shipped to England during the coming night, Ian went around to the loading yard next to the stables. It was close to dusk, and he was riding Foi, who was to go back with James to Castle Cheval Noir. The yard was full of activity, but, as he wove through the bustle, his eye was caught by a figure on a baggage wagon: A small figure with delightful curves and a tiny waist, a sweep of thick, wavy midnight hair beginning to tumble from its knot in shining strands. He knew her at once; his heart leaped up in his chest and, with a quick laugh, he rode up behind her, picked her out of the open wagon, and sat her on the saddle before him, her back against his broad chest. She gasped, twisting to gaze at his bearded face, and then broke into laughter, her eyes wet and shining like jewels, her lips quivering.

"Ian! Have you no manners at all? This is not the way to treat a lady's maid!"

Ian laughed with her. "You are not a lady's maid, my dear Ciel. You are my beloved friend. Lean back here on my arm so I can see your pretty face. Why are you here? Did you make this long trip to tell us all good-bye?"

"Indeed not. I came to go with you! Didn't your sister tell you? Margit is to stay with James, and I am taking her place as Lady Aylena's companion and maid. Isn't it wonderful?"

Ian threw back his head and laughed. "You? A child on an open wagon, packing boxes and sacks? What do you know of being a lady's maid? You could better train a riding mare for her."

Ciel frowned at him. "I shall learn what I lack in being a companion. Lady Aylena has said so. Now put me back on the wagon, for I am helping Thor and the others . . ."

"Not quite yet, little bird. Are you telling me the truth? Are you honestly going to England with us?"

She leaned farther away from him and sternly looked him in the eye. "Have you ever known me to tell a falsehood? Indeed, I am going. And I will be a very good lady's maid.''

Her eyes, Ian thought, were as clear and beautiful as a queen's jewels, and her expression as serious as if she had taken vows. He wanted to laugh, but he held it in, afraid she'd think he was mocking her.

"Then I am pleased beyond words. Both for the sake of my sister and because you and I can continue our friendship. This is a wonderful gift for me, my sweet girl.'' He leaned forward and kissed her on the cheek, then swung her back into the wagon and set her on her feet. "There. And from the looks of it you are nearly through. I'll put Foi in his stall and walk you to the inn and my sister's door.''

Fitting in the last of the several small boxes, Ciel nodded. "I'll be glad for your guidance, Ian. The inn is a tremendous building, and I'd not want to lose my way inside.''

This time he did grin. "Wait,'' he said, "wait until you see the king's palaces, and Queen Eleanor's own suites, and the treasures she left so others could marvel. Your eyes will open so far the eyes themselves will fall out of your face.''

Ciel swung herself down from the wagon, agile as a young boy, but much more graceful. She was laughing like a child, taking his arm as he dismounted, and going along to the stables as he led Foi. "Then I will keep them half shut when I come close to marvels and magic. You must warn me, Ian.''

"And so I will.'' Ian spoke expansively, happier than he'd been since he left Castle Cheval Noir, and wondering why. "I will do anything to protect eyes as beautiful as yours.'' He looked down at her as he spoke and saw a wave of sudden crimson spread itself from her neck to her cheeks. It amused him; she seemed so fresh and innocent after the company of the nobility and the knowledgeable women of the king's court.

Pulling her closer, he put his arm around her. "Why, Ciel, are you blushing because I told the truth? You do indeed have beautiful eyes."

She looked up at him and then away, moving out of his arm and walking sedately. "And you are teasing me, though I am tired and none too clean after the days of travel. Let the compliments wait until I earn them."

He reached and caught her hand. "I was teasing you, my Ciel. I admit it. But it came from sheer joy in seeing you when I had thought our next meeting would be years away. Not many young women would leave their family to travel to a different land."

"Nor would I," Ciel said, "without good reason."

He laughed, holding her hand. "And what was the reason?"

Her glance upward was quickly veiled with her long black lashes; the corners of her lips rose in the beginning of a smile. "There is something I very much want to do," she said, "but it's a secret. If I succeed, then you will know."

Ian smiled. "If I know you, Ciel Valoir, you will do what you plan to do, and it will be done well."

That evening the king called his counselors around him to make plans for the short journey to the shore and the number of small ships waiting there to take them back across the channel to Dover. It was Henry's pride to lead his court, men, women, and supplies, throughout his far-flung domain. This trip would be no different.

The king was cured of his superstitious fear of being blamed for Becket's death, and he wanted it all behind him.

But others worried. William the Marshal raised the question of the king's safety on the road and the possibility of enemies hiding amongst the docks and the waiting ships.

Henry roared at him, like the lion he was. "You see enemies in every corner, William! No longer will I cower here waiting for the pope to pardon me for something I didn't do! Tomorrow I ride avant-garde, leading my people!"

William winced, and there was a rumble of protest from several of his men, but Henry shouted it down.

"Enough!" he said loudly. "Enough! Leave me! I need no squawking, frightened hens to disturb my rest."

Thor's sliding gaze met Ian's startled look, and one eye winked. "Come," Thor said, and stood up. "Sleep is what we all need. Sleep and peace."

They left at dawn, and the noise of their going woke every soul in the Chetexe Inn. Not that the others remaining were angry to be wakened; they were glad enough to know there would be no assassins creeping through the halls in search of King Henry II of England, Scotland, Normandy, Brittany, and Languedoc. None this day envied the man, though they hung from windows to see the caravan winding from the stables and heading for the shore and the straits of Dover.

Not all of the women were riding; some were driving the wagons and carts. Ciel Valoir rode on the wagon that held the Rodancott goods. She had packed the wagon, tied Devil behind, and made a comfortable seat amongst the bundles. And, as the sun behind them grew

in power and lit the nobles riding in the van, she saw
Ian turn in his saddle and look back, his eyes searching.
She smiled, but she was deep in her nest, and his gaze
went over her. Then, as his gaze swept forward again,
he smiled. A great, glorious, happy smile, directed like
a brilliant light at a young and slender blond woman,
wearing a fur-lined cloak and a sapphire velvet gown,
riding an Arabian horse much like the one the Lady
Aylena rode. The woman smiled back, lifting a gloved
hand, her beautiful face pleased and excited.

Ciel knew at once. She looked down at her own
hands, bare of gloves and golden from the sun. Suddenly
heat came behind her eyes and a hard, aching stone grew
in her chest.

"Fool," she breathed, so soft she hardly heard the
word herself. "Fool that you are, Ciel Valoir, how could
you believe that Lord Ian Stewart would fall in love with
you?"

Tears slipped from her lowered lids and dropped
down her cheeks. Until now this wagon, this ride toward
adventure, had been part of a dream. A wonderful, foolish dream, built on the sunny days when she and Ian
had trained her father's horses together and then was set
aflame when Margit came to say the Lady Aylena
wanted her as a companion. She had had such high
hopes . . . and last evening, Ian had seemed so glad to
see her that her heart had rushed ahead of her mind,
leaped gaily over doubt and fallen into joy. Oh, *mon
Dieu!* How stupid she had been!

She drew a square of linen from a pocket and wiped
away her tears. It was too late to change her decision;
she could only hope to play out her role as handmaiden

to Aylena Rodancott and a friend—only a friend!—to the rest of the family. And she would do so.

At that moment, Ian spoke to her. He had slowed his horse's pace and let the first of the train pass him so he could ride beside the wagon where Ciel sat and find out if she had misgivings now that the trip had begun. And it seemed she had. He had seen her tears; he hoped to change the sadness on her young face with a teasing question.

"Missing your home so soon, Ciel? Surely the journey will bring exciting experiences and sights to you. Give me a smile!"

She gave him a smile and wondered if it looked as sour as it felt. Then she lied. "I was worrying about my father. He will be alone now except for the servants."

"I know. But he will seek out friends and, before long, will be looking forward to your return. Neither Thor nor Aylena will want to stay in England once the king is settled and safe."

Ciel nodded. "Of course you are right, my lord. They love their home." Her smile was becoming brighter, and Ian looked relieved.

"You must look forward to new experiences, Ciel. Never fear them, for you will learn much."

Her turquoise eyes flashed up to his concerned face and swept down again before he could puzzle out their strange expression.

"That," she said wryly, "I do believe. I have already noted my astounding ignorance and have begun to learn about life."

"You never have been ignorant, Ciel," Ian said gently. "You are a wonderful person, and more knowledgeable about your father's business than most men.

This trip will, as I have said, teach you much about the world. But what you already know is much more valuable than that which you will learn.''

Her eyes on the van of the train, Ciel seemed not to listen. When he was silent, she gave him another glance. ''There is a lady in the van who is waving you on, as if you are needed. Perhaps you'd better ride forward.'' She watched his gaze leap forward, his smile break through his gleaming beard.

''Indeed,'' he said, ''I'll join her. That's the Lady Serena Bertran, who has been added to the court at the king's invitation. Perhaps you know who she is?''

Ciel nodded. ''I know of her and her father,'' she said, ''for Philippe Bertran often comes to our house. But they live a life very different from ours, and I've never had the pleasure of her company. Do go, Ian. She seems anxious.''

7

 Five large trade boats, double-ended and fitted out above either end with high castles for the archers, waited at the docks for the king, his court, the baggage and horses. Several of the warhorses, bought by English nobles while they were in the fields of Normandy horse breeders, were taking their first voyage.

Being led onto the rocking boats was frightening to the beasts, and they balked and snorted uneasily. Devil was in the midst of them, bigger than most and twice as angry.

Watching with the others of the party, Ciel saw Devil, eyes rolling, foam at his mouth, rear, and strike out at one of the men, missing the man's head by inches with his powerful hooves. She ran to the gangplank and onto the boat, snatching the rope and whip from the hulking ostler and demanding to know where her horse was to be tied.

The ostler's eyes bulged, his red face grew purple with outrage. "Where I please, maid! Get off the ship before one of these raw beasts smashes your foolish head!"

Ciel froze. She was not used to being taken as a servant. "The horse is mine, fool! Step aside and I'll tie him in his place."

The ostler raised a threatening hand. "Off! Off the ship, now, or I'll knock you off . . ." He was stopped in his bellowing by a hand on his wrist, a quick jerk that left the threatening hand twisted up behind him. He winced, swore loudly, looked around, and up, at Ian Stewart's furious face.

"My lord! I meant no trouble. I am beset by this maid and afraid for her bones if she—"

"You will allow her to handle her own horse, man! That brute will kill you if you dare to strike her. Have you no sense? Look at him now, frightened and breathing hard, but standing still for her. Use your head!"

The ostler stepped aside, giving Ciel a quick bow, then pointing at the iron rings set horse high on the bottom of the archers' castle on the bow. "Then, miss, take one of the middle rings and tie him close enough to keep him from rearing. I've two older horses to put on either side. They'll calm him."

Ciel nodded and coaxed the sweating horse forward. His eyes were rolling white, and she understood it well. The bobbing deck beneath her feet felt as odd to her as it did to him. She rubbed his head and whispered to him, and he gentled to her, snuffling her neck with his velvet nose. "There, my Devil. There. You will feel land beneath your feet again before long. Just let me tie you safe and out of harm's way . . ." The task finished, she patted him again and edged out to make her way toward the dock.

The ostler stopped her with another bow. "Lord Stewart said to me that you are Vincennes Valoir's daughter, miss. Had I known that, I would have stepped aside at once. When we land at Dover, you will be welcome aboard to release your big horse and lead him onto the docks.''

Ciel smiled. "Then I will come for him. He will be less trouble to me than to others.''

A light laugh drifted from the dock. "And you will ruin your shoes, maid, walking through fresh manure. Did I hear someone say you were Valoir's daughter?''

Looking up, Ciel recognized the blond beauty who had smiled so brilliantly at Ian. She stepped up beside her on the dock, looking the woman over. A little taller than she, but thin, her features delicate, her elbows and wrists showing small, narrow bones.

"That is true, my lady. Do you know my father?''

Serena shrugged. "I have seen him at my father's home. They say he raises cattle as well as horses on a large farm. My father often buys from him.''

"I see. Then they are friends?''

Serena laughed again. "No, maid, they are not friends. One buys, the other sells, like any customer and merchant.'' She hesitated and then added in an offhand manner. "I suppose that is why Lord Stewart spoke to the ostler for you. He would know you as Valoir's daughter since the Rodancotts live nearby. My father has said that Vincennes Valoir has never aspired to be more than he is—a hardworking horse breeder.''

The woman's voice was amused and lightly malicious. Ciel was suddenly angry. Serena Bertran, as far as Ciel was concerned, was free to act as if she was part of the nobility. But she was not free to belittle her father. She could have her ambition to be accepted by the Normandy nobles, and her excessive pride in her noble blood, tainted though it was, but she could not insult Vincennes Valoir without a challenge.

"Your father was right," Ciel said, turning away. "My father is far too honest to pretend to be a noble and fawn on those who are, and I feel the same. We are both content with our lives."

Watching Ciel walk along the shore to join Aylena Rodancott on the next quay, Serena's eyes were hooded, her small pink mouth tight as if she had tasted something sour. She was sorry to have spoken to the girl, for she'd gotten the worst of it and made an enemy who could do her harm. She should have known from what her father had said that he and Vincennes Valoir had been open with each other about their backgrounds. Now the maid had a story to tell. Walking slowly back to the quay where the nobles were boarding two of the ships, Serena saw Ian waiting for her, his strong face alight and admiring. She smiled, and her confidence returned. The Valoir daughter was in fact very attractive, and Ian had been quick to her side when the ostler threatened her, but it wasn't Ciel Valoir he waited for now. Besides, the maid should be beneath her notice, and his. If a noble felt a desire for her, he would take her as a leman, not a wife.

The trip to Dover was marked by favorable winds and a smooth current. Even for those who had never traveled by sea the voyage seemed swift and comfortable. By evening they were unloading the baggage and putting it in barrows to be wheeled to the big Dover inn. True to her promise, Ciel came to the ship used for the warhorses and found Devil, untied him, and walked him from the ship and onto dry land. Then she handed him over to one of the ostlers to take to the stables behind the inn and followed the Lady Aylena inside and upstairs to a room warmed by a fire crackling on a hearth.

"I know you're tired, Lady Aylena," she said, "and would like a bath. I will order one now, if you wish."

Aylena yawned. "Order a bath for yourself, my child. Thor and I always bathe together. I'll wait for him."

Ciel went to the small room assigned to her and, seeing a maid in the hall, asked for a tub. It came speedily, carried by two menservants and with four scullery maids following with buckets of hot water.

She luxuriated in it, washing yesterday's dust from her thick mass of black hair, scrubbing her fair skin until it glowed. Afterward, she put on a dark-blue skirt with a rose-colored velvet tunic banded in silver, wove her hair into a huge braid down her back, put an apron over her gown, and left off the usual veil and barbette. They were not suitable, she had noticed, for the noble ladies' maids, and she was determined to look and act her part. In Normandy she and the Lady Aylena were friends and neighbors, but here in England she would act within the rules. The Lady Aylena would be criticized if she allowed a maid too many privileges.

She was near the Rodancotts' room when footsteps sounded behind her and a hand caught up her braid and gave it a twitch. She turned, startled, and looked up at Lord Rodancott and a smiling Ian Stewart.

"Playing at being a maid, I see," Ian said, and laughed, still holding the braid. "You'll make many a lecherous old knight ask for the black-haired, beautiful maid to bathe him. I advise you to resist."

Thor gave Ian a look of surprised amusement coupled with constraint. "She might better resist a young knight,

Ian. You are holding that shining braid as if you intend to keep her by your side.''

''I do,'' Ian said, but dropped the braid to place a wide hand on Ciel's small shoulder. ''She's a good horse trainer and a lovely sight to behold. You withstood the trip very well, my dear friend.''

''Indeed,'' Ciel said, friendly but cool, ''I enjoyed it, Ian.'' She turned to Thor. ''The Lady Aylena instructed me to order a bath to be brought to your room as soon as you arrived. I will do so immediately.'' She bobbed half a curtsy and left them, walking rapidly toward the stairs. Her shoulder was still warm from his big hand, her cheeks were hot. *Damnation!* Her heart was her worst enemy.

The next day was a day no man nor woman in the king's party was apt to forget. The road to London ran along the white chalk cliffs of Dover and passed through two notable towns on the way. First Canterbury and then Rochester, before arriving at Southwark and London's bridge across the Thames. It was always a trial when the king came back from Normandy or France, for the citizenry knew when his ships landed and were out in force to cheer and beg, sometimes slowing the royal train to a standstill with a crush of spectators. It was a bother, yet Henry always treated the occasion with good grace.

This time was different. They had set out early in cold, nearly impenetrable fog rising from the sea below, and had barely reached the outskirts of Canterbury when the first ghostly group of hooded villagers appeared through drifting layers of mist and began calling out mournfully.

Their somber cries to God Almighty asked Him to ''witness now the murderer of your faithful follower,

Thomas à Becket, a blessed saint, forever sinless and full of the Holy Spirit.''

The crowd became larger and more daring by the minute. Some picked up rocks and flung them toward the king. They all fell short, whether by chance or by the weak arm of cowardice, no one knew.

Thor rode a ragged circle about the train, exhorted the riders and wagon drivers to close ranks around the women and the king, and, when they had done it, returned to Henry's side. "Have you an order, sire?''

Muffled in his cloak and hood, Henry II turned slowly and looked at Thor. There was no fear in his face, but his eyes were red-veined and sad, his mouth within the glossy beard twisted to one side. "How soon the glory turns to ashes, Thor. These are the same people who welcomed us back on every trip, laughing and wishing me health and a long life. They took the money and gifts we gave them, and praised us all. Now, if they had the courage, they would pull me from this horse and trample me into the ground.''

Thor's face was grim. "A man is fortunate to have three true and steadfast friends in a lifetime, my king. But your rule is not over, nor will it be for years.''

"Perhaps. But not many years. My sons are nipping at my heels, and Eleanor abets them. I—am not sorry. I crave rest. But not even young Henry is man enough to rule. 'Twill be Eleanor whispering behind the throne, no matter which of our sons sits there.''

"We will see, sire. You've many good years ahead. Come, let us pick up the pace and leave the town of Canterbury and its tarnished cathedral behind.''

But Rochester, where they were to spend the night, was not much better. No one called out accusing the king of murdering Thomas à Becket. But the priests and laymen together presented their backs to the king in a way no one could fault them. Rank on rank, they were on their knees in the church, beside the church, on the street in front of the church, and they were all praying loudly for the archbishop's soul.

Dismounting, going into the inn the king habitually used, the members of the train were watchful and wary. But the innkeeper met the king with deep bows, wished him well, spoke not at all of dead Thomas à Becket, but only asked the king's wishes for a hearty dinner.

"We have a roast of beef, your Highness, plump chickens, a leg of lamb and wine aplenty. There is barley soup with herbs, and dried fruit pies. If there is something more you wish, I will send out for it . . ."

Henry swept the thought away with a regal gesture. "You have more than enough delicacies, innkeeper. We will be happy to dine on them."

Ciel Valoir, always at Lady Aylena's elbow and waiting for instructions, listened to this and wondered. His subjects blamed the king for the archbishop's death without a shred of proof that pointed him out. She mentioned that to Aylena as they entered the room that the Rodancotts' would have, and Aylena smiled wryly.

"They are children. The king's enemies rushed to blame the king once the deed was done, for they want to pull him down and end his influence on his people. It is always so with a mob, and will always be. The public wishes to believe lies about the men above them, and the more shocking, the more they will believe."

"Who is his chief enemy?"

Aylena looked at her with regret. "The queen. Perhaps 'tis not so much hate as an overweening ambition. She wants her son on the throne.''

''He is much too young!''

''True. But Eleanor would speak through his mouth.''

''Then I understand. She wishes to rule.''

Aylena nodded. ''Now you have it. Through the years Henry and Eleanor have shared the duties of government; now Henry has taken a leman he loves dearly and put his estranged wife away from him in tiny Aquitaine. I have heard Eleanor is plotting to come back to England.''

''Perhaps she will,'' Ciel said after a moment. ''She is an interesting woman, and very brave and beautiful. I would like to hear her talk and tell her memories.''

Again that evening, after the king's dinner when all the party met in one big room, Ian sought out Ciel. She had slipped outside to stand in the shadow of an immense tree. She needed solitude; she was not used to crowds all day and more crowds at night, but she smiled when she saw Ian coming toward her, his big body towering like a giant in the gloom, his bronze hair and beard catching golden gleams from the torches flaring outside the inn doors. She was suddenly glad that she'd changed into her most becoming gown, one trimmed with red and gold embroidered bands, circling a huge skirt.

''So you are here,'' Ian said, and caught up her small hand. ''Must you always leave a crowd? Come back in with me. There are minstrels there, costumed and beribboned, ready to sing the newest songs from Aquitaine's court of love. Wouldn't you like to hear them?''

''Surely I should,'' Ciel said, half teasing, ''if I am to fit into this constantly changing life.'' Her hand in his was warming, relaxing, nestling on its own into his wide palm. "But—what of your golden-haired lady? Will she be angry to see me with you?"

"Indeed not. I have just explained to Lady Serena that you are my good friend and like a sister to me. She confessed at once that at first she was jealous of you, but now, since she understands, she would like to be your friend, as I am. Come, we will all be together."

There was a dead silence. Then Ciel withdrew her hand from his gently. "Perhaps Lady Serena was generous in her thought, Ian, but the idea has no virtue. It is unseemly for a peasant to look for friendship from a—a noble lady."

Confused and unhappy, Ian shook his head. "You are not a peasant, and my sister clearly considers you her friend."

"Indeed. But I am calling myself her maid, and I would never presume myself her equal in company with her peers. Nor," she added with sudden force, "would I wish to be considered the Lady Serena's . . . ah, equal! And . . . and a good night to you, Lord Stewart."

Ian stared after her as she left, her hands lifting her full skirts an inch or two to clear the mist-wet grass, her small feet in red leather flickering away at a half run.

At noon the next day, under a pall of smoke from the many coal fires in cold and dreary London, the king's party crossed the silver-gray Thames River, smooth as a plain but sliding, silent and shining, toward the east. They made their way slowly over the great London bridge with its shops and homes crowding the wide span, and came into a gray city where a few shivering citizens who had seen them coming across the bridge had gathered along the streets to wave at them.

"Thank God," Thor murmured to Ian. "None are calling out to brand their king a murderer. But always a Londoner is far different from a villager. They are apt to listen to all but judge for themselves."

Ian nodded. He was thinking his own thoughts, and they were about his friend, Ciel Valoir. Tired of the wagons, Ciel had asked permission to ride Devil in the rearguard, and had received it quickly from Thor, who had added that Aylena would be pleased to have her at her side amongst the nobles in the van. Ciel had thanked him but said she would feel more comfortable with the other servants in the rear.

"I will not presume on our friendship," she had told Thor stiffly. "I prefer to keep my place. Lady Aylena will understand."

Thor hadn't argued. He knew Devil was hard to handle unless Ciel had her hands on him. The big horse had been a trial to the men, for he led poorly, pulling back on his rope, nipping, squealing challenges at the horses ahead of him. With Ciel again on his back, he was like an angel. Neck arched, muscles moving smoothly, he carried her proudly, as if he carried a queen. And, Thor thought, Ian's neck must be tired after all the times he'd turned to look at his friend Ciel.

"Take the rear, Ian," he said suddenly. "These streets are narrow. Put the men and horses in close double file. Some of them are wandering off to the side."

With a quick nod, Ian turned and left, cantering along the side of the train, bringing his horse around at the rear. He put men and animals in a tight two lines with a few sharp orders and then joined it, pushing a lackey aside to ride beside Ciel.

"You bring back pleasant memories," he said. "You

and Devil are as beautiful in London's grimy streets as you were in your father's green pastures. It's amazing how good Devil is with you in his saddle.''

She thanked him with a smile and nod. "He's young," she reminded, "and all warhorses have to learn to travel. I think he's doing well in this large and noisy city."

"And I. He's not been refusing to eat, has he?"

She laughed. "No. He gobbles food like a boar."

"Good. Some horses lose weight and muscle when transported."

Ciel nodded. "I know." That was a well-known thing about horses, and there was no more to it than that. There was, she thought soberly, nothing more for them to say about Devil, or anything else. They were constrained, and could no longer tease each other or talk of the future. She looked forward, and, after another space of time, she spoke.

"I think," she said carefully, "that Lady Serena would like to have your company again. She has sent you quite a few glances."

Ian smiled. "I know. But she won't be angry. She never is. She is no longer jealous at all and insists that I must be the same and trust in her when she pays attention to other men. So I have promised to trust her as she trusts me." He laughed a little, watching Ciel. "I see you don't believe me," he added. "But it is true. She feels that trust is a holy thing between a man and woman."

"Why, then," Ciel said, "she must truly trust you. Few women would be so sure of a man's affection. Perhaps I have misjudged her. But do go, Ian. She may be feeling alone amongst the British nobles she barely knows.''

''That's true,'' Ian admitted, and turned off again to the side. ''I'll join her.'' Then he looked back and grinned, a great, wide, white-toothed grin that split his bronze beard and lighted his deep-blue eyes. That grin touched Ceil's heart with his innocence, which she had come to believe was even greater than her own, and she smiled back, feeling a strong tie between them. Then he made it true with words: ''But remember—you're still my most loved friend, Ciel.''

She watched him spur forward and take a place between Serena and another noblewoman of greater age. After a moment, Ciel leaned far forward to rub the broad forehead below Devil's pricked ears, whispering to him softly. ''I am his most loved friend, Devil. Perhaps I should be content with that. 'Tis truly an honor to me.''

They had come to the west outskirts of the great city, and there they passed through immense stone gates that seemed to waver and bend in the drifting fog. Then they were outside the huge, protective Roman walls. But there seemed no threat here, for there were small homes and fenced fields, frozen in a gray, wintry scene of varying shades, and people, most of them hurrying through the streets and byways, stopping to nod and wave at the royal party.

Ciel, watching the faces of the people, hearing scattered cheers, began to change from her uncomfortable discontent to a wondering interest. The citizens who lived in and about London were very different from the grim villagers of Canterbury who would have stoned the king had they not been afraid of retribution. These men and women had friendly faces, red with the cold air but smiling, their mittened hands raised toward their king. Ciel looked forward and saw King Henry sitting straight in his saddle, his hood pushed back from a smiling face and one hand raised in careless salute. She looked over at the ostler riding beside her.

"Our king," she said, "seems to be welcome in London, in spite of the lies about him."

The ostler grinned. "And will be, always. No matter which way the country bends, London is always for King Henry."

Ciel erupted with surprised joy, the clear notes of her laughter echoing in the cold air, and in the front ranks Ian turned to look, smiling at her high spirits. Beside him, Serena Bertran glanced back swiftly and turned to the fore again, her expression sweet but patronizing, ignoring the ripple of chuckles that overtook the train.

Another mile or so, and the wavering fog and coal smoke parted to show the huge bulk of Westminster Hall, the ghostly outlines of huge turrets, a gleam of reflection from long, arched windows. It seemed only a vision, floating in a cloud, but then as they came nearer a deep-throated horn blew, and blew again, and men appeared, running toward them through the gloom, men in mail and helmets, sheathed swords at their sides, who formed up in two rows on either side of a paved avenue.

Ciel Valoir, riding beside the chief ostler, could not make head nor tail of the scene. The train was turning, passing the huge building she had thought must be the king's castle, and traveling now to an even bigger shape in the fog.

Puzzling it out, she saw that they were entering a large courtyard and the train was breaking up, the nobles dismounting, the servants dropping from their mounts and wagons and beginning to unload. Devil snorted and backed uneasily, and she drew him away from the crowd, waiting until she could see an empty space as others withdrew.

Then Ian was beside her, reaching for her reins. "Come, Ciel. The stables are close . . ."

Greatly relieved, she dismounted and smiled at him. "I am thankful to be one of your chiefest friends, Ian. I cannot see in this swirling fog."

He laughed. "Nor I. But I have a nose. Come, we will find the stables." He was leading his own horse, Rogue, and Devil was content to follow. The others had given up their mounts to servants and were like indistinct wraiths, moving away from the hall and toward the huge stone building that Ciel knew must be Westminster Palace.

"What of your lady?" she asked Ian. "Won't she be angry if you leave her to enter the palace alone?"

Ian looked down at her through the darkening air, droplets of fog running down his leathern helmet, glistening in his bronze beard.

"My sister Aylena offered to take Serena in. Of course, the young unmarried women of the court will not stay at the palace except for tonight. They will have other quarters set aside for them, likely in the Tower of London."

"Oh? I thought the Tower a prison."

"A part of it only, and used for noble prisoners, both English and foreign. Here, give me your hand. The bricks at the entry are wet and slippery . . ."

She could have laughed and said she was sure-footed enough to walk without help, but she didn't. She gave him her hand, and felt the warmth of his wide palm, the strength of his long fingers. Her heart swelled thick in her throat, and childish tears heated her eyes. She wiped them away with her other hand and laughed.

"The fog runs down my cheeks," she said, and let go of his hand. Then they passed into the royal stables, lighted by flaming torches, redolent of oats, sweating horseflesh, and manure, and dry as a bone. She looked around, dazzled by light, dazzled by her feelings.

"Oh, what beautiful white horses!"

"Yes," Ian said, studying her in the bright light, "they are Arabians. Queen Eleanor's own palfreys." He turned and handed over the reins of their horses to an old man who came stumping up through the stables. "These warhorses are tinder, John. Be careful not to strike a spark."

The old man laughed softly, taking the reins, smoothing a thick neck and tugging gently. The horses both relaxed and followed him, nuzzling his bent shoulders. The old man turned a bewhiskered face back toward Ian, grinning. "They know," he said, "they know who loves them. They're wiser than men when it comes to that."

8

"We will go in by the kitchens and up the back stairs," Ian said, grasping Ciel's arm as they left the stables. "We'll not bother the steward, Tyler William. He has enough to do, and one of the maids will know where Aylena is to sleep."

Ciel nodded. "Thank you, my lord."

Ian slanted a glance down at her. "You must say 'thank you, Ian.' We are too close for titles, Ciel."

Ciel sighed, walking faster toward the lighted entrance. "That was true in Normandy, my lord. But not in London. I agree it was possible there, and I will always remember our times together and be thankful for them. But here I prefer to treat you the same as I treat Lord Rodancott, and—and all the other nobles." She stopped, breathing deeply, deciding it was the fast pace that had made her voice falter. "There," she added as Ian swung about and stared down at her, "now, you must try to understand. We are friends, of course, but we are of—well, two separate kinds of people, and we are *not* close!"

Staring down at her, Ian laughed. Then he picked her up, cradling her in his arms, and headed again for the lights at the kitchen entrance.

"I do understand," he said before she could speak. "You are just too tired to remember who I am. My name is Ian Stewart, and I am as close to you as a brother."

Ciel caught her breath. "I have two brothers; I need no more. Put me down."

"I shall put you down on the steps, my girl. This path near the kitchen is nothing but mud . . ."

She gave in. She could hear his big boots sloshing in the muck of water and soil. She was silent until he put her down on the top of the steps, and then she moved away a little and thanked him, using his title.

Just inside, an elderly maid dressed in a dark-blue gown and full white apron came hurrying to them across the huge brick kitchen, now odorous with swirls of steam from roasting meat and fowl, busy with cooks and scullery boys, rushing back and forth over the brick floor. The maid's white hair was slipping from her head-dress and her red face was sweating.

"My Lord Stewart! The Lady Aylena has sent me to find her companion. Is this the young woman she wants?"

Ciel stepped forward. "It is. And I am indeed late. Will you show me the way, mistress?"

"Indeed I will, miss. Come along. We cannot keep the Lady Aylena waiting . . ."

Ciel left with her, disappearing into the shadowy hall without a backward glance.

Ian sighed, shrugged, and wandered over to the chief cook, a huge woman wielding a chopping knife on scrubbed salsify. "What can I have to hand, Portia? I'm hungry enough to beg."

The woman laughed and raised a red, beefy hand to point. "Those loaves on the middle table are fresh and hot, Lord Stewart, but take a cup of mead to cool your tongue."

Ian laughed and collected both loaf and mead, glad to be back in England, back in Westminster Palace, which was as much like a home to him as any place outside of Northumberland could be. He took the bread and cup of honey mead and went out into darkness again, standing in the cold, slowly moving air, catching the scent of the Thames to the south, the warm odors wafting from the kitchen, the occasional whiff of the stables. Gradually he lost the feeling of danger that had surrounded the royal party ever since the news of Becket's murder. They were home. They were in London and the king was safe.

Chewing the soft, hot bread, he thought of the oatcakes and ale he would find in the kitchen of his own home, Stewart Castle, so far to the north. He thought of showing Serena the profound beauty of the wild northern coast, the sturdy sheep and the highland kine, shaggy-haired, ferocious beasts with long, curling horns. Even the cows fought the huge wild dogs for the safety of their calves.

While he thought of those things he found it hard to imagine Serena in that cold, bleak corner of the world. But he could easily see her in the castle. He imagined her as his wife, sitting in the sun-filled embrasure of his solar, his accounts spread out for her to copy into his books. Her hair would shine in that sunlight, make a net of glistening gold around her face and spill down her slim back like a golden waterfall. And when he came in, she would raise her lovely face and smile, her eyes as blue as a summer sky. He sighed with happiness. The scene in his mind was so beautiful . . .

"Lord Stewart!" The voice of Tyler William rang in the cold air. Ian turned and saw the small old man standing just outside the kitchen door. Ian grinned. The voice was bigger than the man. "Yes, Tyler?"

Tyler took a deep breath and boomed out the order. "Lord Rodancott has asked for your presence in the chapel. The king and his courtiers will be giving thanks to Almighty God for their safe trip, and the king wants all to attend."

"Thank you. Indeed I will attend."

The chapel was on the ground floor of the palace, an inside room with open fretwork at the top of the walls, to allow the smoke of candles to escape and fresh air to move in. The kneeling benches would accommodate no more than thirty at a time and the altar was not large, but lavishly decorated with carving and gold leaf.

It was beautiful and, Ciel thought as she came in with Aylena, small enough so that everyone could hear the mass yet big enough to hold the guests a king might have. They took their places, and, when everyone had come in, the priest, a man of middle years with a calm expression, closed the doors. He went forward in silence between the kneeling rows and stopped to cross himself before a great crucifix behind the altar, readying himself for saying the mass.

When the ceremony was over everyone rose, their tired faces peaceful, even radiant with gratitude. The king was safe at home, and so were they all, in spite of storm, accident, or enemies.

Then, following Aylena out, Ciel saw Serena Bertran glance at her, then take Ian's arm and whisper to him, her mouth twisted in a derisive smile. Ciel looked away

as Ian bent his head to listen to her whispers. She didn't
care. Whatever Serena might say, Ian would be her
friend. He was a man to count on. That much she knew
in her heart.

A door stood open into Ciel's room, which was next
to Lord and Lady Rodancott's suite, and maids were
going in and out, carrying wooden buckets of hot water.
Ciel looked at Aylena, smiled with relieved gratitude,
and followed them.

Within days, Ciel found herself treated by all as a part
of the Rodancotts. "More like a friend," she said the
morning of the tenth day, "than a maid. You shouldn't
allow your noble acquaintances to think you've taken
me into the family."

Aylena laughed. "But that is exactly how I feel."

"But you should hide it! It is true that we are close,
but rank is too important to others. Your friends will
wonder at you," Ciel added, picking up a brush and
beginning to stroke it through Aylena's silky mass of
hair. "And at Ian. I believe he truly thinks of me as a
sister."

Aylena quirked a brow. "Perhaps. Perhaps not. I am
not sure he knows himself. In any event, you are a real
friend to me, and I hope to keep you near me. Now, will
you seek out Tyler William once you are dressed and
tell him we wish to ride to the tournament field this
afternoon?"

"Oh! Is there to be a tournament today?"

"Indeed. There often is. But this time Ian will be in
it." Aylena shrugged her shoulders. "Not that he wished
to be. He never enters the London tourneys unless notable warriors from other countries are taking part. Se-

rena coaxed him into it before she left for the Tower. She wants to see him fight, I suppose, and have the other young women see him give her the trophy he is bound to win.''

"I see." Ciel went on brushing, her eyes lowered, the lashes hiding her expression in the mirror.

Aylena sighed, took the brush from Ciel's hand, and turned around, meeting Ciel's somber gaze.

"Or," Aylena added, her smile crooked, "she wishes to be pointed out as Ian Stewart's lady. There is no doubt he will wear her colors, and she will make sure everyone sees them together. If you don't want to attend, we won't.''

Color flooded Ciel's cheeks. "Why, there is no reason for us to stay away, Lady Aylena.''

"Then we shall go. Perhaps it will please Ian.''

"I'm sure that it will.''

There was a knock on the door, and Ciel hurried to open it, thinking it a maid with hot water. It was Ian, grinning down at her in her lacy, revealing robe. She clutched the edges of the robe and pulled them tighter, frowning at him.

"What is it you want, Ian?''

"Permission to borrow your horse, dear Ciel. I'm riding in a tournament today, and—though I hate to admit it—Devil is much better trained for it than Rogue. Would you mind?''

"Oh!" She struggled against the surprised smile that curved her lips. "Why, I don't know . . . would it be proper? I mean, is it allowed?''

"Indeed. Otherwise I wouldn't ask.''

"Why, then . . . yes! You yourself taught Devil his tricks and taught me how to control him. I would be ungrateful not to allow you to ride him now. And . . . and I will be watching, Lord Ian. I have never seen a tournament, and it will be a great pleasure for me.''

Ian bowed and took her hand. ''And for me. Many pleasures have come from that field in Normandy, my dearest Ciel. I will do my best to show off the skills of your warhorse.'' He bent to her small hand and she felt the softness of his beard, the warmth of his lips as he kissed her fingers. She took a deep breath and smiled.

''Very few lady's maids,'' she said, her voice trembling with laughter, ''have their hand kissed by a nobleman. I am extremely honored.'' Then she gently took away her hand, stepped backward, and shut the door.

The tournament was held on the windswept Smithfield acres outside the north city walls. The field was often used as a horse fair, when knights, storekeepers, farmers, and noblemen and their wives came to buy or trade their steeds. But now it was bare and open except for the tents and pennons of the knights, and the seats and old Roman walls behind them were decorated with colorful pennants and swaths of colored cloth draped along the seats.

Aylena and Ciel had been accompanied to the field by a trio of the king's men-at-arms. One of them stayed with the ladies after they dismounted; the others led their Arabians to a safe place at the north end of the field, then returned. They had been to many tourneys and were bored with this small one, though extremely courteous to the two women. Aylena explained the scene to Ciel.

At each end of the field there were small tents, each topped by a colorful waving pennon. ''The combatants rest inside the tents,'' Aylena said, ''and many of them pray. The more confident ones visit back and forth bragging.''

"Oh. Which will be Ian's choice?"

Aylena smiled. "Neither. He's at the paddock over there, talking to Devil. He never tires."

"I see. But where is his tent and pennon?"

"Why, right there." Aylena pointed. "Don't you recognize the blue pennon with the silver *claidheamh mor*?"

"I see a blue pennon with a huge silver sword painted on it. Is it his?"

Aylena stared at Ciel and suddenly laughed. "It is. And I apologize. You've never seen the Stewart emblem, and I know Ian would never describe it. He won't brag, either on his skill or on the family honor. But after today you will never doubt his ability nor his goodwill to a vanquished opponent."

Ciel smiled. "You are a truly doting sister, Lady Aylena. After all is said, he must have a fault or two."

Aylena glanced over at a group of young and gorgeously gowned women sitting close together in the stands, talking and laughing, staring and pointing at the men in the field. In the middle of the group was Serena, wearing a dark crimson silk gown that bared the top half of her breasts, and with it her cloak of yellow leather, lined with soft fur. Her red-gold hair was piled on the top of her head, and a net of silver mesh over it was pinned on with sparkling sapphire clasps.

"He has faults, indeed," Aylena said slowly. "Those clear blue eyes of his are blinded by his dreams. But there is nothing I can say to open them. He is caught." The last words came out slowly, and Aylena looked away. "And they will both be miserable if his plans are followed."

Ciel said nothing. She was aware of Aylena's

thoughts, but she had no right to discuss Ian's plans. She settled back in the warm cloak she wore and surveyed the field. It was a sunny day, the skies cold and high. There was little wind, and a word or laugh carried far in the dry air. Against the background of green firs were all the gay colors of pennons and tents, the long, rippling robes on the horses, made of red, blue, and gold silks and velvet, and over that the shining mail the knights wore glittered like silver when the sun struck it. The men and horses were constantly moving, tense and laughing, ready for a signal.

"When will the tourney start?" Ciel asked, and was answered by a horn blaring. She sat up straighter, watching the men and horses come together in the melee, the horses pushing hard against each other, the knights wielding their dull blades in blows calculated to knock an adversary from the saddle. Ian, near the center, swung his broad blade and made a trail of unhorsed knights. Free of the melee, he took a position in front of his tent. He had pushed up the visor on his helmet, and, as he surveyed the crowd of onlookers, he caught Ciel's eye and grinned, raising his sword in salute. She smiled back with an involuntary lift of one hand and saw Serena's quick, angry stare fasten on her face. She looked away, feeling heat in her cheeks and a half-ashamed satisfaction. Serena Bertran needed to know there were other valued friends in Lord Ian Stewart's world . . .

Then the trumpets blew, the knights ceased their efforts, and the melee was over. Each man went back to his tent and the younger knights prepared themselves for jousting, an event where a long barricade, horseback high, was set up with post and board and draped with colorful cloths. Two men, one on each side and opposite ends, faced each other. Each couched his dull lance, pointed it at the chest of his opponent, and at the blare of a trumpet, rushed at the other with the intent of knocking his opponent from the saddle.

It was an event that called out laughter, not groans. Heels in the air, one after another of the young knights flew from his steed and crashed to the ground. Often both of the contestants were parted from their horses. There was only one injury on this cold afternoon, and that was naught but a broken arm. A high note was set for the rest of the tourney; the audience was in a fine, merry mood and waiting to laugh again.

Then came the contests between two seasoned knights. Lots were drawn for the first meeting, and after that the winner must meet the challenge of the first man to speak.

"They leave out Ian's name in the drawing," Aylena whispered to Ciel. "For if he were called first, he would face every man on the field, and some of them are fine warriors. It is not allowed to turn down a challenge unless you are bleeding profusely. Usually, though, the one whose name is drawn will challenge Ian, so that he still meets them all."

"I see." Ciel's face was suddenly white. "Will they rush each other like the others did?"

"No. That is only for boys, not men. They will rush each other, yes, but not with a barrier between them for safety. When one is knocked from the saddle, the other will dismount and they then fight with swords. Judges will stop the fight only if a man is badly hurt, but most of the knights know when they are up against a man they cannot best. They surrender after a token duel."

"I see," Ciel said again. "Then it is unlikely that Ian will be injured. Good. I shall enjoy the rest of it."

Aylena was silent. Her heart ached for the young girl. Ciel was clearly attached to Ian, and Ian was fool enough not to recognize it for what it was. She would have to speak to him, to tell him not to show Ciel affection and raise her hopes. It would be bad enough for the girl when he became betrothed to Serena Bertran . . .

The trumpet blew, and a man on one of Thor's black Percherons rode out, bowing toward the ladies, taking his place on the north side, grinning at Ian Stewart. He gave his challenge in a deep, gravelly shout:

"Come out, Scottish lad, and meet an Englishman!"

Aylena let out her breath. "Lord Abernathy of Sussex, and Thor believes he's one of the best. He's on a horse rightly named Thor's Pride. Ian will wish he came later in the day, when your Devil will have settled down."

Ciel gave her a wild-eyed glance and muttered a rapid prayer before she answered. "Do you believe he will lose?"

"No indeed! But 'twill be a closer match than most. Hush now, the contest begins . . ."

"Oh." The one word squeezed from Ciel's throat and she was still, leaning forward, hands clasped tightly, eyes wide. The two men were as far apart as the field allowed; and when the trumpet sounded they sent the horses toward each other at top speed. Devil's ears were laid back, his lips drawn away from his big teeth, and as he came near to the other horse he called his own challenge, a long, ear-splitting trumpet of anger. Ciel flinched.

"Oh, Lady Aylena! Devil is going to fight!" she said, and tears came into her eyes. "He will! He will fight on his own!"

At that moment the two men came together with a thumping crash, Ian's lance sending Abernathy flying off his saddle to land on his back on the ground. Devil reared high on his back legs, pawing the air with his heavy hooves, shrilling his anger. Ian leaned forward, pulling the horse's head around, and forced him down, away from the prone man and his horse. Then he dismounted and handed the reins to a young knight who had hurried to him. When Devil balked at being led away, Ian slapped him on the withers sharply. Devil still pawed and snorted noisily, but he went along without trouble. Ciel's eyes flew back to Ian, who was loosening his sword in its scabbard as Abernathy, with the help of a servant, stood up and issued a new challenge.

"Swords, Lord Stewart?"

Ian's grin parted his bronze beard. "You're a hard man to conquer, Lord Abernathy. Draw your sword and have at it!"

Aylena laughed softly. "Our good friend Abernathy is no coward. He well knows Ian's skill, but he's putting up a performance I must admire. Watch this, Ciel. Ian is a magician with a sword. Even with the *claidheamh mor*."

"Is that what he has in his hand?"

"No, dear friend. The *claidheamh mor* never leaves Stewart Castle except in war. It is a huge, murderous blade that few men can handle well because of its weight, though Thor and Ian have mastered the skill needed. We pray it will always remain on the castle wall. Now, look! Ian is setting himself for a victory . . . and there it is! He has disarmed his opponent."

Ciel watched Abernathy's sword whirl upward, circle in the air and fall behind him. Following it with his eyes, the knight shrugged, laughed, and came forward weaponless to Ian.

"An honorable victory is yours, Sir Ian. "I'll buy that young horse if you care to sell."

Ian grinned. "The horse is not mine. He belongs to the dark-haired, beautiful girl sitting with the Lady Aylena. I doubt you can tempt her to sell him."

"But I may try . . ."

"Lord Stewart has won!" shouted the trumpeter. "Those who will accept a challenge will come forward!"

A dozen men surged toward the middle of the field, calling out their names. Ian turned, smiling at them, nodding as one called to him, nodding again when another man offered. He acted, Ciel thought, as if he had been urged to enjoy himself at some pleasurable game. She said so to Aylena, and Aylena broke into laughter.

"You are quite right. For Ian, it is much the same. He has never fought in anger."

Ciel's eyes rounded. "Is that true? Then the man who angers him some day may not live long enough to regret it."

"Sit back," Aylena told her, "and watch. You may be proud of Ian's strength and skill, and I shall be remembering my pride in the man who taught him so well."

At the end of the day, when the light began to fail and the men and horses tired, Ian was accompanied by a dozen knights to the center of the field, all of them on horseback. He was given a stirrup cup of French wine and a bag of gold florins gathered from the audience. The Duke of Hastings, an old man but a lover of tourneys, did the presentation of prizes to the victor. Then he handed over a brilliant silk scarf of many colors.

"For your lady, Lord Stewart, to keep for the memory of your success on the London field today."

Ian thanked him. Then he turned and approached the bevy of young women on the seats along the wall, ending in front of Serena Bertran. He bowed to her with dignity and offered the scarf, adding the usual words to the ceremony. " 'Tis yours, my lady, to mark the day."

Serena laughed and rose, excited. She took the scarf, waved it about so the other young women could see it, then tucked it down between her half-naked breasts. Then she threw her arms around Ian's neck and kissed him on the mouth, pressing against him as if she would never let go. Gasping for breath, she leaned away and laughed again, looking down at the scarf tucked in the cleft of her breasts. "You may pull the scarf out, Sir Ian, and push it back in if you like."

The other young women erupted in shocked giggles as Ian turned a brilliant red. "The scarf is yours, my lady, not mine. If I may I will wait on you tomorrow afternoon at the Tower of London. There are things I wish to say. Will you be there?"

Serena leaned forward and kissed him again, her mouth moving sensually over his. "For you, my handsome lord, I will always be where you want me."

At a loss, Ian nodded, kissed her hand again, and left to join his sister and her companion.

The three of them, Ian, Lady Aylena, and Ciel, rode back to the castle together, with the three men-at-arms lagging along behind them, unworried by the thought of thieves in the dusk. London thieves were well educated in their trade and the dangers thereof. None would attack a knight in armor, most certainly not one who rode through the streets with yeomen wearing the king's livery.

9

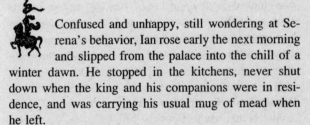

Confused and unhappy, still wondering at Serena's behavior, Ian rose early the next morning and slipped from the palace into the chill of a winter dawn. He stopped in the kitchens, never shut down when the king and his companions were in residence, and was carrying his usual mug of mead when he left.

Now, sipping the warm drink, he headed for the stables. There were things he must do this morning, and the first was to see if Devil had stiffened in any limb—a condition that often occurred after a tourney. When that trouble came, only hot cloths, wound tight around the leg, would ease the pain.

Old John met him at the door, his ancient frame bent and bowed but his toothless grin as merry as ever.

"So, you are another rider who worries about that wild young stud. He is much like you, Sir Ian. Peaceable with the ladies, but determined to win every fight. Come, and I'll show you he needs no attention from you or me."

The stableman led the way to the far end of the building and a high-sided stall off to itself. Ian could hear a soft voice he recognized at once. Stepping around the barrier, he saw Ciel there, her delicate profile lit by the flickering flame of a lantern she'd hung on a nail overhead. She was dressed in an old linen gown that clung to her slender body and accented her high round breasts. Her heavy wool cloak she had thrown over the open, swinging door of the stall. Ian had stepped softly on the hay-strewn floor, and she thought herself alone, continuing her work. She was crooning to Devil and rubbing him down, her small hands red from cold, her black hair in a thick, shining braid. Then, turning, she started at the sight of Ian. It was evident she was embarrassed to be caught in old clothes and behaving like an apprentice ostler. Still, she tried to put a good face on it, throwing aside the cloth she was using and giving him a careless smile.

"Good morning, my lord. You needn't worry about Devil. He has come through the battles as you have, uninjured and ready to fight again."

Ian's spirits had soared at the first sight of her; it took effort to keep from laughing from pleasure. What other woman would be out here in the stables before the sun was up, rubbing down a horse? None, he thought. Only this one.

"I see," he said, "but didn't you know I would come to him this morning? 'Tis my duty to take care of him if he has a strained muscle or a sore joint. No man worth his salt would stay away."

Ciel's smile broke out. "Perhaps 'tis your duty, but 'tis my horse, and my father taught me to be responsible to any beast I own. Besides, Devil is my true friend. Would you think I'd lie in my bed and let him suffer? In the cold of the morning an unnoticed bruise or strain can stiffen and grow painful."

"That is true," Ian answered, "and the reason for my presence here. You could have stayed warm and cozy in your bed."

"Both of you could have stayed in bed," the old man said, disgusted. "I would have seen to that young stud myself. D'you think the king would keep an old man like me in his stables if I wasn't the best in the country?"

Ian and Ciel looked at each other and laughed. It was true; John would have rubbed down the young stud at daybreak and reported any injury at once.

"Come," Ian said, and took her cloak from the top of the stall door, swinging it around her, bringing the catch at the throat together and fastening it. He reached again and tucked the thick black braid of her hair into the hood, then pulled the hood forward to keep the chill away from her cheeks. She pulled away, her cheeks flaming, her body suddenly too warm.

"I can put on my own cloak," she said. "I am no child." His big hands, his warmth and male scent confused her. Delightfully.

"I know," Ian said, "but it pleased me to do it for you. Now, let us go back to the kitchen and see if a cook will offer us breakfast."

The expression on his face was so gentle, his care of her so endearing, that tears came to Ciel's eyes. She blinked them away and took his arm, making herself smile. "They might not cook so early for me, my lord, but they surely will for you. Therefore, since I am hungry, I shall be your companion."

Laughing, they left the stables and crossed the icy ground toward the kitchens. The late sun was rising in the smoky air above the buildings to the east. It cast a cold, yellow-gray tint on the frozen cobblestones and mud, and drew sharp yellow shards of light back from the thick, half-transparent windows of the huge palace above them. Ian drew in a long breath, liking the sharp bite of winter air in his chest.

"Cold," he said, grasping Ciel's arm and holding her steady on the slippery ice, "but not as cold as my land in Northumberland. Were we there, this day would feel like spring."

"And so you are glad to be here?"

He laughed, his warm breath like a cloud wreathing his beard, his eyes merry as he helped her up the steps to the kitchen door. "Indeed not. 'Tis my home, Ciel, and I would rather be there than in any other place I have ever been. There I am myself, the laird of the Stewart clan."

"I see." And, looking into his eyes, she believed. There was a longing, a dream of home in them, shining bright.

"It must be a wonderful place, m'lord. The Lady Aylena spoke of it to me, and I could see her yearning for it. Do they ever visit you, now that they're living in Normandy?"

"Often," Ian replied, opening the kitchen door and letting her go before him. "King Henry likes to have Thor near him, and when he calls for Thor, Aylena comes along and they visit me. She has a love for the old place also." He laughed softly. "And Thor, too. It was his for a time . . . a war prize. But he gave it back to me when I came of age."

"I see," Ciel said again, and looked around.

A cook, standing at the huge iron oven, was staring

at them, amazed. "Up so early, Lord Stewart? Something wrong in the stables?"

"No, Alma. All is in order, except that Lady Aylena's companion and I are starving. Would you be so kind . . . ?"

"Oh! Oh, yes, m'lord. We have sausage and bread cooking, and a sauce of cooked dried fruit . . ."

"Excellent. No need to set places in the dining hall, cook. 'Tis warmer in here. Come, Ciel, and sit by the fire while we wait."

She obeyed, amused but wondering at him. She had never known a nobleman like Ian Stewart. He had no pretensions, no conceit, no overweening pride in himself. He was, she thought, dangerous. She could so easily find herself thinking of him as an ordinary man, though much more lovable and gentle than most. And that would be fatal. He was already in her heart, but, she reminded herself, once he married Serena she would be a friend in far-off Normandy, slowly fading from his mind . . .

They ate, still before the fireplace, and talked together a little, with Ian describing his world to the north. He spoke of the barren ground, the wide beaches along the fast-flowing waters joining the North Sea. He spoke of the ruined castles built in the far past by Vikings; he told of the strength of the Scots and the castles and commerce along the River Tyne.

" 'Tis wild compared to southern England," he said, "and its beauty is harsh, not soft like the meadows and flowers here in the summer. Aye, 'tis sometimes dangerous also. Yet I canna be my ain true self anywhere else."

Ciel smiled at his lapse into Scottish vernacular; she

had heard the same from Lady Aylena and knew the meaning. And, reminded of her lady, she jumped to her feet.

"Look at me! I sit here listening when I should be with the Lady Aylena. She is sure to be rising and needing her maid . . ." She was gone, slipping through the door that led to the back stairs.

Watching her go, Ian still thought of his own home and how lonely it was since Thor and Aylena had turned it over to him when he was barely sixteen and, though they left good men to help him, had settled down to stay in Castle Cheval Noir.

It was right, he knew, and the only answer. A wife went to her husband's home, and Thor had been generous indeed to allow Aylena to stay with her young brother so long. And so a wife was what he needed. Yet he felt reluctant without knowing why. Certainly his ideal woman was right here in London, living in the Tower. His thoughts went to Serena Bertran and his frown deepened. That kiss yesterday—she had made a mockery of the usual chaste meeting of lips at such occasions. And that reckless bit of teasing—the scarf tucked into the cleft of her half-bared breasts, her invitation to him—'twas like a courtesan's eager attempt to catch a noble to take her to bed, fill her womb with his seed and her purse with gold to pay for getting rid of it . . .

But it was likely no more than imitation, he decided as he rose from his seat. Among the young women at court there were always two or three who are caught by their ambition and end up as courtesans. No doubt, he thought, Serena, seeing someone acting like that, had believed it only gay and reckless. He would warn her of

such. And perhaps she would agree to travel with him
and his sister to see the home he offered. But first he
would talk to Thor. If Thor thought the king was in
danger, then they must both stay in London until the
threat was gone.

He found Thor in the great hall of the palace, deep in
conversation with William the Marshal. The young king,
Henry III, stood listening to the talk. Quietly Ian joined
the circle. William, a great, tall, muscular man noted for
his tournament skills and, even more so, his dedication
to the royal family, was frowning heavily as he talked.

"There is no doubt that Pope Alexander means to
make our king suffer, for he's sent word that he must
wear sackcloth and ashes for fifteen days, and must pray
unceasingly for Becket's soul. The king has agreed,
though he will obey the orders only in privacy. My own
fright comes from the threats we have received. Men are
being told by the thieving monks of Canterbury that if
they kill the king, they will spend all eternity in heaven
as their prize."

Thor snorted. "We will see that they don't. Those
who try will die before the king, unshriven." He turned
to Ian. "For a day or so, or until the word of the monks
is forgotten, I will accompany Henry wherever he goes.
If you have other plans, you may continue with them.
But remain close."

Ian nodded. That was settled, whether or no it suited
him. His plan to take Serena to Northumberland must
wait . . . but perhaps he could continue his courtship
here. Certainly she seemed willing to see him, and, when
Thor thought the king safe inside his palace for a few
hours, he would visit her in the Tower.

Later, when Ian heard the king's plan was to remain

in the palace alone for the whole day, he made plans of
his own. The more he thought about it, the more con-
vinced he was that Serena would enjoy an outing with
him. It was likely that she was bored by the lack of
entertainment. The death of the archbishop had brought
about a decided change in King Henry's court, especially now when the pope's wrath seemed to be increas-
ing instead of withering away. There were no state
dinners or musical events to charm the young ladies.
The bevy of beauties had naught to do other than to wait
for a better time. So Ian sought out Thor again and
found him in a small study poring over reports from the
men-at-arms who guarded the palace. Ian interrupted
him long enough to ask permission to leave the palace.

"Indeed," Thor said. "Go, by all means. Our king
wishes to hide and cool his heels. I truly believe he's in
mourning for Thomas à Becket. Angry as Becket made
him, he is now remembering the days when they were
as close as brothers."

"Our king," Ian said, "is more soft-hearted than others believe. He did truly admire Becket, and I believe
he truly mourns, even so. Now, if I am not needed here,
I wish to pay a call on the Lady Serena Bertran."

Thor frowned. He had thought Ian would see through
that vain imposter long before this. "Serena Bertran is
a beautiful young woman, Ian, but she is not entitled to
be addressed as a noblewoman."

Ian frowned. "I know, and I suppose she's doing it
here to make herself seem like the other young ladies. I
don't care for her little conceits, but she may outgrow
them."

Thor shook his head. "To say you are what you are
not—doesn't that count as a lie?"

Ian flushed darkly. "She was open with me in France. Perhaps she will be open and true with me on other things, Thor. I believe 'tis only a fancy for her to pretend herself a true noble and enjoy the entertainments of the king's court. She will settle, once we wed."

"And has she agreed to wed?"

Ian's smile returned. "No. I wish her to see my home before I ask. I am hoping that once the danger has passed for our king, you and Aylena will travel with us for a visit to Stewart Castle."

Thor nodded. "Indeed, we likely will, whether or no she agrees. Have you asked?"

"I will ask her today," Ian said. "I am anxious to know if she's willing."

Thor sighed and turned back to his reports. "I wish you luck and grace, Ian. You may need both."

Leaving, Ian wondered at Thor's words. But then, Thor always saw things as either black or white. And, though it hurt to know that Serena lied, it was, Ian thought, a small and innocent lie compared to many he had heard from real noblemen. Going out to the stables again to choose a horse, he brightened. Except for the meeting at the tournament, he hadn't had a chance to talk to Serena. Today he would surprise her.

The ride from Westminster Palace to the Tower was long and cold. The two buildings were at opposite ends of the city, and the Tower of London around the bend of the Thames. But Ian, used to hunting down his sheep on the barren Northumberland hills and valleys, found the long ride invigorating. The hurrying citizens of the sprawling city, bent against the cold wind and flying snowflakes, gave him wondering glances but no trouble. A big man on a big horse found very little trouble at any time in London. And, when he finally arrived at the gates of the Tower, the guard there recognized him and opened the gate at once. He rode in, dismounted, and handed his reins to a stableboy who came running to take them.

"Are you here to visit the young ladies?" the guard asked, grinning. "There are some beauties amongst them now. And some who would make you a loving wife, Lord Stewart."

Ian laughed. "And surely every man is in need of a wife, Roy. But when there are so many beauties 'tis hard to pick one. Which part of the Tower are they occupying?"

"The gallery, my lord. And a few even higher, on the next level. Go to the solar. Most of them will be there, and those who are not may be visiting the noble prisoners on the lower floor."

Ian had turned away, but now he turned back, eyebrows raised. "They visit the prisoners?"

"Only when the prisoners are young and good-looking, my lord. Then the ladies play at being angels of mercy, bringing the noblemen tidbits to eat and cups of wine."

Ian nodded. "Indeed, why not? The prisoners here are always noblemen from other countries, waiting to be ransomed."

"And some not so eager to go home," the guard said, and laughed. "They only want to be free—in England."

Ian smiled and went on, mounting the stone steps and passing through the wide, carved doors into the great hall and the gallery above it. He felt he could understand that last remark; he too would be happier if free to go where he wished to go. Then he heard the sound of light laughter and headed for it. Someone would know where he could find Serena.

The huge hall was gloomy and cold; the gallery that ran around the walls above it was full of shadows. Only a feeble, sputtering light came from candles in wall sconces. Then suddenly a wide door flew open on the right side of the gallery, and brilliant light and warmth poured out, enlivened by the excited laughter of young women.

"Didn't I say 'twas young Lord Stewart? Was I right? I wish one of you had covered my wager!"

Four young women came sweeping along the gallery, looking down and laughing. Ian recognized the one who had made a wager; 'twas the dark-haired daughter of Philip of Anjou, one of Thor's oldest friends, and having the name of Philippa. He smiled and took her hand, bowing.

"And I will wager you can tell me where I can find the Lady Serena Bertran. Think, Philippa. 'Tis a long, cold way I've ridden to find her."

Philippa's smile wavered. "Why, I . . . I'm sure she was with us an hour ago, but she soon disappeared. Perhaps she has gone to her bed and settled in for a nap. Come along, and I'll knock on her door and see what she says."

"Gladly." Ian straightened and nodded. "Lead on."

"You'll be wasting your time, my lord."

Ian turned and met the gaze of a tall, well-proportioned young woman with lemon-blond hair and a pair of cold, intelligent eyes. Philippa stepped between them and smiled nervously. "May I present the Lady Constance of Salisbury, daughter to the earl, Lord Ian?" She turned to the tall blonde without waiting for Ian's answer. "I will find Serena, Constance, without your help. Please excuse us." She took Ian's arm and marched him away, toward the stairs. Behind them, a hum of low voiced conversation rose, the tone argumentative.

"Philippa?"

Her dark eyes looked up at him and then away. Holding her full skirts aside, she concentrated on each broad step they were climbing. "Yes, Lord Stewart?"

"Are you sure this is the most likely place we will find the Lady Serena?"

There was a silence while they took the last few steps and stopped on the gallery floor. Then Philippa raised her eyes to his and shook her head. "No, my lord. 'Tis much more likely she is visiting the prisoners. She—ah, seems to enjoy cheering them up."

"Then why are we here?"

Philippa crimsoned. "Some of the noblemen who come here to visit us are angered if they find us . . . uh, consoling the prisoners. I was afraid . . ."

Ian's face relaxed into a smile. "I see. However, I am not offended. Were I a prisoner here, I would more than appreciate a kind word and the opportunity to converse with a lady. Take me to the cells, then. I haven't a great deal of time to waste." He turned and started down the stairs again and Philippa suddenly joined him, taking his arm and smiling.

"That will not be necessary," she said, pointing. "There is the lady in question. See? Serena is just entering the hall."

Taking the last few steps, Ian looked and then smiled broadly. Flushed, half laughing, Serena had never been more beautiful. Her usually neat coil of red-gold hair was loosened enough to make stray ringlets around her face, and her blue eyes sparkled like jewels. Nor was she as formally dressed as usual. She wore a loose violet silk gown that seemed to float around her, and a warm cloak of deep purple wool edged in vair. She came across the marble floor with her hands outstretched to Ian and offered him her cheek to kiss.

"My lord," she said gaily, "how wonderful that you found time to visit me in these dangerous days! Tell me, is all well with our gracious king?"

Looking down at her, Ian could hardly speak. This was another, entirely different Serena. So joyous, so full of spirit, such kind words and thoughts. He took her small hand and held it as he answered.

"The life here must agree with you," he said. "You are so alive, so beautiful and charming!"

Serena turned pink. "Do you really think so? Perhaps it is only my pleasure at seeing you. I am truly surprised! I thought you'd be with Lord Rodancott, helping to guard King Henry."

"And so would I be, my lady, but the king is confining himself to the palace, and both Thor and William the Marshal are there, along with the palace guards. 'Twas the first chance I have had to visit you, and Thor agreed to it."

Serena smiled and took his arm. "Then let us make the most of it. I have a chamber of my own, and a small sitting room. Come, we will be alone."

There was a murmur, quickly silenced, from the other young women. Serena ignored it. Head high, she took Ian's arm and led him upstairs. The hall was carpeted with woven rushes, and their feet made only a rustling sound. She took him nearly to the end before she stopped and opened a door.

"Here," she said, waving at the neatly furnished sitting room, "we can be very private. These doors are thick, and the walls the same. No one will try to listen; and none could hear if they did."

" 'Tis a lovely little room," Ian said, stepping inside, glancing through to the bedroom. "But no one will have to try to listen. We will leave the door open while we talk."

Serena looked up at him incredulously. "Do you not want to—to be alone with me, Ian?"

He turned and put his arms around her loosely. "Serena, my angel! Indeed I do. But not until we are wed. Your virtue must not be sullied by the smallest suspicion."

Serena looked at him searchingly. Slowly her face changed; her look of puzzlement faded into poorly concealed amusement. "You," she said, "are truly a holy, parfit knight, straight from the court of King Arthur. How . . . ah . . . wonderful!" She stepped away from him and indicated a chair.

"There," she said, "that is my largest chair. Sit down, and I will sit on the smaller chair across from you—and I will also leave the door open. Does that satisfy you?"

Ian looked at her carefully. She had lost the bubbling enthusiasm, the flirtatious manner, the smiles and bright eyes. Still, she was friendly, and he didn't mind being teased. He nodded, glad the argument was over.

"I think it right, my lady. I came to tell you of my plans for the spring. Lord Rodancott has promised that the Lady Aylena will accompany you to my home, for propriety. I want you to see the castle and grounds before we wed. Naturally, I intend to send word to your father of our plans . . . or . . ." He slowed, seeing the sudden displeasure that crossed Serena's face. "What is it, my lady? Had you already sent such news to your father?"

"No. Nor had I taken your suit seriously." All at once, Serena was perturbed by what she saw for herself. He was serious, and she was caught in a trap. This large English knight who lived in a freezing land and had naught but sheep wool and meat to make his fortune was altogether too determined to marry her! To be stuck in an icy castle close to wild Scotland without a court of noble lovers and poets would be disastrous. She would fade away and die of boredom!

She jumped to her feet, whirled away from him, and spoke harshly. "You have taken entirely too much for granted, Sir Ian. It was not my plan to consider marriage to you when I came to England."

Ian stood and towered over her. "That is not true. You mentioned your interest in me to others, including the king. If you have since met a man you prefer to me, then so be it."

"I have met no one I wish to marry. I prefer court life as a single woman, as many do!"

Ian stared at her. "Do you mean as a courtesan?"

A look of boredom settled on Serena's face, and she turned away, going to peer through a small window. " 'Tis true I thought perhaps we would marry, but I have met a—a Spaniard who has intrigued me. It is not love in the way that you call love, Ian. Only a different way of living. Of enjoying life. Of taking what one wants . . .

when one wants it, and never tying oneself to a dreary circle of duty."

Ian stared at her, wondering if she knew what she was saying. From the look on her face, she did. He turned away, bitterly disappointed. "I believe I understand. There is naught to explain, Serena. I wish you well and happy."

He stepped from her open door and saw Philippa standing between him and the stairs. He went toward her, and she came to him and spoke.

"There has been a messenger here with a note for you," she said, and pulled a scrap of paper from a pocket. "I—I wasn't sure I should interrupt your conversation with Serena, but it speaks of trouble at Westminster Palace. Here it is."

Down the hall, Serena stepped from the door, looked at them both, then disappeared again. Philippa flushed red. "I am sorry, Sir Ian. I heard words between you and Serena, and I want you to know I will not repeat any of it. I detest gossip."

Ian nodded. "As do I. And I thank you, both for the message and for your honest remark." He glanced at the paper and saw that Thor had written to ask him to return to the palace immediately. He shoved the scrap of paper into his belt pouch and looked at her dark, pained eyes.

"I must go, Philippa, though to be fair, I will return to visit Serena again. It is possible that she will regret her words."

Philippa looked him in the eye. "She may, Lord Ian. But for your sake, I hope she doesn't." She turned and left, going swiftly toward the solar.

10

Ian, entering the courtyard behind the palace, saw old John waiting for him. Dismounting, he tossed the reins to John and left, knowing the old man would have help from an ostler in removing the heavy saddle and rubbing the horse down. It increased Ian's worry to realize that John too knew there was reason for him to hurry inside. He went in rapidly, passing through the kitchen and halls, going at once to the room where the king met with Thor and his other advisors. He knocked, and was answered by the door opening.

"I'm sorry to cut short your visit to your lady," Thor said, stepping back, closing the door as Ian came in and locking it. "But we have received new threats against the king. They may be false, meant only to disturb him."

The room was small but crowded. King Henry was there, his usually ruddy face pale and troubled. William the Marshal sat near the king; the others included the young King Henry III, also pale, and Philip of Anjou, Thor's right-hand man. Now Ian came in, and his size made the room seem even more crowded. He sat down, ready to listen. William reached over and handed him a paper.

"The rest of us have read it," William said, "and none of us can agree as to the threat. Read it for yourself."

Ian took it and read it. The message was simple. "God will avenge his servant Thomas à Becket, the great archbishop of Canterbury who was beaten to death at his own altar. His murderer will meet the same death and in the same place."

Ian looked up. "A madman has written this. No one could promise such punishment. Even if they were able to capture the king, which is near to impossible, they would be caught on the way to Canterbury. It means nothing, other than to prove the writer insane." He tossed the paper aside. "We will make sure of the king's safety, and most of his subjects will help us. Perhaps 'tis only a few men plotting against him in the hope of putting a rival on the throne."

King Henry laughed abruptly. "Young Ian has the right of it, Thor. There are always some who use any excuse to dethrone the king they don't want and put their own choice in his place. I will ignore the threat—though I'll not disobey the church. 'Twas an evil deed, and it came from my temper, if not from my hand or will. When the church finally determines my punishment, I will take it."

There was a growl of dissent from the others, but the king waved it off. "I would rather bow to God's church than to consider myself above it. Leave it be."

Later, leaving the room and heading for the midday meal, Thor and Ian spoke together. "What you said was right," Thor told Ian. "Except for those playacting fools in Canterbury, few of the English subjects have blamed

the king for Becket's death. I see no problems ahead
that we cannot handle."

Ian nodded and was silent. After they had eaten, he
sought out Thor again.

"If you need me here," he said, "I am content to
stay. If not, I will go home soon. It is time I did."

Startled, Thor gave him a quizzical look. "What of
your lady, Ian? Is Serena Bertran ready to brave the ice
and snow on that long, cold way?"

Ian gave him a humorless smile. "Serena Bertran is
not ready to brave that long, cold way. Nor, now that
she has seen and enjoyed court life, is she interested in
marrying me."

Thor put a hand on Ian's shoulder. "Better to hear
that now than later, perhaps. As for the trip, go if you
wish. When the trouble around Henry subsides, we will
follow and be with you for a time before we go back to
Normandy."

"Then I will. But not tomorrow. I believe I should
see Serena Bertran again. She came here to England and
London because of me, and if she means to return I
should help her."

"Then by all means go. 'Tis better to do your duty
at once rather than put it off."

"True. But I am not looking forward to it."

In the morning, Ian set out again for the Tower. The
day was even colder than the one before, he thought,
and then wondered if it was only in his mind. His dreams
of beautiful Serena had disappeared, leaving only the
responsibility he felt, and he was not eager to arrive. But
the guard, Roy, greeted him with an open gate and a
conspiratorial grin.

"May you manage to stay for a while this time. They say some of the young ladies can be very entertaining."

Ian hardly heard him. He was composing the words he must say to Serena. She might need help in getting back to Normandy, and he wished to ease her way and thereby ease his conscience. He had gone over in his mind the various things she had said, and he also thought he should look at this man who had so fascinated her. No doubt he was handsome and well spoken, but it would be well to judge his character. He handed the reins to Roy and posed him a question.

"Is there a young, personable man amongst the prisoners?"

Roy's heavy brows shot up, his wide mouth stretched in a grin. "Two or three, my lord. But only one Spaniard. Spaniards are always popular with the young ladies. They like to flirt."

"And his name?"

"Leon, the Count of Aragon," Roy said, rolling his eyes. "He claims royal blood, but 'tis mixed with a hot Catalonian peasant brew. He awaits the ransom from Aragon that he has promised to King Henry. While he waits, he enjoys good food and the company of young, pretty ladies."

"I see. How do I get to the prisoners' cells?"

Roy laughed. "The noble prisoners' cells are merely small rooms, Lord Stewart. Comfortable but locked and confining. Take the entrance there behind the small gate. You'll find a guard or two inside. They can direct you."

"My thanks." Ian flipped a coin into Roy's waiting hand and went rapidly toward the gate he had pointed out.

When he swung the gate open and started in, two

burly guards got up from a bench and started toward him, hesitating when they realized his size. Then one of them recognized him and laughed.

" 'Tis the Scot who won the tournament, Tom. Rodancott's young man, Lord Ian Stewart." He came toward Ian and bowed. "What can we do for you, my lord?"

"There is a man inside—a Spaniard claiming noble blood and awaiting a ransom. He calls himself the Count of Aragon, and I wish to see him and talk with him."

"Nothing easier, Lord Stewart. Follow me." The man turned and went at a smart pace toward the inner wall and another iron gate. Holding it open and letting Ian go through, the man spoke again. "You've no weapons on you, have you, my lord?"

Ian's brows rose. "A long knife, guard. But I have no enmity to any prisoner inside. Why?"

"There are times when men come to take vengeance on the prisoners, my lord. The king would blame us if he lost his ransom."

"I see." Ian stared ahead, surprised to see that the cells were, as the man had said, like small rooms, as if for servants. They had ordinary doors, though all were closed.

"Strange," he commented. "But no doubt better than iron bars, like a cage for animals. They have their privacy, then."

"Oh, yes, m'lord, though we watch them at times," the guard said, and winked. "Some of them don't care. See the little square bars in the next door? Yes? You're tall enough to put an eye to it. We must use a stool . . ."

Ian paused at the tiny square, looked for a frozen moment, and straightened, his face a dark red. The guard laughed softly. "Look again if you want, m'lord. Once I knock they'll be scrambling to get their clothes on."

"Knock, then." Ian's face showed angry disbelief and shock. "Is this the Spaniard I asked for?"

The guard was still chuckling as he knocked and twisted the key. "Yes, m'lord. He's a fine stud. Night an' day he's at it, and some of the young ladies fight over him." He looked up and grinned. "It's always the same. Most of the young ladies are pure, but the others . . . ah, yes! Yes, indeed! Those others will make you wish you were a prisoner too."

Ian didn't bother to answer. Fists clenched, he waited for the door to open. He was enraged, but he had no idea what he was going to say or do. What little he had seen proved Serena was no virgin nor was she sadly giving in to a man. Ian was not so innocent that he hadn't heard from other men the pleasures one found in high-class brothels, though to say truth he had thought the stories exaggerated.

But what he had seen was Serena, naked as she was born, sitting astride a man's loins and taking him into herself, while he thrust and groaned and moved inside her, caressing her small breasts. Certainly she hadn't been forced. Indeed, from the look of hot pleasure on her face, it seemed she was more than eager to take part in the act. Was this what she had planned when she asked him to her room? Was that all she had wanted from him? It was impossible to think it true . . .

"There you are, sir. The count is coming to the door."

Ian looked at him. "Is there a priest in the Tower, guard?"

"Oh, yes. Father Blaine of Southwark. But for what, sir?"

"We may need him later." Ian stared at the opening door, seeing inside Serena's flushed, laughing face looking up at the Spaniard. They had thrown on their clothes, somewhat rumpled and unbuttoned. Then she looked around and saw Ian. Her face fell, the smile fading.

"Why . . . Ian! Why are you here?"

"I came to meet your friend," Ian said, "since I wanted to know enough about him to let your father judge whether you should stay or go back to France."

Behind Serena the so-called Count of Aragon had seen Ian and turned a greenish white. He pushed past Serena to speak.

"She was not a virgin when I took her, m'lord. She is well practiced in the arts of love. I did not despoil her."

Fury reddened Ian's face again, but he held it in. "Is that true, Serena?"

She hesitated, looking from him to the Spaniard. After a moment, she shrugged. "It is true. I have had many lovers, and hope to have many more." She laughed suddenly, her eyes sparkling. "And I would like you to be one of them, my Lord Innocent. Perhaps now you will come to my room again and allow me to shut the door. You'll never regret it."

Ian's mouth curled cruelly and his eyes grew stonehard. "When I am in need of a whore, Serena, I will find an honest one." He turned, facing the guard. "There is no reason to bother the priest now. I'd not saddle the Spaniard with an unwanted wife."

"Aye, m'lord. If you'd like to see that the lady returns safely to her friends upstairs, why, take her arm and go.

I'll show you the stairs that go up to the great hall and the rooms for the young ladies.'' The guard's face still held a look of amusement and a suggestion of being a willing accomplice, but Ian's face was a frozen mask, turning away.

"She found her way down, guard. She can find her way up again. In the meantime, I thank you for your guidance. I will see myself out the same way I came in.''

That afternoon at the palace Ian packed his necessary belongings of clothes, blankets, dried foods, and weapons in two big bundles that would hang from his saddle. He knew how, and he worked precisely and well, taking all he would need and with nothing extra. It was a long trip to Northumberland with only one horse, but he knew Rogue could do it and he didn't want the management of an extra animal. He wanted to be free. And alone.

When he had finished his preparations, he sought out Thor and asked him to join him in a private room for a talk. He told Thor what had happened.

"I was a fool,'' he ended. "I had seen her faults but looked right through them to her beauty. If you wish, you can tell Aylena what I have told you, but no one else. I'll not start gossip about Serena, even so.''

"You can't,'' Thor said gently. "Gossip about her began on the tournament field when she accepted your token, and every day it grows. It will continue to grow, no doubt, but not from what we say about her.'' He hesitated. "Do you want to tell Aylena yourself?''

Ian blushed a dark red. "No. She will know I've been a fool, and I don't want to see her pitying glances. I need no pity. I am damnably lucky to have escaped.''

He turned away, toward the door. "I will leave early, Thor. Tell Aylena and my dear friend Ciel that I am on my way home and will be very happy to see them both when you visit me."

"I will." Thor hesitated, and then asked flatly: "Have you an agreeable serving woman at your castle? One who will accommodate you occasionally?"

Ian paused in the doorway but did not turn around. His broad back was stiff and still. "There was a woman who offered. I refused. I'll not refuse the next one."

"Good. 'Twill satisfy your body and keep you from foolish dreams. Then when you truly love, you will know it."

This time Ian turned and looked at Thor wonderingly. "I am amazed, Thor. Except for my father, I have never known a man to be as faithful to one woman as you have been."

Thor nodded. "True. An 'twill be true until I die. But I was far from being an untried lover when we met. Be sure the serving woman is willing and clean, then take my advice. Too many love-hungry men marry the first pretty face and regret it later."

Ian's white teeth gleamed momentarily in his bearded face. "You've taught me all I know; perhaps this will be the last lesson." He came back into the room and clapped Thor on the shoulder. "By the gods, you've never been wrong in your advice."

Thor grinned. "Then pray I am not wrong now. As for what I may say to Aylena, the advice I've given you will not be included. My loving wife still believes you rival King Arthur's legendary Galahad."

Ian's grin grew broader. "My sympathy to Thorwald and Bruce in the near future. And may the threats against our king turn out to be no more than words, and you'll be heading to Stewart Castle soon. I will be waiting for all of you.''

Thor went with him to the stables, carrying one of his heavy bundles, and helped him with the saddling. Rogue fought the bridle, throwing up his heavy head and squealing loudly. Ian soothed him, rubbing his ears, speaking softly.

''He thought his work over for the day,'' Ian said, ''but a trip to the Tower and back is nothing at all. Not even enough to tire a pony. Enough, Rogue! We'll not travel far tonight.''

Just far enough, Thor thought, to keep from answering Aylena's questions. Another few months and Aylena will realize Ian has become his own man, and the questions will stop. Thor watched as Ian mounted the big horse, calmed him with a few words, then looked again at Thor.

''Till we meet in Northumberland, my good friend.'' Ian felt his heart lighten as he said the words, and his smile came, gleaming through his bronze beard. ''I'm going home.''

11

Ian rode hard, for the rest of the day and most of the night. He went as far as St. Albans, where he found a tavern and an inn. When he woke the next morning his heart was aimed like an arrow toward Northumberland. He took a loaf of dark bread, a pound of cheese, a leather flask of ale, paid for his lodging and food, and left.

It was bitter cold. There were few on the road, and that few bundled up and miserable. It took three grim, desolate days to reach Manchester, a city at the rolling base of the Pennine hills. There he found a large tavern and a fine, well-built stable. Rogue showed no signs of tiring, but after seeing the comfort and warmth in the inn, Ian decided to give them both a rest by staying an extra night. He ordered a rubdown and a double ration of oats for Rogue, and a bath for himself. The maids filled the tub with steaming water, laid out the dish of soap, the washrags and towels, and left. The last one, an elderly woman, turned at the door and asked in a knowing manner if he'd like a maid to wash his hair and back. He thought of what Thor had said, opened his mouth to agree, then shook his head. It was too soon, too careless. He wanted no woman who spread her legs for money.

He washed thoroughly, rinsing his hair and beard with the bucket of clear water they left, then dried himself and called the maids back in to empty the tub. He helped, filling the buckets for them, setting them out in the hall. They thanked him, took their tips, and left.

Ian yawned as he locked the door and went back to bed. He slept until noon, then rose and dressed. He packed away the clothes he had worn and carried his belongings down with him. In the publick room he asked for a hearty meal and ate it. Then he went out into clear, cold air and headed for the stables. He was rested enough; and the day was before him.

He stopped at dark in a rough tavern in York, rose early the next day, and left before the sun was up. With any luck, and with Rogue seeming stronger every day, he'd be at Tynemouth before full dark. Now his heart drove him hard toward his home. A night with Godwin and Drusilla in Godwin's Inn; another two days, perhaps, or three, depending on the trail and the weather, and he'd be at Stewart Castle.

At dusk he was close enough to Tynemouth to smell the cooking fires. The Tyne ran toward the sea to the east, but now only as a shallow trickle between two great slabs of winter ice. Rogue snorted at the slippery footing but held his way, agile and strong, as they crossed over.

The streets were dark and empty; the houses battened against the cold, the smoke from their chimneys rising in slanting plumes against a lowering sky. They went on, a big horse, a big man, solitary and silent, sure and confident. Then came the main thoroughfare, lighted with flaring torches along the frozen river.

"There," Ian said, aloud. "There is the inn, and

lighted well. You'll be in a warm stall and eating your oats in less than a half hour . . ." Hearing himself, he laughed and felt foolish. 'Twas time he found friends who could talk back.

He took Rogue around to the stables and saw him comfortable before he entered the inn as he always had—through the kitchen door.

Drusilla, still plump and rosy as ever in her old age, turned from the stove and stared angrily at the snowy giant who had just entered. "Now, you look here! If you want a room or a meal you must go around to the entrance . . . oh! oh-h-h, *Ian!*" She rushed to hug him. "How good to see you! Are you alone?"

Ian kissed the round face and laughed. "I am alone and starving, my dear friend. Have you a bed for me?"

Drusilla chuckled. "If I haven't, I'll roll one of our guests out on the floor and give you his. Sit down over there and I'll feed you first."

Ian let out a long breath and stretched. "Leave your guest be. All I'll need is a thick blanket or two and I'll sleep on the floor. 'Tis worth it to be amongst friends."

"We'll do better than that," Drusilla said firmly. "Now sit down while I fill a plate. Godwin will be coming in soon for his own dinner, and he'll want to talk. And so will I. I want the news you carry about our Lady Aylena and Lord Rodancott."

That night Ian slept dreamlessly and long, waking after the sun was up. Godwin had told him that one of the young Stewart cousins had been in Tynemouth only two weeks ago, and he had said the sheep and the shaggy Shetland cows were in fine shape. That had eased Ian's worries, though he had learned that his careless young cousins were more easily pleased than he. Still, he had expected losses, and none were mentioned.

Once awake, he moved fast. Two days he had given himself, and one already started. Godwin refused to charge him for his board and room, and said he'd expect a low price on the young rams in the spring. Ian had laughed and dropped the money on the table where they sat.

"You should know better than to barter with a Scot," he told Godwin. "Take the money now or take the loss later."

It was a glorious day in spite of the cold. Rogue sniffed the salt air as they came to the cliffs that led north, threw up his handsome head, and neighed loudly, as if he remembered his home and the salty Normandy winds. Ian laughed at him. "The mares you are calling are far away, my friend. But there's one or two where we're going. Keep up the pace!"

That evening he came to the old Norman castle where Thor and Aylena had camped when Ian was a child. It was now only a few pieces of wall, but a better choice than the windswept beaches. Ian had brought along blankets and rations for himself, and oats for Rogue. It had been months since he'd camped, and even in winter weather he enjoyed it. He tethered Rogue out of the wind and gave him his rations. Then he built a fire of driftwood against a bit of wall and cooked his meat. When the fire was only embers, he rolled up in a fur cloak and slept, waking at dawn to find himself covered by snow and still warm.

The next night he spent in a shepherd's empty hut. He had come to his own land and wanted shelter. The shepherd, Orn Thoma, belonged to Stewart Castle and would have news. But Orn was gone, though his clothes, his dried meat, and even the bags of winter hay for the sheep were there. Ian went to the big winter corral among sheltering trees and found no sign of sheep nor shepherd, only trampled and muddy paths that soon disappeared in the fresh snow. Ian felt shamed and guilty. As the laird, he was caretaker of his sheep and his men, and he feared for old Orn's life.

After a restless night Ian rose early to search again. He found nothing and, angry and worried, turned Rogue to the north and kicked him up with his heels. Orn Thoma was honest. Someone had happened by . . . a thief, or an enemy. And not long past. There had been no dust on Orn's table or bed.

Halfway to the castle, when he could see the top of his ancient keep in the gray sky, he came near to a dark heap along the worn path. It was half covered with snow, but his heart told him it was Orn.

He dismounted, tied Rogue to a sapling, and went to look. When he turned the body over, he saw that the frozen ground was smeared with darkened blood from a gaping chest wound. Tears came to Ian's eyes. Old Orn had been a faithful friend of the old laird and had given his full allegiance to Ian in turn.

Carefully Ian wrapped Orn's small body in a heavy cloak, tied it tight, and carried it to his horse. Rogue blew and snorted, backing away from death, rolling his eyes. Ian spoke to him calmly, insistently, and at great length, still holding the body as if it were part of him. Finally Rogue stilled and, quivering, allowed the frightening burden to be laid across his already laden back and tied to the saddle.

Riding away, his eyes on the tall keep of his castle,

Ian was grim. The joyous homecoming he had expected was only a childish dream, for his absence had led to losses and an old man's death. He had been gone too long, and some enemy had become confident enough to take advantage of old William Stewart and Roderick, William's son. Guilt settled over Ian like a gray winter fog, giving a straight, angry line to his young mouth and a deep cleft between his heavy brows.

He was recognized by his men-at-arms when he was still a quarter mile from his castle walls. Trumpets blew crazily; the drawbridge came down with a ground shaking crash, and people poured out to gather themselves into two lines and stand there waving, laughing and weeping a little.

Ian knew they expected him to kick his new warhorse into a gallop. That had always been the custom, and it set off the beginning of a day-long celebration. But with Orn's dead body behind his saddle there would be no holiday. He came on slowly, and gradually the crowd quieted and moved about, talking and wondering. Two of his men-at-arms mounted horses and came to meet him. He saw the question in their eyes and shook his head, indicating the body behind his saddle.

" 'Tis Orn Thoma, young Gerald. Someone has stolen his flock and killed him, leaving his body beside the path."

"Before God!" Gerald said, shocked. "I visited Orn two days ago an' sat in his hut talking for an hour. The old man was hale an' hearty then, an' his sheep fat as butter."

Tom of Leckie, the other man-at-arms, nodded vigorously. " 'Tis true of all the winter's sheep! Old Harald, who has the big flock toward the Tweed, says he has never had any fatter than these. We have been riding out often to talk to the shepherds, for William has sworn that you'll find your sheep in better fat and wool than ever before.''

Ian's face twisted. ''If I find them at all. Orn Thoma had a big flock.''

The crowd gathered in front of the drawbridge grew more and more quiet as the three men came on. They sensed trouble and grief from the scene. From the top of the wall, William Stewart, the old man of the clan, shook his head and said a prayer, the air so quiet now that the ones below heard and crossed themselves, echoing his amen.

The young laird, huge and silent on his immense black horse, rode between the two men-at-arms, who looked small and serious on either side of him. Ian was as deep in sorrow as ever he had been in his life. Anger and guilt consumed him. Yet, looking at the shocked faces turned up to him, he knew he must show courage. They were his people, and his duty. He stopped in the center of the courtyard and dismounted, giving Rogue's reins to Gerald, and told him to see to old Orn's body. Then he waited until William and his son, Roderick, came down from the wall and joined the crowd. Ian came to them and put his arms around old William, kissed him on both cheeks, and stepped back to shake Roderick's hand vigorously. Then he went back to the steps that went up to the door of the keep and stood on them to address the hundred and more men and women of the castle.

''As you have seen, a Stewart man has been killed by a coward,'' he said, ''secretly and in the dark. Old Orn Thoma, a good and honest man, is dead. And the thieves have stolen the two hundred sheep that Orn kept on the southeast pastures. Now we must see to the other shepherds and their flocks. When a thief is successful, he will try again.

"You men who have been checking the sheep and shepherds these last months will ride again tomorrow, and will each choose a man to ride with him. You will leave after the ceremony of Orn Thoma's burial." He stopped there, his gaze sweeping the men and women, the wide-eyed children and the old ones, bent and rheumatic. They stood, their eyes still on his face, waiting. Waiting for him to claim them as his clan, as each laird must do when he speaks to his people. And, slowly, Ian found a few more words to comfort them. What they needed now was a righteous anger to give them hope and strength.

"When a faithful man dies from a coward's hand, it leaves his friends too sore and angry to celebrate the good in life. But I will say to you that I thank God every day for my own men and women who fill this courtyard, and ask Him to bless you now. And when we have discovered and beaten back our enemy, we will celebrate— louder and longer and better than ever before. I swear it on the *claidheamh mor*!" Ian's arm shot up, his big hand clenching into a fist, and every man in the courtyard roared assent, their fists rising and punching the air as high as they could reach.

"For the Stewarts!" The cry rang out from every man. Red-faced and angry, they bellowed it again and again.

Finally Ian held out his arms and quieted them. "Orn will be buried tomorrow morning. Five men will be chosen to build a fire on the burial grounds and keep it burning all night to soften the frozen plot. Roderick will choose from all who show a wish to help.''

A number of young men surged forward toward Roderick as Ian turned and went into the castle and keep, followed by the staff of women and young boys who worked indoors. Old William, Ian's uncle, kept step beside Ian. They stopped and stood together silently in front of the wide fireplace Thor had planned and built on the north side of the great hall, to replace the old, center fire pit with its choking smoke and soot. Both Ian and William were silent, staring at the glowing coals. Then the seneschal, Robert of Bourne, came to Ian quickly, bowing, his lean face showing anxiety and a desire to please. ''I'll take your cloak, sire, and bring you ale. Are you hungry? There is boar meat roasting.''

Ian gathered his thoughts and pushed away his pity and anger, knowing his staff and his clan were shaken and wondering. He put a hand on the seneschal's shoulder. ''Boar and bread and good dark ale will set me to rights, Robert. It's good to be home.''

12

 The priest, sent for when the gathering of the clan was over, arrived in midmorning. By then the grave had been dug in the fire-softened ground and the body laid out on a bier, covered by a funeral robe. All had known Orn Thoma, all had liked him for his droll wit and his knowledge of sheep and land. He had no relatives to mourn for him; his wife had died many years ago in childbirth, and his newborn son with her. But he had been a Stewart on his mother's side, and the whole clan grieved at his death.

The cook and her staff had worked through the night, baking the funeral meats and breads for the gathering clan. And men had been sent to the outlying shepherds to tell the news and to stay to guard the sheep. The shepherds would want to come in and honor one of their own.

With them came Rory mac Kenloch, the laird of the Kenloch clan, who brought with him another priest, one who had been at his castle to perform a wedding. Hearing of Kenloch's arrival, Ian came down into the courtyard to greet him. The two men embraced, pounding each other on the back. The Kenloch laird was only three years older than Ian; they had met often as friends and fought each other in tournaments and games. Now they left the crowd and went up to the solar and sat together before a roaring fire, taking a glass of wine and settling down to talk for the half hour before the funeral.

Rory, a strong man of medium height with the red-brown hair and green eyes of his clan, seemed shaken by the fact that the murderer—or gang of thieves and murderers—had managed to get away with two hundred sheep.

"But how?" he kept asking. "How could men, even a small number of men, drive so many sheep through snow without leaving a wide trail? Though the snow kept coming, 'twas light snow. There should be enough sign to show the way they went."

"I thought the same," Ian admitted. "And I deem myself a good tracker. But I saw no part of the snow on the meadows to be lower and darker than any other. I will go back there after the funeral. It has not snowed since, and I can stay in Orn's cabin and search more thoroughly tomorrow."

"If ye consent to it," Rory said, "I will go along. As yer friend, and also because of my ain folk, for it could happen to us. Tha sheep are our livelihood also."

"Then I am indeed willing."

Ian had left the door ajar, and Robert of Bourne came to knock discreetly. "The mourners have begun to gather, sire."

Ian rose. "Stay here by the fire if you like," he said to Rory. "Or come with me."

Rory stood. "I honor any man who dies doing his duty. I will march with ye and add my prayers for the old shepherd."

* * *

Afterward, the two lairds met with the other Stewart shepherds to talk. None of the men had lost any sheep except for a ewe that died of old age and a young ram that had run into a wild Scottish cow with her calf and had been trampled to death by the cow. None of the men had seen any other men near the flocks, and they rode the snowy pastures every day.

"It's because Orn Thoma was off to himsel'," one of the other shepherds said. "The thieves could know that. Had it not been for our laird coming by when he did, those sheep would'na been found missing for days, likely till 'twas Orn's turn for an overseer to come counting. But where are the animals? Where could a man hide two hundred sheep?"

Starting out late in the afternoon, riding with their backs to a dying wind and the same snowy fields before them, Ian and Rory were still considering those words.

"I come this way seldom," Rory said, wrinkling his brow. "But I have been here before, and I remember no valley nor thick patch of trees where a flock of sheep might be held. But ye did say there were trees behind Thoma's cabin and that ye went into them to a winter holding pen, to see if some of the sheep might be there. And ye found nothing. Is there more woods about the place?"

Ian shook his head. "It may seem to you that there are many trees, but in truth there are few. Only enough to shelter the sheep from icy winds. But you can hear the sheep when they are in there."

"But there was no sign?"

"None."

" 'Tis passing strange. Still, no snow has fallen since.

Together we may find out what has happened to yer sheep.''

It was coming night by the time they reached Orn's hut. Ian had brought blankets and food; there was firewood enough inside. They ate and slept, waking to a still, icy morning.

"No wind at all now," Ian said, coming in after a look outside. " 'Twill be easy to hear. We'll eat and be on the way.'' Before they left, they doused the remaining half-burned logs with a bucket of snow water.

"I'll be putting more sheep here, and another shepherd," Ian said, "but not until I find out what happened. Somewhere there will be a sign.''

They spent two to three hours looking for sign in the meadows. There were Rogue's hoofprints and the boot tracks made by Ian as he hunted before. Finally he turned back to the woods again to show the winter pens to Rory.

The woods looked deep, the trees large enough to make good timbers, the undergrowth heavy enough to hide the woods beyond. And the flat space where the pens were kept was nearly bare of snow.

Sitting his horse and looking around, Rory shook his head. "Ye tell me this is a small woods, but I find it hard to believe. The trees to the east seem to grow higher and more numerous, as if they joined another woods farther on.''

Ian smiled. "Were this a windy day like yesterday, you'd not think those thoughts. You would hear waves crashing on rocks. Come, I'll show you . . .''

Rory followed as Ian wove through the trees. The ground rose, at first slightly and then, as the trees grew farther apart, steep and rocky. The horse's hooves slipped and they slowed, picking their way carefully. Then they emerged from the last of the trees and halted on a granite cliff that had reared itself high above a low, flat beach. Below them was the gray, ominous surge of the icy North Sea and, in the far distance, a fishing boat battling the current.

Rory stared. "I had no knowledge of this. Ye are much closer to the sea than I thought."

"Only at this point," Ian said, "for we came straight from the castle toward the east, though it often seems to strangers that we are moving south. We treasure this place, for it gives us wood for our building instead of only stone."

"Ye are fortunate. We have no woods like this . . ." Rory had ventured closer to the edge to look and now he dismounted quickly and kneeled, leaning to look straight down. He cursed luridly and stood again, looking at Ian's surprised face.

"We have found yer sheep, Ian."

Ian dismounted and joined him. It was true. The narrow, rocky shore far below them was littered with dead sheep. Ian stood up, his face red with anger. "Someone has driven them over the cliff," he said, "and killed them all. Out of anger, or out of hatred. There was no profit in it for them. Who, then, is my enemy?"

Rory, still on his knees, shook his head. "The laird of the Stewart clan has no enemy in all of Scotland except for the Barwicks, an' I canna believe a Barwick would come so far to wreak mischief. They are a lazy lot, and cowards."

Ian nodded. "But as full of poison as a snake. Perhaps they had another reason to leave Scotland for Northumberland. If they were passing here for other reasons, they would hunt out some mischief to inflict on the Stewarts.''

"True, nae doubt of it.'' Rory got to his feet, his strong-featured face tense with anger. "The Barwicks are a slur against Scotland itself. Time and again, my old father advised the other clans to put the curse on the Barwicks, an' all they did say was tha Barwicks needed pity instead.''

"If I could be certain about the sheep,'' Ian said slowly, "I'd curse them myself, and see it carried out. 'Twould rid the world of an evil and murderous clan.''

"If ye curse them, I vow to join ye. The mac Cullenan will join, an the Dounes and Crichtons. Then others will hasten to our side.''

Ian nodded. "Friends, all. But I must know 'twas done by Barwicks before I speak. If I know them, they will brag on the deed if 'tis theirs. We must wait and listen.''

Later, after riding south far enough to descend a trail leading down to the shore, they walked amongst the frozen, pitiable bodies, counted them and found twenty gone, figuring the sea had taken them. The others, they thought, would be eaten by vultures following the first thaw.

"When I set a flock there this spring,'' Ian said on the ride back to the castle, "I will see to it that the shepherd is young and strong, and armed to fight. And I will set another flock to the west, so the two shepherds can watch over each other. Two Stewarts can take half a dozen Barwicks. Had I done so before, Orn Thoma would still be alive.''

Rory gave him a sidelong glance. "Never blame yer-self, Ian, for crime done by evil men. Ye will do enough damage from yer ain ignorance wi'out takin' on theirs.''

Ian had to smile. ''I fear 'tis true, Rory. I thought myself a well-educated man as well as a good warrior, but in the past few months I have learned otherwise. I came back from Normandy and London with a new humility.''

''Ye'll not tell me someone bested you in a tourney?''

''No, not that. Nor will I tell you how I became more humble. But I will say that in the ruins of a dream I have found the beginnings of wisdom.''

Rory burst out laughing, leaning back in his saddle. ''Ye speak like a troubadour, laddie! A singer of great deeds and hopeless love!''

Ian managed a smile. ''Nothing so grand. I canna call protecting a frightened king a great deed; and as for love, I canna believe in that. 'Tis only an urge in a man's loins, after all.''

Rory laughed again. ''An' thank God 'tis true! Had our fathers less of it, we would have no life.''

They rode on, the old castle walls now in view, gray stone against a lighter gray sky. The drawbridge was down over the dry moat, waiting for them to return. There were men-at-arms on the walls and some, fully armed, wandering back and forth in front of the drawbridge. Ian's gaze took in the scene, then rose to the silken blue and silver pennant hanging above the keep. On the clear blue, the silver shape of the great, two-handed sword called the *claidheamh mor* glittered in a shaft of weak winter sun. His heart swelled in his chest.

''And so we live,'' he said finally, ''and we shall do the same with great pleasure, and hope for many strong sons. The clan is all.''

* * *

Rory stayed on for another day. He had an older sister, Marian, who was skilled, he said, with words and numbers. Sitting that evening by the fireplace in the solar, he told of her.

"She tallies the stores and tallies the lambs, an' our seneschal expects his orders from her rather than from me. She wastes nothing. 'Tis a pity she's past marryin' age, Ian. She would make ye a good wife, I swear. But she nears thirty."

Hastily Ian changed the talk. He remembered the long nose, the haughty look and speech of Lady Marian mac Kenloch.

"An' you, Rory? Have you found a young woman to wed?"

Rory laughed. "I have more time to look than ye. If I fail to produce an heir, my brother James will provide. He is already the father of two strong boys, though he is younger than I by a year an' a half."

"Then your clan is safe. Mine is not. My uncle, William, is ancient and peaceable, and all know it. His son, Roderick, is weak and without judgment to my mind. If I were mortally wounded, I believe I'd ask Rodancott for his second son, for with Aylena as a mother, he's as much Scot as Norman. And he is named for my father."

"Purrrhaps," Rory answered slowly, " 'twould be right. He will undoubtedly be well trained and schooled." He looked up at Ian and grinned. "However, I hope 'twill be ye for many a year. I have few friends as close."

Ian stretched his huge frame and yawned. "That is what I intend—many a year in mine own castle, looking to the health and happiness of my people. But I am also sworn to protect the English king. When I am called, I must go. Thor will end his duty as the king's man when he returns to Normandy this time.''

Rory was silent for a time, taking that in. ''There are Scots who would call that treason, Ian. They canna like the English.'' He smiled at that. ''Not that they've tried.''

''Aye, 'tis true. But King Henry has left Scotland to the Scots, which few English kings have done. An' his wife, Eleanor, is a Frenchwoman. Remember how long the Scots and the French have been friends on the battlefield.''

''Only,'' Rory said in a droll tone, ''as long as it takes to fight back at England together. But, be that as it may, each man must choose his own life.'' He rose from his chair, stretching and yawning. ''I intend a trip to Carlisle within two weeks, and I'd like to have company. What say you?''

''Why, I have no business in Carlisle, or none that comes to mind. However, since the markets in Carlisle are the best in the whole of north England, I will have a talk with my seneschal . . . why are you grinning like an ape?''

''There are some very charming women in Carlisle, Ian. None, perhaps, who would make a good wife, but all of whom will give you a wonderfully pleasant evening for a bit of siller. I go there often.''

Ian shook his head. ''Call me foolish if you wish, but I have no desire to plow strange fields. I'd not leave a child of mine to grow up in a whore's nest.''

Rory laughed. ''As ye wish, Ian. I'll not have to share.''

*   *   *

In London, the wrongful death of Thomas à Becket had been pushed aside for other gossip. Those who prized their positions at court lined up on the side of King Henry II, and Henry—no longer white with fear—welcomed them back with a series of royal dinners and other rich entertainments. The Westminster palace was full of visitors and guests, and Thor Rodancott, now seeing no reasons for staying to protect a newly popular king, began thinking of home. He grabbed an opportunity one late morning, when Henry had slipped from the suite where his lovely Rosamund slept, and was walking alone toward his own room. Thor followed, and spoke softly as the king reached his own door.

"Your Highness, I would have a word with you."

Henry turned and looked at him mildly. A month before he would have whirled, his hand seeking his dagger. His fear, Thor noted, had disappeared in the security of his palace and London.

"I think I know the word, Rodancott. 'Tis 'home,' is it not? You have grown overly fond of your own hearth."

Thor smiled. "You know me well, sire. My lady and I will travel to Northumberland for a visit to her old home and Ian. Then we'll be back, to leave for Calais and Castle Cheval Noir. The laird of the Stewart clan will be your man now, ready to come to you at a moment's notice. He is as able as ever I have been, and considerably younger."

Henry bent an inquisitive eye on Thor's black-bearded face. "But not as wary and well seasoned. Still, he will learn. And what of the young lady pretender he loved so well? Did she go with him to Northumberland to marry there?"

"Indeed not, your Highness. The Lady Serena Bertran would die before she would leave London to live in Northumberland. Her place amongst the other young ladies in the Tower suits her well."

"I see. And was Lord Ian disappointed?" There was a glint of humor in the king's eyes.

Thor smiled faintly. " 'Twould be more truthful to say his eyes have been opened and he is no longer dreaming. The lady is where she wants to be."

"Good. He needs a woman with courage. No doubt he will find one in that harsh climate." The king paused, his smile disappearing. "When do you wish to leave?"

"Now, sire. If you stay in London, you will be safe. But if you call up your men-at-arms and head for the Norman Marchers in Wales, you will be safe in the whole of England. There is much turmoil over Wales."

"True." The king's face was thoughtful. " 'Twould be a popular war and easily won, until the Marchers rise again. A good omen for these days . . ."

"Then I may go?"

Henry laughed and put a heavy hand on Thor's shoulder. "Go, my good and faithful servant. You deserve your time with your family and your home. From now on, I will send for Ian Stewart when I need a champion. He will come, I know."

In their rooms, Thor told Aylena they were free to go. "So we travel north," he ended, "to Stewart Castle. We should take the time to see to your revenues from Castle Belmain, but Ian can do that when he attends the king. Two months or more from today, you'll see your home again, and your sons."

Aylena laughed and kissed him. "You know my weaknesses better than your own. And I know yours.

You're pining for Cheval Noir and the salt air of Normandy.'' She hesitated, and then asked: "And have you told King Henry 'tis your last duty to him?"

Thor's thick brows went up. "Indeed. He has known for some time that this would be the end of it. He has accepted Ian as the king's man."

"I wish a man from another family would take it instead," Aylena said, frowning. "The Scots will not like one of their own acting as an English king's protector."

"The Scots," Thor said deliberately, "are too easily inflamed. Henry has been a friend to them, setting up trade with their fishermen and miners and staying out of their arguments amongst the clans. Sometimes I think the Scots have more pride than good sense."

Aylena laughed again. "I'll not argue with that. My father was ever proud and seldom sensible in his opinion of the English. But I am happy to be going to Northumberland. I must tell Ciel!"

She left him, going into the sitting room she shared with Ciel. Ciel was in a chair by one of the tall, arched windows that gave good light even on a gray day, and she was embroidering a wall hanging in wool and silk. Ciel immediately laid down the handiwork and stood up when Aylena entered the room.

"Sit," Aylena commanded testily. "I am not a queen! When will you learn I am your friend, not your mistress?"

"You are both, my lady." Ciel was trying to hide a smile and having a hard time doing it. "Allow me to give you the respect you deserve."

Aylena sat down. "I have news! We start tomorrow for Northumberland and a few weeks there with Ian, then we come back here and set sail for home. Does that please you?''

Ciel sank into a chair. She had known Ian had returned to his home. But that was all she knew. No one had wished to speak further on it, nor would she ask; so she didn't know if he had taken Serena along. Or, perhaps, Serena was to follow now . . .

''Ah . . . will Serena Bertran travel with us? Not that I object, but I would like to know.''

Aylena, who knew nothing except that Thor had said Ian was no longer interested in the Bertran girl, smiled. ''No, for which I am grateful. 'Tis a hard trip for anyone, and Serena would be horrified by the distance and the lack of comforts. Which is just as well. I understand from Thor that Ian's interest in Serena has died away.''

''I hardly think that possible,'' Ciel said slowly. ''Ian was truly entranced by her beauty.''

''Aye, he was that. But he is also a discerning man. Serena is not an intelligent or useful woman. Thor has said Ian learned that in time.''

''I see.''

Ciel's heart was in her throat, beating rapidly. She rose and went to a frosted window, peering out between the white traceries. Harsh and gray, London loomed in the distance. She had tried hard to forget Ian, for she knew she could never have him. But now, knowing she would see him again—and in his own castle!—she was warm and excited. She would know how he lived; she would have memories to keep all her life . . .

''Is it a long trip, my lady?''

''Indeed. Nearly as long as all England. And 'twill seem longer in this cold winter weather. We must take our warmest clothes.''

"Then should I begin the packing? Some things may need a cleaning or brushing. What of Lord Rodancott? Will we pack for him also?"

Aylena's smile came again. "You have been bored, I think. Your enthusiasm for the trip is growing. Thor will have his man pack for him. Now, let us go through the gowns and cloaks we brought along and see to the washing and freshening."

A few days later they set out, in the company of the king, a great number of knights, many men-at-arms and camp followers. Wagons filled with supplies for war set a slow pace, and the Rodancott party, which consisted of Lord and Lady Rodancott, Ciel Valoir, Philip of Anjou, and the Reeve brothers, Martin and Nicholas, were glad to come to the parting of their ways on the second day. They took the east road toward Manchester, while the king and his troops took the west, heading for the battlefields in Wales.

"Another five or six days," Aylena said dreamily, "and I will see my old home. And Ian! How I miss him."

Ciel only smiled. She would never tell her own feelings about Ian, though she suspected Aylena knew and kept the secret. Now, when she thought of seeing him again, her heart pounded in her throat. 'Twas a stupid heart, she thought to herself, yet honest. It told no lies. Nor was it faint or frightened. If a time came that Ian wanted her, she would give herself to him gladly, for however long they had before the Rodancotts took her home . . .

* * *

It was freezing cold, and colder as they made their way north, but little snow fell. They made good time, and on the fourth night had dinner with their friends at Godwin's Inn on the north side of the ice-choked Tyne River. All of them talked half the night. Riding north again the next morning, Aylena told Ciel they would have a night, perhaps two nights, in shelters the men would put up for them.

Ciel was amazed. "What wild country! Are there thieves about?"

"Not in this weather. But in the summer, yes. However, few are foolish enough to attack even one armed knight."

Ciel glanced about at Thor, Philip of Anjou, and the Reeve brothers, seeing that the four of them not only carried axes and swords but had them handy, swords loose in their scabbards, the axes held only by a leather thong below the shining double blade.

"I see," she said, "we are well protected." She lapsed into silence until they topped the cliff and saw the cold North Sea below them. " 'Tis a dreary prospect, Lady Aylena. Gray and misty, with those sharp rocks in the swirling water, black as the devil's heart."

Aylena looked at Ciel's beautiful face and saw the faint echo of sadness she tried so hard to hide. Her own heart ached for the girl's hopeless love. Ian was such a fool!

" 'Tis home to me, Ciel. I know this land well. 'Tis cold now, but in spring and summer it becomes magical, turning into a different land, beautiful as a dream."

Ciel was silent for minutes before she spoke. "If you say so, I believe it. But I will never see it for myself."

Aylena was silent. She still nursed an insistent hope

that Ian would see for himself the value of this young woman.

After two days—the nights spent in shelters built of cut poles and coverings of cowhide they had brought along—they came within sight of the ancient keep and the blue and silver pennant of the Stewart clan. And on they came, while men with sharp eyes watched from the walls, wondering, then sure, and then yelling and cheering, rushing to let down the drawbridge and open the inner iron gates.

" 'Tis Lord Rodancott and his men! And praise God, our own Lady Aylena, the old laird's daughter!"

Old William, sunning himself in the courtyard, jerked to attention as he heard the shouts and struggled to rise from his chair.

" 'Tis Rodancott, you say? And our Aylena? My gracious lord, call for Roderick! Call for Robert of Bourne! Our laird is off with Rory mac Kenloch again and not here to greet them!"

13

A day later, riding alone through what passed as a bright winter day in Northumberland, the laird of the Stewart clan came home to his castle. He was a little the worse for drink, sorry he had even tried the smoky whisky Rory mac Kenloch had offered him. But when the gatekeeper told him the Rodancotts were there, Ian's gloom disappeared. He went at once to see them, and found them in the great hall, talking to old William and Roderick, while Philip of Anjou and the Reeve brothers sat at the fire and remembered their earlier days here.

Ian embraced them both. "I thought the king would keep you far longer than this, Thor! What has happened?"

Thor laughed. "He is harrying the Norman Marchers and gaining approval from all of England. Soon he will be the hero to them that he has always been."

Ian laughed with him. "The Marchers thought it a good time to harass the Irish, then. Instead they are forging a new halo for the English king." He still had an arm around Aylena, and now he looked down at her again.

"Where is my Ciel? She came with you, didn't she?"

"Indeed! I'd not let her go back to Normandy alone, would I? Nor would I leave her in London. She is here, and likely to be in the stables, looking after Devil."

Ian's smile was suddenly crooked. "She mistrusts my ostlers? They are good men."

"I know. But what can you expect from her? Remember, she trusted neither the king's stablemaster nor you to look after Devil in London."

"True." He smiled, remembering. "Devil will be cozened all his life, I vow. I will go and find her . . ." He was gone, his long stride carrying him swiftly through the hall, through the kitchens, outside and around to the open stable doors. He stopped there and stood silent, conscious of a suddenly tight throat, a heat in the back of his eyes. Small and graceful, wearing a dark, heavy wool gown but with her shining black hair pulled back on her white neck and tied with a bright silk scarf, Ciel was currying Devil's thick, furry winter coat of steel gray and talking cheerfully to white-haired Harald, who sat nearby and listened with a smile.

"Oh, yes," Ciel was saying, " 'twas Lord Ian himself who taught me to manage this imp of Satan and turn him into my good friend. But, be that as it may, Devil does seem particular as to who may ride him . . . he much prefers women. The Lady Aylena is as able on his back as I . . . oh!" She had felt big hands grasp her shoulders, turn her around, and slide down to her waist. She looked up and saw the shaky smile in the bronze beard and tears welling up in Ian's blue eyes. He leaned down to her and kissed her on both cheeks, and for a moment she thought she would burst into tears herself. She had tried to pretend that when she saw Ian again he would be as ordinary to her as any good-looking knight.

It was not so. For in her eyes he was the same, the magical hero light still shimmered around his broad shoulders as he drew her close.

"Ciel! By the gods, you are as welcome as spring, and twice as beautiful." His hands were warm and trembling on her small waist. "Come, leave the rest of the grooming to Harald, and sit with us all as we talk."

She managed a laugh but shook her head, blinking away her tears, trying with no success to calm her runaway heart. The look of him, the clean scent of his crisp beard and the deep, warm tones of his voice had undone her again. She struggled to make her own shaky tone light as she answered.

"That I cannot do, m'lord. Harald has more than enough work here, what with your horses and the others we brought. Besides, I am almost through."

"Then I will help." He looked at old Harald, who leaped up and, hiding a grin, brought him a currying brush. Holding it, he circled the big horse, looking for a rough patch. There were none, and when he looked at Ciel he saw she was avoiding his gaze and a mounting blush was pinkening her cheeks. He felt heat in his eyes again and began currying the thick, arched neck as if it needed it. Then, as Ciel's own unneeded efforts slowed, he handed the brush back to Harald.

" 'Tis done," he said, and took her brush from her hand and handed it over. "Now, trust Harald to put your mount in a warm, dry stall, feed him his oats, and give him water. You and I will join the others."

He had noticed her cloak thrown over a door to a stall, and he took it up now to swing it around her as he had done in the past. He pulled up the hood and tucked her hair into it as if she were a child. Then he found the ties that fastened it and tied them with suddenly awkward fingers. "There," he said hoarsely, "now you are ready." He took her arm and led her out of the stables and into the snowy courtyard, looking around to see if anyone else was there. No one was, and he tried to calm himself, wondering how to tell her something he had just now discovered . . . something that shook his heart.

Ciel's every emotion had been called into play by those warm hands, that caring touch that tucked her hair into place, the shaky smile on Ian's handsome face. She was hot with wanting, surprised and almost ashamed of herself. Her wet eyes, a brilliant, shining turquoise in the gray and white of sky and snow, met his gaze for an intense instant and then looked down again.

"I am Lady Aylena's maid, Ian. You know that. It is not right for me to join the company of nobles in the castle . . ."

" 'Tis more than proper," Ian broke in hotly. "You are as much a lady as Aylena herself. And . . . and if you will consent to marry a fool who has only just recognized his ain true love, you will also have a title! Ah, Ciel . . . say you love me!"

Ciel caught her breath in amazement. "Why—I cannot!" She whirled away from him and fled toward the kitchen entrance.

He caught her in two strides, and wrapped his arms around her. "Say it!"

"I will not!"

He laughed unsteadily, his heart full enough to burst. Her wet, worshiping eyes told him a different tale. "Then you must say you don't love me, Ciel, and never will!"

She was silent, snug in his arms, her gaze searching

his eager face and the burning dark blue of his eyes, full
of passion. She had fallen in love with him the day they
met, and now, as the short winter day faded into dusk,
she saw in his eyes the startled desire, the sweet hot love
of a man. She put her hands up to his face and held his
bearded cheeks, her eyes soft but full of pain.

"You know I cannot say that, Ian. I do love you, and
I know I always will. But I cannot marry you. 'Twould
be wrong for us. You have a proud tradition here, noble
family to noble family, and I'll not be the one to tear it
down."

He couldn't answer. She was too close, too tempting.
He held her closer and kissed her cheeks, tasting tears.
He lapped them up with his warm tongue and kissed her
open mouth, feeling a strong surge of pure passion as
she yielded to him, her slender hands slipping around
his neck, her body snuggling closer. He was on fire, even
as snowflakes drifted on them.

"This," she whispered unsteadily, "you may have,
always. I have never been with a man, but I will be with
you if you want me. We can never marry. Your people
would not want you to marry beneath yourself."

He drew away, but only in inches. "They would never
fault me, my love! In the clan, some order and some
obey, but they are all the same otherwise." He frowned,
realizing now that he was in for a long battle. He wanted
a wife, not a leman, nor did he want to take her without
vows, for she was an honorable woman.

"Come," he said, and turned her toward the kitchen
entrance again. "Our family waits for us." Moving
through the kitchen, Ian wished her expression less serious. She took everything too hard, he thought. But she
would learn that at the Stewart castle there would never

be questioning glances nor whispers behind a fan. In this harsh country, faced by extreme weather and long, hard spaces to travel between hamlets and homes, each man or woman was ranked as high as another in importance. The least of the peasants and servants received the same treatment as the nobles when they were hurt or ill, and all felt pride in their own work, as did the nobles who ordered them. He thought for a moment on whether he should tell Ciel that—and then put the thought aside. She would find out herself, and therefore would believe it entirely.

That evening the great hall was to be used as it should be, for there was now another excuse for the gala celebration they had missed when their laird returned home. Already the air echoed with talk and laughter. Standing near the high table in a noisy, excited group, Ian had offered the prime seat at the head of the table to Thor, who raised a thick black eyebrow and shook his head.

"Thank you for your generous offer, Ian, but 'tis your place now. Your clan will not want to see a Norman lord in your chair."

"Ah, but they know you are the man who took the Stewart castle and then gave it back to us. Their gratitude is overwhelming. Perhaps they would cheer you if they saw you sitting there in honor."

Thor grinned. "We'll not tempt them, Ian. The Scots are quick to anger if they think one of their heroes has been slighted. They will enjoy seeing their conqueror come back and sit quietly in a seat near to their clan's laird."

Ian laughed. "You may be right. They can be amused by other tricks, but most of them have thin skin when it comes to the pride of the clan. We'll sit, then, and end their doubts. Where are our ladies?''

Thor looked around. "Aylena is there, near the fireplace, and talking to Ciel. Come, we'll take them to their seats.''

"Yes!" Ian smiled and went with Thor, pushing through the crowd of men and women. "I shall have Aylena on my right, and on my left my ain true love, Ciel Valoir.''

"I thought you might come around to that, once you forgot the spoiled daughter of Philippe Bertran.''

Ian reddened. "I was a fool there, I vow.''

"And lucky to get away," Thor agreed. "All London is talking of her now and laughing. But that's enough . . . we're drawing close to our lovely ladies, and neither of them knows nor need to.''

Ciel had admired the old castle from the first view across snowy fields. Now, on this festive evening, she was trying to take in every embellishment in the great hall. The high table, reserved for the laird and his important guests, was covered with white linen and decorated with red silk across the front, a long band caught up in drapes and folds the full length of the table. The other tables, for the household workers, were covered with heavy blue cloth, fluttering gaily with varicolored ribbons. And there was a pleasant scent like that of sweet hay, for the old, dried grasses and reeds that covered the stone floor had been swept up and carried away, and a thick new layer had been put down.

Wide-eyed, Ciel let her gaze travel upward from the huge fireplace to the wall above, and was seized by wonder. The great sword they called the *claidheamh mor* glittered there, shining like silver. Only two men, she remembered with awe, were able to swing that huge blade with one hand . . . Her gaze came down slowly and met the dark, desirous blue eyes of one of them. Blushing, she turned away and continued to look at the huge room.

Precious tapestries, normally kept in a locked room, had been brought out and hung high on the walls. Thick with embroidery, and sporting fringes of heavy gold strands, the tapestries celebrated battles between the clans as well as between countries. Along with valuable household goods like silver goblets and the drapery of velvet and silk, they gave an air of great importance to the celebration. Ciel's eyes were full of the beauty, and she mentioned the glorious tapestries to Aylena, who looked at them with pride.

"My mother embroidered four of them, as other Stewart wives had done, and you'll know them by the brighter colors, for the older ones dimmed in the swirling smoke of the old fire pit. It takes half a lifetime to do so much . . ." Aylena turned and smiled as the men broke through the crowd. "Is it time, then? Is everyone here?"

"Here and hungry," Thor told her, and took her arm. "Come along."

Ciel took Ian's offered arm in silence, her eyes lowered. She still felt out of place, yet she was fascinated by the scene, and the people in it. Some of the household servants were dressed nearly as well as their superiors, and the seneschal, Robert of Bourne, was more splendid in his velvet tunic and heavy silver necklace of keys than Ian was in his best. She watched from the corners of her eyes and marveled. Then they were there, and the women taking their seats. At once, the others in the hall surged toward the tables set for them. Seated between Ian and the older Martin Reeve, one of Thor's trusted knights, Ciel felt awe as she saw the women take their seats while the men continued to stand, waiting to hear Ian, who was waiting for quiet.

This gathering, so different in every way from the formal dinners at the Westminster palace, was to Ciel far more impressive. For a king she had expected, and seen, a deal of formality, but for Ian, the laird of the Stewarts, there was feeling of another kind. There was ardor, pride, and a great outgoing of something much like love. It shone like a beam of light as they stood and faced him, and she wondered at it.

Ian smiled. "So," he said, "the Stewarts are growing. Not only do I notice this great crowd of sturdy men and women, I have also been told by my seneschal that the fruitful wives of our strong men have brought thirty-four more Stewarts into the clan during this fall and winter."

Silent and amused, he let the laughter and cheers die down, then spoke again. "I am proud of you, and of Robert of Bourne. No Stewart, I am told, has gone hungry or cold this year. But as most of you know, one of us, Orn Thoma, is dead by the hand of an unknown enemy. What you may hear of it from others could help us discover the murderer. Bring any knowledge you have or find to me, no matter how little nor how late. We must avenge Orn, and we will. But now, with all of us gathered here to celebrate, Orn would be the first to say we should set sorrow aside and enjoy ourselves." He reached for his silver goblet and raised it high. "For the Stewarts!"

The mass of men and women roared it back: "Aye! for the Stewarts!" Then, as Ian took his seat, a great noise of talk and laughter began, along with scraping benches and chairs. The rest of the dinner was carried in steaming pots and placed on the tables, where ale, wine, bread, and bowls of melted fat already waited. All fell to, piling food in their wooden bowls, passing the torn loaves, the pitchers of ale.

Food this night was plentiful. The swirling odors of roasting meat and soups, the pleasantly sharp tang of ale and the yeasty warmth of fresh bread had made every mouth water. Two huge boars had been roasting over hot fires for hours, and the tender meat was falling off the bones. Soup made from lamb and dried herbs began the meal, and with the meat from the boar there were loaves of bread baked in the courtyard ovens. And, to end the feast properly, there were puddings made from fresh milk and dried fruit, flavored with spices.

Ciel was enthralled. She had been shown the pomp of Henry II's court and had been greatly impressed. But this—this was like a small country all its own, taking care of its own problems, its own citizens. In the cities of England and France people died of the cold, died of starvation, even died for want of a single friend. But here everyone watched out for the others, and offered fealty and the strength of their arms to their laird, and their laird—she glanced at Ian and his proud grin as he looked over the crowd—their laird would die for them! She knew that as well as they did. That was where the ardor and pride came in when they cheered their laird, and that outpouring of silent, flowing love. He was their champion, and they gloried in his strength.

She looked down, swallowing, hiding a sudden awe, a glisten of tears. Ian was truly a wonderful man. A knight who could have held his own in King Arthur's court. She raised her eyes to his face and smiled.

"They are so proud of you, Ian. And so am I. The Stewarts are fortunate to have you as laird." Amazed, she saw his cheeks redden above the beard. She had embarrassed him with the praise, rather than pleasing him, and she was sorry she had spoken. Still, it was true.

"They did very well for themselves while I was gone," he said, "and I am proud of them. I feel guilty, and wish I had come home earlier. I might have saved Orn Thoma's life."

"No," Ciel said, "no more so than any other man here at the castle. No one could have known when the murderers meant to strike. Had you ventured out to see if Orn was safe, they would have melted away into the shadows and chosen another night for their mortal sin. Men like that would not ride to meet you with a challenge. They are always cowards."

Ian turned and looked into her eyes, his brows lifting, his expression grateful and warm with feeling. "You have the right of it," he admitted, "I could have done no more than anyone else. Yet I still wish I had been here."

"You will find them out," Ciel said, "I know you will. But tonight you celebrate with your clansmen." She smiled and lifted her goblet. "To the Stewarts, m'lord!"

Ian picked up his wine and raised it to her, his eyes dark with emotion. "And to you, my dear and beautiful Ciel."

On his other side, Aylena smiled and turned to Thor. "I do believe," she whispered, "that young brother of mine is courting Ciel Valoir."

Thor smiled and touched her satiny cheek with a light caress. "I agree. I believe 'twill come to pass as you wish. They are well suited in many ways."

Midnight came and went, and the crowd dwindled down to a dozen or so sitting around the fireplace, the older men recounting long-ago tales of bravery and strength, their voices hushed and reverent, their eyes staring into the coals as if seeing visions. Old William grew teary in speaking of his brother Bruce Stewart, father to Aylena and Ian.

"Aye, Lord Rodancott, the old laird was savage in his hate of King Henry and, had his ailin' heart held out, would have done his best to kill ye when ye came to our gates. And he would hae been wrong. Ye hae ever been a great friend o' the clan and our young laird, Ian. Why, 'twas ye and our own Aylena that went clear to Black Island to fetch the boy home through a horde of enemies. Well I remember that and always will . . ."

Ian rose from his seat beside Ciel and took old William's arm, helping the old man up. "And you, Uncle William, had kept me there. And I was foolishly angry, to be truthful, but always safe from harm. Come now, and take your rest. Tomorrow will see us all settled in for a time." He looked back at Ciel and nodded. "I will be back. Wait for me then, and I'll see you comfortable myself."

But when he came back both Ciel and Aylena were gone. He looked at Thor and frowned.

Thor, a goblet of brandy in one hand, shook his head. "They were tired, I am sure. And you will have three or four weeks of your friend's time, Ian. 'Twill be that long before we leave."

"But I meant to see her comfortable."

"Aylena will see to that. Young Ciel will have warmth and a good bed. Sit, and tell me of Orn Thoma's death and who you believe was his murderer."

Ian sat and picked up his half-full goblet again. "I have no real cause for suspicion, Thor. Yet even Rory mac Kenloch came up with the same name. He said the Stewarts had no enemies in Scotland except for the Barwicks."

"That may well be true, though they are a lazy lot and the distance between us great. But tell me all that you saw and thought, both the first day and the second, when you and the Kenloch laird went over the place together."

Ian sighed but obeyed. He told the story slowly, for he knew Thor wanted everything described, every thought mentioned. Even so, he almost left out the number of animals missing. Realizing he had, he added it hurriedly, explaining that both Rory and he had thought the North Sea had swept away the twenty missing sheep. And Thor's interest, which had begun to flag, came back with a rush.

"I will see the place," he said, rising and stretching. "You will show it to me tomorrow. As I remember the width of that strand of rock and shale, there is enough space below the cliff to contain all the sheep that Orn Thoma cared for."

Ian opened his mouth and then shut it. He firmly believed that the rough water of the North Sea had stolen the twenty dead sheep. But he knew Thor. Thor would insist on seeing it for himself. Besides, he would welcome a day on horseback with him. He had known great loneliness here since Thor had taken Aylena to live in far-off Normandy.

They climbed the steps to the gallery together, silent because of the servants and knights sleeping in their blankets around the great hall. The broad stone steps ended near to the door of the solar, the room used by the laird for sleeping, for privacy, for going over his accounts, for writing messages and receiving honored guests. They paused there, and Thor clapped a hand on Ian's shoulder. He spoke quietly.

"I doubt we'll see anything that will help us, Ian, but 'tis wise to go over the place again. Now that you've had time to think you may find new signs."

Ian nodded. "True. And with a man more knowledgeable of thieves and robbers." He grinned and added: "Since we are now alone, I will admit that your experience is greater than mine in cases such as this. Good night, my friend."

"Good night."

Ian watched Thor's upright and powerful body stride away in the gloom, then a streak of light from an opening door, a glimpse of bright golden hair and the sound of Aylena's voice, murmuring and sweet. Ian sighed and went into the solar to doff his clothes, bank the fire, and seek his empty bed.

Now, looking back on his own stupidity about Serena Bertran, he found it hard to believe. But it had straightened itself out in his mind. He had thought his beloved sister a perfect wife and the most beautiful of all women. It had been Serena's resemblance to Aylena that had made her seem ideal to him. Even when he had dreamed of Serena here, seated in this room and writing down the records, the dream was nothing more than a memory of his sister doing the same, with the sun shining through her golden hair and her bright smile when he came to her with some childish question.

Pulling up his fur bedcover, sewn of heavy wolfskins that still carried a whiff of the wild, Ian knew he had been lucky to see past Serena's beauty. One of the Carlisle whores would have been a better wife. They, at least, were honest about their profession. And he had recognized at last the strong emotion he had for Ciel Valoir. What he felt now he knew was real love for a flesh-and-blood woman, not a mooning dream about a fanciful ideal.

There were problems ahead for them, one of them so foolish—why would she care whether she was a recognized noblewoman or not? She was not only the most beautiful woman he had ever met, she was also brave and resourceful. A woman who could stand this frigid climate; one who would want to have children, and, yes, one who could laugh at the problems of a harsh life. If she would only agree to wed, they could begin to live . . .

Cold, gray February light seeped through the glazed windows in the solar, and in the room split logs tumbled from a servant's arms and clattered on the stone hearth. Ian recognized the sound and pulled the wolfskin cover close around him, peering from beneath it and recognizing his body servant, old Hunter Blake. Blake saw him peering and grinned.

"Lord Rodancott routed me out, Laird Ian, an' set me this task here. He is havin' a breakfast o' bannocks an' honey, an' washin' it down with hot mead. He says ye'll profit by it yersel', since the weather is freezin' cold an' apt to go colder. If I was to be ye, I would listen to that man. I never knew him to chance bein' wrong, an' I hae listened to him many a time. Now, if ye know what clothes ye wish to wear, I will bring them, an' if ye don't I will search for the warmest . . .''

Ian nodded quickly. In times before, he'd tried to stem the tide of Blake's quavering voice, but he had learned not to try. The man had brought hot water for his face and hands, and he rose to wash hastily and dress. He too had learned to listen to Thor.

Cold mornings meant breakfast in the fire-warmed kitchen. The iron griddle was steaming with bannocks, the mead warming on a rack near the fire, and the cook was spreading honey on the flat cakes for· Aylena and Ciel, seated with Thor at the kneading table. Ian's heart lifted at the sight. He came to them quickly and sat beside Ciel, who looked warm and ruffled, still half asleep but startled into a smile.

"We are going with you," she said, excited, "and Thor says 'twill take a day and a night of traveling!'' She saw his forehead wrinkle and his smile disappear. "But . . . do you mind?"

Ian's frown deepened. " 'Tis a hard trip in thick snow, Ciel. Not, I think, for women." He looked at Thor, who shrugged his shoulders and maintained silence. Ian's gaze traveled from Thor's studied indifference to stop on Aylena's smiling face.

"I have made the trip to Orn's cabin in all possible weather," Aylena said to him sweetly. "And I do not intend to remain here when there is a chance that I can help in your search. Besides, I need to stretch my weakening arms and legs into full strength again."

"And I," Ciel said, keeping her lids lowered and her tone properly sedate, "am going with my mistress. She may, ah, need me.'' She looked up at the two disapproving male faces and added quickly: "If only for female company, you know. A long ride can be dreary.''

"This ride,'' Ian said flatly, "will be dreary or worse, for there is deep snow to travel through and perhaps other dangers. Think it over carefully, Ciel. You may regret it.''

"I will think it over, then,'' Ciel said shakily, and looked away, staring down at her plate. Amazement was in her clear young voice. In all her life she had never met a man who would allow a wife to make her own decisions in a case like this. Yet Thor Rodancott, a mighty warrior and a strict father, had not argued once when the Lady Aylena said she would go. Until now, she had thought Thor would wait until they were all together and then refuse her, perhaps to make it plain to the others that his wishes would be obeyed. But he hadn't said a word. She raised her eyes and looked at Ian's disapproving expression.

"I have thought it over,'' she said, "and I will go. If there truly is danger I will be able to help if I am needed, for I ride a well-trained warhorse. Neither I nor Devil will make your task harder.''

Both men looked at her, disapproving but silent. She smiled brightly. "And why would I have trained my horse to fight, if he's to be held back?''

There was no answer to that. The men looked at each other and rose from the table.

"We'll see to our mounts, and yours,'' Thor said. "Wear your warmest clothes, and bring with you the bags the cook will give you. And make haste. The day is well started.''

14

 The snow had ceased. They rode in a single line, first Ian on Rogue, then Thor on a Percheron stud he had brought from London, then Aylena on her Arabian, and, at the rear, Ciel on Devil. Devil was sullen and hard to hold, for he wanted to lead. Even one horse in front of him was too many, and here were three, all plodding along slowly.

Tired of Devil's sudden plunges to the side, angered by his flattened ears and the way he jerked at the reins, Ciel asked Aylena to pass the word along that she'd like to break the heavy snow for a while, now that there were trees looming up in the distance, and she could take them as a goal.

"Devil needs to know," she added, "that you can't gallop in this heavy fall. At least, not for long."

The word was passed, and Ian turned to catch Ciel's eye and raised a hand to motion her out and around to the front. Ciel reined Devil toward the high drifts alongside and spurred him. He leaped to obey, his big hooves throwing snow as high as his head, but in a few minutes was slowing and breathing heavily. Still she pushed him on and ended in front of Rogue, who was tiring and glad for Devil to make a trail in the snow. Ciel looked back at Ian and laughed, her face pink with pleasure.

"Another lesson learned," she said. "My good friend Devil will not be so anxious to lead the next time. He has never been in snow as heavy as this."

" 'Tis rare here also," Ian said. " Stay close, so you don't find a danger that might change your mind." He could hardly take his eyes from her now. His thoughts and plans seemed to fly like birds over his head, wheeling and calling to him to hasten, to bring her home . . . to take her as his wife. He thought of their kisses in the courtyard yesterday and was consumed by love and hot desire . . .

"I will, m'lord."

"Good. Then I will trust you to keep yourself safe." Even to him his words sounded shaky and foolish. He shut his mouth and followed her along the path made by Devil's big hooves until they entered the first sparse trees that marked the site of Orn Thoma's cottage, where the snow settled into drifts around the trees. Then he turned out around her.

"Move back and join Aylena," he said. "I expect no real trouble, but if there are strangers here, this is where they will be—in or near to the only shelter."

Ciel nodded and turned back, seeing Thor spur his black stud past to join with Rogue, and Aylena coming on slowly, her smile in place, her eyes full of interest.

"It is passing strange," Aylena said, still looking about in front of them. "These trees that enclose the old cabin were only saplings when we left. Now they are big enough to make building boards . . . Ciel!" She whirled her horse and looked behind her. "What did you see? Your eyes are enormous . . ."

Ciel passed her at a thundering gallop, heading toward thick, snow-covered brush beneath a large tree. Her face was white, her voice flew back to Aylena, full of fury and fear. *"Attaquez, mon Devil! Attaquez!"*

"Attack? Ciel! No! Come back!" Aylena's face went pale, her voice strained. She had seen the brush move and knew Ciel had seen more. But Ciel's eyes were blazing, her voice commanding Devil, and Devil was responding eagerly, his squealing challenge echoing through the woods as he plunged forward. Then he was rising on his back legs to attack the two men leaping at him from the dense thicket, their long glittering knives poised to strike. The unexpected blows from his hooves stunned them and they fell, screaming with fear, and Devil plunged down on them, a ton of fury, rising again and again, stamping their jerking bodies into the ground, squealing his war cry.

Ciel calmed him, turning him away from the broken bodies in the trampled, bloody snow, stroking his neck and murmuring to him, though now her face was greenish white and her voice shook. She saw Ian and Thor galloping back toward them, their faces like granite masks. She looked at Aylena, now beside her. "They would have *killed* you," she said, and burst into tears. "They had d-daggers out, Aylena, and—and there was nothing I could do but kill them! Oh, *mon Dieu,* I did! I did! They are dead!"

At that instant Ian arrived and lifted Ciel out of her saddle and into his arms, pressing her streaming face into his warm neck, holding her tight, whispering to her. "My love, my brave little Ciel. You saved the life of an innocent woman. Why do you cry? I am proud of you!"

Aylena, seeing his purpose, took Devil's trailing reins, turning her face from the bodies and the bloody snow. When Thor motioned to her she left the two alone, sure that Ian could comfort Ciel better than she could. She went toward Thor gratefully, in need of comfort herself. Behind her, Devil was calm again, following her little Arabian as a colt follows a mare. Thor sensed her feelings as she came up to him.

"I'll take his reins," Thor said, "and he will stand. Take your place beside me now. We were fools not to think of men put on guard around this place of murder and thieving. I cannot blame Ian, for he thought it a solitary thing, an attempt to hurt the clan. I am sure it is more than that."

"And I." Aylena was still white, not for fear for herself but for the dangerous action Ciel had taken. Ciel herself could have been killed except for Devil's expert training. Those knives had been murderous, and the men themselves vicious, ready to use them. "I wonder," she added in a low tone, "how many men like that are in our woods. And why? Surely the risk of dying cannot be equaled by the meat of a few frozen sheep. Why are they here, Thor?"

"Until I capture one of them I have no way of knowing, my love. Perhaps they were only hungry."

"But 'tis too dangerous and hard to kill those sheep for meat at this time of year!"

"Then perhaps they were hungry for goods to sell, my love. Sheepskin brings a good price in a cold winter."

"Yes! Sheepskin is twice as warm as woolen cloth. That must be why they came, to strip more hides from the frozen bodies." She turned to call back to Ian and

Ciel, but they were coming along slowly, Ciel clinging to Ian, her head on his shoulder, her cheeks still white with shock. The look on Ian's face was all that Aylena wished for. He had found his beloved. She turned back to Thor.

"What shall we do, then?"

"Wait. 'Tis Ian's land and Ian's sheep. He must say."

"Yes. At times I forget."

Thor laughed. " 'Twould be more honest did you say at times you remember. What must the man do to make you stop seeing a child when you look at him?"

"I truly don't know, m'lord. Perhaps I never will. But they are coming to us . . ."

Thor turned and waited in silence. When Ian arrived with Ciel they were both calm. Ian helped Ciel into her own saddle. Her face was still white, and there were tearstains on her cheeks, but she smiled and thanked Aylena for leading Devil to the clearing. "I was foolish to cry," she added, "for Ian says 'twas no mortal sin to kill men bent on murdering an innocent woman. But I hope I never have to kill again."

Thor turned to Ian. "No life in either man?"

"None," Ian said calmly. "Ciel and I prayed for their souls, on the chance they were Christians, and left their bones to be found by their friends and buried with their families."

They went on, finding the old hut full of cobwebs and the tracks of mice. The sacks of food for the sheep were there, full of mouse droppings; the dried grains Orn had kept for himself were moldy, and the fireplace still contained the same half-burned logs that Ian and Rory mac Kenloch had snuffed out when they left.

" 'Tis strange," Thor said, "that no one sheltered

here. Come, we'll take a look from the top of the cliff.''
Ian led them by the path he'd traveled with Rory. At the
cliff, they saw two fishing boats, not far from the shore
below them, beating their way east by southeast. Ian's
eyes went from the boats to the rocks and mud below,
and his thick brows came together in an angry frown.

"There are our enemies," he said, pointing at the
boats. "And, by the gods, I should have known before.
When Rory and I stood here and saw the dead bodies
of the sheep below, there was a boat there where those
two are now. Look down, Thor. The marks are there
where they dragged their boats into the water again. And
I see no sheep bodies at all. How stupid I've been!"

"Not stupid," Thor said. "Who would think pirates
would steal sheepskins off the sheep? But the lists of
crimes grow every year. Those must be fishermen from
the Frisian Islands, men who have no land to farm. If
you wish to continue a fold of sheep near here, provide
a fast horse and a good rider to bring the news of pirates
landing."

Ian shook his head. "No. By the time we came up
here, the island men would have grabbed what they
wanted and set sail again. But, say a month or two from
now, I will put out a flock with heavy fleece and make
sure they can see them from the water. Then we will
make a place for a company of men-at-arms to hide and
await them. They'll stay away from my sheep after
that."

Thor gave him a surprised grin. "Set a trap, will you?
I believe it would work, if you can keep your men well
hidden until the thieves have landed and started up the
trails. Only remember to let a few go free, and let it be
as if they'd managed it by themselves."

Ian frowned. "Why? All should be punished."

"No. If none return to the islands, 'twill be thought they sailed into a storm and drowned. That happens often enough to be believed. Then others would try. You need a man or two to say they escaped, but the others were captured and killed."

Ian's face eased from frown to an embarrassed grin. "You have the right of it, Thor, as you always do. We will be careful, then."

They went back to the hut, for the bitter cold of night was dropping like a deadly curtain around them. They took wood from the shed to keep the fire blazing, and Ciel found a worn reed broom to scrape the worst of the dirt from the floor. The horses were covered with woolen cloths, tied close in the shed and given oats and snow water, and the steam rising from their huge bodies made warmth for the night.

The cook at Stewart Castle had sent along a supper of meat, bread, and pies, and Robert of Bourne had added two skins of ale. Dazed by the experience with the two thieves, Ciel ate little and found a corner of the big ragged bed to spread her cloak and lie down. She dreamed of warmth, of pleasant male scent, and dropped into deep sleep, waking once in the still night to feel arms around her and to see, outlined in the faint light, the strong, bearded profile and thick, waving hair of the man she loved. She slept again, safe and warm.

By morning the freezing weather had moderated. It was still cold enough to keep the heavy snow from melting, yet the sun cast a pale yellow tint from a clearer sky. The trip back to the castle seemed short, for with no wind or new snow the path they had trampled the day before was like a lane.

Coming within sight of the castle walls, they saw the drawbridge lowering for a single knight on horseback. Ian, leading the rest, turned and grinned at Thor.

" 'Tis Rory mac Kenloch, Thor. He will be glad to see you and Aylena. He speaks of you often."

"A strong man," Thor said, "though from a family overfond of gaiety and tournaments and less than happy with work. Has he wed?"

"No. Not yet. Ah, he has seen us and is coming our way. He's been bored, I suspect, and is looking for company."

Rory had put his horse to a gallop, staying in the beaten path their horses had made yesterday. His rugged face beaming, he came up to them and pushed back his hood to nod to Thor and Aylena.

"A pleasant surprise, my friends," he said, and, as his eyes discovered Ciel's young and beautiful face inside her hood, he laughed and added: "Pleasant indeed! Who is this lovely lady?"

Aylena smiled. "Her name is Ciel Valoir, of Normandy, and a friend of mine."

"And soon to be my wife," Ian said, moving to place Rogue beside Devil. He smiled down at Ciel's crimsoning face. "And far too shy to admit it. But 'tis true. Rein in your galloping thoughts, Rory."

Rory sighed. "I see I must." He turned to Aylena. "Have you other friends of such beauty?"

Aylena laughed, enjoying Rory's foolishness. "Not at the present, Rory. But I'll keep an eye out for a lady to suit you. Now let us go on, for we are all tired from our trip and need rest and food."

They moved out, the two younger men in the van, talking seriously now, for Ian was telling Rory about the men who came to the shore and took the sheepskins to sell, or—as Rory pointed out—perhaps took them to have their wives make warm tunics for them.

"God knows," Rory went on, "the life they lead is hard. But we canna allow them to steal an' kill. Orn Thoma must be avenged."

"Orn has been avenged," Ian said flatly. "Though not by my hand. You see the gray warhorse Ciel rides? The beast is hers, and she has trained him. Two lurking men came after Aylena, holding daggers aloft. Ciel turned her mount and ordered him to attack. He killed them both with his front hooves, without a wound for him or for her."

"That young girl?" Rory was incredulous. "What courage! And such skill in training. Who taught the horse?"

Ian flushed, looking away. "She gentled him to ride and obey commands. I helped with the training for war. But the horse is a natural fighter. It took little time to show him the tricks."

"By the gods," Rory said, looking back at Devil and letting out a held breath, "I would pay twice for that horse. I'll try to bargain for him, if you don't mind."

"Do so," Ian said, and laughed. "Ciel will be courteous, but the answer will be no." Their horses' hooves rattled the planks of the drawbridge and trumpets blew from the wall above, letting the Stewarts know their laird had returned. Then a small blue pennant ran up a pole on the keep and fluttered just below the big silk flag with the image of the silver *claidheamh mor*. Rory knew the small flag meant the laird was in residence. He regarded the flag with a half smile as he dismounted.

" 'Tis more an English habit than something a Scottish laird would do, Ian. You might better be wary of other Scots' opinions. There is some talk of your thick English blood o'ercoming the thin Scottish trickle."

"Thick English blood? If we have trouble with England it will come from their own thick Scottish heads! What is it they wish me to do? I stand between them and the English raiders who come this way to do mischief." Ian was angry, his face flushed red above his close cut beard. He swung down from Rogue and handed the reins to an ostler. Turning back to Rory, he added: "King Henry has ever treated them fairly, and England's traders pay well for the wool and coal we bring to the market at Tynesmouth. What more do they want?"

"An occasional fight," Thor said, dismounting behind him. His deep voice sounded weary and disillusioned. "A battle between you, Ian, and the English. Not that the Scots would care to join in, for they are much too weary from their own battles with each other. But 'twould be something to drink to when the whisky flows."

Ian swung around, frowning. "You speak of them as if they were children, Thor."

"I do indeed. With good reason. And, from what Rory has said, I will wager that within six months— when the weather clears—you will have a battle. But not with the English."

Ian turned back slowly to face Rory. "Do you think the same, mac Kenloch?"

Rory looked away, hiding his expression. " 'Tis pos-

sible, my friend. There is much grumbling over the price
of wool. The men believe the buyers are lying to them,
saying the wool coming in from northern Europe is finer
than theirs. They feel cheated.'' He looked back at Ian
and shrugged. ''I'll not fight ye, Ian, but neither will I
fight beside ye. I believe ye honest and true in yer bar-
gainings for wool and coal, but I doubt your heart is still
true to Scotland.'' His eyes went to Ciel, and warmed.
''Nor can I blame ye now. She's a lovely, lovely lady,
but no Scot. Happen she may like it here, but if not, ye
may be spending more time in London or across the
Channel in Normandy. Yer old Uncle William canna
tak' yer place here, an' well ye know it.''

Riding slowly away with Aylena, Ciel heard every
word in Rory's clear voice. Her back stiffened, even
more erect than before.

Aylena glanced at her and spoke. ''Rory mac Kenloch
is ambitious, Ciel. He would like to wear Ian's boots,
but they'd never fit his hesitant feet. Like many a man,
he is all froth and opinion.''

Ciel nodded. ''I thought the same. However, he has
made me see even more clearly. The Scots will want
one of their own to sit beside their champion and raise
strong sons to protect their lands in the future. They
would not want a Norman peasant girl sitting there.''

For once, Aylena didn't argue. She laughed. ''You
know Ian well, but not so well as I. Mark these words.
Either the other clans will welcome the Norman peasant
girl, my dear Ciel, or they will be saying farewell to Ian
Stewart.''

Tears glittered suddenly in Ciel's clear eyes. ''That I
will not have. He belongs to his clan, and they trust
him.''

"Of course! Nor would one of the Stewarts, neither the sheepmen here nor the fishermen on Black Island, ever say a word against their laird's lady. They will love and revere you, Ciel, and be proud of your skills and courage."

Ciel looked at her doubtfully. " 'Tis a strange breed of men, Aylena. Nothing like the Normans, nor the French. In ways they are like honest children, yet brave and skilled . . ."

They had made their way around to the kitchen court-yard and the stables while the men had entered the keep. Now they dismounted and gave the horses to Harald. Aylena went at once to the kitchen door, and when Ciel would have gone with Harald into the warm stable the old man stopped her with a smile.

"Today we've gained four visiting ostlers, an' all anxious to work. Ye take yer rest, my lady. I will see that yer prime fightin' beast is comfortable an' well fed. All have heard of yer courage an' quick action an' are thanking the good Lord. There'd be wailin' an' tears from here to Cromarty if ye hadna preserved our Lady Aylena's life."

Ciel went a brilliant red. " 'Twas the horse only. He is well trained. And I thank the good Lord, like the rest of you. The Lady Aylena is—is very dear to me."

She fled, her small feet flying up behind her as they always did, and Ian, who had walked through the castle and now emerged from the kitchens, caught her up and swung her onto the gray stone stoop. He set her down, looked her over, and settled the fur-lined hood of her cloak around her astonished face.

"We have important company, my dear lady. Come and be presented."

Ciel stared at him, shocked. "Ian! I must slip away . . ."

"Indeed not. I wish to present you as my future wife."

" 'Twill be a lie!" she said quickly, and blushed.

He laughed and drew her to him, turning to go back through the kitchens, his long stride hurrying her along. "I never lie, my dear love. Nor would I start now. 'Twould be insulting to begin such a habit while entertaining the King of Scotland, William the Lion."

15

Entering the great hall on Ian's arm, Ciel stiffened her spine and managed a gracious smile.
The room echoed with an excited hum of voices
and the movement of men trying to be quiet and failing.
There were men-at-arms removing their hauberks—
short-sleeved, hooded jackets of chain mail that reached
to their knees. They had put down their arms at the double doors of the entrance and removed the heavy conical
iron helmets from their heads, placing them with their
spears, their large, triangular shields and their single
handed, double edged swords. Now, laying aside their
burdens, they took seats at table and began drinking ale
and eating from big platters of food placed along the
middle of the table. The constant movement and clatter
was deafening. It seemed to Ciel that a whole army had
moved in.

However, the king himself was not bothered by the
noise. A broad, well-muscled man of medium height,
William the Lion had a shock of long, dark-gold hair.
He was resplendent with jeweled silver and gold chains
hanging on his black velvet tunic. He was standing and
talking with Thor and the Lady Aylena at the fireplace.

Robert of Bourne, pale and nervous, was standing apart, ready to leap at the first command.

Ian took Ciel directly to the king, who turned from his conversation with Thor to raise his brows in surprise and smile at her, revealing strong, yellowed teeth.

"So, Laird Ian, I do indeed understand your pride in your young bride-to-be. She is not only a brave and resourceful woman who kept your sister from mortal harm, she is also a great beauty."

Amazed at the Scottish king's perfect English, Ciel stumbled over her reply. "Thank you for your gracious words, sire. I but did what anyone would do. I used my—my only weapon to save my dearest friend."

The king smiled at her. " 'Twould seem a deadly weapon, from the story Thor has told me. The beast would be worth his weight in siller, I vow. Now, let me wish you a peaceful time during the rest of your visit here to Scotland, so that you will remember it as what it is—a wild but lovely country."

Ciel took her arm from Ian's grasp and curtsied, glad the king had ignored Ian's claim to her hand in marriage. Perhaps now Ian would understand that his king and his peers expected him to marry a noblewoman.

"Thank you, sire. 'Twas most kind of you to greet me." Rising from the curtsy, she moved away to allow the men to talk privately with their king. Aylena joined her as she went toward the stairs.

"I have ordered food brought to us in my chambers," Aylena said, her usually clear forehead furrowed in thought. "The king seems anxious to talk to Thor and Ian. But he spoke very coldly to Rory mac Kenloch."

"Coldly?" Ciel asked, wondering. "You believe he dislikes Rory?"

"I believe," Aylena said, lowering her voice, "he has lost trust in some of the clans, and perhaps one of them is the Kenlochs. In any event, he quite clearly told Rory to leave because he had problems to discuss with Ian."

"Oh!"

"Yes, 'tis odd. But here is a fine tray being brought to us by Robert of Bourne! You should have called for a servant, Robert. God knows you must have had a burdensome day . . ."

Bearing a huge, heavy tray of food, Robert smiled at Aylena. "This duty is the first I've enjoyed, my lady. I was taken aback indeed when the king and his minions came marching to our gates an' all of ye gone! We sit on a sharp edge here, ye know."

Aylena laughed, helping Ciel clear a space on a low table for the food. " 'Tis true, Robert. But you must always greet our king as if you were certain of his trust and he of ours! 'Twould be insulting to doubt him."

"Yes, m'lady. An' I always will, until the Stewart tells me otherwise. But still . . ." He shook his head. "King William is a crafty man."

" 'Tis the Scot in him," Aylena said, "as well you know. Every Scotsman is suspicious. Some more so than others."

Robert laughed abruptly and turned to the door. "Indeed, my lady. I canna think of a Scot who doesna' hold a suspicion or two about his neighbor. We are a strange and touchy breed, 'tis true."

Aylena and Ciel washed their hands in a laver, dried them on rough linen, and sat down to make a meal. After the long ride and a skimpy supper in the hut, they were ravenous. They said nothing until they were both satisfied with the mutton stew, fresh bread, and ale. Nearing the end of a long harsh winter, there were few dried berries and fruits, but they did not suffer. The cooks had brought out the mincemeat, honey, and spices, and the pies were delicious.

With a satisfied sigh, Aylena leaned back in her chair. "Undoubtedly the king will stay the night and perhaps longer, along with his men. But if I know William the Lion, he will have brought a deer or two and perhaps a boar, all to be cooked in our kitchens. We will not starve."

"Then he is a fair and thoughtful man in his way," Ciel said, surprised. "He has a care for those he governs. That is good to hear."

"But," Aylena said slowly, "I believe there may be one problem between King William and Ian."

Ciel's gaze swept up to Aylena's face. "I think I know, Lady Aylena. King William will have heard by now that Ian has become the English king's man and will go to Henry's side when needed." She sighed and curled back in her chair. "King William will not like that."

Aylena nodded. "Indeed. 'Twas different with Thor. Thor was not a Scot but a mercenary. And as long as he kept the border free of trespassers, none of the Scottish lairds objected. Besides, the Scottish king at that time was Malcolm the Maiden, a man too timid even to marry! This king is well named the Lion. If he feels Ian is too friendly with the English, he is likely to withdraw his own friendship."

"He would regret that," Ciel said, and Aylena's eyes widened at the sudden anger on Ciel's young face. "He would lose an honest friend and a mighty warrior. None but a fool would doubt Ian."

" 'Twould be shortsighted on William's part," Aylena agreed pleasantly. Now she was sure at last that Ciel truly loved and admired Ian in every way, but she was wise enough not to mention it. She went on, talking of the future.

"This castle watches the border, and both Scots and English mercenaries respect it and the fighting men in it. But William, like many others, wants his own way. The Stewarts are Scots, and he wants every Scot in his fold, obeying his command like sheep obey their shepherds. Ian will not take to that."

"Never," Ciel said. "Ian is not a sheep, nor is that proud little man a true shepherd. And from what I have learned of the Scots, he may have as many enemies as friends."

"I do wish," Aylena said slowly, "that we could stay longer. Ian will need Thor to advise him. But Thor must be in Normandy soon. The early-spring foals must be handled with the greatest of care, as you know."

Ciel's suddenly frightened gaze shot to Aylena's face. "I do know! But still, my lady, the earliest of spring foals will not appear for another month and a half."

Aylena smiled at her sympathetically. "True. But the journey is long. Think, dear Ciel, how far we are from London, and, once there, how often the weather keeps the Dover boats in port and we must sit and wait. We can stay here no more than another two or three weeks."

Rising quickly, Ciel tried hard to hide her dismay. The time was too short. Her plans had turned into impossible dreams. She crossed the room to stand in the deep embrasure that pierced the eight-foot-thick wall and looked out. The heavy glass, braced with slender rods of black iron and full of bubbles and ripples, made the dim courtyard outside seem to weave and move, as if in a dream. She shook her head to clear it. " 'Twill be hard for me to leave him," she whispered, and in the silence Aylena heard the soft words. She rose and came to Ciel, putting an arm around her young shoulders.

"And harder for him," she said. "He needs you now!"

Now. After a moment Ciel nodded. "I know. I must think on it."

"You could marry here."

"He is a proud man. I will not shame him!"

"You couldn't." Aylena watched Ciel's face go pale.

"My lady, think! I have no title. I am not a noble."

"None of those things matter here, Ciel. Thanks to your father, you have an excellent education for a woman. Better, I would say, than most of the young ladies at court. And once you marry, you will be Lady Ciel Stewart, wife to the laird of the Stewarts."

Ciel shook her head. "That can only be pretense, my lady. I would be taking Ian's pride and hiding behind it. I would still be called a Normandy peasant masquerading as a noblewoman. I will not pretend!"

Aylena frowned and turned away. "You speak of his pride, Ciel, but I hear your own. You fear that others will talk of you and whisper that you married to become a noblewoman. 'Twould be nothing but jealousy, so why would you care?"

"I would not be another Serena Bertran!"

"Ah, now we have it. You are afraid someone may point out the similarities between you and that young courtesan! No one who knows you would ever think you were alike."

Ciel's eyes changed from anger to a look of sadness.

"But we *are* alike, Lady Aylena. More alike than different. Our fathers are both bastard sons of Geoffrey Plantagenet, and we are their daughters. Serena pretends it ennobles her; I know it doesn't affect me at all."

Aylena shook her head impatiently. "Ian loves you, Ciel. He cares nothing of noble blood. Don't break his heart."

Ciel's eyes filled with tears. "Don't even say it! I will explain my feelings to Ian, my lady. He will see 'tis best."

Aylena sighed. "I doubt that. But I'll not argue more. Thor and I must visit amongst our old friends in other clans during the next week or two, but if you wish you may stay here. Perhaps Ian can set this a'right when you two are alone."

That night, readying herself for sleep, Ciel thought over her plan. She knew it was wrong. She knew she would be doing penance for many years to make up for it. Yet if she didn't follow her heart, there would be no wonderful memories of love with the only man she had ever wanted. She had looked ahead at what her life would be without even a memory of Ian's kisses and lovemaking, and it had seemed an empty desert of duty and boredom, stretching from here to infinity.

Then she brightened. Thinking of the Rodancotts leaving them together here at Ian's castle, she felt that fate had softened toward her and had given her this time alone with Ian. She would have her nights of love and passion with her beloved, and it would be worth the pain when they had to part. She knew the possible consequences—she could shut her eyes and see her father's agonized face if she had to tell him she carried a fatherless child. And if in the future her father approved of another man to wed her, then that man too would have to be told she was not a virgin.

But none of that mattered. She would have Ian Stewart now, and forever after she would have a heart full of memories, dreams, and a wonderful love . . . never, never to be forgotten.

She blew out her candles and slid into bed. Her yearning body, warm from her thoughts and dreams, kept her awake for a long time. Then the two hard days of riding took over and she slept, dreaming of love.

"Ciel?"

Morning light touched her face as she opened her eyes. Seeing Aylena by her bed, she sat up and swung her legs out to stand up. "Oh, my lady! I am sorry to have overslept . . ."

Aylena smiled. "Sit down, my little one. I came only to say we are leaving. I needed no maid to help me put gowns into a box and shut it! Thor has said we shall return in ten days or a little more, and then you will be indispensable. We will all need to ready ourselves for the long trip home."

Ten days, or even more. Ciel sat and felt her cheeks flush with excitement. "Then . . . then the Scottish king is also leaving this morning?"

"Yes. He has already made his farewells and added a bit of advice, which Ian calmly refused to accept." Aylena looked amused. "Even William the Lion should have known better than to tell Ian Stewart whom to marry."

Ciel gasped. "Oh, my lady! What did he say?"

Aylena laughed and sat down on the edge of the bed beside Ciel. "Let me try to remember his exact words

. . . oh, yes, I remember now. Our king said this: 'Your Norman lady is exquisitely beautiful, Ian, and I see the great temptation you face. However, 'tis time now for the Stewart clan to return to their Scottish roots. As it happens, I have no daughters, but I do have a lovely niece. Come with me now and we'll see how the two of you will suit . . . ' "

"See?" Ciel's tone was accusatory and frightened. "Don't you see now that I was right? His king has objected! Ian must go with him and meet this Scottish princess . . ."

"Indeed he will not!"

"What? Why, he must, Lady Aylena. A man must obey his king."

"Not in this case," Aylena said. "And I am sorry that I spoke. I thought you would laugh, as I did. I forget you know so little about the Scots. They are all hardheaded and seldom take advice that wars with their own opinion. Ian has already refused the girl, quite politely, and King William has departed, leaving him gifts of food and weapons."

"Oh." Still flushed and embarrassed, Ciel slipped from her bed and drifted across the room in a cloud of fluttering white muslin, looking for a robe. "I will dress quickly, Lady Aylena, and help you to make everything ready . . ."

Aylena came and stopped Ciel's attempt to find her robe by putting an arm around her waist and a farewell kiss on her cheek. "All I need do now, my friend, is mount my Arabian. And if I falter, I have Thor and his three knights to hoist me up! And you, my dear, have some deep thought and praying to do. Don't break Ian's heart—nor yours."

Ciel's throat was too tight to allow another word. She
hugged Aylena and then turned away, wiping her eyes
and listening to Aylena's quick steps fade into the distance. It was true, she thought, that she must take every
precaution to keep Ian's heart and pride from any hurt.
She loved him; she must not hurt him. Even Aylena
would hate her then.

Turning to her wardrobe, she brought out a simple
gown of fine blue wool, trimmed at the wrists and high
neck with white embroidery, and fitted to her slender
body from neck to a few inches below her waist, where
it widened into a full, trailing skirt. She thought the
gown the most flattering of all her clothing, and she
meant to attract Ian's attention more than she ever had
before. There was no holding back now. Either she must
lure him into her bed or find a welcome in his. 'Twas
her only chance to know love, and she meant to have it,
for she was sure she would never love anyone else.

Dressed, with her long hair shining like rich black silk
beneath a silver headband set with jewels, she went
down the stone steps from the gallery and found Ian
standing before a dying fire at the large fireplace that
centered the north wall of the keep. She spoke and startled him from a reverie.

He turned, his face brightening, and came toward her
to take her arm. "Ciel, my dear love. How beautiful you
look this morning. You are rested?"

She reached for his hand, moving close to him, feeling
the heat from his big body, breathing in the faint masculine scent. "I am indeed. I slept so late Aylena had
to waken me to say farewell. And now I am hungry.
Have you eaten?"

"Only a bite with the king, who left before dawn. He

had a long day of travel before him. Come, we'll begin our day with a solid meal.''

The door at the entrance of the great hall opened and closed, and Rory mac Kenloch stepped inside, shaking the snow from his woolen cap. He nodded at them and came forward to the fire, rubbing his hands but avoiding their eyes.

"Did I hear a mention of food? By the saints, I am as hungry as a wolf." He looked quickly at Ian and then away, frowning at the empty hall.

"Then you will join us," Ian said politely. "We have much food. There is venison and boar and perhaps a small pie."

Rory laughed, suddenly relaxing. "Ye tempt me to stay for two meals, friend. But first, I'll speak to the king."

"You'll not catch him, Rory. He and his soldiers left well before dawn for the road north."

"Gone so soon?" Rory was suspicious, his face hardening. "Why? What brought him here for such a short time?"

Ian shook his head. "He said little and gave only personal advice. He said nothing of any other clan. But I have a feeling he might be happier with another clan leader at the border."

Rory frowned heavily. "There is no large clan near to the border but yers and mine. 'Twould have made sense for him to speak with me about it. My clan has no English blood, nor Norman." His gaze swung over Ciel and away. "Only Scottish."

"He may speak of it to you later," Ian said, but Ciel turned away to hide a frown. There was something in Rory's eyes and voice that made her feel unsettled, or

perhaps wary. Today his show of friendship was like a
swirling cloak that hid a sharp weapon. But it wasn't for
her to speak such thoughts . . .

"Come," Ian said, and took her arm, smiling. "Let
the three of us fill our bellies and perhaps our tempers
will subside. A hungry dog growls."

"True," Rory said, and made an effort to hide his
discontent with a wide grin. "An the dog fierce enough,
he will be fed well. Lead on, my friend."

In deference to his visitor, Ian ordered a late breakfast
brought into the great hall and placed before the remains
of the fire. Three places were set, and Ian took the middle. He was well aware that Ciel was not overfond of
Rory mac Kenloch. Her eyes gave her away. But as they
finished the meal, she was courteous in answering Rory's questions about the lengthy training she had given
Devil. She ended by giving Ian most of the credit.

"I am too short-tempered to train my own warhorse,"
Rory said carelessly as she finished. Leaning back in his
chair, he watched her closely. "But if I could find a man
with knowledge of such things, I would hire him. I will
give ye a fortune for yer own horse, Lady Ciel." He
gave her the title with a mocking smile, but she only
looked aside.

"Devil is not for sale, m'lord, and 'tis just as well.
There are few men who can handle him."

Rory laughed uproariously, slapping Ian on the shoulder. "Yer fair lady believes me too weak to handle her
horse! What say ye?"

Ian looked at Ciel and Rory, then smiled and
shrugged. " 'Tis her horse, and she knows him well. Let
it be."

Rory shook his head and pushed back his chair. "Ye

talk like a man who sees two sides at once," he grumbled, springing to his feet. "An' neither of them wrong! Tak' care, Ian, that ye don't become a king's advisor, talkin' from both sides of yer mouth."

"At times," Ian said mildly, "there are two sides to be considered, and both with virtues. Can I give you a haunch of venison to take to your family? We have meat to spare."

"Aye, I'll take it. Ye are greatly favored by our king, I see."

Ian stood, towering over Rory mac Kenloch, but smiling. "Then come an' choose the joint that suits you. I'll send a man to bring your horse an' I'll see you well away."

Ciel slipped off toward the steps to the gallery as the men strode toward the kitchens and the cold room where the venison hung from huge and blackened beams. She ran up the stone steps and found her heavy cloak, one Aylena had given her that was lined with sheepskin. She had a great desire for fresh air and the crystal purity of snow and ice. Only a few breaths and she knew she would feel wonderful again. Pushing the great door open, she stepped outside.

There had been so much anger in Rory mac Kenloch this day that she was frightened and repelled. Yet she knew it was mostly jealousy on Rory's part. Dismissed by the king yesterday and ignored this morning, Rory had cause to be worried. 'Twas likely, she thought, that the mac Kenloch clan was one the king didn't trust. But then, that was no affair of hers, nor Ian's. She stood still on the stone entry, her hooded cloak about her, her short boots on her small feet, and smiled at the young boy sweeping snow from the steps and shivering.

"The air is so cold it is like breathing ice," she said to him. "Shouldn't you be wearing a warm cloak?"

"No, m'lady. I am in an' out a dozen times on a snowing day. 'Twould wear my good cloak into ribbons were I to . . . Ah! good morning, Laird Ian! A pleasant day to ye. Would ye care for a ride? I'll bring yer horse if ye want."

"Not this time," Ian said, and reached for Ciel's hand. "Perhaps later, if the afternoon clears. This is a day to sit by a fire and plan a new life. Come with me now, my lady."

16

 Her plan had begun. Ciel found courage enough to smile and put her small hand in his. She felt warmth and strength in his hand, and an odd tremble as his fingers closed over hers.

"The fire here is banked," he said as he drew her inside. "The hall is too large to heat in this weather unless 'tis needed. The castle staff gathers in the kitchen, and the huts outside each have a hearth. For us, I had a fire laid in the solar. I want to be alone with you."

Ciel nodded and turned with him to the worn stone steps that went up to the gallery, her eyes down, her heart suddenly beating rapidly. They would be alone, as she had wished. What he had said had taken her breath away. Had he too decided not to wait for a ceremony? She was afraid to ask. She would wait and see . . . and hope.

The great hall was empty. Even the hunting dogs, the wolfhounds that usually stayed by the smoldering fire all day, had deserted the cold floor for the kitchens. They went up the wide steps in silence, and when they reached the top he led her into the solar, loosing her hand and turning to shut the heavy door, sliding a thick iron bolt across to hold it there.

She had caught glimpses of the solar when passing along the gallery, but this was the first time she had been inside the luxurious room. The room she had been given when she came here had seemed wonderful to her, for it had a thick rug and a very comfortable bed. But the solar was as fine as a king could ask for. Warm as midsummer with that blazing fire on the hearth, and the whole floor covered with rugs, covered twice in front of the chairs and along the sides of the huge bed by thick sheepskin pelts over the woven wool. She stood still, taking it all in, with her small hands clasped in front of her, and her eyes shining.

" 'Tis a wonderful room, Ian. So comfortable."

"Aye." Ian came to her and stood by her side, staring into the flames. "Thor and Aylena changed many things during the years they stayed here waiting for me to grow into a man. Thor brought a Frenchman who was taught in hearths and chimneys, and he built this one and the one below, then filled in the fire pit in the middle of the hall. The air is much sweeter now."

"Indeed, I am sure of it." Gazing at the fire, she could almost feel the waves of desire flowing between them, hot and insistent, matching the heat of flames. It was strange to her to feel a weakening in her thighs, a mesmerizing heat growing low in her belly. When Ian put an arm around her and pulled her to him, she drew in a long breath. She must tell him, ask him . . .

"Ian."

He looked down at her, and in his eyes was a man's desire, a man's instinct to take the woman he wanted. But an iron will held him back. She was looking at a war and she was afraid it was already lost. Still, she would try. She turned in his arm and put both of her hands flat on his chest, moving them slowly up to his broad shoulders.

"Ian. Look at me and say what you see in my eyes."

He did. Then he put both arms around her and pulled her close, burying his face in her thick hair and saying, muffled: "I see a long life and a happy one, with a woman I love and who loves me."

She sighed with happiness. "Then take me to your bed."

Startled, he raised his head and looked into her eyes again. "What are you saying, my sweet girl? You are young and virginal, and when we marry . . ."

She leaned back against his arms and put her slim fingers over his lips. She had expected an argument and was ready for it. And confident now, for she had seen the leap of hot desire in his darkening eyes.

"But that could be forever and a day, Ian! Why, anything could happen! I want you now. I want to make sure, on this very day, that you have known me, that I have lain with you, skin to skin, and that you love me, and I you. And I swear to you, 'twill always be the same in my heart. I will never love anyone else nor let another man have me. In my soul I will always be yours."

"My love! My dearest Ciel . . ." He spoke against her lips and then crushed them with a deepening kiss, pulling her slim body against his. She felt the strong arousal of his loins and for a moment felt a virgin's fear of penetration. She forced herself not to stiffen, not to move away. He would sense her fear and that would be the end of it. So she did something else, something she instinctively knew would convince him. She tilted her hips and moved, soft and warm and insistent, against his bulging loins.

"We want each other," she whispered in his ear. "Why should we lose this chance when we are alone here? Don't we both want the joy and the belonging? Why should we wait?"

He answered her with an impassioned groan and swept her up into his arms. "I canna resist you," he said hoarsely, and strode toward the bed, carrying her like a child. "Aye, you are my dearly beloved, my beautiful angel. I take you now as my wife, so no other can ever come between us . . ."

Ciel smiled and put her face against his neck, so he couldn't see the triumph in her eyes. Nor, perhaps, the fear. Not that she feared the mating. Her work with the mares and stallions, the ewes and rams, had taught her much. She knew to expect pain on the first encounter; that was also true with a first breeding for either mares or ewes, but she had seen how quietly they stood for the next breeding. They were no longer afraid . . . nor was she, except for the time to come when she must refuse to marry him. That thought chilled her to her bones. Ian would be furious then.

"Are you frightened, my dear love?" Ian had stopped at the edge of the dais where his bed awaited them and let her slide down to stand with him. "Have you changed your mind? Don't hesitate to tell me, Ciel. I'll not be angry."

She looked at the wide bed, thick and comfortable, the coverlet of wolfskins, the pillows covered with white linen. Shadows of the fire's flames danced and played over the soft pillows. This wonderful bed would be their world for the little time they had.

"My mind stays the same, my dear lord." She took

his hand and held it beneath her left breast. "Can't you feel my heart? 'Tis beating hard, wanting much."

Then, with a sudden quiver of excitement, she saw Ian's face changing, taking on a male dominance, a look of heat and passion. Still gentle, but suddenly hot and trembling, his hand curled around the shape of her breast under the thin, silky samite of her gown, and the heat of his palm and trembling fingers stiffened her small nipple. Ciel drew in her breath in a quick gasp and felt as if the room swayed beneath her feet. His hand had ignited a flame in her breast, and the flame had darted down to her most secret place.

"Ian? Should I . . . should we . . . ?"

He bent to her mouth, kissing her, his lips and tongue taking possession, his arm holding her close as he caressed her breast.

"We should," he said against her soft lips, "and we will. But for now, let us take our time. I wish to make a long and tender mating with my beloved."

Ciel nodded, not trusting her voice, and shut her eyes. She wanted to feel every hot thrust of his tongue, every touch of his long, shaking fingers, now sliding between the loosened ties that held her bodice together. Then, vaguely aware of his insistent attempts to get rid of her clothes, she wriggled and pushed her way out of them, so that it seemed that all of her clothes had fallen away and the furs on the bed had been pushed aside, and she was in it, trying to stop gasping for breath and watching Ian's broad, golden-furred chest emerge from his tunic and his long, muscular legs emerge from his chausses. Then he was in the bed with her, and they reached for each other and clung, glorying in the heat, the smoothness of bare skin, the wonderful longing, the promise of paradise in each other's arms . . .

"When we mate," Ian whispered to her, " 'twill hurt you, I fear. But only the first time."

"I know. I won't mind. 'Tis soon over."

"You needn't be brave, Ciel. You may cry and blame me. I have to be brave enough to hurt you. I have never made love to a woman until this day." He smiled suddenly, thrusting his hand into her silky hair and smoothing it back away from her face. "And I will be faithful to you all my life. Like my father—and like Thor. We are all faithful men."

Ciel felt a sudden stab of guilt. "No promises," she said quickly. "Think of nothing serious today, my dearest lord. Think only of love, and teach me how to please you."

Ian drew her closer and their lips met again, their bodies clung and moved together, hard muscles against soft skin. Then she felt the fiery heat of his shaft, the length and size and weight of it, and the strong, hard-muscled loins burning against her slender thighs. Then she was frightened, and he knew it. Ian reached out to touch her cheek with a gentle hand and took his mouth from hers.

"If you want to stop you must tell me, my love."

"No, my lord." Her voice was shaky with fear, her eyes huge. "I very much want to give myself to you. It's just that now I cannot believe—we will ever fit!"

He held back laughter. She was truly frightened, and he'd not shame her. He turned to his side, lifted her slender legs across his belly, and widened them to stroke her soft, quivering flesh and the springing black curls at the joining of her thighs. He thought her like a young foal, curious, affectionate, but ready to run at the slightest threat. An innocent. Like him, yet more afraid; more sensitive . . .

"Now," he said, pressing her thighs apart, "we shall discover if we have any hope of fitting ourselves to each other. You won't mind if I see what can be done?"

"Indeed not. I only hope I'm wrong." There were tears in her turquoise eyes, tears of fright.

He nodded. He no longer wanted to laugh, only to show her that the pain she would feel was soon over, and, according to what he had heard, nothing to the wonderful pleasure she would gain afterward. He stroked her gently and with awe, fingering the soft folds and the hot, damp path between them, then finding the pulsing tempo of her aroused blood. And gradually, over the silence and warmth of his caring for her, her fear began to lessen, her whole body became pliant and soft. And then desirous. He knew it; he felt the slight lift under his hand, the sensuous movement against his palm that asked for more . . .

Passion drummed in his wild heartbeat. He felt a towering desire for his woman burning his caution aside. But still the desire came with an awful fear of frightening her, of hurting her enough to turn her from him. It was time to make the decision, and still he was undecided and wary . . .

"Ian?" Her voice was soft and sensuous, like words said in a dream. "Take me now."

His hands traveled upward on her small body, sliding over her damp, silky skin, finding her thrusting white breasts and the tight buds of pink that centered them. He caressed them, his big hands trembling. "You are sure, my dear love?"

"I am sure, my lord. I ache inside, and 'tis as if I want you there."

He couldn't speak. He felt as if the life they would live together would depend on the next few minutes, a time in which he would either ruin all or ensure a happiness few men ever had with their wives. At last he wished strongly that he had taken Thor's advice, so that he would know when the best time had come, but that was too late now. He was close to praying as he slid from beneath her and rose over her, his body huge and gleaming in the shadows. Then he spoke, breathless.

"You may stop me at any moment, Ciel. Remember it . . ." And then his eager body pressed into the cradle of slim thighs and his shaft found the throbbing velvet path that invited him in. An instant later the guardian hymen inside ripped like thin paper against his powerful thrust, and he had gained the tight, hot center of her body. He lay still, and so did she, astounded by the heat and weight inside her, and by the slow growing triumph and relief on the strong face staring down at her in the light of the flickering fire.

"Are you hurt, Ciel?" His voice was full of concern, even now, when he knew the entry was over and easily done.

She smiled and ran her hands up his braced arms and around his neck, whispering. " 'Twas a small pain hardly worth complaint, my dear love."

He gasped and moved within her, unable to stop the urgency in his body from taking him over. "Then . . . then move with me, Ciel. Oh, yes. Yes, like that. Ah, my love, my beautiful girl . . ."

During this time she hardly knew the man he had become, yet he was part of her. Her body ignored her and answered to him, moved with him, took part in a strange, shuddering bliss that grew bolder and hotter every moment. She heard small cries of great pleasure and knew they came from her throat; she felt her legs embrace his plunging body in a wild dance. And then from a deep thrust of his strong loins, she felt a hot, sensuous delight roll through her in squeezing waves, shaking her, making her cry out, helpless against the storm.

Afterward, they lay there, entangled, panting . . . and then, looking at each other, laughing. Laughing with pleasure; laughing with relief.

" 'Twill not be such a rush and awkwardness another time," Ian said breathlessly. "We—we mate very well, I think."

She nodded, still too spent to speak. And amazed. She had thought the real pleasure for her would be to please him. But the pleasure she had felt herself still coursed in her veins, throbbed in her belly. Oh, 'twas cooling now, losing the hot, sweet thrumming of a few minutes ago, but as it cooled it left a wonderful feeling of ease and happiness. She had thought before that it would be very hard to leave Ian after they had declared their love; now she wondered if she had the strength to leave him at all. To leave, to be parted forever, knowing she would never feel this strange bliss again . . .

Ian insisted that they dress. "My men speak with me in late morning; they come as they have always come to my door here to tell me of lost sheep or sickening amongst the pigs, or if a horse has gone lame. We must act our parts. I'll not have them saying in the courtyard that you were here with me and half dressed."

Ciel nodded. She understood that. Once dressed, she

straightened the tossed bedclothes and went to her own room to change her gown and braid her hair, then came back to the warm solar to sit before the fire and work on a tapestry, in plain view of anyone walking along the gallery. Ian went to his accounts, which had been neglected for days.

"Once we're wed," he said, smiling, "I shall be more than happy to turn these over to you. I'm in great need of a wife."

Ciel was suddenly ashamed. She had spoken no vows, she had made no promises. But what she had done was implicit in its meaning. She had given herself to him. He had every right to believe she intended to marry him. Yet she would not. When this brief, happy time ended, she would go back to her father and live out her days. And Ian would find a woman of noble blood who would bear noble children for him. Thus the blood of the Stewart clan would continue unblemished by a Norman peasant. She sighed and laid the tapestry aside.

" 'Tis a bright day," she said. "I will put on a warm cloak and visit my friend in the stables. Devil will treasure a small bowl of oats."

Ian laughed. "'Tis no wonder that horse loves you," he said. "You spoil him." He was sitting in an embrasure, his work before him, his pot of black ink and quill pens close to his hand. His books, sewn sheets of yellow parchment made from the split hide of his own sheep, were spread out for marking. Sunlight from the thick glass struck light from his blue eyes and brightened his tousled hair and dark beard. He looked content, or more than content. He looked like happiness itself.

Silent, Ciel turned away, heading for the door, knowing at that exact moment the pain that would await her when she left this man forever.

17

 Ciel passed that afternoon full of regret for what she had done. Remembering him at that moment, with his face alive with faith in her, would scald her heart with longing for the rest of her empty life. But there was no thought in her mind to change her decision and ruin his life instead of hers. He would find a wife amongst the noblewomen of Scotland. Perhaps the Scottish king's young relative, after all . . .

But that evening at dinner, when they sat together with old William Stewart and Roderick and listened to tales of the clan in times past, Ian looked at her with such love in his eyes that it brought tears to hers. Once old William and his son had left the table for their beds, it took only one smile from Ian and she knew they would sleep together again that night.

They had little fear of talk amongst the castle serfs. Nor did they wonder what William and Roderick thought. Robert of Bourne might notice, but no seneschal spoke of things private to his lord. Still, Ciel went to her own room, turned down the covers, and rumpled the bed as if it had been slept in. Then, taking her tapestry and yarns along, she went to the solar to sit in front of the fire and sew by its light. Ian came in, shutting and locking the door behind him. He came to her chair and leaned over her, taking the tapestry from her hands and setting it aside.

"I canna sit and watch you sew, dearest love. Come to my bed. My arms ache for you, and my body begs!"

She rose from the chair, smiling and silent, and went to the wall wardrobe beside the dais that held the bed. No candles nor lamps were lit, but the light from the fire showed her the way. She opened the wardrobe and began removing her clothes and hanging them up. Ian took little time to remove his own clothes. Then he watched her disrobing there in the deep shadows, but she made no attempt to beguile him by pretending modesty or teasing him with seductive movements, as Rory described how the women in Carlisle heated a man's blood.

When she shut the wardrobe and turned toward the bed, he went to her and held her small, naked body close to him, feeling the delicacy of her soft skin, the smoothness that was like satin.

"I love you." His deep voice was rough with feeling. "You've blessed my life." Looking down at her, he saw the shine of a single tear dropping down her shadowed cheek. He licked it away carefully. "Are you sad, my dear love?"

She smiled up at him, shaking away her thoughts. "Women," she said, "are full of tears, and they often overflow. Make love to me, Ian. I'm hungry for you."

He swept her up in his arms as he would have swept up a child. "In our bed, my love? Or on the sheepskin in front of the fire?"

She stared at his firelit, smiling face in astounded silence, then broke into sudden, shaky laughter. "Why, on the sheepskin, certainly! 'Tis a fine rug of pelts, and a pride of the Stewarts. I shall feel honored . . .''

That night they were like seasoned lovers. There was no holding back, no doubts, no hidden questions. In Ian's arms Ciel forgot the future and thought only of the now, the love, the passion that roared like a hunting lion in winter, and sang like a bird in spring.

After a first quick coupling to ease them, they lay together on the soft, woolly pelts, and, with the firelight dancing on gleaming skin, they teased and laughed softly. Ciel became bold, her small hands moving over him, fingers threading through the dark-gold, curling hair on his chest and then down, down far enough to touch and ease the silken shaft with soft, warm fingers. And Ian caressed her, his fingers cupping her breasts, his lips taking in her stiffened nipples, rolling them with his tongue, sucking gently, nipping . . . moving slowly down her body.

"If you think anything wrong or hurtful," he whispered, "tell me, and I will stop."

Ciel stretched her small body luxuriously. "Everything you do feels wonderful. How could it be wrong?"

He raised his head and smiled at her, his face golden in the glow of flames beside them. "Between us, nothing can be wrong; nothing can hurt us. We love each other."

Ciel was silent. Those last words were true; the others weren't. She would hurt him—and soon. And hurt herself. But the sharp pain would fade away in time. Better that than to pull him down forever into obscurity and a sad half-life with a peasant woman, a man pitied by his peers.

Stop, she told herself. Don't think of that. This is the now, the part of her life she was giving him and giving herself. She would make the uttermost best of it. She sat up, leaning over him, admiring his smooth skin, the clearly delineated muscles, the strong masculine lines of his huge body. Then she bent and kissed him.

"Tell me," she whispered, raising her head to see his eyes, "tell me how to please you best."

Ian laughed softly, threading his fingers through the curtain of silky black hair around his face. "If you please yourself you will please me best, my angel."

She had to move. She could no longer stand the rippling passion inside her, the throbbing, swelling ache. She rose over his muscular flanks, moved to find the exact place she wanted, and then lowered herself gently until she had enclosed his rigid shaft. Then she wriggled, taking her time to settle herself solidly before she lay forward on his chest.

"There," she whispered, "right there . . . isn't that good?"

Ian's eyes had closed as she settled herself, his jaw had firmed, his body had become unnaturally still beneath her. Now his lips moved only a little. "Indeed."

She raised herself a little to look at his face, not satisfied with his answer. "You aren't comfortable?"

He let out his breath and dragged it in again. "I am very comfortable. Indeed."

She sat up again, her light weight and warmth pressing down on his loins and making her wriggle with the hot sensation. " 'Indeed'?" She spoke wistfully. "I'm sorry. I thought you might like it more than that . . ." She stopped speaking and clutched his rearing body with her knees and then her arms as he rolled her over on the sheepskin and took her like a lion, growling deep in his chest. Then, dazed and panting, he felt his control return to him.

"Are you hurt, Ciel? Did I bruise you with my weight? I am so sorry . . ."

Her heart pounding, Ciel lay there smiling at him. "You did not bruise me, my love. Nor did you hurt me in any way. It was my fault to tempt you so."

Ian shook his head. "You always will, whether you wish to or not, I fear. Come and stay in my arms."

She moved even closer, against his side. Radiating heat enveloped her, his pleasant scent was an aphrodisiac to her. She sighed with pleasure and began again to tease him sweetly.

"If I sleep, I won't waken until morning," Ciel said much later. "I must go now, or the whole castle will be talking of the careless lovers."

She slid out of the huge bed on the dais where they had ended their lovemaking and went to the wardrobe again, feeling inside for her chemise and gown. She dressed quickly, then tied on a scarf, looked at Ian, and smiled.

"I know I should feel wicked," she said, "but I don't. I feel wonderful."

He went with her, around the gallery and to her room. There were men below, stretched out near the deep red coals of the huge fire they had tended, and fast asleep. No one saw them passing quietly around the gallery; no one sleeping behind other doors heard them and came to look.

" 'Twas meant to be," Ian said cockily. "Fate is kind to us. We belong together."

She was smiling as he spoke, but turned away when her smile slipped with his last words. "Good night, my love,'' she whispered, slipping through the door to the room she had been given. She turned to shut the door, her eyes shadowed, looking away from his open gaze. ''Sleep well ... who knows what trouble another day may bring?''

Hesitant, Ian touched the handle of the closing door, wanting to ask her why she feared the future, then dropped his hand and turned back toward his own room. A woman's vagaries, he had heard, were often taken too seriously. There was nothing he could think of that would spoil their plans, and there was no use in hunting trouble. Tomorrow they would ride again in the afternoon and she would brighten. Devil and his antics would see to that.

Ian was sure of his reasoning the next day. Ciel was happy and cheerful, delighted with the promise of a ride and the clearing weather. The sun was a pale-yellow disk, making the gray sky shine and the white snow and ice turn golden in its morning rays.

When Ian said they would ride that afternoon, Ciel seemed even happier. She bundled up and went to the stables to curry Devil until he shone. And then, when it was time to ride for an hour or so, the north wind gentled to a mere breeze, so they must loosen their cloaks around their necks and put their minds on suddenly spirited horses. Both Devil and Rogue needed to be reminded of their training.

Just outside the walls that protected the courtyard was a fenced training field where the snow hid no holes or obstructions to lame a horse. They took the excited horses there and calmed them down with practice in battle maneuvers. They were on their way back to the courtyard gate when Rory mac Kenloch and one of his men rode up and called out to them. They both stopped and turned back to greet him.

But as they neared, Rory's expression spoke of anger. Ian looked at Ciel and cocked his head toward the court-yard entrance. " 'Tis a man's ear he'll want," he said, "and not a woman's. Go, and have an ostler help you to rub down your horse. I'll be there soon."

She nodded and turned willingly. Her feelings toward Rory were not the best at any time, for she thought his temper like that of a foolish boy. And 'twas worse ever since the king had found no time or favor for him.

Ciel was still in the stables, rubbing the dampness from Devil's thick winter coat when Ian came in, leading Rogue. He handed his reins to old Harald and came to her side, speaking quietly. "There is trouble in the clans," he said, "an' Rory wants my nod for the Ken-lochs. I have told him I canna give it until I talk to the others. I must know both sides to be fair."

Ciel caught her breath. "Then you must do some trav-eling, then?"

"No. I will send for men to come to me and say their grievances. The Renfrews have sided with the Gowries and Callandars against the Kenlochs and Dounes. Rory would be satisfied if I would only throw my name in with his, but I canna do that unless I know why they are at it again."

Ciel frowned, slowing her strokes on Devil's shining coat. "Did he not say?"

"Oh, yes. He always says. But much of what he says is only what he believes others are doing and saying. He has no facts; only suspicions."

" 'Tis from his disappointment when the king ignored

him," Ciel said, and shook her head. "He is a boy, not a man, for all that he is older than you."

Harald chuckled. " 'Tis true, Laird Ian. Kenloch has been feeding his anger against the king since William turned his back on him. 'Tis foolish, but all the same— we should keep an eye on him. He is a jealous man."

Ian nodded. "I hear you, Harald. And you may well be right. I will be careful."

Ciel put down her currying brush and led Devil into his stall. She could hear Ian still talking to Harald though she couldn't make out the words. Nor did she want to. She had thought Ian would be alone with her for a full week, and now he would be in the company of other men every day! Weak tears came to her eyes, and she felt ashamed. Then, reaching for her cloak, she felt it swirled around her and fastened at her neck by a pair of big hands. As always, Ian had come to make sure she dressed warmly before stepping outside. She looked up at his blue eyes and saw concern.

"Yes," she said, keeping her voice low, "I was indeed weeping. I wanted my full week alone with you."

"You'll not miss a day, my darling. I have told Rory I will not enter the fray until I have reports from all five clans, saying the disagreements as to the pastures and flocks and the killing of other men's sheep. Then and only then I will travel to their homes and see what they can show me."

"That may take weeks!"

"True. A Scot will argue to the end of time. But once I start out to hear it all, I'll not listen to it twice." He was smiling now, touching her soft cheek, seeing the color come back into her face.

"There," he said gently, "you look happy again. You

have a bit of the child still about you, my love. Surely you have patience enough to think of the long life ahead and the love between us, and can wait for my return.''

Ceil lowered her gaze and nodded. "I will be less— less demanding, Ian. I am sure you are right." The words were hard to get out. The more she realized the depth of his feelings for her, the worse she felt. She was living a lie and he would soon know it. She put her hand in the crook of his arm and went with him, back to the lovely, ancient castle she would never forget.

She spent some time alone while Ian called in four of his men-at-arms to tell them the threat of war, and then sent them riding with messages and questions to the quarreling clans. It took some time. Each written message had to be memorized by the man-at-arms carrying it, for none of them could read and, though it was never mentioned, some of the lairds could no more read than they.

Afterward Ian went seeking Ceil and found her in the kitchens, going over the supplies of grain and oils with Robert of Bourne, who had asked for her help. The seneschal raised his brows when Ian questioned him.

"Lady Ceil is well used to sorting out mildewed grain and rancid oils, Laird Ian. An' she says to remove them quickly, before they spoil the new. We are in the midst—"

Ian nodded impatiently. "And you can finish it, Robert. You've a good nose and eye. Come, Ciel, and rest before my fire. You've had a long day."

She went with him as far as the great hall and then turned away. " 'Tis time for my bath, m'lord. 'Twill be ready soon. Your maids are always prompt."

Ian stopped, raising his thick brows. "I see. An' I

hope the bath is not as cool as your tone. Are you angry with me?''

She looked up at him, and her eyes glittered with sudden tears. "Never, Ian. Surely you know that. If I am angry, 'tis only with myself.''

He put an arm around her and pulled her closer. "And why are you angry at all? Tell me.''

"I would rather not.''

"Ah? Should I command you to say?''

"No. You would be disobeyed.'' There was a slight glimmer of a smile with that, and Ian laughed ruefully.

"Then I'll not. Go luxuriate in your tub, then. But remember to come to my room later.''

Standing before the fire in the great hall, Ian watched Ciel mount the stairs to the gallery and disappear into the shadows of the center hallway. Her small, slim body moved quickly and silently, her head bowed a little, as if the weight of the luxuriant mop of her black hair was too much for her slender neck. But he knew her strength, both of body and of mind. Something was worrying her, and it puzzled him. She loved him; he never doubted that. And she had given him that love in generous measure, fully and freely. He had been happier than ever before in his life, knowing she loved him, knowing she would be his wife. But all the same, he wished she would tell him what she had on her mind. Whatever it was, he thought, it was something that worried her greatly . . .

A few days later, the times changed. The shepherds had begun to move the pregnant ewes toward the lambing pens, and the stores of hay and grain in the castle stables were being taken in carts to the pens by both men and women of the castle staff. The weather was still cold, but the worst of it gone. The workers were glad enough to get out in the pale sunlight and stretch their legs. The sound of their laughter in the courtyard made Ian smile.

"They are strong people," he said to Ciel. "They don't complain at the bitter weather. But still they welcome the smallest sign of spring."

They were alone, standing together on the steps that led up to the kitchens, and he put an arm around her shoulders and pulled her closer. "Spring," he added, "is a wonderful time to marry. What say you?"

She glanced up at him and then away, wondering who had heard him. It was becoming much harder now to keep the subject of marriage out of their conversation. Yet she must. Another day or so, and Aylena and Thor would be riding in. And the dream would be over.

"You are in the midst of an argument that might turn out to be a war amongst the clans," she said, trying to make her voice cool, "and that would spoil any happy event. What news did you have from the man who came in early today?"

Ian shrugged. "Much the same as the others. All the clans swear that someone has carried stories to King William and put doubt in his heart."

"Do you think that possible?"

Ian sighed. "I think it probable. A Scot is always suspicious and feels it his duty to report to the king. However, I believe the rumor is dying for want of bloodshed. If we can continue the peace until they tire of it, 'twill turn the problem away."

Ciel smiled, thinking of the jealous Rory. "And do you believe Rory mac Kenloch will be satisfied?"

"Rory is more than satisfied. He's tiring of it now. The season for making trouble is nearly over, and in a month or so there will be new lambs in the fields and salmon in the rivers. We'll not have the spare time then to go about killing each other."

Ciel shook her head. "Is it the winter, then? The cold that keeps a man brooding in front of his fire? Or is it that he has more time to think?"

"Why, we can ask," Ian said, staring off to the north. "There is Rory now, riding toward our gates. He'll have a favor to plead for, I vow."

Ciel sighed. "He is here more often than ever, now that the threat of war has gone by. He has offered again for Devil, and I have refused. What more can I do?"

Ian laughed. "No more will be necessary, my love. This time I shall say he should ask for his mares. Devil won't mind giving one or two of them a prize foal."

Startled, Ciel shook her head. "No. I—I would rather not lend my stallion to him."

Surprised, Ian shrugged. "Then I'll not offer. 'Tis your horse, not mine." He went down the steps to greet Rory, who was entering the courtyard, and Ciel turned to go into the kitchens, angry at having to refuse a neighborly gesture, but knowing she couldn't risk having Devil at Kenloch's stables when Thor and Aylena returned. They would be in a hurry to leave.

She was busy in the storerooms when Ian came looking for her. He looked half angry, half disgusted, his head bent to miss the low-beamed ceilings, his big body squeezing past the rows of shelves.

"Rory has called in the Dounes for a meeting, and they have asked for me. I must go. If the Dounes force a fight over the pastures, all will lose. I'll not be gone over two days, my love."

Ciel nodded, not wanting to speak aloud until she could do so without showing her disappointment. She had been making a list of what various spices and dried fruits were in low supply and she took the list now to put on the cluttered table where Robert of Bourne did his tallies.

"There," she said, swallowing her disappointment, "that much is done. Now I'll help you gather what you need . . ."

"No, my love. Hunter Blake will see me packed and ready. I have already told him what I want. I'll go now to the stable and see that Rogue is saddled. Once these quarrelsome fools are able to air their complaints, the air will clear."

"Then what can I do?"

He smiled, touching her cheek with a gentle palm. "I'd ride away with your kiss on my lips, and know 'tis the promise of more."

She moved into his arms to hide the tears in her eyes. "Then the kiss will be there, m'lord."

In less than a half hour Ian strapped his leather bags on Rogue's saddle and then mounted, riding to the high steps that led to the kitchen entry. Ciel stood there, silent, her wet turquoise eyes startling, as brilliant as jewels in her white face. When Ian stopped and held out an arm to her, she put both of her arms around his neck and kissed the warm mouth within the frosty beard.

"I love you," she whispered. "I always will. Please remember me."

18

 At dusk the dark figures of a mounted party came into view on the snow-covered barrens to the north, riding at an easy pace straight toward the Stewart castle.

A man-at-arms strolling the top of the curtain wall saw them and grinned, then wound his horn in one long howl of welcome. Old Harald came from the stable doors and looked up at him, his whiskered face curious.

" 'Tis Rodancott, then? Gi' the man a signal to come to us instead of the drawbridge. We'll open the coward's way an' let them in."

The man-at-arms grinned. "Aye. We'll shorten their trip an' cut their time in tha saddle." He put the horn to his lips and blew three quick notes. Across the patches of dark rock and snow the horses lifted their heads and snorted, picking up the pace. And, in the van, Thor's black stallion turned and came directly toward them, leading the rest.

Inside the warm stables men were shoving back a section of wooden planks, exposing the stone of the thick curtain wall that surrounded the whole courtyard and buildings. A narrow, buttressed passage appeared in the otherwise solid wall, winding to the east, turning west sharply for a horse's length and then north, hiding its outer entrance with the bulk of a watchman's tower. Known as the coward's way to escape if a battle turned sour, it was also a quick way into the castle grounds.

Led by Aylena on her Arabian, Thor and his knights came through the narrow passage one by one, and into the warmth and light. With sighs of relief, they all dismounted. Thor clapped old Harald on the shoulder and thanked him for the quick thought.

"And where is Ian?" Aylena said, looking around. "Does he know we're here?"

"He's off to the Kenlochs, my lady," Harald said, "making peace amongst the clans. Yer little maid will be glad to see you, I vow. She was sorry to see him go."

"Oh! Of course. She is alone and lonesome."

"She is indeed. But Robert of Bourne will be looking out for her. He is well pleased with our laird's plan to marry the girl."

Aylena laughed, delighted. "So, they have spoken again of marriage? I must hear this now. Take care of my horse, Harald. We leave again tomorrow." She was gone, rushing from the stables, hurrying across the snowy courtyard and into the kitchens.

The cooks looked around, startled. "Lady Aylena! How many to sit at the table?"

Aylena slowed for only a moment. "Besides my friend Ciel and me, three hungry men!" Then she was gone, running up the stone steps to the gallery. "Ciel! Where are you, child?"

In the shadows of the long hall a door opened and Ciel stepped out. "Lady Aylena! I heard nothing of your arrival. Oh, my lady, I am indeed happy to see you."

Aylena put her arms around her and kissed her, finding the salt of tears on a satiny cheek. "You are lonesome since Ian left, I am sure. Will he be back tonight?"

"Oh, no. He only left at noon. He believes 'twill take a full day or two to convince the Scots that all is well." Ciel, dressed only in a gown and shawl, shivered in the cold air. Aylena drew her along the gallery to the solar and opened the door. A heap of red-hot coals on the hearth still warmed the room and brightened the shadows.

"Sit here with me for a moment," Aylena said, and found a chair, wondering at the silence. Young women in love were apt to chatter and laugh constantly. She watched Ciel as she dragged over a stool and sat down, gazing at the coals. Looking at Ciel's face in the firelight, Aylena's heart dropped. The affair had gone amiss, there was no doubt of it. She broke the silence.

"What are your plans, Ciel?"

"The same as they were, Lady Aylena. I will return to my home as you will to yours."

"The servants here believe you will marry Ian."

Ciel looked away. "I know. But they are wrong."

"Have you and Ian quarreled?"

"Oh, no!" Ciel's eyes came up to Aylena's face. "Ian is never quarrelsome. He has been wonderful to me."

"Then why leave him, Ciel? You know he loves you."

Ciel stood up, suddenly determined. "And I him! Enough that I will not ruin his life. Nor will I listen to any advice, even from you. 'Tis my life too, and I've— I've told him good-bye."

Ciel looked away after those last words, her face reddening. But it was true, she told herself. There was a carefully written letter on Ian's table where he tallied his sheep and bales of wool. He had not seen it yet, but when he read it he would understand.

Aylena sighed and rose. "Then I will not take you to task again, my dear little friend. You have made your decision. Have you packed? We leave tomorrow at the break of day. Thor is anxious to be gone."

Ciel let out her breath and moved away toward the door. "My belongings are ready to go. And I too am anxious. My father will need me in the fields this spring."

Aylena forced a friendly smile. "Yes, I am sure he will. And perhaps 'tis best for you, after all. This dreary place has little charm for a woman brought up in your beautiful Normandy."

Ciel's gaze came up to Aylena's face in surprise. "Do you think it dreary, Aylena? I have never been in a place so full of joy and love as this beautiful old castle. Perhaps not every clan is like the Stewarts, but there is nothing sad nor gloomy here. I will remember it as the most wonderful place in my life."

Aylena stared at her. "Yet you would leave it?"

"I must."

There was a long silence as they looked into each other's eyes. " 'Tis your choice," Aylena said finally. "I will say no more. Now, come with me while we eat. Then you must ready yourself for travel. I have stretched our time here well past what Thor thought enough. We leave at dawn."

Three days later, Ian Stewart came back to his castle, tired, disgusted, and yet hopeful. Rory mac Kenloch had opened a hive of bees when he invited the laird of the

Stewarts to attend that meeting. All of the hotheads from other clans had been there, loudly demanding their rights and denouncing the English traders. It had taken all of Ian's patience and wit to set them on the right path. And Rory was the loudest. Ian lost a great deal of his friendly feelings toward Rory mac Kenloch, and, now, with his own castle rearing up before him, he yearned for warm greetings and the sight of his beloved Ciel.

The guards had been watching for him. He was barely in view when the drawbridge came crashing down and his men-at-arms came out, lining his approach, grinning and raising a few scattered cheers.

Rogue was far from being tired, and with the castle in plain sight and the drawbridge settled, the big horse lengthened his stride, galloping toward home. The port-cullis that separated the castle itself from the busy court-yard was kept raised in times of peace, and Ian looked past it as he entered, hoping to see Ciel waiting for him on the steps of the keep. She wasn't there, but he thought it likely she was absorbed in some of the duties she had already taken on and knew nothing of his arrival. He thought of surprising her and his tired face broke into amusement. He went on around to the stables and dis-mounted, handing the reins to Harald.

"Send one of the ostlers inside with that baggage," he said, "I'm in a hurry."

"Yes, sire."

Ian had already turned toward the kitchens, but he glanced back, wondering at Harald's subdued manner. Yes, *sire*? Harald had long forgot that formality. But then, the man was old now, and here and there a change would show . . .

Ciel was not in the kitchens. He spoke to the kitchen

workers as they chorused a welcome and kept on walking. She'd be in the solar, then, for the day was still
cold. He went up the steps two at a time and opened a
door on a dark, chilly room. He paused, fighting a sudden, undefined fear. From the feel of it, no fire had been
lit here in over a day. 'Twas like a tomb, he thought,
and went in, his heart beating rapidly. *Where was she?*
There was nothing of hers about. He stared at the wide
hearth. A fire had been laid but never lit. He turned to
the door as old Hunter Blake came in with a lighted
candle in his hand.

"I'll just gi'e ye a bit of warmth here," Hunter said,
folding down his bony body in front of the dry logs.
"God knows ye'll need yer comforts with yer lovely bit
of a lady gone far away. All of us hated to see her
go . . ." His shaky hand held the burning candle to the
dry twigs beneath the logs. "Now, there . . . the flame is
beginning to catch . . ."

Ian's broad hand grasped the back of Hunter's heavy
cloak and lifted him straight up until only his toes
touched the stone hearth. Hunter's jaw dropped, his pale,
rheumy old eyes filled with fear as he saw the rage in
Ian's face.

"S-s-see here," he got out, "yer actin' against yer
elders! No true knight would harm a helpless old man!"

"If you value what's left of your useless life," Ian
said grimly, "you'll tell me where she went. I want her
back now!"

"Why . . . why she went to Normandy, Laird Ian. An'
in the company of our own Lady Aylena. An' all in a
fearful hurry to be gone, an' worryin' about the spring
foals in Rodancott's herd. They came in the night of the
day ye left an' were gone by daybreak of the next day.

Why, they must be close to London if the roads are
clear, an' soon over the Channel. An' the girl droppin'
tears all tha way, I'd swear. She looked to cry her heart
out.''

''Shut your babbling mouth, Blake! Did she leave me
a message?''

''N-not with me, sire! Nor does anyone else claim she
spoke to them about leavin'. But—but there is a paper
there on yer tally table, weighted down an' written on.
Maybe it's . . .'' Hunter staggered as Ian let go, got his
balance, and reached for the guttering candle he'd
dropped. Then he left the room at a shaky but rapid pace,
never looking back.

There was still light enough from the window to read
what Ciel had written. Ian flung himself into his chair
and unrolled the sheet of parchment, his jaw set grimly.
It tightened to iron as he read the first line:

> I will not ask you to forgive me, Ian, nor do I de-
> serve it. I wanted the love and joy only you could
> give me, and the memories I have of our time to-
> gether will make the rest of my life worthwhile. But
> I could not stay, for I never intended to marry you.
> I knew your peers would scorn your peasant wife
> and call your sons pretenders. You would hate me
> then.

''I hate you *now!*'' Ian gritted out loud, and flung the
parchment aside. There were tears in his eyes and a rage
rising in his throat that threatened to choke him. The
woman had *lied* to him! She had used him like a man
uses a whore, just for the pleasure of it! And she was
still lying, still claiming that she loved him! He stood,

shoving the table away, rocking it and spilling his records across the stone floor. He rose and strode across
them to the door. Flinging it open, he stood on the gallery and roared for Robert of Bourne, his voice echoing
like thunder through the hall.

The seneschal came into the hall below at a half run.
"Yes, sire!"

"Send me a pitcher of Normandy wine from the cel-
lar, an' be quick about it! An' a loaf with a slab of goat
cheese."

"The cooks are close to finishing a good dinner, sire,
an' you—"

"By the gods! Is there no one here who obeys me? I
need no slops from the kitchen! I want wine, damn you!
Wine and bread and cheese! Now!" He turned and went
back into the solar, slamming the door behind him.

The men below looked at each other and left the hall,
Robert heading for the cellars and the others stripping
the high table of the linen cloth they had just laid. They
folded it in silence and put it away in the linen room,
then edged out to the kitchen to eat there. None of them
had seen their young laird in such bitter anger ever before, nor would they want to again.

In the firelit room Ian walked back and forth, mutter-
ing to himself. He passed the piece of parchment each
time he turned, and finally he picked it up and began to
read the hastily written end.

"I cannot ask you for understanding," Ciel had written, but you mustn't be angry with the Lady Aylena.
She believes we agreed to part. And she knows nothing of what went on between us in our time alone . . .
though she is a wise woman and she may guess. And

now I must leave. I know you will never believe me again, but I will love you until I die.

"Liar!" he shouted, and tears came to his eyes, tears of either sorrow or rage. Which, he did not know. He crushed the parchment in his powerful hand and turned toward the bright fire, flaming high and ready to rid him forever of her lying words. But somehow he couldn't toss the wrinkled ball into the flames. Instead, he took it across the big room to a heavily carved chest, jerked up the lid, and tossed it in, saying to himself that if he ever forgot her treachery, he could get it out and read it again. Staring at the carved lid of the chest, another thing came into his mind. He could take it along when he went to fetch her. Yes. Yes, he would fetch her. He would bring her back here and teach her obedience. And if he needed proof of her lies, if he needed to show Vincennes Valoir that she had accepted his offer of marriage and then had run away, the parchment was proof.

That night he sat in front of the fire in his wood and leather chair and drank the whole pitcher of the strong Normandy wine, finishing off the loaf of fresh-baked bread and goat cheese. He slept there for a while, then woke after midnight as the fire guttered out, staggered to his feet, and headed for the bed, dropping clothes as he went.

At daylight, Hunter Blake eased the door open and peered around the edge, his wrinkled face tense.

"Shall I see to the fire, Laird Ian?"

Ian opened red eyes, winced, and shut them. "Indeed. Have a serf bring an armload of wood. And tell the maids I wish a bath, once the fire warms the room."

"Yes, laird." Hunter eased the door shut and let out

his held breath. "Ye heard that, did ye?" he added, looking at Robert of Bourne. "A bath, on a freezin' day like this? He'll be riskin' death . . .''

Robert sighed with relief. "He'll be fine, old man. Gi'e him a day or two. The lambs are dropping, an' he'll be too busy to grieve. Come! He needs food, once he's up. Then we'll have him back to himsel' an' numberin' tha lambs in his book.''

At that same hour the Rodancott party left Manchester for the last two days of travel to London. From the first day after leaving Stewart Castle until this morning the air had steadily warmed and the stiff, cold winds had become only chilly breezes. Everyone spoke of it and said their luck was perfect. Ciel listened and nodded and agreed politely. She wouldn't have noticed a snowstorm. Aylena had seen that. It was as if Ciel had her own sad little world, and she was in it alone. Not that she neglected her duties to Aylena. She was a perfect lady's maid: pleasant, helpful, and quiet. So very quiet it brought tears to Aylena's eyes.

Then, a day or so later, they were in London and at the Westminster palace, and the weather was still fine. King Henry ordered a private dinner of venison from his hunting preserves and sparkling wine from France, in honor of Thor, Thor's family and friends. And, for the first time, Aylena and Ciel met the king's paramour, the young and beautiful Rosamund. Small, slim, and dark-haired, Rosamund was friendly and smiling, her eyes going often to the king with a look of adoration. Ciel broke her quiet mood as she and Aylena left the party for Aylena's room.

"She does not look well," Ciel said hesitantly. "Perhaps she is tired."

"She is ill, Ciel. But no one speaks of it in the presence of the king. He cannot bear to think of losing her."

"I see." Silent again, Ciel went on to the door of her room. She was stopped there by Aylena's hand on her wrist.

"Think," Aylena said softly, "how far apart the king and Rosamund are in their positions. And how happy they are."

Ciel flushed. " 'Tis not the same! The king can do no wrong, nor would anyone dare to say he has. He could take the lowliest of the low to his bed, and no man nor woman would chance even a whisper about it. But I do have sorrow and respect for the lady, for her feelings about the king are as clear to my eyes as mine own feelings for Ian."

"And Ian's for you! You surely are not suffering alone, Ciel. My brother's feelings run deep."

"Please! I cannot bear to speak of it, my lady. 'Tis over!" She slipped through the door and closed it, leaving Aylena in the hall. Thor spoke behind Aylena and came to take her arm.

"Come to bed, love. You needn't fight Ian's battle for him. He's noted for his victories, not for his losses."

Aylena took his arm and leaned against him, her eyes sad as they went toward their own door. "You may be right. But 'twas simpler in our time," she said, and Thor snorted.

"Your memory fails you, then. We fought many a battle before you gave in, my lady."

19

March and April sped past at Stewart Castle. In mid-April Ian stationed a force of men-at-arms in the woods near old Orn Thoma's sheepfold and placed a healthy herd of unsheared sheep to toll in the thieves from the Frisian Islands. In ten days two boats arrived at night on the rocky beach. Men came up the trails quietly and met their death when they began herding the sheep toward the precipice. As Thor had advised, the men-at-arms allowed three men to get away and take the tale home. The bodies of the other men were placed in the remaining boat, which was set afire and shoved away from the beach to drift.

"Vikings they were once," Ian had said grimly. "Let them have a Viking funeral."

He had said it to a subdued Rory mac Kenloch, who had come to him to make peace after war flared in the north of Scotland. The Earl of Orkney had brought a claim to the land from Moray Firth to Caithness, and William the Lion, leading his troops in battle array, had no time now to listen to acid complaints amongst the quarrelsome clans. And now Rory had no more thoughts of being the judge between England and Scotland. He said openly that he'd not want the problems that would be coming once King William conquered the earl.

But when the fight between the thieves and Ian's men-at-arms was over, Rory was as glad as Ian to see the Frisian funeral boat float away in flames. Riding back to the Stewart castle together, he spoke of it with confidence.

"They'll not try it again, Ian. They may be dishonest, but they're no fools. And with yer number of healthy lambs dropped this season, ye have exceeded yer loss even so."

"Indeed," Ian said. "This spring weather has favored us all." He looked up, his gaze sweeping the rocky, sunlit meadows, the spring greening of the few trees, the patches of grass springing up on the barrens. Then his eyes lit on the ewes and their frolicking lambs in the distance amd his hard face gentled. " 'Tis truly a wonderful change."

Rory brightened. "Aye! 'Twas an anxious winter, with troubles enough between us. A trip to Carlisle is what we both need. I must confess that England beats Scotland in the quality of her whores."

Ian glanced at him and laughed without humor. "I doubt the English would find that a compliment, though I can't judge for myself. However, I'm afraid I can't join you. I have been called to London an' must leave tomorrow."

Rory's quick look was full of suspicion. "Why? Does that king of yours plan to take over the Scottish lowlands while William fights the Earl of Orkney?"

Ian shook his head, half amused and half disgusted. "You have a devious mind, Rory, but a lack of judgment. Henry has more than he can rule now, an' if he's fool enough to decide to add to it, he will add more of France. Scotland is too poor to tempt him.''

"Then why are you going?''

Ian sighed. "I am the king's man. Had you forgotten? When he calls, I go. He will tell me why when I get there.''

Rory frowned. "I wouldna like that, Ian. What if 'twas a thing you didna wish to do? Must you do it whether or no?''

Ian broke into laughter. "To be a king's man means you protect the king against secret assailants. That is all.''

"Then when he sends for you, he believes there is a threat to his life?''

"Indeed.''

"Which will be a threat to yer life, then?''

"Naturally. For the assailant must remove the king's man to get to the king.''

Rory shook his head. "Nay, I wouldna like it.''

"It is not so hard,'' Ian said, still chuckling. "The king is a good friend to have. He sent the message by way of two men-at-arms, both trained in the arts of war an' sworn to protect my life on the road to London. They wait for me at the castle.''

"And these men so clever at murder canna protect the king theirselves?''

"They are trained only with war weapons. In a crowd around a king the sword and ax are dangerous to all.''

Rory stared at him and then slowly nodded. "True, Ian. An' ye so quick with yer hands and yer slim dagger. Lord Rodancott taught ye those tricks, I know. I did hear once that Thor could kill an armed man with no more than his bare hands. Was tha man who told me lying?''

"He was not lying. But there's danger in it."

Rory sighed. "You need not warn me, Ian. I will fight for my clan an' hunt for our meat with the weapons I am versed in, but I'll not try your methods. I am far too cautious."

"That is the best way, Rory. You will live a less dangerous life, and stay near your home." Ian was slowing his horse, waiting to turn toward the Stewart castle, looming off to the north. "I have found a strong and able man to help out old William and Roderick while I am gone. His name is Angus Cline, and he comes from Cromarty. His mother was a Stewart, and he seems an honest man. Robert of Bourne knew him before and gave him a good name. He might enjoy company while I'm gone."

"I'll visit him, then." Smiling, Rory turned his mount to the northwest. " 'Twill be good to hear talk of another place an' other people."

That thought came back to Ian the next morning, when he and the two royal men-at-arms set out for London and the Tower, where the king was staying. Had the last two months not been so busy, he would have been miserably lonely in his castle. It lifted his spirits now to have the two men with him, ready to tell stories, to laugh, to brag of their victories. It was wonderful entertainment, for they were both seasoned warriors with many stories to tell.

They dropped along the coast for two days and ended up in Godwin's Inn for a night. Godwin and Drusilla set out a dinner for them and asked Ian for news from the Rodancotts. It was the last of the easy part of the trip. Ian sensed the men's growing attention as they passed

Manchester and then Tichfield and Coventry, where the king had left a favorite baron in a wooden castle. They spent a night there, then set out again, refreshed, for London. At last, when the myriad of church spires reared in a misty gray sky behind ancient Roman walls, and the three of them rode through the north gate, Ian asked a few questions. The two men-at-arms stared at him as if struck dumb. Ian laughed.

"Well enough, friends. You needn't answer. I have noticed your eyes going to well-dressed men and priests. And you, William Baird, even loosened your dagger when you saw a monk. I believe I know from whence the threat comes."

"We know very little," William Baird said. "We were only told to watch out for several men to draw near to us at once and to keep a distance between them and you." He smiled a little. "Indeed, the king is chary of words this time. But from the look of those two big men on our left and the three coming toward them from the right, we may get an invitation to dance in tha street. What say you, Tom Golden?"

"I say you are right." Tom gave Ian a measuring glance. "What weapon do you prefer, Lord Stewart?"

"On a horse, my sword. It lengthens my reach. You?"

"The same. And William likes swinging a mace. Yes, they are setting themselves to fight . . . *now! Have at them, William!*"

Screams erupted from men and women passing by on the narrow street as they ran for safety. The five men afoot and the three on horseback came together in a clash of sword against shield, angry roars, and a noise of clattering metal. Two of the mounted men, Tom and

Ian, sent the swords of their assailants flying from their hands, and William's mace caught two heads in one swing. Both men staggered away and collapsed in the gutter. Instantly the man who had missed his blow threw down his weapon and fled, dodging through the crowded narrow streets and out of sight. Ian laughed and turned to William.

"You gave us fair odds," he said, "with that mace of yours. But . . . are you bleeding?"

William looked down. "Indeed you are right, but a nick on the thigh only." He laughed and turned to look back as they rode on. "He blooded me, an' I brained him, for he still lies back there with the other one. I'll leave him as a warning."

An hour later, at the formal entrance to the Tower, the king's chamberlain greeted Ian with a smile of relief and took him up the wide stairs at a fast pace, talking constantly.

"The king is not in the best of humors, Sir Ian. He despises this necessary confinement. But there have been threats to his life, and a plot uncovered."

"A plot?"

"So it is said. A plot by defrocked priests. Once the talk about Thomas à Becket subsided, the king quite rightly called in the new archbishop and gave him a list of the criminals who evaded his laws by becoming priests, though continuing in their criminal activities. Of course the archbishop defrocked them."

"Indeed. 'Twas the least he could do. But the pope has intervened?"

The chamberlain paused and stared at him as they reached the top of the stairs. "How did you know?"

Ian smiled. " 'Tis what he would do. The pope considers every priest as his emissary. He feels that if they need punishment, he should be told. Then he will act. Either to pardon them or give their souls to the devil.''

"Exactly! He has ordered the king to reinstate them.''

"And has the king obeyed?''

The chamberlain shook his head and turned again in the wide, dim gallery, going swiftly toward the large solar. "He is considering it.'' He glanced back at Ian and shook his head. "He is also considering a claim against you, Lord Ian. But he will tell you of that.''

Ian's brows rose. "Against me? For what reason?''

"I cannot say. However, I wanted to warn you. Be careful in what you tell him.''

"I will say only the truth, James. I have nothing to hide.''

The chamberlain nodded and smiled, reaching to open the double doors. He escorted Ian into the large room, bowed to the king, bowed to Ian, and bowed himself out, pulling the door shut in his own face, which was still smiling properly. Ian went forward with a feeling of relief, dropped to a knee before King Henry II, put his hands together in Henry's firm clasp, and murmured: "My hands in your service, my king.''

"And thank God you are here,'' Henry said, stepping back. "Come, we'll have a glass of wine to settle our nerves.'' He glanced up at Ian's calm expression and gave a short laugh. "You may be in as much trouble as I, my friend.''

"If I am, I have not heard of it,'' Ian said amiably, and as the king settled into his chair, he took another one across the round table. "What do you need of me?''

"Your protection,'' Henry said. "No more, no less. The criminals who Becket pardoned and anointed as priests have protested to the pope and the pope is considering their pleas and mine. In this time of waiting, they hope to take my life.''

Ian leaned back in his chair, stretching his long legs. ''They'll not take your life, sire. Thor has taught me well.''

''I believe you. But there is another problem I must present to you.'' The king's face held both sympathy and a touch of wry amusement. ''I have heard from Thor that your affection for the Lady Serena Bertran has died away. Is that true?''

Ian nodded. ''Thor had the right of it there.''

''Then I am sorry indeed. I am in a strange position with my pretty little unclaimed cousin. She has come to me for help. She is big with child, and she has informed me that you are the father. You must marry her, Ian.''

Ian stared for a silent moment. ''The father,'' he said finally, ''is Leon, the Count of Aragon. Or perhaps another one of the cosseted foreign nobles in this half-prison, half-royal residence. 'Twas not I who took her to bed and gave her a child.''

''But you cannot be sure!''

''Indeed I can. I never bedded her.'' He hesitated. ''In fact, I had never bedded any woman until after I left her.''

King Henry laughed out loud. ''Now that is hard to believe, Ian, and if 'twas any other man I know I would never think it true. But Serena swears 'twas you who fathered her unborn babe. She wants you to wed her now and let her reside in Belmain. She has heard of the fine castle there, the fine trade with Flanders and Normandy, and says she will take wonderfully good care of it all.'' He was trying hard to seem serious, but Ian heard stifled laughter behind his words. "And I am sure she would. Not you nor the Lady Aylena would ever be bothered by having to count your money from Belmain again."

Ian settled back in his chair and let go of his fears. He had caught the king's intent in his amused eyes. "I see by your face, sire, that you do not believe her. And well you may doubt the woman, whatever she says. But she was truly fond of the Spaniard. Is he still here?"

"Indeed. The nobles of Aragon have refused, so far, to pay the tribute I asked for. They seem quite content to leave him here. However, 'twould be worth a decent sum to get rid of them both."

Ian sighed. "My small trickle of Scottish blood warns me that you will ask me to add to your young cousin's dowry, and that I will. 'Twas my foolish admiration that brought the slut here, an' I will pay my share. But I may ask another favor of you in time."

"And I will listen. Will you see and talk to Serena before she leaves?"

Ian's eyes met the king's stare. "Only in your presence, my king. God knows what new lie she would tell if I met her alone."

"Then go to the door an' tell the chamberlain to fetch her here. I wish to hear what she says to you."

Ian rose and complied, telling the chamberlain that Serena Bertran was to be brought to the king at once. Then he came back and sat down.

In minutes, the door opened. "The Lady Serena Bertran," the chamberlain announced, "at the king's pleasure."

Serena swept in, gowned in her best but straining at the seams. She made a small genuflection toward the king, then rushed to Ian, taking one of his hands in both of hers. "My darling Ian! Oh, how I have missed you since you left me! Promise me you'll never leave me again!"

Ian rose from his chair, freed his hand from her clinging fingers, and brought another chair forward, putting it on the other side of the king. "Sit down, Serena. I want to hear your lies with my own ears."

Serena looked from one to the other and sat down. "So, there is none left of the attraction you once felt. And I see I'm caught. Who tattled on me, my king? I know without asking that it wasn't Ian."

"Half of London, my dear. What tricks you might get away with in Bures are child's play in London. You were soon found out. And Ian has told me there was no mating between you. Your own lies caught you up. Is the child's father Leon, the Count of Aragon?"

Serena's pretty face twisted. "Most likely, sire. That is, the father's name is Leon, but whether or no he is a count is still to be seen. However, he pleases me, and if you decide to send him back to Spain, I would go with him."

"Then it is done. You may tell the man his prison days are over, and you will be taking along a dowry for his future." The king smiled at her and made a gesture that she should leave. "You do have courage, Lady Serena."

Rising, smoothing down her tight gown, Serena gave him a brilliant smile. " 'Tis the Plantagenet blood, sire, I am sure of it."

The two men watched her sail out, head high and still smiling. "A liar, yes," the king said thoughtfully, "but no dithering coward. I like that in a woman, though that woman is indeed a poison to men."

Rising, Ian nodded. "She is that. Am I to stay here, in the Tower? Or should I find other rooms?"

The king laughed. "I am no dithering coward either, but I am more confident when you stay near. Ask the chamberlain to give you a room near to mine and set you a place at table."

That evening the close friends of King Henry gathered in the solar for a meal together. The huge room was lit by a blazing fire on the hearth, and ranks of silver candlesticks poured light on the dining table. Even more candles were set about on the tops of tables and chests. Yet shadows still flickered and moved in the dark corners, as if the ghosts of long past kings watched and listened and breathed out sighs.

William the Marshal was there, big and stolid, his face never giving away his thoughts. And the young king, Henry III, pale and frightened, was in attendance. He came at once to Ian and greeted him with gratitude.

"Thank God," he said, "we are safe enough here now. In the streets the priests and monks are all afire, speaking the pope's recent words against the crown."

"Like a fever," Ian said to him for comfort, " 'twill run its course. Some new thing will attract their empty minds."

But curiosity made Ian stare at the three big men who came next, wearing gleaming shirts of mail. They stood at the door to allow a servant to remove them. Then, in their velvets and silks, their jewels and gold chains, they came to the king in his chair and greeted him with vows of fealty. These were the men Ian had known only by their deeds, though Thor had often spoken of them, calling them the king's three magnates.

Now, with Ian there as king's man for the first time,

each of them came to take his hand and wish him well, as if he had become a member of a secret order. An odd chill ran up Ian's spine as he realized these were the men who had beaten Thomas à Becket to death.

The oldest of the three, if white hair and beard could be believed, was the leader. He spoke as if for all of them, saying that they had left their men-at-arms outside the solar door to make sure of no rude interruptions. His eyes, sharp in spite of his age, rested on Ian often, as if he were measuring the new king's man. Then, when all were seated and were drinking their wine, he turned to Henry. "What word has come from the pope, my king?"

Henry flushed red. " 'Tis always the same. He ignores my wishes and has refused to agree to the archbishop I chose to take Becket's place. He insists on having the names of the men who killed him. He never wavers on that." He paused, turning even a darker hue when he spoke the next words. "Also, he refuses to accept any punishment but death for them."

The three men looked at each other swiftly and then settled back in their chairs. "What do you intend to do?"

Henry stood, his jaws set, and began walking jerkily back and forth before the fire. "I will tell Pope Alexander I cannot name the men who did it. And if he wants to punish someone for Becket's death, he should punish me. My damnable temper was the cause of it, as we all know."

The older man with the white hair sighed and got to his feet, restless. "The death," he said, "was not intentional. The archbishop became insane with rage and flung himself down at the altar, grasping the sides with both hands, swearing no one would drag him away from it. A blow from a club, which was meant to loosen his grip on the altar, missed his arms and hit the back of his head when he suddenly reared up. He died within minutes. Yet no one there wanted him dead.''

There was a long silence. The three men stared at the floor; the king continued to pace. Ian sensed the tightness of their feelings, and his own thoughts changed. He and others he had talked to had believed the killing intentional, but there was the ring of truth in the older man's voice.

Then Henry II came to a halt, turning to gaze at the others, now all standing again in a loose semicircle. He looked at each of them in turn, his eyes dwelling longest on his son, the young king, who gazed back at him fearfully.

''I will take the blame,'' Henry said slowly. ''And the punishment. 'Twas my fault that an old friend of mine was killed, and I bitterly regret it. 'Twill make me whole again to be punished, for I know the responsibility is mine and none other's. I will inform the pope of my feelings.''

''No!'' William the Marshal spoke up heatedly. ''You are our king. You cannot be touched by inferiors. I say no!''

''And I!'' ''And I!'' There was a chorus beginning, but Henry held out his hand, palm forward.

''Enough. I have made up my mind. There is no more to say or do until I send word to the pope. Then I will gather you together again. But now we will sit and have our dinner.''

The next day Ian sat silent as the king composed his message to the pope, wrote it on parchment, and sealed it, putting it in a leather pouch and giving it to a trio of knights to take to Rome. When they had left for Dover and the king was alone with Ian, he gave Ian the liberty to stay in London or to go home again if he wished.

"I will be safe now until the pope decides. It will be at least forty days before I receive his answer, and that if he replies promptly, without asking his cardinals for their advice. Too much time for you to sit and cool your heels. Do as you will."

Ian was taken by surprise. "Are you sure, my king? What of the priests who threaten you?"

"They will be told the message has been sent. They'll not risk the pope's fury by interfering now."

That was undoubtedly true, Ian thought. The pope was a hard master. But forty days? He could be in Normandy in less than four days. 'Twas time for Ciel Valoir to learn that he would not put up with her fancies and her disobedience! The girl was ripe for a lesson . . .

20

 Ian crossed the Channel and planned to arrive at Castle Cheval Noir on the evening of the fourth day. He had spent a night at an inn halfway between Calais and this rich, rolling pastureland and had wakened before dawn with an urge to set out again that drove him on without breakfast. He told himself that what pushed him was the righteous anger inside him. Ciel Valoir would soon hear what he thought of her.

But now Rogue had sensed his first home. He threw up his handsome head and bugled, breaking into a wild gallop as a mare's whinny answered, a clear sound of welcome echoing through the green valley that led up to Cheval Noir. Ian laughed, his heart suddenly light in spite of his anger, and pulled him up to set him again at a comfortable canter. He leaned forward and patted the stallion's thick neck.

"Soon, Rogue. Very soon. Your former master will be glad to turn you into the pasture with his mares this spring. And I will allow it, though I will need you when I visit the Valoir family."

Then one of the men-at-arms, seeing an ebony horse and a tall man with a mass of dark-gold hair glinting in the sunset light, blew his horn. In minutes the courtyard gate swung open and ostlers came grinning to take Rogue's reins and help young Lord Stewart untie his belongings.

"Ian!" Aylena rushed from the kitchen door and ran to put her arms around him. "How wonderful! How long can you stay?"

Ian hugged her and laughed, his eyes soft as ever when he looked at his sister. "Near to a month only. But enough."

"You've been in London? We've heard some tales concerning the man Henry chose to be the new Canterbury archbishop. It seems the pope disagreed with Henry's choice."

"And you heard right, then. The man Henry chose got rid of the so-called priests who had sought the safety of the church after committing murders and theft. Many of the priests he defrocked have attempted to blame our king for their troubles, and have sent all manner of lies to the pope."

"And you are here? Does the king not need your talents?"

"Not for forty days, of which I have used only four. He has sent a message to the pope, and the rest of it hangs on the word from Rome. We must wait, and I chose to wait here."

Aylena stared up at his youthful face, noting the thinning of flesh, the new, hard lines in the set of his mouth, and the frown lines between his blue eyes. "And do you plan to see Ciel Valoir?" She watched his jaw harden, the rush of blood to his cheeks.

"Indeed. I have much to say to that young woman. Little of it will please her."

Aylena drew in a long breath and turned away. "She has never said a word against you, Ian. All I know of her is that beneath her sweet, calm face she is desperately unhappy."

"And beneath that she is a cheat and a liar!"

Aylena whirled back to stare at him angrily. "That I do not believe!"

Ian's jaw snapped shut. He turned and took up the bundles of clothes and weapons the ostlers had removed from Rogue's back. "Then I will say no more. Show me the room you have for me."

"Then come," Aylena said stiffly. "And we shall not speak on that subject again."

That evening Thor asked all the questions and, when supper was over, took Ian off to a small study and went over the problem between Pope Alexander III and King Henry.

"Neither will want to give in on the archbishop," Thor said, "and yet Henry knows that any archbishop picked by the pope will welcome the defrocked priests into the church again, even if 'twould be only a show of his power. And those thieves and murderers will lord it over Henry and continue their wickedness. 'Tis an impossible fight to win."

"Still, we shall try. Henry has asked that the punishment be given to him because of his anger and rash words. 'Twas his own fit of temper that sent others to drag à Becket from the cathedral."

Thor shook his head. "He has given the pope an opportunity to do whatever he likes, and that I regret. I am amazed that the magnates allowed him to do it."

"I will be with him, Thor. If the punishment becomes

too harsh, I will stop it whether Henry says yea or no. I am, after all, the king's man.''

Thor looked at him and nodded. '' 'Tis all you can do, and all I could do if I were still in your place. Now, let me ask a question on another subject. When we came to your castle and found you gone, Robert of Bourne mentioned a problem with some of the clans. Has the problem been remedied?''

Ian shrugged. "For the summer, no doubt, for their work keeps them busy. But another long winter and the clans will begin quarreling again. 'Tis always so.''

Thor smiled. "Indeed. I learned how to stop that. Listen carefully to what the man has to say and then forget it. Another week, and he too will forget. Wait until a war starts, Ian, and then join the right side. You may have to wait years until a cranky winter quarrel goes that far.''

"I don't doubt it," Ian said, relieved. '' 'Tis the chance to complain that they like. I'll take your advice.''

"Will you take more?''

"From you? Gladly.''

"Careful, now. I speak of love.''

Ian's relaxed face froze into stone. "Not a fit thing for you to speak of to me, Thor. I know what you think. But I have every intention of taking Ciel back to Northumberland as my wife. First I must talk to Vincennes.''

"You sound too bitter to be a bridegroom, Ian.''

"Bitter I am. She lied to me!''

"Lied?''

"She said she would marry me.''

Thor sighed. "Are you sure?''

"Naturally! I wasna going to take her before the vows, but she put it in such a way that I felt 'twould be right. And she said . . . she said she would never love anyone else nor let another man have her, for in her soul she would always be mine. That is plain enough, I think.''

''I heard no words like 'I will marry you,' '' Thor said gently. ''Did she ever say them?''

''Why, let me think. She must have done . . .''

There was a total silence in the small room. There was an open window across from where they were sitting, and the faint sounds of flying insects whirred now and again, while the deep blackness of the night grew lighter from the rising moon. Finally Ian left his chair and went to the window to look out. His voice came back to Thor, calm but distant and cold.

''You are right,'' he said. ''I have searched my mind for every word she said, and not once did she ever say she would marry me, only that she would love me all her life. Always she said I would be ruining myself if I married a peasant girl.''

'' 'Tis her own blindness,'' Thor said quietly. ''She cannot see that in this family and in your clan no one cares whether blood is noble or common. She is a beautiful and wonderfully able and loving woman, but she is stubborn in her belief.''

Ian turned and looked at Thor. ''Tell me, then. What should I do?''

Thor smiled. ''Go to her, Ian. Say the truth. Say you cannot be happy without her. She too has been sad and lonely.''

''Lonely?''

''Indeed. She haunts those meadows where you taught her to train warhorses, though no colts will be ready for lessons until fall. I see her there often, sitting alone under a large tree while Devil browses on the thick new grass.''

Ian turned back to the window, his throat thick. He knew that tree. He thought how stupid he had been not to take Ciel in his arms under those huge branches. He had known then that she wanted his arms around her, yet he had been foolishly dreaming of Serena Bertran.

''Then I will try those meadows tomorrow afternoon. If she isn't there I will go on to the farmhouse and hope Vincennes Valoir is still willing to allow me to enter his home.''

By noon of every day Ciel had the Valoir household running smoothly. She had a washerwoman and a maid, and a cook, though she worked beside all of them. Always she looked for more work, more tasks to consider, more changes to be made. It kept her busy. But these first soft summer days called her outside, took her to the far pastures and brought her memories that warmed her heart, and, sometimes, nearly broke it.

This new day was lovely and dry. Golden weather, and deep green shade beneath the huge trees. In the far meadow, she put Devil through all his paces, determined that he would never forget the skills that Ian had taught him; nor would she forget how to teach them to other warhorses.

Thinking of that, she thought of that day when she told Devil to attack, and he had killed the two men threatening Aylena. Then tears of gratitude came to her eyes. Ian had wiped away all the horror she felt, and had held her and kissed her and shown her that what she did was right, and the only way to save Aylena. Thinking of the kisses, she shut her eyes. Lovemaking . . . by all the saints, had she known how much she would miss it, she wouldn't have begun it! She sighed, turning Devil toward the road again. Time to start home.

Coming along the road from the south, Ian looked to the east and the rolling meadows and saw a horse and its rider heading north and west, making a slanted course between the trees. He knew at once who it was. The rider was unmistakably Ciel, for her shining black hair and small size gave her away, and the horse was Devil, for he saw the shine of his gray satin pelt. Ian's heart leaped into double time.

Joyful, yet afraid to trust this meeting to be welcome to her, he touched Rogue's sides with his spurs. But then, just as he started to call out her name, he saw her slow Devil to a walk and turn him toward the shade cast by the gnarled boughs of the old oak. They had often rested there on a cushion of soft leaves to talk together. Now, while he watched, he saw her slide from her saddle, tie Devil to a small tree, and disappear into the deep shadows beneath the huge limbs.

His heart still beating fast, Ian slowed Rogue and went on, wondering. Wondering and fearing, for he thought Ciel might have stopped there to meet a new lover. The fear grew as he neared the big tree, and he stopped at a strong sapling, slid from Rogue's back, and tied him to it. There was no sound of talk or laughter, so he went closer, and as he ducked beneath the low-hanging branches, he saw Ciel with her back to him. She was sitting in a patch of flickering sunlight, her small body bent forward, her arms crossed on her upthrust knees, her forehead resting on her wrists. For a moment he was afraid she was crying, for the constant whispering rustle of leaves above her would drown the sound, but when he moved closer he saw her body was still, not shaking with sobs.

Then, inexorably drawn to her, he went as close as he dared. He was quiet, though he thought she might hear the pounding of his heart. When he was within arm's length he eased down on the thick leaves and sat, waiting and wondering. And, in the silence of another few minutes, Ciel raised her forehead from her crossed wrists and looked at him.

She was jolted, only half believing he was real. Her eyes widened, her mouth quivered. Still staring at him, she tried to speak and burst into tears instead. He reached across the small space between them with his long arms and lifted her over into his lap, wrapping his arms around her tightly.

She clung to him, her hands moving around his broad chest to his back, holding tight. She put her wet face in his neck and cried some more. Then he coaxed her mouth up to his and kissed her thoroughly, running his hands over her warm body, pulling up her skirts and seeking her smooth thighs, the gentle curve of her satiny belly and the silken curls that hid her womanhood. When he felt the heat there, he lay her back on the rustling leaves and reached under his tunic to loosen the chausses that bulged tight at his loins. After pushing them down, he entered her, moved slowly within her, kissed her and whispered of his love, and in only a few minutes she came up to him, arching high and pleading with her writhing body. Then he knew it was right; it was what she wanted, and he felt the throbbing, rolling ecstasy of her passion. He closed his eyes to feel more completely, and then his triumph roared out like a lion from deep in his chest, shaking him, bringing tears of happiness to his eyes.

And the heat between them dried all their tears. She sat up and leaned against him, stroking his bearded cheek, gazing into his eyes, her own eyes soft and full of love.

"Why are you here, Ian? I thought you'd hate me."

He smiled at her. It seemed so simple now. "I came to fetch you, my heart. My bed at home is cold; nor is there any warmth inside me when you are gone. All is winter without you. And will you come home?"

Ciel hid her face in his neck. "Surely I will if I can, though you must promise not to harry me about marriage once you get me there. I will be your leman, Ian. My father is too angry to speak to me except about our work and the horses. I—I told him all of what I felt and what I did, and he believes me a silly fool."

"We shall see. I will talk to your father."

Ciel's eyes came back to his. "My father has a terrible temper."

"Aye. That I knew. Let us go now and find him."

Vincennes Valoir's busiest days were on hand. The fields of wheat, the work in his vineyard, the birth of piglets, calves, and foals now kept him running from dawn to dark.

Vincennes had welcomed the extra work, for it gave him little time to think of his foolish daughter. Though, at this moment inside the huge barn, he was thinking of her and almost smiling. He was gently wiping down a newborn foal with a piece of coarse linen, reminded of her and her pride in her horse. The new foal was large and handsome, and his shining pelt was a beautiful satin gray. He thought of how Ciel would smile to see Devil's get from the last breeding season . . .

"Father?"

Vincennes looked up and saw the towering Lord Ian Stewart standing beside his daughter. His face flamed red; his whole stalwart body turned to iron. In spite of knowing that Lord Stewart had not been at fault, Vincennes was a father first and a friend next. He stumped forward, glaring.

"You! How dare you come into my home!"

Ian smiled. "You yourself gave me permission. I think I recall that you invited me, and added that I could stay as long as I liked. Am I wrong?"

"But I never gave you permission to take my daughter's virginity!"

"Father! I told you all that happened! 'Twas my fault, not Ian's. And . . . and I lied to him!"

"Enough!" Ian said, and said it loud enough to ring through the big barn. "I am here to make amends. I wish to marry your daughter, Vincennes."

Ciel whirled and stared at him. "You promised . . ."

"I made the promise, and I know what you said. I will never mention to anyone in Northumberland that we are married. Surely that should content you."

"You are making a fool of me!"

"He is not," Vincennes said, turning to her angrily. " 'Tis yourself who is making a fool of you. The man wants a wife, not a silly girl. Why are you so determined not to marry a lord?"

Ciel rounded on him. "My Lord Ian is the king's man! We will be in London, and I'll not be talked about as a peasant pretending to be a noblewoman, like Serena

Bertran! She will talk about me to others and claim a relationship . . ."

"She'll not," Ian said gently. "She has been sent away, big with child. She has been banished to Spain with one of the doubtful nobles who was in a cell in the Tower, a man named Leon, the Count of Aragon, whom she said was most likely the father of the babe she carried. The king provided for her, but she cannot return."

"Oh!" Ciel looked from Ian to her father, her face pinkening. "But still, I should not be called a lady. I have no noble blood."

"I think," Ian said, hiding a grin, "the lady protests too much. From what I have heard, the blood she carries is indeed not merely noble. 'Tis part of the royal Plantagenet stew. Should we call her Queen Ciel?"

Vincennes roared with sudden laughter. "A queen she is, Ian! The queen of my house now, and queen of yours, once you are wed. What say you, Ciel?"

Ciel looked from one to the other. Both of the men who meant the most to her were happy, grinning like apes and beaming at each other. She felt her eyes grow wet. It was wonderful, after all the blame and anger.

"Then," she said impulsively, "if you mean to keep your promises, I say yes." And all at once, as if she understood only after she heard her own words, she laughed with happiness, flung her arms around Ian's neck, and kissed him. "And you will be my true and much-beloved husband, though few will know."

Over her glossy black hair Ian's dark blue eyes met Vincennes's gray ones, and one of them slowly winked.

21

Aylena, upset by Ian's anger at Ciel, had seen him ride away toward the Valoir farmhouse near noon. And though she thought he'd be back within an hour or so, it was close to dark when she saw him from her window, coming toward the stable-yard and the open gates. She watched, holding her breath, to see if in the dimming light she could determine whether he was still angry. Then he looked up and saw her there, leaning on the broad stone sill and staring down at him. He laughed and reined in his horse.

"Vincennes has sent for the priest, my sister, and the wedding will be tomorrow, just after midday. Does that lighten your heart?"

"Thank God! You know it does! 'Tis honestly true?"

"Every word! I shall go back to England with a wife."

"Wonderful! I must tell Thor!" The window frame was immediately empty; her clear voice echoing back as she ran for the stairs. "Thor! I have fine news!"

Ian grinned and went on toward the stables. Fine news, indeed. They could learn the rest of it later.

At dinner Aylena began the questions. "How does Vincennes expect the priest to marry you two at such speed? The usual time is ten days for the banns to be posted, is it not?''

"It is more. But the priest will listen to Vincennes.''

"I see. But—Ciel has no wedding gown.''

"She has her mother's, and she says it fits well.''

"I see,'' Aylena repeated, but frowned. "And the guests? Haven't they friends or relatives that may want to attend?''

"We want you and Thor there, and naturally the house servants, that is all.''

"But I am sure Ciel must have friends in the village. Other young women. What of them? They might want a new gown for the ceremony.''

"Ciel wants no guests.''

Aylena looked at Ian and shook her golden head. "That cannot be! All brides want guests. There must be some young women she knows . . .''

Ian sighed and pushed back his chair. "I see I must tell you. Ciel wants no one except family, for she will not admit to being married. That is why there will be no guests.''

"Why? That is *wrong!* Others will believe she is—is your leman!''

Ian grinned. "You have the right of it there, my dear sister. That is exactly what she wants. And I wish to please her, as does Vincennes, since she will not agree to marry unless we do. Afterward it may be a different story.''

"Then I will say no more. 'Twill be as she wishes. And now I must find Thor again and tell him he must be ready to witness a secret wedding!''

*   *   *

The Valoir home had a tiny chapel, a room with an altar and silver towers holding candelabra on either side of it. There were pictures of saints and the holy family, and thickly embroidered altar cloths, the best of which had been brought out and laid reverently on the polished altar.

The village priest, Father Donne Farranda, was old and mellow, and fond of Vincennes Valoir and his lovely daughter.

He heard the confessions of the young couple before the ceremony, absolved them of all sins of the flesh, and brought them into the chapel himself, his wiry old hands firmly holding their arms and leading them to the altar, where they sank to their knees to pray. Taking his own place behind the altar, Father Donne nodded and smiled at the bride's father and the sister and brother-in-law of the groom.

Aylena caught her breath when she saw Ciel. Ciel's mother had died long ago, but the wedding gown itself was worth a caught breath. The finest of white silk, light enough to float in the air, and the most intricate of lace on each of many fluttering ruffles. It was low cut, with matching lace circling down to caress the swell of rounded breasts, then hugging her small waist and leaping out in huge waves, billowing and swaying as she walked. Ciel was beautiful, her eyes like wet turquoise stars, her smile soft as she looked up at Ian. The ceremony was powerful in its meaning. The old priest was smiling as he began.

"Ian and Ciel, you have come here today to seek the blessing of God and of his church upon your marriage. I require, therefore, that you promise, with the help of

God, to fulfill the obligations which a Christian marriage demands.''

The sonorous words went on, the questions were put: "Ian, you have taken Ciel to be your wife. Do you promise to love her, to comfort her, honor and keep her . . .''

Tears in her eyes, Aylena listened and remembered her own vows and took Thor's hand to hold. His fingers closed around hers warmly. She looked at him and then past him, at Vincennes, whose red face was smiling but damp with tears. Behind them a group of house servants and workers from the farm stood quietly and listened. And then the tension broke and everyone was suddenly at ease, for it was over, the final blessing said, the wedding acknowledged. Relieved smiles and nods came as they quitted the chapel.

In the dining hall a wedding feast was spread. Done quickly, but a boar had roasted all the night before and the cook had made use of the extra heat to bake new bread and pies. Wine flowed and toasts to the bride and groom were made, while excited laughter filled the hall.

And when Ciel went up to change from the wedding gown to an ordinary riding gown, Vincennes came to Ian and his family.

"I will be lonely now," he said, "but happy to know my daughter is well loved and cared for. She has a different view of life than I, but soon Ian will make her see the truth—she is as much a lady as any noble-woman.''

"Indeed," Aylena said strongly. "More of a lady than some I know. We will convince her, Vincennes, or life itself will.''

Then Ciel came down, smiling and happy, and telling

her father that she would be back for the rest of her
clothes and belongings, for Ian had said they would soon
leave for England again. She turned then and spoke to
Aylena as they went out.

"Ian has told me we will leave soon for London, but
'twill be a month or more before the king needs him.
So he plans to spend the time in Castle Belmain. He
tells me 'tis small and out of the way, but comfortable."

Aylena smiled, amused. "Belmain is indeed comfortable, my sister. Far more so than the Stewart castle. You
will have a pleasant time."

"But—what lord owns the place, Lady Aylena?"

Aylena smiled. "No lord at all. I own it. The Belmain
line comes down through the women, not the men. My
mother owned it before me."

"Oh! Then I shall feel at home there." She turned
and smiled at Ian, who brought up Devil for her to
mount. "Thank you, my lord. No, no, you needn't lift
me . . ."

Ian swept her up, kissed her laughing mouth, and
swung her into the saddle. "I am well aware you are
able to mount your horse, my dear love. But 'tis a pleasure to help you. Would you take the honor away from
me?"

Ciel laughed. "Oh, no! You might then find another
woman to toss about and kiss."

"Never." Ian's smile was intimate, his eyes clearly
possessive. "There is only one woman I want. That
much I have learned under the sheltering branches of a
Normandy oak tree."

That night, in a comfortable room in Castle Cheval
Noir, they spent the first night of their marriage.
Somehow, they felt awkward and uneasy with each

other. Yet both were anxious and wanting to show their love. But in the morning Ciel saw a golden cloud in a deep-blue sky, a courtesy from the rising sun behind them. She rose, drawn to the sight.

" 'Tis an omen," she declared, turning back to see Ian still in bed but watching her. "It promises us happiness and good fortune."

A pale golden light came through the deep window and outlined her body in the sheer muslin of her bedgown. Ian smiled, holding out his arms.

"If you return now to our marriage bed, I will feel it good fortune indeed."

She laughed and bent, catching the hem of her voluminous gown and pulling it off over her head. She tossed it off to the side and stood for a second, naked as she was born, pretending a shy reluctance. Ian was out of the bed in an instant, catching her up in his arms. She laughed and teased him, then caught her breath as he sank again into the luxurious bed, keeping her atop his urgent body.

"Now tell me," Ian whispered, "are you glad we married?"

"Indeed." Her eyes were slumbrous, half closed, her lips were parted and her breath came deep and slow. She caressed him, softly smoothing back his thick, dark-gold hair, threading her fingers through his beard, touching his lips and gently parting them. Then she leaned down and licked them, her tongue sucking them into her mouth to nibble.

"By the gods," Ian whispered, "by Eros himself! You are casting a spell on me . . ."

She barely heard him. Her passion swelled inside her, her instinct led her on. She moved down his chest, finding and gently scraping with her small teeth the flat nipples inside the golden haze of hair, then followed the narrowing golden trail to his navel and beyond. His huge chest rose and fell like a giant bellows, and as she touched the silken tautness of his heavy swollen shaft with her soft lips, his hands came down, grasped her waist, and lifted her high. She laughed softly and braced herself with her hands on his thick arms.

"Are you then afraid of what I might do, my love?"

"Indeed not," he got out, half strangled. "Only of what you might make me do. I do not wish to die of passion, though it might be the greatest of pleasures."

"Then let me down. I will stop tantalizing you. Only . . . let me down slowly."

"Why?"

"Because . . . no, I cannot explain, but you will see." He saw, for she settled herself on his loins, slowly taking him in, and her body slowly accommodating itself to him. The dawn light had brightened, and he saw the desire in her eyes, the throb of her heart in the soft flesh of her neck as she felt him fill her. And he thought of Serena. Was it really true that a woman could have a passion that was hard to control, just like men?

Then the thought was gone, and he knew only the softness, the wet heat, the loving and the passion coursing through him, and then his own deep cry of completion ringing in his ears.

And as he came back he thought of Serena again. Perhaps it had not been as strange and lurid as he had thought, though her habit of moving from one prisoner to another showed a far different character than that of her half cousin.

* * *

A day later Thor and Aylena joined them on the ride to Calais.

"We must go," Aylena said to Ian, "for I know the best of the Calais dressmakers and Ciel is in need of fashionable gowns. Good silks and woolens, and the newest styles. She may be in London for weeks."

"We have little time."

"You have more time than you need. Would you shame your lovely wife by letting her wear old clothes at court?"

Days later, Thor and Aylena saw them off, with Ciel's baggage bulging with gowns of silk, bright woolen cloaks, and the newest of the new, two silk gowns painted with flowers. There were gauzy wimples and headbands of stiffened wool and linen, set with colorful gems. All of the gowns swept the floors, needing to be lifted to clear the filthy streets or decks. Ciel thought the length a bother, but she was much too happy to care.

The trip across the channel to Dover was rough, but neither Ian nor Ciel suffered from *mal de mer,* and by nightfall they were in the Dover Inn and hanging up the gowns and tunics that had dampened on the way across the Channel.

Ian was amused. Ciel had devoted herself to the role of a leman instead of a wife. She hurried about, advising the maids to make sure of smooth beds and plenty of bathwater. She wore a plain gown, along with a white linen cap, nearly like that of the maids, and left her thick, shining hair to swing and and stray like thick black silk over her shoulders. She looked, he thought, as tempting as any leman could be. He followed through on her pretense, chucking her under her chin when the maids were about, and pinching her round bottom to make her jump.

She was red with fury before the maids giggled their way out of the room, casting back flirtatious looks at Ian, as if they thought he might change his mind about that sharp-tongued female, pretty though she might be, and choose one of them for the night. He stood in the middle of the room and waved them on, grinning.

"I will call on you," he said to them both, "if I am in need of anything at all. And so will my . . . er, friend here." They burst into laughter and ran down the stairs.

"I am surprised," Ciel said, clipping out words sharp as a knife, "that you would treat me so in front of those silly girls! They will think us rude!"

"And so we were," Ian said, "but if you wish to be considered a leman I canna treat you as I would treat an honorable wife."

She gave him a dark look. "And why not? The king treats Rosamund as if she came down from heaven on angel wings."

"Aye. But all know he has a wife and that Rosamund is his leman. He has nothing to prove."

Ciel did not answer. She dressed in her best for the dinner the inn served, but was somber and quiet throughout. Leaving the table, she refused his offered arm and followed him up the stairs in silence. Then, when she blew out the candles and undressed in the dark, she put on her heaviest nightgown and joined him in bed, taking up only a foot on the edge of the wide mattress, lying on her side and presenting a dim view of her back to Ian. He waited for a time, then tugged gently on the soft mass of her silky hair.

"Surely you are not practicing the arts of a leman," he said, his tone injured. "A leman cossets her man always. I want you to please me and make me smile."

Cool amusement spread through her, softening the hurt. She smiled, knowing he couldn't see her face. She sighed, as if deploring another duty to take care of, and crawled from the bed. Standing, barely seen in the light of a rising moon in a dark sky, she removed the heavy nightgown, pulling it off over her head. She could see the bearded face turned toward her and thought she could make out a glisten of teeth, as if he smiled.

"Now, m'lord," she said, quite calmly, "what entertainment appeals to you? I warn you now, I am not known for singing."

"I can sing," Ian replied, startling her. He sat up, taking both pillows and stacking them at the head of the bed so he could lean back comfortably. "I know several songs beloved by our minstrels. Perhaps if I sing them, you will dance for me."

She stared at his dimly seen face and thought a grin was tugging at his mouth. But she had started this, and she felt she should follow it through.

"Then sing," she said, "and I will see if your song tempts me to dance."

This time, she did indeed see a shine of teeth within the beard. "Then I will," he said, and began singing slowly in a rich, pleasant voice, the melody deep and sweet:

Then if the flame of love be true, 'twill ne'er go out,
an' you an' me will love more with ev'ry day that
*   passes.*
An' when our love grows so great an' pure that 'tis
*   seen by all who doubt,*
Then shall we be the envy of all the jealous lads an'
*   lasses.*

His voice died away as if he had swallowed the rest of the song. His eyes were on Ciel, who was circling and swaying, a lovely, curved body in the growing moonlight, her movements as graceful as a soaring bird, her arms outspread, her breasts taut and gleaming, her head thrown back and the black hair sweeping around her as she twirled.

Ian was out of the bed and reaching for her, picking her up and turning back to the glisten of white sheets, the warmth of wool blankets. Her flesh was cool, for the night was cold, but when he fastened his mouth on hers he felt the heat of her passion, the warmth of her love.

"My woman," he whispered, laying her down again in the muddle of blankets and sheets, "my darling wife. I will love you forever."

"And I you," Ciel whispered, and circled his neck with her arms. "Let me show you . . . let me be your woman now. There are things I want to do . . ."

"Then show me." He lay back again, feeling the heat of the slender body lying atop him, the soft, wet mouth touching his closed eyes, his ears, the flat nipples on his chest. She was like a flame traveling his body, finding the places that she could touch and kiss and give him pleasure. Each time she found a place that increased the heat of his hands and body, made him groan, made him tremble, she told herself to remember it. This was the power she wanted. He had shown her his power and now she needed her own. But even so, she was nearly crazy with her own desire, her consuming passion. She was on the edge of begging when he finally took her in a helpless rush that left her limp in a swirl of emotions.

They slept late, rising an hour before noon. They were still tired from the strain of the wedding, of buying clothes in Calais, and the trip over. They decided to stay another night before they began the trip to Belmain. The night was much like the one before, full of passion and delight. Thinking back on the lovemaking they had done together at Stewart Castle, they agreed that it now seemed like the first fumbling efforts from a virginal couple.

"But still," Ian said, stroking the warm, slender body that lay against him, "still 'twas a wonderful thing to me. I thought myself in heaven."

"And I," Ciel agreed, and sighed contentedly, "but we had only begun."

Leaving Dover, staying another night in an inn along the road to London, they saw the church spires of the huge city near noon of the fourth day. They dallied, riding slowly along and seeking views of the gardens and the young animals sporting in the fields. Here in the south of England the weather was lovely, soft and warm, with the scent of early roses rising from thorny thickets along the roads.

Once in the city they went at once to the Tower. The chamberlain greeted them, motioned to servants to take in their possessions, then took them along to a room on the gallery.

The chamberlain was an old man, devoted to the king and trustful with Ian. He spoke at once of the king's unhappiness and his wish to have the ordeal of the pope's sentence over.

"Not even Rosamund," the chamberlain said, "can bring his good nature to the fore. He mourns."

"Mourns?" Ian asked, puzzled. "For whom?"

"For à Becket," the old man said, ushering them into their room. "For his friend. 'Twas only the archbishop's overweening pride in his new position that brought on his disobedience to the throne. Few know that, Lord Ian. Our king loved him like a brother. 'Twas all a mistake.''

"That last I knew," Ian said wonderingly. "But I did not know they were close friends. 'Tis more of a pity than I thought.'' He looked down at Ciel's serious expression as the old man left and touched her cheek lingeringly.

"In some way," he said to her, "I must see him through his sorrow and doubt. He is a strong man.''

"Yes," Ciel said, "you must. He is strong—but he is also in his late years. You must be strong enough for both of you when the time comes.''

"And I will. Are you content to stay alone in this room while I meet with the king, or should I ask the chamberlain for a maid to join you? The king may keep me late.''

Ciel glanced around the luxurious room and smiled wryly. "I am content, m'lord. I need no one to keep my spirits up.''

But when the chamberlain brought servants with laden trays of food, the young and beautiful Rosamund accompanied them. Coming into the room, Rosamund smiled at Ciel and came to kiss her cheek.

"I have been lonely for a woman friend," she said frankly. "And a bit of gossip. The king is sad and morose. I am very glad you are here." She stood back and looked at Ciel's gown. "How beautiful! I have heard of the painted flowers, but this is the first I have seen. I must ask for a new gown." She smiled and added: "But not at this time, Lady Stewart. My dearest Henry is sunk in gloom and foreboding. I shall comfort him instead of asking for a present. Come, now. The food is steaming and good.''

Lady Stewart. Uncomfortable, Ciel glanced away and saw the servants leaving the room, closing the door. She turned back to Rosamund. "I have no noble blood, my lady."

Rosamund shrugged. "Nor I. But I am loved." She laughed a little, turning toward the laden table. "And I would say you are too. 'Tis better than a title. But I will confess I thought Lord Ian had married you."

Surprised by the words, Ciel silently followed the graceful figure to the table and the comfortable chairs placed beside it. Dishes held early spring berries, tart but fresh and juicy, jellied preserves, fresh bread and roast lamb, and greens cooked with herbs for flavor. They looked at each other and smiled. Two women alone needn't pretend to merely pick at the food—and they were both hungry. They ate, and spoke little, only to mention a flavor or recommend a tender piece of the meat. They sighed with repletion at the end and leaned back in their chairs when the servants came to take away the dishes.

Ciel noted the respect the servants gave to Rosamund. They knew who she was, and they knew why she was here, and the king's own aura of power wreathed Rosamund's slender shoulders like an impenetrable cloud. She was fully protected by what they knew. When the servants shut the door behind them, Ciel turned to the king's favorite again.

"You were right, Lady Rosamund. Lord Ian did marry me, I suppose for the sake of my father's pride. But I do not intend to bruit it about—for I will not pretend to be of noble blood."

Rosamund smiled. " 'Twould make no difference to the Scots, dear Ciel. Few lairds look for noble blood to wed, for noble blood at times runs thin and lazy. And the Scots call their laird a king in many ways—and his bride the queen of the castle. 'Tis not a prancing, primping world like the French nobility, nor even so fancy and foolish as our English nobles who brag of their superior blood but have shed none for their homeland. As our king has said, the common men who fight for England are worth far more than the mincing fashionplates in court.''

Ciel was silent, staring at the shaft of light from the setting sun that brightened the cozy room, turning the age dimmed rug to a rich crimson at their feet. Then she spoke slowly. ''I see I have been foolish and stubborn. My family—and Ian's—told me the same thing, but I thought they said it only to persuade me. I was wrong.'' She turned to Rosamund and smiled, her face brilliantly happy. ''Then I too will be called a lady—the lady of the king's man. And I will be as proud as any in the court.''

22

Two days later a party assembled in the courtyard of the Tower. Lord Ian Stewart, the king's
man, Lady Ciel Stewart, his bride, and four
husky men-at-arms, sent by King Henry II to travel with
them. Ian had objected when he saw them, saying nothing to the men, but going back into the Tower to tell the
king that he and his wife would be safe enough in England to ride alone.

"We will not take that chance," the king said flatly.
"Soon I will need you—and my enemies know it." He
had smiled, a small ghost of his usual hearty grin, and
added, "I am dependent on you for my courage now,
Lord Ian. I fear for my life."

Ian left the king's room with a feeling of pity. It
seemed that Henry had lost all when he put Eleanor from
him. He had four sons, and only one of them showed
any concern for him—and that was the young king,
Henry III, a weak, easily frightened boy, who gave his
father affection but still went secretly to his mother,
Queen Eleanor, for advice. The power and glory of the
English throne had been shattered by the war between
the royal couple.

Coming down the flight of stone steps and into the

cool, sweetly perfumed air of mid-May, Ian looked up and saw Ciel, gowned in dark-red silk and wearing a dark-blue hooded cloak. She was seated on Devil's back, watching her husband come down the steps. He saw the worry in her eyes and smiled at her quickly. She gave a little nod and smiled back, relieved.

"I was frightened," she said later as they rode side by side through the gates, "because of these men. Why are they here?"

"To protect us," Ian said, "though we don't need it. Were we alone, no one would notice us—the king's man is never recognized, for all eyes go to the king. But I canna convince him of that."

"I see. So we must be protected. Where will we stop on this first day?"

"At one of the few wooden castles Henry didn't burn when he became king. There is a grateful, elderly baron there who will make us comfortable."

"Oh? Have you been there before?"

"Often. There is commerce between that baron and Belmain. We often send his wool along with ours when it goes to Flanders, and it saves him half. He is more than friendly."

"And then?"

Ian laughed. "Must you know all? Next we come to one of Henry's favorite towns: Winchester, where he built the first of his courts of law. There is a fine but small castle there, with well-trained servants, and we are welcome to use it."

"Then we will be royally treated. How many days follow before we reach Belmain?"

"Two. We will stay at an inn in Petersfield, then rise early and have breakfast in a small town called Haslemere, and that afternoon we will be in Belmain.'' He smiled down at her. '' 'Tis as beautiful as a fairy tale, my love, and the castle staff will welcome us as if we were a king and his queen. The days we spend there will fly by like the wind.''

Ciel laughed, tossing back her ebony hair, looking up at the soft blue sky with happiness shining in her eyes. ''Then this Belmain must be an enchanted place, my love. Suitable indeed for lovers.''

On the fourth day, following a worn path on a high green meadow full of lazy sheep, the men-at-arms from the Tower in London, riding guard around Lord and Lady Stewart, topped a smooth rise and looked down at the castle of Belmain. None of the party except Ian had ever seen it before. A deep ripple of admiration ran through the men. And Ciel's turquoise eyes widened, glanced at Ian, and then were drawn back—back down the slopes of thickly forested land, ribboned by a net of winding brooks shining like silver, to a lush green valley and a small, purling river in the distance. And there, built in the center of the valley, was a small but beautiful castle, its pink ashlar walls touched and warmed by the afternoon sun, its turrets gleaming, its many blue banners rippling a joyous welcome in an errant breeze.

Ciel shook her shining head in wonder, nearly dislodging the band of chased silver set with jewels that she wore to keep her hair from blowing around her face. ''There is no place as beautiful as this. 'Tis a dream only. I will wake up soon.''

'' 'Tis all true,'' Ian said, smiling, ''though it always surprises me with its beauty. Once away from it, one forgets. But come. They have seen us, and the gates are opening.''

Ciel was silent all the way down. The paths were steep, but not too steep for a horse, so it wasn't the hillside that kept her from talking. She was simply amazed, finding it all too much to believe. And the feeling grew as she came closer.

Finally she spoke. "They are letting down the drawbridge and raising the portcullis. How can they know who we are at this distance?"

Ian laughed. "They do not see our faces, my love. But they know the king's livery. Until my sister claimed Belmain many years ago, King Henry had taken it for his own. And even now the men there are used to seeing his men-at-arms ride in, for Thor never traveled here without them. Our king takes good care of his protectors.''

Ciel lifted her chin. "As he should," she said, and looked at Ian with pride. "He has the best."

Then they were on the level road that led to the castle, and there were men-at-arms coming out to line the drawbridge as an honor guard. Ciel straightened her already straight back and nodded to them pleasantly as she passed.

Two men, one elderly and one young and large, stood on the steps of the keep. "The thin, white-haired one," Ian said quietly, lifting Ciel from her saddle, "is the seneschal, Cedric Wye. The other, as you can see from his robes, is a priest. I have never met him, though I was told old Benet had died last year. Come, I will present them to you."

"Lord Ian!" Cedric Wye's wrinkled face broke into smiles. "I should have known you by your size. There are few so tall.'' He extended a hand and Ian took it, turning to Ciel.

"I present to you Cedric Wye, the seneschal of Belmain, my lady. A man long trusted and admired by our family."

Ciel nodded, smiling, and Wye bowed deeply. "I am honored, Lady Stewart." He turned and brought the young, heavily muscled priest forward. "And, this is our new priest, Father Boise de Hebert, who arrived yesterday from France."

The priest stepped forward quickly, took Ciel's hand, and kissed it. Then he turned to Ian and bowed, smiling as his quick eyes measured Ian's height and weight, widening as he stared. Watching, Ciel saw a familiar flicker in the priest's eyes, a measuring look she had seen in the eyes of knights who vied with Ian in the tournament. But then she put it aside. The priest was a large, strong man, and before he took his vows he might well have been a man proud of his strength. He was smiling now and speaking courteously to Ian.

"Indeed I am at your service, my lord, and will be happy to see you and your lady in chapel." He spoke in French, and bowed again to them both, his black eyes traveling over Ciel warmly. "How long a stay can we hope for? It is pleasant indeed to have visitors from the Stewart family."

Ian smiled, though his eyes stayed cool. Watching him, Ciel felt his doubts. She was suddenly sure that Ian had found a trait he didn't like in the tall young priest. But she was not willing to worry about it. Surely the seneschal would speak to the priest about his forward manner, and as far as his too-friendly behavior, the new priest would soon remember his duties and dignity. If not, Ian would speak to him.

The housekeeper, an old but tall and strong-looking woman, stepped forward from the rear of the great hall as they came in. She acknowledged Ian's grin with a smile of her own and came to them.

"The solar is ready for you, Lord Ian, and your bride. And we are preparing a feast in honor of your marriage." She turned from Ian and looked down at Ciel, her broad face kind and gentle. "I am Blanche, my lady. May I send a maid to help you unpack?"

Ciel smiled, startled. "Why, yes! I would like that."

"Then it is done. I will send you Edda. She is clean and careful with other's possessions." Excited, Blanche hurried off. Ciel looked up at Ian, wondering if he would think her lazy for wanting help.

"I thought it wise to agree," she said. "I have found that many of the ladies in the court have a maid to gossip with, and in turn the maids listen to other maids and soon you know all there is to know about the place . . ." She hesitated, taken aback by the grin on Ian's face. "Am I wrong, m'lord?"

"Indeed not. 'Tis the maids in this world who bring the news and spread it about. My sister will give you lessons on how to extract the real truth from a shy servant . . ." He laughed and caught her hand, bringing it to his lips. "And you should have a maid, if only to brush your beautiful hair. If this one suits you, we will take her home with us if she wishes to go."

That night in the solar, lying together in the great bed after their lovemaking, they talked of the future. Ian was open with her, saying that while their home would al-

ways be Stewart Castle, they would often be in London
or in Aquitaine and Normandy.

"A king's man is always traveling, and it brings in
many favors. Not only the king is generous to me, for
there are always men fawning upon the king's man and
giving him gifts of gold and silver. They know he trusts
me, so they wish to have me as a friend."

Curled in his arms, Ciel listened and took in his
words. Every day she felt more in love with him, and
more in awe of what he was and of the trust the king
had in him. She burned to help him, though she could
think of nothing she could do. She was a strong woman
despite her size, but no match for a grown man. Her
heart full, she put an arm across him and slept.

They discovered a feeling about Belmain that was almost like a dream. It was as if they fashioned it while
they slept and wakened to climb dream paths that led
upward to the high pastures, to drink the cold, bubbling
water of the brooks that leaped down into crystalline
pools, filling them to the brim, then played and leaped
again, to the next pool below. There was no level spot
on the sides of the hills that didn't contain at least one
pool.

At first they had ridden the paths and enjoyed the
scent of blossoming wild roses. They visited the arbors
of ripening grapes, the fields of plums and apples and
berries. But after the first two days, they left the horses
in the stables and climbed the paths themselves, eating
the ripening fruit, drinking from the pools, and, finally,
throwing off their clothes and braving the chilly water
for a bath. They laughed and swam, held each other and
kissed while their teeth chattered. And they were caught

one day stark naked and in a deep, cold pool by the new priest.

He had appeared silently, his big shoulders straining the black cassock, his silver and gold crucifix on a silver chain around his neck, and his bearded face sly and triumphant within his hood, as if he had found something he had been searching for. Ciel saw him first, for she faced that way. She turned her back at once and whispered his name to Ian. Ian turned, looked up at the bank, and was immediately furious.

"So, Father de Hebert, you follow and spy on us! For a priest, that seems indeed a sinful weakness. Get you back to the castle!"

Ian could hear Ciel's shuddering gasps behind him, and his temper rose even hotter when de Hebert stood still, gazing at him defiantly. He surged through the water and climbed the sloping side of the pool, a huge and naked warrior. "Go, false priest," he growled, "or take a beating!"

De Hebert's gaze swept the sides of the pool and stopped for an instant on the pile of clothes on the other side. Then his right hand slipped smoothly through a slit in his flowing black robes and came out again, holding a long, slim dagger. He smiled slowly at Ian.

"Now," he said softly, "the king's man dies. And I will be rewarded with the alluring body of his wife to play with for a time. I will truly be repaid for doing my duty."

He threw back his head, laughed, and leaped forward, knife held high to thrust into Ian's broad, naked chest. But Ian leaped toward him at the same moment, and his hands shot out and flickered in the air, grasping the priest's thick arms. De Hebert sailed over Ian's head like a huge black bird, coming down with a tremendous splash in the center of the pool. Ciel leaped for the other side and her gown, pulling it over her head and down her wet and shaking body, then whirling to look at the struggle. Her eyes widened, her hand came to her mouth to hold back a shriek.

Ian had de Hebert's knife in one hand and was using the other to keep the man's face under water. The rest of de Hebert was under Ian's crouched body, frantically fighting the superior weight and muscle, but drowning, drowning now, this very minute, sending up his last breath in a wavering column of silver bubbles growing smaller and smaller and then gone. Horrified, Ciel looked once at Ian's face and then away, swallowing. A wolf. His eyes as cold and clear as winter ice.

Afterward, Ian dressed quickly and they left the pool to sit and dry themselves on sunlit rocks along the path. They didn't speak of what had happened until they were on their way to the castle, and even then Ian cautioned her to silence.

"I wondered," he said, "when I first saw the man. He was not like a priest. Yet I canna believe the church would send a murderer to kill me just to make Henry easier to capture. And I doubt the pope had anything to do with it. Likely de Hebert was one of the London murderers Henry had defrocked. I have heard they banded together."

When she said nothing, but only wiped her eyes, he took her hand and held it. "I know how you feel, my dear love. But if I let him go, he would try again, and he would be much more careful. It was not an easy death, but better than hanging. A shepherd or serf will find his body and think he fell in and drowned. He will be given a Christian burial.''

Ciel nodded silently. She was sure he was right. She was, she told herself, glad of Ian's skills. Glad of his training. And most of all, glad he was alive. But she wanted very much to forget the look on his face when he knelt on de Hebert's chest and watched him drown.

At the castle that evening Ciel waited tensely to hear someone mention the absence of the priest. And at the time of evening matins she heard one of the kitchen workers ask Blanche where the priest was and should she simply enter the small chapel alone and pray for her sick mother. Blanche gave her permission to do so, saying that Father de Hebert had been called to the deathbed of one of the older sheepmen and would stay with him until he was gone.

Relieved, Ciel took that news to Ian, who was speaking to Cedric Wye in the great hall. She waited until they had finished the accounting of the first spring shipping of wool to Flanders and then joined them.

Ian turned toward her, smiling but with a look of warning in his eyes. ''Our seneschal has entreated me to take the family share of the wool profits to London and see that they are banked. He also reports that our wool this year is more plentiful than ever, and the prices good. He does not want a fortune in gold here in the castle, where some brigand might steal it all.''

''I see,'' Ciel said, and smiled at Wye. '' 'Twould be a real temptation even to an honest worker, I would say.''

Wye nodded eagerly. ''True! And with Lord Ian going to London soon, with four of the king's men-at-arms riding with him, 'tis what you might call a golden opportunity! I would feel better with the load in the London bank.''

''And I,'' Ian said slowly, ''have a feeling now that our king—alone in the London Tower—may also be in danger. Ciel and I will leave tomorrow.''

Ciel felt a wave of great relief and turned away to hide it. Beautiful though it was, she wanted to leave Belmain. There was a scene fresh in her mind that she hoped to cover over with new views. But still she managed to put a bit of disappointment into her soft voice when she spoke.

''If you feel we must, my dear lord, I will begin the packing.'' She turned and looked at Wye. ''If I take Edda with me, will I be putting you out? She is willing to go, and she suits me well.''

''Why, not at all, my lady. Edda will do well with you, and we have no trouble here finding maids.''

Ciel smiled at him and then at Ian, who looked dumbfounded. ''I will vouch for her, Ian. She is a good maid, and clever. You'll not regret it.''

''I am sure you are right,'' Ian said as they walked away. ''But to save my life, I canna remember which one is Edda.''

''Edda,'' Ciel said calmly, ''has bright red hair, a quick laugh, and disappears like a wizard when she sees a man. But she's a wonderful lady's maid.''

23

 "We'll not go tomorrow," Ian said that night. He and Ciel were alone, sitting together in the southern embrasure before going to bed and watching the brilliant stars come out in a black sky. "We'll stay until the priest is found and declared a victim of drowning. We'll not give the church another puzzle to discover, nor give our seneschal even a remote suspicion as to his death."

"Our seneschal will not suspect us, Ian. The false priest told Blanche he was on his way to a dying worker and would stay until his death, no matter how long. Clearly he meant to leave here as soon as he managed to kill you, and 'twould be necessary, of course, to kill me also. Then he'd be gone."

"Ah! The man had much too much confidence in himself. Still, he suffered little. It was over in only a few minutes. He will find more time and punishment given to him in hell."

Ciel winced. "Thank God 'tis over," she said. "He is now in the devil's hands. And in the early morning, when the workers bring in the ripening grapes, they will discover his body. That is the path they take."

"True. I had forgotten." He dropped into silence,

staring out again at the starlit sky, the faintly silvered treetops and the narrow, gleaming ribbons of brooks on the hillsides. Then, after a few moments of thinking back, he added: "I do not believe that Pope Alexander sent the man to kill me. The pope believes the king, but feels he should be punished for the rash words that sent his magnates to rid him of the archbishop. He has never mentioned death."

Ciel sat forward. "What are you saying? Could that be true? Would a priest dare to take your life and pretend it was his superior who sent him to do so?"

"No, no priest would do that. But 'twould be sensible if the false priests who wish to kill the king would first kill the king's man. And that, I believe, is what happened. The defrocked priests will not want the punishment to be less than death for Henry. They are all hardened criminals, without a care for their afterlife. Nor do they love the king's laws."

"I see." Ciel's heart was beating rapidly, but she tried to hide it. "How many of these criminal priests are there, m'lord?"

"Not all of them have stayed in Canterbury," Ian answered. "Some have been bored, and have willingly gone back to their trade and are no doubt happy in it, pilfering purses and murdering for money. But there will be some who will come to see the king take his punishment, if they are allowed to enter."

Ciel was silent, watching his calm, thoughtful eyes, thinking of that scene at the pool. No one man could ever take him, she thought, but half a dozen might.

"You must take others with you," she said. "Men you trust."

He looked at her and smiled. "I will. I will have an

honor guard—and I shall pick each and every man." He stood and reached down for her, picking her up and stepping down from the embrasure. "But for tonight I mean to forget my worries while you, my sweet Ciel, give me the kind of love that makes my bed a heaven."

Her arms around his neck, she smiled at him enchantingly. "Naturally. After all, I was named for the blue sky that contains the true heaven. Like every woman who truly loves, I want to give all of me to you."

He stopped on the way to their bed and looked at her. He knew she was teasing, yet he could see the tenderness in her eyes. "All, my dear wife? Love and faith and trust? 'Tis a hard promise."

"Yet I make it, m'lord. And I mean it. My life and my pride lie in your arms."

"Safely," Ian said, and hugged her close. "Safe and warm. No one will hurt you; no one will bring trouble and trials to you. You are my heart."

They had come through a fire that day, Ciel thought, and they both felt it. When Ian eased her down on the wide bed, she felt his trembling passion, the aroused heat of him, the growing ardor. She knew he needed her love to take him past the memory of death, the sorrow of having to kill. She reached up and put her arms around him, pulling him down to her parted lips, wanting the thrust of his tongue, that warm, wet promise of true mating. When it came she shivered with delight and felt her breasts tighten, the small nipples drawing into hard peaks. Desire took her over; she felt her thighs widen the space between them, her hips rising . . . and then she heard a strangled oath.

"By the gods, you tempt me to tear off your clothes! Get them off, m'lady, or see them torn."

Laughing, she wriggled away from him to stand beside the bed. In minutes she was bare, and stepping away
from a puddle of silk and muslin. Fast as she was, she
was no faster than he who had kicked off his boots, flung
his tunic on the floor, and let his chausses drop. He
picked her up like a baby in his arms and fell into bed
laughing.

"And now, temptress, we shall see which of us will
beg for more."

She laughed with joy, twisting away from him, rising
to her knees and bending over him, shadowing both
faces with her shining black hair.

" 'Twill be me, my dear lord. I am hungry for you."
She began kissing him, her lips moving over his hard
face, her tongue nudging his lips apart and then moving
to his ears, to his neck, and just as he thought he might
suffocate from passion she was gone, moving down to
explore with soft, inquisitive hands that paused and lin-
gered when he moaned with pleasure.

Amazed, Ian lay still, nearly afraid to move for fear
she would stop. But she had given him all her confidence
now; he felt the bonds of her shyness loosening, giving
her the freedom of her desire. And he felt the smoothness of her palms, the tender touch of her warm lips on
his body, the sleek warm fountain of her silky hair swirling on his belly. He trembled, his huge body in thrall to
her small hands, her soft mouth.

"Ciel . . ."

She murmured an endearment and moved on, her slim
fingers stroking the sleek, tight skin of his shaft, then
taking the taut sacs below into her palms. He heard her
whispering, and made out a few words: ". . . fearfully
and wonderfully made is man, and these—these cradle

the seeds of great warriors." Ian reached down and grasped her shoulders, dragging her up his body. When her face was above his, he let go and wrapped his arms around her.

"Now take me inside you," he said hoarsely, "and I will give you a warrior to raise."

Her eyes were huge and dark, the pupils so large that only a rim of clear turquoise remained. Still she smiled and kissed him, licking his lips open and tantalizing his tongue. "Then I will, my lord. I am fit to burst with wanting . . . but still I think you should overcome me."

He rolled them over with a growl and thrust into her hot and throbbing body. She laughed and then gasped, and gasped again, winding her slender legs around him. "Oh, yes . . . yes, my darling, yes, my dear lord . . . like that . . ."

Ian had purposefully set the time of leaving at first light. He would have it that they made Petersfield long before dark, for now they carried gold. It had been portioned out in bags and slung over every horse, except for the small, quick little mare ridden by Edda. Ian had taken time to talk to her as they readied the train for the trip, and he told Ciel later that the girl seemed both intelligent and thrilled by the chance to become a lady's maid.

"She rides well," he ended, "and is not afraid. She is only unused to men."

"I knows she stays away from men," Ciel said slowly, "but I do not know why. Some day when she has learned to trust me I shall ask her."

They were ready to mount when the first of the serfs who brought in the grapes arrived, dragging a litter with

the body of the drowned priest laid on it, hands folded
over his chest. Shocked and sorry, everyone came out
from the castle to view the body and to make the sign
of the cross over it.

"On his way to heal the ill," lamented the man who
found him, "and a misstep took his own life. 'Tis sad,
but God knows the hour of every man's death, and no
doubt Father de Hebert is with his God now."

There was a swelling of low-voiced agreement, but
Cedric Wye, his face alive with doubt, spoke softly to
Ian.

"I had meant to speak to you of that priest," he murmured. "He seemed no priest to me. What say you?"

Ian nodded slowly. "Much the same, seneschal. But
if he was priest or pretender he is neither now. I will
send you a gentle and well-mannered priest to take his
place."

Wye nodded, relieved. "Then I thank you. I had many
doubts about this one, though certainly I never wished
him dead by accident."

Ciel, listening, shook her head. She took Devil's reins
from one of the king's men-at-arms and mounted. Then
she turned and looked at the maid she had come to like,
and saw that Edda had mounted and turned away from
the sight of the dead priest. Ciel moved to her side and
saw that her face was white, her eyes fearful.

"Don't be frightened," Ciel said comfortingly.
"Death comes to all, but your death is far in the future.
You will be cared for and happy in your new home."

Edda's round and freckled face twisted with anguish.
"But 'tis not my own death I fear, my lady. I wished
the priest dead! And I feel guilt now. God will punish
me, I know."

"His death," Ciel said firmly, "had nothing to do with your wishes. If all of us could wish those we dislike into death, few of us would be alive." She saw Edda's green eyes blink and a tinge of color coming back to her cheeks as she took that in. Then Ciel added: "Now let us lead off and get these hesitant men started to London."

Edda straightened her plump body in her saddle and nodded. "Yes, m'lady. I will do as you say."

The day was bright, the horses fresh, and the riders anxious to cover ground. They came into Petersfield in late afternoon, hungry but proud of their ride. Ian went to each of the men as they dismounted and made sure they carried the bags of gold into the inn and into a guarded room.

"If the bags get to London still unopened, each of you will earn a fee of five sovereigns, over and above your pay. But if opened, 'twill be your neck."

The four men-at-arms grinned and nodded, hoisting the bags and taking them along to the room, which would be guarded by one and then another while they ate their dinners. And for the night, all four of them slept beside the bags. Five sovereigns meant a fortune to them, and they had no wish to swing on a gibbet for trying to steal more.

Edda followed Ciel like a puppy, carrying their clothes while Ciel, knowing Ian's strength, handed him her bag of gold to carry with his own. He grinned at her.

"A heavy load," he said, "can make a heart light. Aylena will be pleased."

They were all anxious to have the trip over. Ian ordered food prepared to take with them, and they ate as they rode the next morning. Until the towers of Winchester Castle reared before them, gleaming in the golden light of evening, they had not stopped except for a quick trip into woods or behind a hedge.

Edda's eyes widened as she saw the guard bow to Ian and rush to open the gates and let them in. She turned to Ciel and whispered a question.

"We are to stay in the king's own castle, m'lady?"

Ciel smiled. "Lord Ian is the king's man, Edda. He is welcome in any of the residences the king uses. We will be treated as honored guests."

" 'Tis past belief! Never did I expect to put foot in a royal castle. How glad I am you chose me for your maid!"

Laughing, Ciel rode through the gates with her wide-eyed companion. "I, like you, would not have believed such luxury possible for me. We have both been surprised by fate."

Ian turned his horse and waited for Ciel inside the gates. When she looked at him, she knew at once that he had something pleasant to say, for he smiled at them both.

"You see the huge cathedral down there in the town? That is where Thor and Aylena married, some seventeen years past. I remember it well, for I stood with Thor and held the ring. Now, come have a good supper and a good night's sleep without worry. We are safe here."

The next night was spent at the Baron Tunbridge's wooden castle, and the baron's news included an attempt made by a false priest to enter the Tower and kill the king.

"But the men-at-arms were suspicious," he concluded, "and they captured him when he tried to enter the king's rooms. I understand he has been burned at the stake as a warning.''

''Then I am needed now,'' Ian said flatly. His face was hard and still, his eyes an angry, burning blue. ''We will leave early for London.''

Edda, who had joined the kitchen help and was helping to serve, looked at him and then stole a glance at her mistress. Later, while brushing Ciel's windblown hair, she spoke of it. ''I saw naught but anger in Lord Ian's face,'' she said, ''and naught but fear in yours, m'lady. Give your lord his due. The king's man will win against the murderers.''

Ciel felt helpless, full of fear. Ashamed of herself, she made herself smile. She remembered too well the dark halls of the Tower, the prisoners in the cells below, the many priests who came and went, ministering to them. Too many to watch, she thought, and the robes of a priest could hide the black heart of a murderer. That much she had learned at Belmain . . .

''Good advice, Edda,'' she said ruefully. ''Now to make myself take it. The trial approaches, both for King Henry and for my husband, for he is sworn to uphold him. I hope the pope will be lenient on our sorrowful king.''

Edda nodded. ''And I. Will we be allowed to go as witnesses to the trial, m'lady?''

''Oh, no. This punishment of the king will be carried out in private, I am sure.''

''Why, m'lady? Isn't it supposed to be public?''

Slowly Ciel's hand moved up and took the brush from Edda's swooping strokes. Then she turned to look up at her. ''Now that I think of it, Edda, you are right. All church punishment is done in the presence of priests, important laymen, and family members, so they can swear it was carried out. I will bring that to the attention of my husband.''

The sun was setting the next day as they rode across London's bridge and into the city. Now Edda rode in the van, taking directions from the low but distinct voice of Lord Ian. All of the bags were now on the strong backs of Rogue and Devil, and the four men-at-arms rode a close square around them, their weapons at the ready. Turning to the east, they proceeded at a fair pace toward the Tower without a word said.

When they came to the iron gates, the gatekeeper rushed to let them in and called ostlers to take their horses. They all dismounted, and the men-at-arms carried the bags of gold into the Tower and to the double-locked, steel door that led to the treasury. The king's chamberlain let them in and locked the door again when they came out. Then they went back in the soft summer twilight to carry in the baggage, left on the stone steps by the ostlers.

Ciel sighed with relief, picking up her smaller bundles herself and smiling at Edda, who had helped with the gold and was overwhelmed by what she had seen inside the Tower. ''Now we will have a warm bath and clean, soft beds. 'Tis better by far than traveling.''

''Indeed, m'lady. 'Tis a wonderful, magical place, like a fairy tale inside these walls! But as guarded as a prison.''

''Not for us, Edda. We can come and go as we wish. You will surely see more of London before we go back to our home.''

Beside them, Ian was listening to the man who had let them in.

"Thank God you are here," the gatekeeper was saying. "There has been an attempt to kill the king while you were gone."

"I heard," Ian said tersely. "How did the man get in?"

The gatekeeper winced. " 'Twas my fault indeed. He killed one of the Tower priests, m'lord, and dressed in his black habit. I recognized the clothes that evening and didn't bother to make him push back his hood. I am lucky to be free."

"You are indeed," Ian said, surprised. "Our king does not overlook carelessness."

"And I was shamed, m'lord! I confessed at once, and expected a lashing and a prison cell for a good long time, but the worst that happened to me was two days on bread and water, and the promise of a gibbet did it happen again."

Ian laughed. "Then surely his heart grows softer."

The gatekeeper laughed with him, but added: "Not for the false priest who came in to murder him, m'lord. That one burned at the stake."

"Well enough. One less to get rid of, then." Ian turned away, shepherding both Ciel and Edda toward the huge, deeply carved doors that led inside.

The royal chamberlain had seen that the Lady Stewart had found a maid for herself, and he provided a room for her, a few doors away from the room Ian and Ciel shared. Edda was hurrying to it when the door of the solar opened and King Henry stepped out, his hair a vivid red halo in the light from blazing candelabra inside. He hailed Ian with a loud, relieved curse and followed it with complaints.

"By God, Stewart, 'tis time indeed for your return.

This time you stay with me.'' He glanced past Ian and saw the two women behind him. ''Come,'' he added roughly, waving an arm toward his open door. ''I have news for your ears and for no other.'' He slipped in, pulling the door nearly closed, and Ian followed, turning to motion Ciel and Edda on.

Ciel looked at Edda and smiled in relief. ''Our king,'' she said softly, taking Edda's arm and heading for their rooms, ''is usually courteous. But at this time he may be excused for bad manners. Forgive him.''

Edda gazed at her as if she spoke a foreign tongue. ''Forgive him? A king needs no forgiveness, m'lady. He can think and do whatever he wishes. But I am amazed. I never thought a king of England would have hair as red as mine!''

Ciel laughed softly. ''And ten times the temper, I am sure.'' She glanced back at the seneschal and the servants following them with their baggage, to make sure they couldn't hear. ''The king is chafed by his position now. 'Tis as bad as being in prison to him, and I see we must stay until he has his freedom again.''

A smile broke out on Edda's round face. ''I'll not mind, m'lady. This living in castles and being a lady's maid is wonderful to me.''

24

 During the last days of waiting for the pope's decree, Rosamund guided Ciel and Edda to the best of the seamstresses in London. There were many, most of them in the Street of the Weavers. Within the city walls there was a show of Britain's finest architecture and the kingdom's richest shops, which displayed a wealth of jewelry and fabrics—gold, silver, and fabulous cloth that rivaled anything found in other countries—even in Florence, one shopkeeper told them proudly. Ciel needed little more than she already had, for the gowns she had acquired in Calais were of equal value and style to any in London. But Edda was thrilled by new gowns and a fur-lined cloak Ciel insisted on buying for her.

"'Tis far too expensive," Edda said, shocked, "and surely unneeded! I have a woolen cloak."

"You have never seen a Northumberland winter," Ciel answered. "You will be glad enough of the fur." She liked Edda more every day and considered her a confidant. They were often with Rosamund, who was pale and losing strength daily, though she wore a smile in spite of her illness. She confided in Ciel, telling her how lonely she had been.

"I have often wished for a true friend," she said, "but no noblewoman will have aught to do with me. Eleanor still wields a power in England almost as great as that of our king."

"Indeed, I have seen it," Ciel agreed. "And now even the young king has left the company of his father. Perhaps he too is in Aquitaine."

Rosamund nodded but, since they were entering the gates to the Tower, said no more. Ciel's thoughts went on, and that night as she and Ian were dropping into sleep, she remembered it and turned in the circle of Ian's thick arm to speak of it.

"Where is the young king?"

Ian pulled her closer to his warm and massive body. "With the rest of the family, waiting for the end."

Ciel rested her cheek over his heart, feeling the strong, steady beat. "The end? Well, yes, I understand. The end of the waiting, the worry, and, the worst of it—their father's public punishment from Pope Alexander. But I had hoped Henry III would stay here with his father as a comfort to him."

"The boy lacks the strength of will to go against his mother. She rules her children." Ian was silent a moment, and then added: "You spoke of public punishment. I hope you are not planning to attend."

"It seems to me," Ciel said slowly into the darkness, "that some of those present should be friends of the king, wherever the punishment occurs. I doubt if many will go. To be close to the king now is a dangerous position, yet none could expect the king's man and his wife to be against him."

There was a silence. Then Ian spoke heavily. "In

ways you are right, my love. But your safety is more important to me than anything else. I forbid you to go."

Slowly Ciel spoke again. "Ian, listen to me. Rosamund is my good friend, and she will ask me to accompany her that day. Can you not trust the king's men who will be watching over her? She will be safe with them, and so would I."

"No. Nor do I wish to hear more of this!"

Ciel settled down to sleep, irritated but not conquered. Vincennes Valoir often had felt forced to forbid her from taking a path he didn't approve of. She had learned a woman could not convince a man against his will . . .

Ten days went by, and the clear weather disappeared. Fog set in, dismal and gray, cloaking the church spires and even hiding the walls around the Tower. From any window looking south there was nothing to see but thick fog hanging over the Thames, and other views offered even less. The men ignored it and went about their various duties, riding out in twos and threes for safety against unseen thieves. But the women, who seldom had any necessary errands, grew restless.

Rosamund, coming into Ciel's small sitting room on the sixth day of heavy fog, was pale and unsmiling. She sat down in a chair beside Ciel and again motioned Edda away. Edda went quietly from the room and shut the door. Her glance at Ciel as she left plainly said she realized the visit must be of great importance.

Ciel sensed it. She had been sewing, but now she put it aside and gave her full attention to Rosamund.

"The king," Rosamund said quietly, "has the message from Pope Alexander. The pope requires that Henry must receive the same beating in front of the altar at Canterbury as the Archbishop Thomas à Becket received from the king's magnates." She paused and looked straight into Ciel's eyes. "He has added that the beating is to be seen by as many of his subjects who wish to see it, and that the beating must be hard, though he has also added that it must stop well short of death."

Ciel let out her held breath. " 'Tis monstrous, Rosamund! Our king never ordered that beating for Thomas à Becket, nor do I believe his magnates meant to kill the archbishop. I think it wrong to beat our king like some common criminal!"

"And I," Rosamund answered. "But Henry has agreed to it. I think this long, miserable time of waiting has made him willing to undergo anything that would put it behind him, so he can return to governing this stubborn England."

She rose from her chair, and as she did so she seemed to waver, catching herself with a slender hand against the wall. "No one," she went on, "has ever realized what Henry has done for this country. His laws and his courts of true justice will someday be praised to the skies. But I doubt he will hear it. If he lives through this, Eleanor and his sons will be his death . . ."

"Don't say it!" Ciel went to her and put an arm around her thin waist. "Never think it! He has real friends—men who would die for him. And he is a man of great strength and will! Somehow he will come through this horrible plot."

Rosamund looked at her with brimming eyes. "I dare to hope that he will. And I want to be near when 'tis over, to comfort him. Will you . . . can you travel with me to Canterbury?"

Ciel held the small, thin body close. "I will, Rosamund. I will be with you and help you all I can. But you must not mention that when Ian is nigh. He has said I cannot see the king take his punishment.''

"Oh, Ciel! He may beat you if you disobey him.''

"If he does, I will accept it. He'll not beat me hard. I must go with you, for you need me.''

'"And indeed I do. You are a true friend, and it will be our secret. I will hire men and horses for us.''

Ciel nodded. "Yes, though I must tell Edda. She will help me hide my absence.''

"If only this could change England back to what it was afore that overweening woman tried to take all of it away from Henry . . .'' Rosamund coughed and tried to speak again, then failed, overcome by the coughing. Her hand servant, a plump older woman, came quickly along the hall and took her arm.

"Come, m'lady. You need your rest.'' Without a glance at Ciel, the woman grasped Rosamund's arm and took her away, speaking to her in a low, complaining tone.

Ciel saw that the door to Edda's room stood open. She whisked down the hall, stepped in, and shut the door, her face white with fear and foreboding. Edda, sitting at the window and repairing a split in one of her petticoats, jumped to her feet and offered Ciel the chair. Ciel shook her head, her turquoise eyes glittering and wild.

"You look as if you have done something wrong, and hope to get away with it,'' Edda said. "Whatever could it be?''

Ciel laughed without humor, catching her breath as if she had been running. Then she quieted and took the chair, running her fingers through her thick, tousled black hair. "I have promised to accompany Rosamund to Canterbury Cathedral, to view the punishment to be given to King Henry." She was facing the window but now she turned and stared into Edda's astounded eyes. "They are going to beat our king! The same way, it is said, as the archbishop was beaten. Fortunately, Rosamund doesn't know how that beating was done. Our king will be forced to kneel at the altar and allow the monks of Canterbury to scourge his bare back with whips."

"No! May the blessed Virgin Mary take away his pain! A king should not have to suffer such insults."

"But he will. Rosamund says he has agreed to the pope's terms and is anxious to have it over with."

Edda sighed. Her usually pink and smiling face now was as white and frightened as Ciel's. "When I saw the Lady Rosamund come through our door, I was afraid of trouble. Lord Stewart will be furious, my lady."

Ciel shook her head. "I know," she said. "But Rosamund has no other friend. Not even that nurse of hers that the king hired would help her. In fact, that bossy woman would be the first to warn the king and his guards."

"You mean the king doesn't know Rosamund will attend?" Edda's eyes were huge. "Has he forbidden it?"

"I think not. Rosamund didn't say. But she did offer to find men and horses for us, which he would have done had he thought she would go. I am sure the king thinks her far too ill to attempt such a tiring venture."

Edda sat up straight. "I am going with you, m'lady."

"You must not! I will need you here to lie and say I am out shopping, or, if 'tis evening, I was tired and went to bed. Can't you see you must be here?"

"Why? If you've already gone there is nothing your lord could do! Or if you leave after him, he will never know! He has to be with the king, and he'll not go chasing after a wife who has taken her maid and left without leaving a note to say where she went! He might well believe we have gone shopping again. Let it be my way, my lady. I want to be there if I am needed."

Ciel looked into Edda's green eyes and saw all the courage anyone could ask for. "Then that is done and agreed upon! None of us must let a word slip. Both you and I must pretend we know nothing of the arrangement."

"And Lady Rosamund . . . will she speak of it before your husband?"

"I doubt it, for I believe she is keeping her plan from the king. But I will make sure she says nothing in Ian's presence."

Edda grasped Ciel's hand in both of hers. "I say we should all go together so the Lady Rosamund will have help! Did she say she would hire men for the trip? That way we will all be protected along the way."

"True," Ciel said doubtfully, "but still . . ."

"I say Edda is right," Rosamund said, slipping through the door and closing it softly. "The men I have hired are from the best of the king's troops, and I have sworn them to silence."

Ciel turned and went to her, shocked again by the gray-white tinge of illness on Rosamund's face and the burning purpose in her sunken eyes. "My dear friend," she said, taking a small hand and feeling the heat of fever in the dry skin. "Let us go in your place. You are too ill . . ."

"I must go," Rosamund said clearly. "I must be there

to comfort him after his punishment. He has no one else.''

Ciel felt hot tears spring to her eyes. It was true, what Rosamund had said. The king had men to do his bidding and servants who were in awe of him, and he had other men as friends. But none of his family would mourn for him when he was hurt, or come to help him heal.

''I will say no more, Lady Rosamund. Edda and I will be with you when the time arrives.''

Rosamund nodded. ''I heard your worries, but you may put them aside. We will leave after them. They plan to be there by noon of the second day, so the king can rest for the ordeal, which is to happen near ten that night—for that was the time Thomas à Becket was beaten to death.'' Her faltering voice cracked near the end of her speech, then resumed to add: ''You are both wonderful to help me. I will remember you always in my prayers.'' She turned away. ''I must return to my room before that woman comes back and finds me gone again. She told me to rest. And I will. I am extremely tired . . .''

Edda rushed to take her arm. ''I'll help her, my lady. No one will believe she has been plotting with a maid! Come, Lady Rosamund . . .''

In the next few days Ciel discovered how well her husband kept a secret. She had thought he would tell her the decision handed down from Pope Alexander as soon as he could find a few moments of privacy. She knew he trusted her not to carry tales; he had often told her other secrets, only adding at the end that she must not repeat them. This time she realized that he was making sure she would not know of the punishment until it was over. He knew her well, and he knew how she felt, and, she thought, he was not entirely sure she would obey him.

Then, as the time drew near for the shriving of the king's guilty soul, she began to keep his thoughts away from it by flirting with him outrageously. She knew now what caresses tumbled her lord's reserve, how seemingly innocent words intrigued him. She caught up with him in dark corridors, snuggled against him, touched him daringly, making him laugh, making him want her at once. In bed, out of bed, she teased him; even in company when she could catch his eye and exchange an intimate smile. The king's man went about in the Tower of London in a state of warm half arousal, erotic imaginings filling his thoughts, and spent half his nights in making them come true.

Ciel knew before Rosamund knew that the time had come—for Ian had changed into a stern and cool stranger in the space of one morning hour and had left the Tower early, telling her he had to see to his duties. She ran to Rosamund's door and knocked.

Rosamund opened the door herself. She smiled at Ciel and took her hand to lead her in. "The old watchdog is gone," she said, "and good riddance! She was nothing more than a spy for Queen Eleanor! Now that we've learned that news, I am much relieved. Our kitchen help told our seneschal that the woman has been giving me opium in those weak soups, saying that I needed rest. He ordered her off at once and I am feeling much stronger."

Shaken, Ciel spoke in a low tone. "She could have killed you! And I hope I'll not send you to your bed again with this news. I believe this day is—is the day before our king's punishment.''

Sudden fright made Rosamund pale, but she recovered quickly. ''I will find out,'' she whispered, for there were men marching upward from the hall below. ''I have a loyal man-at-arms who will tell me. Wait for me in Edda's room.''

Rosamund was still pale when she knocked at Edda's door and came in, but her voice was firm and her thin body straight as a lance.

''They have already left, Ciel. We must leave soon.''

Within an hour the women trooped down to the court-yard and mounted three dark Arabian mares. The five men-at-arms who accompanied them had chosen the fastest of the warhorses. The one who had befriended Rosamund led the group through the gates silently and turned toward the great bridge that led south. The way to the bridge was swathed in blankets of fog that dulled the sounds of their passing, muffling even the hoofbeats of the heavy Percherons.

The women were silent, their heads and necks wrapped with soft woolen scarves that covered all but their eyes, their shapes indistinguishable in the great cloaks and thick layers of skirts. They depended on speed to arrive when they must, so they had no wagon of goods. They had packed only a change of clothes wrapped into bundles behind them.

On the bridge the fog was wet and heavy, smelling of the river. They saw the others only as dim, gray shapes floating beside them.

Kent Grover, the man-at-arms Rosamund trusted, came to ride beside the women and encourage them.

"Once away from the Thames and into the country lanes beyond we'll find the air colder and clearer, my lady. Then we set a quicker pace."

Rosamund agreed. Pale with fright and weakness, she was still utterly determined. "Thank you," she said, and added a small smile. "We are in your hands, Kent. Lead us carefully."

"That I will, Lady Rosamund. Our king needs friends amongst his enemies."

Within an hour of quitting the bridge, the fog was lifting, letting a pale gleam of early afternoon sun brighten the roads ahead. The men-at-arms relaxed; the women looked at each other with warmth and hope. And as the air grew steadily clearer, the party picked up the pace and went cantering south toward Rochester. There was a wet and rutted road to travel on part of the way; they prayed for no accidents there. If they could keep up this speed, they would spend the night in a Rochester inn and not along the way at some small and uncomfortable farmhouse. And, well enough, they rode into the Rochester inn's stables just as twilight turned into darkness. They congratulated themselves, the women smiling at each other, the men quitting their saddles, bending over and rubbing their stiff thighs. Then just as they gathered at the open stable doors, Ciel recognized Rogue, who whinnyed at her from a dark corner. She reached out and grabbed Kent Grover's sleeve, whispering to him.

"'Tis Rogue over there, Grover! If we go into the inn we will be recognized at once and sent back under guard!"

Kent Grover grinned. "Indeed not, my lady. I thought 'twould be like this. We will enter by the back door, say to the innkeeper that we are servants from the castle, come to see the king punished for causing à Becket's death. We will be shown to the servants' quarters, which I can recommend. The price is smaller and the food and comfort the same.''

Ciel stared at him, and then nodded. "Well done, then. No one will know." She glanced over at Rogue, who was eyeing her hopefully, wanting a treat or a touch. "No one but him, and he'll not give us away. Take us in.''

Beside her, Edda whispered, shooting a glance to the side where a slender figure leaned against a supporting post, tired and weak. "Will Rosamund be all right, my lady? She is used to being cosseted.''

"She will be fine, Edda. Like us all, she is only tired. Tomorrow will be when she needs our care.''

25

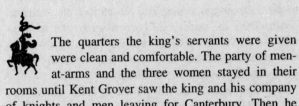

The quarters the king's servants were given were clean and comfortable. The party of men-at-arms and the three women stayed in their rooms until Kent Grover saw the king and his company of knights and men leaving for Canterbury. Then he went to knock on Edda's door. When she opened it, he looked into her green eyes, then swept a warm gaze down her lushly curved body. When he looked up again he grinned.

"You may tell your mistress and the king's leman that we can leave when they are ready. The others have gone."

Edda blushed at his examining look. Swinging the door almost closed, she peered around the edge and nodded, her glorious, flame-colored hair spilling over one white shoulder.

"Thank you, Grover. I will tell them immediately." She shut the door and leaned against it, catching her breath, listening to his heavy tread going toward the stairway. Then the steps stopped, turned, and came back.

"Edda?"

His voice was muted, as if he didn't want anyone else to hear. She swallowed. "Yes?"

"You are very beautiful in that thin gown."

"What? Oh, you shouldn't have looked! Shame on you!"

There was a silence and then a whisper. "I'll not say I'm sorry, Edda. There is not a man in the world who wouldn't look at you in that skimpy gown. Now, go clothe yourself and tell your lady 'tis time to eat and go."

She listened again and heard his solid tread on the floor of the hall, the quickening steps as he took the stairway down. Then she turned and hurried across the room to waken Ciel, ashamed of herself. For much more than a few moments she had completely forgotten the serious problems that faced them all this day.

Ciel had heard it all. She smiled at Edda and sat up. "We will give the king's party time to get well ahead of us," she said, "and while we wait we will make plans. Dress yourself and waken Rosamund. Then go down and ask for a hearty meal. The men too will be pleased by full stomachs." She paused and her smile widened. "But watch out for Kent Grover—he seems to have his mind on you."

Edda blushed. "Yes, m'lady. 'Twas my fault entirely. I went to the door without—without putting on enough clothes. Any man . . . oh, never mind! It won't happen again. What would you like for your meal?"

"Anything the cooks put out. But you must ask Rosamund what she can eat. Now go!"

By midmorning the horses were saddled and mounted. The men-at-arms led the three women away from the inn and out on the main road to Canterbury. As they rode, Kent Grover spoke of how they could enter the cathedral quietly and be seen by few.

"I was raised hereabouts," he said, "and I know the

cathedral well. There is a small, nearly hidden door in the southeast transept, far from the main entrance, that we used as young boys ...'' He stopped and glanced at Ciel and Rosamund, a smile flickering across his bearded face. '' 'Twas much quicker to use its small door than it was to march the length of the building, but few used it, for most wanted to be seen parading to the altar. We can go in that way and miss the stares from most of those who have come to watch a king be beaten.''

Rosamund made a small sound deep in her throat, and her eyes clouded. ''I cannot believe it even yet,'' she said, and shook her head. ''His people seemed to love him, but they have turned on him like wolves, excited by the thought of having a king treated like a disobedient slave!''

'' 'Twas always so,'' Kent said somberly. '' 'Tis no different now from the time of the Roman games. The Romans all attended when the best and most holy of Christian men were flung to the lions.''

Looking ahead, Ciel made out the walls and towers of a city, some of the Roman style, others new. The land outside the walls was bright with sun and growing crops and flowers. It was far from the deep fog and angry citizens throwing stones at the king when they had come past here from France.

''Are there many farmers here?''

''A few. The main business of Canterbury is minting. 'Tis noted for its coins, both silver and gold.'' Kent smiled across at Edda, who turned pink. ''But none of that will help us. What we need is to find an inn and settle ourselves.''

''Indeed,'' Ciel said, and looked around at Rosamund.

The sad eyes looked back at her, the thin but beautiful face smiled sweetly. Even tired, Rosamund showed an improvement over the days when the false nurse fed her opium.

"We do need rest," Rosamund agreed. " 'Twill be hours before the—the punishment begins. I would sleep for some of those hours . . ."

Listening to her faint voice, Edda nodded quickly. "And I will bring fresh fruit and herbs for you, my lady. Surely I can find them in a market." She looked at Ciel and nodded. "I can, truly. No one will notice me. If I see someone I know I can slip from their view."

"There," Kent said, pointing at an ancient stone building on the city square. "That inn will be fine for us. The king will be in the big one nearest to the cathedral. And I will go with your maid and see that she finds what she needs for Lady Rosamund. I know the city well."

Ciel glanced at Edda's suddenly happy face. "Then that is fine," she said. " 'Tis true the Lady Rosamund needs to eat and rest. We will do as you suggest, Edda."

They took rooms in the old inn on the square. They were comfortable and clean enough, and the faint must- iness cleared when a maid removed the bedcovers and put on new. Rosamund went straight to bed, tired and weak.

"The Lady Rosamund will feel better once I find a market and bring her the things she can eat. I'll ask Kent Grover which way I should go," Edda told Ciel, finding her in the ajoining room.

Ciel smiled. "Don't risk going alone. Take him with you. He may tease you, but he will keep strangers in their place."

Edda smiled back shyly. "Once I ask directions, I hope he offers to take me there as he said. But if he doesn't, I will ask him to accompany me. I am not too proud to keep myself safe." She turned and found her warm shawl, knitted of light-green wool in a lacy pattern. After draping it over her head and around her upper body, she took a basket and a purse Ciel had filled and went toward the door, opening it, turning back to speak again.

"I'll not leave without finding Kent," she promised, looking back at Ciel. "I'd be afraid without him." She turned to go and stopped, blushing. Kent stood just outside, grinning at her.

He bowed and offered her his arm. "I am pleased by your trust in me, Edda. I will take good care of you."

Speechless, Edda took his arm and left without a backward glance.

Later, worried about Rosamund, Ciel rose from her chair and went into the adjoining room. Asleep, Rosamund was white with fatigue, but she was breathing normally. The constant congestion she had in London had disappeared in the country air. Ciel studied the beautiful face, the perfectly carved features, the abundant, shining hair. Tears of pity came to her eyes and she turned away, wondering if it were true that Eleanor had plotted death by slow poison for a woman whose only crime was falling in love with King Henry!

Taking a chair, Ciel pondered that question. Rosamund had asked for no recognition, for no great fortune, nor for anything except the love Henry felt for her. And, Ciel thought, the chance to comfort him when he was ill or hurt! Queen Eleanor showed no sense of mercy for him at all and likely wished for a chance to laugh at him while he was beaten . . .

"My good friend," Rosamund said from her pillow, and smiled. "There! I made you jump. Your expression was sad, Ciel. Please, do not think of this coming night—only of the days that will follow. At last, Henry will be putting this horrible affair behind him. I think him noble for taking the blame, when we all know he is innocent."

"True," Ciel said, and returned a matching smile. "By midnight 'twill all be over, and you will be comforting the king." She stood up, hearing footsteps in the hall. "There! That must be Edda, with food for you. I'll let her in."

While Rosamund ate the early fruits and berries Edda had bought and spread butter on the fresh loaf of bread, they all sat together in her room and planned the trip they would make that evening. Kent Grover, quiet and thoughtful, pointed out that moonrise would come a scant hour after darkness fell.

"If we wish to be unnoticed as we enter the cathedral, we must use the early dark to get to the southeast transept. Once in, and the public seated, they cannot prevent us coming from the transept and choosing places for us all. The pope's decree says all who wish to attend are welcome."

Ciel's heart fell, thinking of how Ian would feel when he discovered her there. There was no doubt he would see them all once they were seated. She glanced at Edda, who was looking at her anxiously, and shook her head, smiling.

"I must take my chances," she whispered into Edda's ear. "Don't worry about it."

But later, when all had been decided and the party dispersed, Edda went out again with Kent Grover as a guide and came back later with another purchase.

"I have brought you a black veil, my lady. 'Tis thick and dense, so your features will not show through, yet the upper part of it will allow you to see. And you have your black cloak and shoes. If you sit apart from us, your husband will never know you are there. All will believe you are a recent widow."

Ciel stared at her. "But . . . I am not sure I wish to fool him, Edda. I may rather take the punishment later."

"But I'll not like hearing your cries!" Edda's green eyes sparked with anger. "No man should ever raise a hand to a woman!"

Ciel sighed and gave in. "I'll wear the widow weeds, if you feel so strongly, Edda. 'Tis true he'll not recognize me behind that thick veil. If he sees you, he might well believe I sent you with Rosamund, as a companion on the trip."

From a vantage point on a rolling hill where they had stopped to wait for the dark, the tense group of friends saw the great, sprawling cathedral shining in a bloodred glow from the setting sun. They made the sign of the cross, fearing the thought of the royal blood that would be spilled before the altar this night. Behind her black veil, Ciel watched Rosamund's white face and wished that nurse who had been poisoning her had been caught earlier. She was still too weak and unwell to be where she could see her beloved king beaten . . .

"It is growing dark," Ceil said, turning to Kent.

"Perhaps we should station ourselves at the southeast transept now. 'Twill be better to go now than stumble about in the dark."

Kent let out a breath from his deep chest and nodded. "True. But now that the beating looms before us, I feel guilty. As one of the king's guards, I will think myself a coward when he is beaten and I stand there doing nothing to help him."

Ciel nodded. "Think of my husband, Kent. He is the king's man, sworn to protect Henry or die. He will hate this even more than you, for he lives his vow."

Kent's wide mouth twisted into a strange humor. "True. I'd not wish to be the next person to attack the king when Lord Stewart is present. He is said to take down armed men with his bare hands."

Ciel's eyes closed behind the veil. A macabre scene rose from dark memory, a scene in a grassy field where two men had planned a murder and, instead, lay twisting and screaming in pain, their long, sharp knives useless on the ground. And near them stood the man they wanted dead, his face like an iron mask, without a sign of pity or remorse. And then, the face of the false priest at Belmain, so still beneath the icy water—God help us! How many men had Ian Stewart killed? No innocent men, please God! She turned away, her eyes on the growing twilight.

" 'Tis true," she said quietly. "I have seen it. Now, 'tis dark enough. Let us make our way to the small door you spoke of, and wait."

She looked around as he nodded, seeing the other women, silent but enduring, and the other men-at-arms, now uncomfortable and looking to Kent for what they must do. She looked to Kent herself, and as he reined his horse toward the huge mass of the cathedral, she followed, hearing the others take in deep breaths, speaking to their horses, and to each other, in soft whispers.

What Kent Grover had said was true. They were the only people who entered the cathedral through the southeast transept, and when they came quietly to the pews facing the huge, ornately decorated high altar, those already seated paid no attention to them, other than to allow them space to squeeze past them and find seats.

Sitting there, Ciel breathed in the same odor present at tournaments and races, a smell of intoxicating fear and great excitement. Spurts of tense whispering ran through the crowd as the sound of measured footsteps were heard, echoing faintly from the long choir to the west and growing clearer as they came toward the presbytery below the high altar. Then behind her a woman's strained whisper caught her and made her reach for Rosamund's hand.

"I see the king!" the woman hissed. "He is barefoot and wearing rags! He looks like any shamed beggar . . ." She made a quick sound of pain, as if someone had poked her, hard. "But he does, goodman! I only told the truth."

A man's voice growled. "Best you keep your flapping mouth shut! The priests are enraged and bold—watch quietly!" Rosamund clung to Ciel's strong hand, and kept her eyes down. But when the men-at-arms marched by with the king in their midst, she glanced up and caught a glimpse of his white, anguished face, his eyes fastened on the altar. Her hand clung even tighter, and she lowered her face as tears fell from her eyes again.

"If he can bear it," she whispered to Ciel, "then surely I can. But my heart is hurting overmuch." She looked up just as the men came to a stop and allowed the king to go forward alone to the altar. He seemed half dazed, but his jaw was firm as he went to his knees and prayed, the soft mumble dropping into silence as he murmured his amen. His head was still bowed.

There had been no sign of clergy until now. While the king prayed at the base of the altar, the present archbishop, Richard of Dover, a dignified man, came quietly from a passageway on the left. He was dressed in the full white robes and tall, pointed headdress that proved him a prince of the Roman Catholic Church, and he wore the gold chain and sacred medal depicting the crucified Christ. He approached the altar and stood there, waiting for the king to look up at him. When Henry's eyes rose to the calm face, the archbishop nodded.

"You are here, Henry Plantagenet, to do penance for your sin against the church. Have you come willingly?"

Henry cleared his throat, seeing that four muscular men in monks' attire had followed the archbishop from behind the altar. All of them carried the braided leather whips used for penitents. But he answered clearly.

"I have come willingly."

"And you know your penance?"

"I do. I am to be beaten by the Canterbury monks."

"As Thomas à Becket was beaten by your special friends. Is that not so?"

"It is so, your Excellence."

"Then we will begin. These are the first four of twelve monks chosen to carry out the penance."

He turned to the monks and admonished them, saying they must remember that the blows should be hard but not death-dealing. Then he went behind the altar again and sat down in a red leather armchair, ready to watch.

With the first whistling blow that crossed King Henry's broad shoulders, drops of blood appeared where the braided leather tore through the cloth and bit into his fair skin. Rosamund moaned softly and fainted, falling toward Ciel. Ciel caught her in her arms, but Edda, reaching out from the other side, took the slight burden away from her and held it against her sturdy body, her white face frightened but determined.

"Pay no attention, m'lady," she whispered to Ciel. "Your lord glanced this way! You are supposed to be a stranger to us. Remember it!"

That was true, Ciel thought wildly. She must not show concern for a stranger. But with every blow—and they came fast and furious now—her stomach roiled and tightened, threatening nausea. She looked at Ian, standing behind the kneeling king and watching every blow. Ian's face was like white marble, carved by anger and pity, his big hands clenched into fists. His huge body seemed to vibrate as the monks wielded the whips with all their strength. But as the beating continued, the monks themselves began to breathe hard. Their blows had begun to weaken, merely to slash the air instead of whistling. The archbishop, wearing an expression of grim suffering himself, rose and came forward to hold out his arms and stop the blows.

"Your time is over," he said to the panting monks. "Send the others to me."

One monk hesitated, his dark face cruel, his arm rising again. But the archbishop turned to him quickly. "Another blow, and you earn the same beating for yourself, Leland."

That monk skulked away toward the crowd and took a seat to watch. The others took their leave, retiring to the small room behind the altar as four other monks came forward and took their places. Still on his knees, the King of England reached forward and put his hands on the floor, his head hanging limply, his bruised and cut back dripping blood. The archbishop came closer and, eyeing the king with pity, declared the beating would continue. As the four whips whistled down to the raw and bleeding back and sent blood splattering up in a red mist, the king uttered his first sound—a deep moan.

Ciel watched Ian's huge body turn to rigid steel. He was fighting himself now, fighting the flare of fury that overtook him, shaking with the effort to stay calm, knowing this time he could not intervene. Ciel watched him fearfully through the dark veil, seeing with her knowledge of him how close he was to springing forward and stopping the bloodshed. Then she saw him raise his eyes to the stolid figure in white and gold that sat behind the altar. The archbishop looked back at Ian steadily and shook his head. It was clear then. The punishment would go on.

The king's deep moan was not followed by cries for mercy. Only by the sound of whips cutting through the air, cutting through torn skin. And finally, halfway through the third set of monks with whips, there was nothing on his back but broken flesh and running blood that pooled on the floor and ran in streams toward the altar. At the end of the beating, which had lasted close to an hour, the king slid down and lay helpless in his own blood, only half conscious. The archbishop rose from his chair again and came forward.

"It is ended," he began, but stopped at a stir in the watching crowd, whispers and muffled exclamations and then a shriek as Ciel leaped to her feet and cried out in alarm.

"Ian! Behind you!"

Ian whirled, taking a slanting blow on his forearm that was meant for his head, his hands grasping the ugly monk who had stayed to watch the whole beating. Ian's hands wrapped around the monk's thick neck and squeezed until he lost consciousness. Then he flung the barely breathing man down, picked up the iron bar and the knife the man had as weapons, and turned to the silent archbishop, holding up the weapons so all could see them. There was a dead silence in the cathedral. None of those watching moved or spoke, only stared and waited.

"Now," Ian said hotly, "you may order your man as you will. He is one of the well-known criminals who became Canterbury monks to hide their thieving and murders. We will remove our king, who has taken a bloody beating for what this man and others caused. And see to it that other false monks are not hiding in your church to escape punishment for their mortal sins."

His words fell into a deep silence. No one moved. Even Ciel, a shaking hand at her throat, was still standing in the aisle and staring at Ian. He turned and gave her a long, cold look of fury before he turned back to his men.

"Bring in the litter and put our king on it. He will need many days to mend enough to ride back to London. But thanks to God, he has done his penance. He will live free."

From the seats behind Ciel, Lady Rosamund staggered to her feet and came forward, her anguished eyes on King Henry.

"I will accompany him," she said to Ian, "and nurse him until he is well. He will want me there."

"And you strong enough for it, 'twill make him heal better than any herb or ointment." Ian's look at her was almost friendly. "There is room for you in the wagon we brought. If you have baggage, we will send a man to pick it up."

Rosamund glanced around at Ciel, who had pushed back her veil when she knew she was caught. Ciel's face was white and frightened.

"Lady Stewart will bring them to me," Rosamund said. "She and her maid." She looked back at Ian, and added: "Ciel is my true friend."

"Undoubtedly," Ian said, furious and hurt, "a diso-bedient and lying wife must have one virtue, though I see none in her! I will send one of my men for your baggage. I can trust them."

"But . . ." Rosamund turned to speak to Ciel and saw nothing but a head of shining black hair and a somber cloak of black wool fluttering back from a slim body, disappearing into the southeast transept between Kent Grover and Edda. Then she turned back to protest Ian's decision and saw men putting Henry on a soft litter. She hurried to him, and his tortured, red-veined eyes wid-ened at sight of her.

"Rosamund!" Tears came to his eyes at last, and he reached out a shaking hand. She took it and kissed the palm.

"My darling," she whispered, "my lover. 'Tis over, Henry. We can live again . . ."

Ciel was silent on the way back to the inn where they had stayed. Edda watched her closely in the wavering light of the lanterns. Ciel's face was pale and still, her eyes dark pools of misery. But when Edda tried to comfort her with whispers, she only shook her head.

"Let it be," Ciel said quietly. "'Tis my own fault for disobeying him." Her face was white but determined. "And I would do it again, were Rosamund to ask me."

"Oh, mistress! You must not say that to him! He is already furious, and he may well beat you for it."

Ciel sighed and shook her head. "No doubt he would, but that will not happen, Edda. I will not look on his angry face again. I will live with my father in Normandy."

"But you are his wife! You cannot leave him!"

Ciel shook her head. "You heard him, Edda. He doesn't want me. Now he will understand why I said he'd be better off with a woman of his own kind. No lady in London would do what I did. They would have ignored sad little Rosamund and said her flagrant sins were being punished."

Edda's green eyes flared with sudden anger. "True enough! You have the right of it, m'lady. They would never blame the man who took her and taught her to love him! I will go with you, then. I have saved my money and will add it to yours."

Ciel smiled, her eyes wet. "You are a faithful friend, Edda. You needn't give me your money, for I have much of my own. We will have more than enough. My father will give you work you will like, and I will work beside you."

They were at the inn, and going up the stairs when one of the men-at-arms who had accompanied the king arrived to take Rosamund's baggage. He was well spoken and friendly, and was careful to tell Lady Stewart that the king's party would stay in Canterbury for at least a week, allowing the king's wounds to begin to heal.

Ciel and Edda put Rosamund's baggage together and gave it to the man. "If you can," Ciel said at the end, "say to Lady Rosamund that we are happy for her, and wish her well. And, of course, give our profound sympathy to our king. He took a terrible beating to protect his friends, and did it with great courage and grace. Thank God 'tis over!"

The man promised that he would deliver those messages, and left. Ciel and Edda went on with their packing, this time with their own clothes. There was nothing now to hold them in this friendly inn, Ciel thought, nor, for that matter, anyplace in England. Her heart was aching like a sore tooth, and she could think of nothing that could relieve the pain except for the strong arms and steady love of Vincennes Valoir.

26

 When seven days had gone by, the lash cuts on King Henry's back had closed and begun to heal. Henry had always healed easily and was no complainer. He said little about the pain, but spoke at length about the sense of freedom he felt after having been relieved of the curse of à Becket's death. His eyes were always on Rosamund, his hand reaching for hers, and she was always there. For the first time, Ian realized the strong love between them.

Like himself and Ciel, he thought, though he admitted to himself that he and his wife were at odds now. Ciel's strange action of doing what she pleased whether he forbade it or not had made a wide rift between them.

Gradually his sense of failure receded. He knew it was stupid to feel as if he had failed in his vow to keep King Henry alive and unhurt. It had been torture to watch the monks beating the king. His whole big body had been tense and murderous. He had held in a fury that knew no bounds. He also admitted to himself that some of that evil anger had been expended on his own wife—if only by words. But he gave himself some little credit. He knew many men who would have beaten her right there, with the whole crowd watching.

Then, as the week ground toward an end, he admitted to more, though only to himself. Angry as he was, he needed Ciel, and wanted her with him. Of course she would have to be punished for disobeying him. Every wife's duty was to obey her husband, and Ciel had failed miserably at that. Finally he decided to go to the inn where she was staying and speak to her. It would save sending one of the men to tell her when they were leaving.

He took some pains with his appearance. During the past weeks he had been careless of his untrimmed beard and hair; now he found a barber in the town and had that remedied. Then he set out for the small inn in the middle of town, his heart lighter than it had been since they left the Tower to journey here.

The landlord of the inn was welcoming a family on their way to France, bowing them into the cozy downstairs room that served as a dining room as well as receiving newcomers. When he spotted the king's man, he hurried across the room to welcome him.

"How can I help you, Lord Stewart? Have others arrived and need more rooms than the Canterbury inn can provide?"

Ian smiled. " 'Tis tight at the seams, landlord, but the rush of friends has trickled away. They have gone back to London satisfied to know our king is gaining strength every day and soon will be on his feet. Now, I have come to speak with my wife, the Lady Ciel Stewart. Can you direct me to her rooms?"

"What? Why, no, my lord, I cannot." The landlord's genial face was suddenly suffused with a rosy tint. "She and her maid and man-at-arms left my inn the morning following the trip to the cathedral. From what I heard, I would say they were headed for London. I thought they had brought the—the king's leman to his side and were going home again.''

"I see." Ian stood staring at the landlord and it was clear that he was confused. "Back to London, you say?"

"Yes, m'lord. And in a dreadful hurry. They were gone at dawn of the next day."

"No message given to perhaps a forgetful servant?"

"None. I have no servants who would have forgotten a thing like that! They would have been running to the Canterbury inn in great haste, m'lord."

For once Ian was at a loss. " 'Tis unlike my wife," he said slowly, and the first real doubt came into his mind. "But perhaps she was . . . undone by the scene she had witnessed and wanted to leave immediately. No doubt I will find her waiting for us in London."

"Oh, yes! Yes, indeed! Had there been an accident, that man-at-arms would have let you know . . ." The landlord's voice came to a halt. The king's man was out of hearing and had left the front door swinging wide to the cold air.

Now, with the king unable to ride hard, the return to London took four days. When they crossed over the Thames and set out for Westminster Palace, crowds lined the streets and called encouragement to their valiant king. Londoners, as usual, were on his side. Not so with some of the churches—their muffled bells took note of the new saint, for Thomas à Becket had entered sainthood as a sacrifice to a king's evil anger and the priests were praying to him, their newest and now most popular saint.

Riding with his king, Ian Stewart chafed with impatience. He must see Henry to his rooms, make sure no enemy lurked in the palace, and then set guards at every entrance. Until those things were done he could not set out for the Tower.

It was coming on dark this short winter day when Ian finally rode into the Tower grounds, handed Rogue over to a stableboy, and hurried inside. He heard chatter and laughter in the solar, and his jaw clenched, hard. Undoubtedly his wife would be there, enjoying herself, perhaps flirting a little. And if her attitude toward him wasn't subdued and meek, he would see that it changed rapidly. He strode to the solar and flung the door open.

Inside, the young ladies of the court were entertaining each other with songs and games, while a few young men enjoyed the scene. The songs and laughter stilled abruptly at the sight of the king's man. Ian looked about, then centered his gaze on Philippa, the only one of the group whom he knew well.

"Where is my wife, Philippa? Is she in her usual room?"

Philippa came forward and curtsied. "Good evening, Lord Stewart. Lady Stewart is—ah, not in the Tower at present. Come, m'lord, and I will tell you what I know of her absence."

"Absence? What do you mean?"

"Shhhh! Come this way, m'lord." Philippa turned and went rapidly to the door, beckoning him to follow. There was a complete silence in the solar until the door shut behind him, then a rising wave of hushed voices and choked laughter. Red-faced and furious, Ian followed Philippa's quick stride. At the end of the gallery, the young woman turned and faced him.

"I will tell you what I know," she said, "and though

she gave no excuse for it, I hope you will consider that what she did was done for the sake of both of you.''

''For God's sake, Philippa! All I need to know is where she is now!''

Philippa drew a deep breath. ''Normandy. She went home.''

Ian uttered a loud and lurid curse. ''Her home is in Northumberland, and she well knows it! Was she fool enough to go to Normandy alone?''

''Oh, no. She was accompanied by her maid, and . . . and one of the men-at-arms named Kent Grover. He is known for his good character and able use of his weapons. She was undoubtedly safe enough.''

''Good God! She gave me no hint of that action! When is she coming back, or did she say?''

Philippa blushed heavily. ''Why . . . she uh . . . she had no plan to return, Lord Stewart. She gave me to understand that her marriage was over. She said 'twas caused by her disobedience to you, and she was sure you would rather be single. She said to tell you she would not fight an annulment if you asked for it.''

Ian swallowed, easing a tight throat. ''Naturally I was angry when she disobeyed and went against my will. But all she had to do was repent and promise it wouldn't happen again.''

Philippa nodded, her gaze drifting away from his. ''Aye. I told her the same. But still she left. She said she could not make a promise always to obey. She . . . she said very clearly that in her opinion, only horses and dogs should have to obey without question.''

''My wife said that?''

Philippa's cool gray eyes came back to his face. ''She did, Lord Stewart. And to say the truth, I think her right.

'Tis the reason I have not married. Single, I do as I please.'' She smiled at him, her plain face lighting up with wry humor. "And I can remain honest instead of becoming a liar.''

Ian turned away, struck by an awful fear. "I will think on't, Philippa. What she did was . . . not entirely dishonorable. We all thought Rosamund too ill to watch the beating of our king, but she was invaluable as a nurse and companion. The king was greatly eased and helped by her presence.''

That night, alone in the room where he and Ciel had been together in the Tower, Ian considered what he had heard. It was clear now. His wife would do as she thought right when a friend needed her help. And, thinking about it, he knew it had been stupid of him not to have expected it. Her heart was always her leader, and she followed it faithfully.

The next day he went back to Westminster Palace and found King Henry sitting at table and eating like a well man. He still wore bandages and ointment on the deepest of the cuts and winced when he leaned back in his chair, but his spirits were high, his laughter easy as he told Ian his news.

"I have heard today from a bishop in London, saying that Pope Alexander III had sent word to all of them that once the beating was done and over, there would be no more attempts made on the life of the King of England by any priest or churchman. Anyone disobeying that edict will be tortured to death. And since all priests know of the tortures used by the Roman church, I feel safe indeed.''

Ian smiled, looking from the king to Rosamund, who

sat near him. "Then you have no need for me, my king?"

"You may make your own plans, Ian! You have a place in this palace whenever you want it, and so does your brave little wife! How thoughtful she was to help my Rosamund when many a woman would be afraid to take the chances. Do as you please, for I owe you much. It was good of you to allow your wife to bring Rosamund to the church, for my heart was healed at sight of her. Go, then. I will send for you if I need you."

"I will come," Ian said, "as long as I am the king's man." Bowing to them both, he turned to the door and left hastily. Within an hour, his clothes and weapons repacked and Rogue saddled, he made a late visit to the usurers who kept and lent and doubled the gold of Belmain. He left their coffers with his purse full, heading south to Dover. Icy winds accompanied him on the way, but he was warm and hopeful, urging tireless Rogue onward.

Ciel had fallen back into the work at the Valoir farm as if she had never been away. And Edda, before she became a maid at Belmain, had been the daughter of a farmer who grew apples, pears, and berries. This big farm with its Percherons, chickens, and cattle, its men to feed and big house to clean, swallowed both women into its busy life and myriad tasks. And they were glad of it, for they were strong and needed something useful to do.

In the beginning Vincennes was shocked by his daughter's tale of misunderstanding and anger. He had sat in silence while she told him the story of the beating and the scene that followed, when Ian had named her in public as a disobedient liar he could not trust. She told it in detail, and with a cold and distant air, as if it no longer mattered. But Vincennes saw the tears in her eyes and knew she mourned for her husband.

"A wife," Vincennes had pointed out gruffly, "obeys her husband. 'Tis your own fault, Ciel. You should have bent your stiff neck and let him have his way."

"I could not desert my friend," Ciel said. "Nor will I ever bow to a husband who does not respect my serious feelings. I was in no danger."

"But you were! What of that mad monk and his weapons?"

"The knife," Ciel said, "was not for thrusting into my back, 'twas aimed at Ian! Had I not seen it and called out, he would be dead." Tears came to her eyes and she wiped them away. "For that alone I am glad I was present to warn him!"

"Why would the monk want to kill Lord Stewart?"

"Because he is a wall that must be destroyed before one can kill King Henry. Undoubtedly the monk would have killed the suffering and helpless king once he had murdered my husband."

Vincennes shrugged his heavy shoulders. "Perhaps you are right. But with you so hardheaded there was bound to be a strong quarrel between you sooner or later. However, if I know Lord Stewart, he'll not let you go."

"He'll not let me go? Hah! He will thank me for ending a marriage that has turned sour for him!"

Vincennes smiled wryly. "We shall see. I'll not blame him if he decides to find another, more tractable woman."

Ciel nodded. "Nor I. There are many pretty, titled

ladies who will please him far more than I, and be more inclined to obey his orders. He will find his match."

Vincennes's smile slowly disappeared. "If he does, your heart will break," he said finally. "You will feel your life is over."

Ciel rose from her chair and dropped a kiss on her father's forehead. "My heart will hurt," she admitted. " 'Tis aching now. But I will still have a life and friends who trust me. And now I am off to the stables to take out one of the yearlings and begin his training. The fields are cold but clear of snow."

She continued to ride the frisking young colts every day, and left most of her kitchen work to Edda, who had no interest in breaking the tremendous warhorses. But when Kent Grover received an order to return to London within two weeks, he and Edda came to the field where Ciel was riding and told her they were both leaving. They would marry in Calais, where Kent had friends and distant relatives. Ciel hugged Edda, wished them both good fortune, went back to the farmhouse with them, and gave Edda a generous sum of money to buy a wedding gown. She smiled and waved as they left and then ran up to her bedroom, shut the door, and burst into tears.

There was no one now to remind her of her happiness with Ian. She had instead the unremitting daily activities of the farm; of the training of the horses; and the sight—occasionally and only at a distance—of Ian's sister.

She was too hurt to try to explain any of it to Aylena yet. Ciel continued to put off a visit to her sister-in-law and was surprised when, one morning, as she was finishing a lesson on one of the yearlings, Aylena came along the road, riding her Arabian and staring incredulously at Ciel. She reined in, not waiting for an invitation, and crossed into the meadow at a brisk canter.

"Why, don't say you two are here in Normandy, and I have had no word from my brother! Where is that rascal?"

Ciel's eyes filled with tears. "I—we—we are no longer together, Aylena. I hesitated to bring bad news to you, though I am sure 'twas my duty to let you know. But . . ."

Aylena's eyes widened. "No longer together? I cannot believe it! What has happened?"

"We . . . quarreled. I did not obey him."

"What? Is that all? Tell me more."

Ciel wiped her eyes. " 'Tis too long a story, my lady. You would tire of hearing it."

"I'll not. Come, let us get out of the wind and into the sun, there on those dry rocks. I want to hear what my foolish young brother has done."

Ciel's heart warmed. Aylena was still her friend. She turned her big horse to follow the small Arabian and dismounted with Aylena when they arrived at the sun-warmed outcropping of gray stone.

"Now," Aylena said, smoothing down her heavy skirts, "sit here with me and tell me all, straight from the beginning."

"Well," Ciel said, staring at her feet, "I became very close friends with Rosamund . . ." She looked up. "Perhaps you don't think I should make friends with the king's paramour, but Rosamund is a—a different sort from most of the paramours I have seen. She truly loves the king . . ."

"I know."

"Yes! And she wanted so much to be in Canterbury

when he was—was to be beaten. She wanted to help him, to soothe his hurts, to bring back his spirit. And she did. She was better than any physician. I heard that before I came home."

"I believe you," Aylena said, nodding. "But what has that to do with you and Ian?"

"Ian . . . well, I asked permission to go to the cathedral, and he said no. But my maid, Edda, and her friend Kent Grover, a man-at-arms, helped me. I—I wore a widow's apparel. 'Twas black, and the veil thick. But—but a crazed monk drew a knife and started toward Ian and I jumped up and warned him. He knew my voice." Tears came to her eyes and flowed like silver brooks down her cheeks. "And he—he said unforgivable things to me! He called me a disobedient wife, and a liar, in front of everyone there! And when we all left the cathedral, he took Rosamund with them, but he left me and my maid in the same small inn we had chosen apart from them, and I packed up and came home! He *hates* me!"

"He loves you," Aylena said sternly. "And you know it. You should have given him time to tell you precisely what you did wrong. 'Tis not right to run away when the issue is not yet spoken of and solved. Besides, it rather mellows a man to have his wife agree to her sins."

"Oh? I talked to Lady Philippa at the Tower, and she agreed with me when I told her the tale! I said no one but a dog or a horse should have to obey without question, and she heartily agreed."

"Philippa is not married."

Ciel stared at her, searching Aylena's lovely face. " 'Tis true," she said finally. "But she said 'twas the reason she had not married."

"One of the reasons, perhaps," Aylena said, "but not the only one. She is extremely particular. And lonely. Almighty God made very few perfect men." Her lips curled sweetly upward. "I, of course, have one of them."

Ciel wiped her eyes and stared at the ground. "It seems I have ruined my own life. My father thinks the same."

"Ruined it? Because of one mistake? Think it over, my little one. He loves you dearly." Aylena rose from the warm rock, dusted herself off, and whistled the Arabian over to her.

Taking the reins in one hand, she stepped into the left stirrup and swung up into the plush-lined saddle. "You'll see. He will find you."

"He will be too angry to look for me!"

Aylena laughed softly. "He will be too hungry for you to be angry, Ciel. Just remember to be charming and a little bit sorry for your sins. 'Tis all it takes."

At last a shy and reluctant smile lighted Ciel's face. "I hope you have the right of it, Aylena. And likely you do. 'Tis the boy you raised yourself. I'll put my trust in that."

Edda, resplendent in a traveling gown of dark wool and the fur-lined cloak Ciel had bought for her, walked proudly with her husband, Kent Grover, toward the Calais docks. There was a large English cog being warped in to dockside, and in it the arriving passengers were moving about, gathering up their possessions, laughing and talking. Glad, Edda supposed, because they had made the voyage with no trouble.

"Will we sail on that cog, do you think?" she asked Kent. "Or will we have a French boat?"

Kent's eyes sharpened as he gave the cog a look. Then he turned Edda, swinging her around on his arm, starting down the docks toward land again. "The king's man," he whispered, "is aboard that cog and working his way toward the gangplank. I wonder if he's here to see Lady Ciel?"

Edda gasped and then smiled after taking a quick look over her shoulder. "If he is, he is likely to find her! He knows where her father lives. Perhaps their marriage will turn out well, after all."

Minutes later, Kent felt a hand grip his shoulder and turned, looking up at Lord Stewart.

"Kent Grover, is it not? And Edda! Is your mistress here in Calais?"

"No, Lord Stewart. Only Kent and I, for we came here and have married. Now we are to sail back to England."

"Then—she isn't here at all? Did she leave?"

Edda shook her head. She wanted to tease him, but the eager hope in his eyes made her sympathetic.

"Your lady," she said, "is with her father. She is breaking in the yearlings and teaching them tricks in the far pastures. And . . . and she is watching the road for you, every minute of every day, though she never admits it."

Ian's eyes widened, and a moment later his teeth showed in a dazzling grin. "You mean that, Edda?"

"I do. But you must not say I told you that. She is very proud."

Ian grabbed Edda's shoulders and planted a kiss on her cheek. "A kiss for the bride," he said, laughing at Kent's startled face, "and gratitude with it! I had very little hope when I came here—but now—now I dare to be happy!" He clapped a heavy hand on Kent's shoulder and, still smiling, disappeared in the crowd, hastening toward the cog again.

Still staring at the tall, broad-shouldered man, now taking Rogue's reins from a sailor who had brought him onto the docks, Edda smiled. She turned back to Kent and took his arm. "Somehow," she said, "I believe we stand a good chance yet to belong to the Stewart clan. 'Twould be a nice life for us both."

A day and a half later, still hopeful, Ian arrived at Castle Cheval Noir. It was past noon, and the courtyard was deserted, though footprints in a light fall of snow crossed the space between the barns and the doors into the kitchen. He took Rogue into the barn and found no one there except for restless horses with empty troughs and a sleeping stableboy, warm and snug in a thick blanket. He routed the boy out and asked him if he'd fed the beasts. The sleep-flushed face went white as fear drained away the warmth of his blood.

"No-o, m'lord! I'll do it right now!"

Leaving, heading toward the kitchens, Ian looked back and saw Rogue receive the first, full measure of oats. That set off a chorus of whinnying from the others, loud enough to wake the dead. Then a kitchenmaid stepped out to dump a basin of dishwater on the icy ground, saw him, and whirled back to the door. "Cook! Send a scullion to the solar to tell our Lady Aylena her brother is here!" Then she turned back and bobbed a curtsy at Ian, her face pink with pleasure, her eyes admiring.

"Welcome, m'lord! You'll make a dreary cold day warm an' sunny for your lady sister, I vow!"

"I hope so," Ian said, stepping up beside the maid and giving her a smile. "But uninvited guests are not always a pleasure. Where is Lord Rodancott?"

"In the fields, m'lord, he and his two sons, riding his yearlings. His boys ride almost as well as he does."

"I see..." Ian turned as Aylena came swiftly through the door and flung her arms around him. He hugged her, smiling, and kissed her cheek. Then she waved the kitchenmaid away, stepped back, and spoke quietly. "Now, come! I have heard from others that you have had trouble with Ciel. I have several questions for you."

Frowning, Ian shook his head. "No prying into my life, I pray. Trouble I have, but I am not here to listen for words of wisdom or blame. I need no advice, my beloved sister."

She frowned at him. "That sounds as if you have already made a decision and are ready to bear the consequences. But I'll not argue with you. Come with me, little brother. There is a hot fire in the solar."

"I'll be glad of the warmth, my dear sister. My life at late has been both cold and barren."

When Thor came in from the fields, Thorwald and Bruce were with him, tall, strong boys with the look of Vikings, both bragging loudly and stamping their feet on the stone floor of the kitchens, knocking the ice and rime from their boots. When they heard the voice of their mother's brother up in the solar, they took the high steps two at a time, burst into the solar, and came to a stop in front of Ian, grinning foolishly.

Ian stood and embraced both of them, giving each a hug and a slap on the back, then standing away to look at them and shake his head.

"Weeds," he said, looking behind him at smiling Aylena. "Only weeds grow so fast. Tomorrow they will be taller than I."

Coming into the warm room, Thor laughed. "I hope not. Two like you would be impossible to feed." He came forward and slapped Ian's back, then turned to his sons. "You will leave us now. You may join us at dinner." He watched, with unconscious pride, as they both bowed and left the room, silent until they shut the door and then as noisy as ever, talking, laughing, and clattering down the steps to the great hall.

Thor turned back, grinning, to Ian again. "What

brings the king's man to these shores? Surely Henry is not traveling yet?"

"Not for another month or so," Ian said, his smile disappearing. "The king is mending, but 'twill take time. No, this trip has naught to do with Henry. I have come to take my wife home."

"If she will go," Aylena said behind him. Color came up above Ian's close-clipped beard, but he didn't answer her. He continued as if she hadn't spoken.

"She has been here long enough, and I have been lonely. Have you spoken to her, Thor?"

"No," Thor said, and looked at Aylena. "But your sister has. Perhaps she will tell you what she knows."

"She will tell me I am a thoughtless brute," Ian replied, without even a glance at Aylena. "And give me not one word of encouragement. If I listened to her, I would surrender now and go home without my woman."

Behind him, Aylena smothered a laugh. "The king's man," she said in a calm and wondering tone, "is a coward. He is afraid of his wife."

"I," Ian said, still looking at Thor, "am afraid of my sister, not my wife. My sister still thinks of me as a boy who needs advice. However, I forgive her. She was very good to me when I was young."

Aylena broke out in laughter and stood up, dropping her embroidery work. "And since you became old, I have been cruel?"

Ian turned, showing a small smile. "You have changed sides, my sister. Not one word in my defense will come to your lips now. I have learned that women band together."

"And men do not?"

"Simply put," Thor broke in, his dark eyes glinting,

"we are always fair and always right. All men see clearly. In fact, men are never wrong. If you could keep that one truth in your mind, Aylena, we would never disagree."

Laughing, Aylena came to kiss him. "I know that, m'lord. But it took time for me to learn. Perhaps young Ciel is also having a bit of trouble with it."

Heaving a sigh, Ian left the solar, heading toward the room he always used. He found it ready, an iron bucket with glowing coals for warmth, another full of warm water and a wooden bed made up with a goosefeather mattress and thick wool blankets. He washed and changed his clothes, wondering if he had time to bathe all over. But then that could wait until tomorrow, when he readied himself for the visit to Valoir's farm . . .

In late afternoon Ciel rode slowly toward her home. It was cold but still, and without wind to penetrate her woolen cloak she was warm enough to take her time. Solemn and lonely, she gazed across snow whitened fields dotted with bare stone.

It was strange, she thought, that even with the healthy evergreen trees and the comfortable house appearing in the distance, it seemed a barren land to her. One more day had gone by without a sign of Ian, nor even a written note brought by a traveler heading this way. No matter what Aylena might say, it began to seem as if Ian had given up his wayward wife. Or perhaps he was waiting to see if she would return to him and beg his forgiveness.

Even thinking of doing such a humble thing made her wince. Not only because she hated to humble herself in any way, but because it would put her forever in the wrong. Never again could she have an opinion that went against her husband's. He could—and would—immediately remind her of the necessity of obeying him and taking his decision as her own, whether she liked it or not! She thought about it all the way home and again as she bathed and dressed for dinner. And yet again as she fiddled with her food in the company of her silent father. And then she burst out at him.

"Would it be possible to have my marriage to Ian dissolved by the church? Or is that favor reserved for kings and nobles who wish to marry someone younger, richer, or more beautiful?"

Vincennes turned red. "No daughter of mine will ever ask to have her holy vows of matrimony dissolved! Never mention that again!" He stared at her for several minutes and then broke out again. "Who is courting you? Don't lie now!"

"No one!"

Vincennes flung down his spoon. "I said no lies! Who is it?"

Ciel drew a deep breath and calmed her voice. "I do not lie, Father. You know that. I would not marry again. I only want to be free of the vows."

"That is the truth?"

"It is."

Vincennes sighed and pushed back from the table. "Perhaps you are right, Ciel. In time to come you may decide to marry again and have children. 'Tis bitter, I know, to be alone. And it does appear that Lord Ian is no longer willing to be a husband to you."

Ciel winced at those last words. "Ah . . . tomorrow?"

"Yes, if you wish. If it is possible, still it will take a great amount of time for the church to act."

"Thank you, Father," Ciel said stiffly, and rose to

clear the table of their few dishes. "I am, uh, glad you agree."

That night, lying sleepless between the feather mattress and the thick woolen blankets, Ciel finally accepted some of the guilt that had parted them. What she had done was truly unforgivable to Ian. And it was true, what her father said. It did appear that Ian no longer wanted to be married to her. Surely he would have come searching at her father's home.

But only if he wanted her. Only if he still loved her. The more she thought about it, the more she doubted his love had survived his deep anger. Tomorrow, she thought, I will ride over to Rodancott's castle and talk to Aylena again. If she will tell me where Ian is, I will send a message to him, avow my own faults . . . and ask his forgiveness. And there was one more thing she would do—she would offer him his freedom. For no man should have to live with a wife he could not forgive . . .

By morning Ciel had lost her courage. Even thinking of sending a cool note offering Ian his freedom made her heart drop and flutter like a wounded bird. And when she met her father at the breakfast table, she told him she had changed her mind and no longer wanted him to talk to the priest to see if she could win her freedom.

"I would rather wait and allow Ian to approach the church," she said, her eyes on her plate. "He is a decisive man. I left word that I wouldn't fight an annulment, and if he wants to remarry, he will move heaven and earth to dissolve our marriage. Let him do what he believes is best for him."

Vincennes gave a grunt of relief. "True, my girl. He

knows what he wants. Nor will we object, whatever it is. The quarrel was your fault.''

Ciel gave him an angry, wounded look but said only, ''And I have that yearling to handle. I will need the whole day to settle him down.'' She downed her cup of warm cider and stood up, anxious to end the conversation. ''I will take along a loaf and butter. The day is warmer, and I'll not come home for a midday meal.''

Vincennes nodded and gazed after her with combined worry and pride. But he no longer sent a man with her, for none was needed. After what had happened to the first men who tried to shame his daughter, there had been no more. It was whispered in the village that his pastures were full of evil spirits who commonly mated with the Valoir girl and were violently jealous. Of course they had heard that the girl had married a noble, but they were sure an evil spirit had assumed the body of Thor Rodancott's brother-in-law. How else would an ordinary man without a weapon be able enough to break the arms of two strong and determined peasants wielding knives? It had all happened because Vincennes Valoir had made a pact with the devil himself, and every field was haunted. How else to explain his constant success in the markets? A few pious old women prayed weekly that the unfortunate Vincennes Valoir would see the awful fate awaiting him and change his ways before he faced eternity in hellfire.

So strong was Ian's wish that he woke that morning from a dream of lovemaking so powerful and seemingly real that he reached out for Ciel with both arms, and found nothing but pillows and rumpled sheets. He was never superstitious, but his disappointment reminded him that he still had no real reason to think she wanted him back. What he had said in anger there in the cathedral had come back to haunt him several times, and each time it seemed more cruel and unforgiving.

Bathing, choosing his cream-colored wool chausses and golden-brown velvet tunic, the words he had used that night rammed through his hopes and scattered them again. Ciel was proud. Could she forgive him for calling her a disobedient, lying wife without one virtue? Did she remember he had refused to trust her with Rosamund's baggage? And that he had turned his back on her, leaving her to stay with her maid and Kent Grover while he took Rosamund—cause of the trouble!—to the Canterbury inn? He sighed, fearing the day before him. It could go badly. He hoped she would be in the pasture with a yearling, so her angry refusal of him and his love would not be heard by anyone else.

Ian had been taught to move noiselessly in spite of his size. He went past the closed door of the solar, past the double room used by Thorwald and Bruce, and down the steps to the great hall, where several men-at-arms and castle servants still lay on pallets before the glowing red embers of the big fireplace. He didn't wake them, only went through to the kitchen, full of scurrying workers, heat, and tantalizing odors of baking bread and meats. They grinned at him, and he grinned back, liking the friendliness. His stomach growled, and he pacified it by grabbing up a hot loaf, cutting a trench down the top crust and shoving in chunks of butter. Chewing on it, he swung his cloak around him and went out into the chill air, heading for the stables.

He took his time saddling Rogue. It was early yet, and he wanted Ciel to be in the pasture before he got there. He wanted to observe her from a distance. What Edda had said about Ciel watching the road had given him hope; he thought now that if she seemed to look toward the road it would be an encouraging thing to him. He was not superstitious, but recently he looked for signs. And when he mounted Rogue and started north he said a small prayer and crossed himself. It was, he thought, good to use all the ways of asking for help. He finished the last of the loaf, wiped his buttery fingers on his saddle cloth, and straightened himself. The sun had risen above the cold, misty fog in the east and was sending warming rays across the fields. It was time. His eyes turned to the east, to the wide yellowed fields of winter-killed grass and dark evergreen trees, and his heart jumped and began beating fast. She was there.

Ciel had dismounted near to a thicket of trees, for the young horse she was training was limping awkwardly, his left hip giving beneath him even at a walk. She tied him to a sapling and went to lean against his hip and pick up the leg by the fetlock, to look inside the rim of the upturned hoof. True enough, there was a stone jammed inside. She reached in her pocket for the smoothed piece of thin iron bar she carried to pry out stones, and, after a few minutes, she succeeded in removing it. Then she mounted the horse again and began putting him through his paces, giving him orders in a clear voice, but still watching closely for further signs of weakness in the leg. There were none, and after a few tests she relaxed, patting his neck and whispering to him. Then, out of habit, she turned him toward the road and, passing the thick clump of trees that cut off her view, turned again toward the south, looking as far as she could see, shading her eyes from the growing sunlight.

There was no one in view. She sighed, and her whole small body drooped as she slowly turned north again. Behind her, motionless beside the clump of trees, Ian cleared his throat and spoke.

"Don't leave me now. I have come a long way to beg your pardon."

She froze, unable to look around, feeling her heart in her throat, knowing she couldn't speak. His deep voice seemed to flow over her like warm cream, and there was a yearning in his tone, a sound that brought tears to her eyes. She heard his saddle creak, then the tread of his boots, and he appeared beside her.

"Will you sit with me and talk, Ciel?"

She nodded dumbly, and he reached up to clasp her narrow waist and set her on the ground. He took her reins and tied her horse near Rogue. Then they looked at each other, and, as if they had planned it, they joined hands and went to sit on a smooth, dry rock east of the trees. And, gradually, they began to talk.

"I was a fool to deny you when you wanted to help Rosamund, and a worse fool to let my vile anger out at you in the cathedral. I know better now. Will you forgive me?"

Ciel's eyes filled. "Surely 'twas all my fault. I should never have plotted against your wishes. I should have shown you—told you—that it was something I had to do. Rosamund had to be with our king, Ian, and no one else would take her there. Had you been a martyr to the church, like the king, I would have been there to comfort you, even if I had to crawl."

Tears came into Ian's eyes, but he smiled. "You still love me then?"

"Always and forever."

"Then we'll go home."

"Yes." Ciel's arms went around him, her hands nestled in thick bronze hair that touched his shoulders. She kissed him, long and sweet, her tongue moving sensuously against his. "Yes," she said again breathlessly, "we will. My memories of our solar in Northumberland are rich and varied. I can still see that roaring fire, with the soft sheepskins beneath us . . ."

Ian groaned. "You are testing my patience, love. This rock is hard and cold and you are warming my blood past endurance. Another kiss like that, an' I canna wait . . ."

Ciel sprang to her feet and reached for his hands to pull him up with her. "Tonight, my love! And tomorrow I will pack my clothes and say farewell again to my father. But there is a maid and a man-at-arms in London whom I hope will want to join us and come to live in Northumberland. What say you?"

"I say yes! They gave me courage."

"Did they? How?"

He stood there, gazing down at her beautiful face, at the love and happiness in her eyes, and saw the long, wonderful years ahead of them. Always together, in good years and bad. His smile came, his arms pulled her close.

"Never mind. You may ask them."

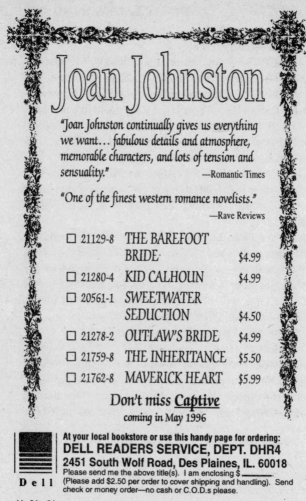